AN AMERICAN ASSASSIN

To my Poker buddy Ray

Joey

AN AMERICAN ASSASSIN

LOUIS DE MARTINIS

Copyright © 2016 by Louis De Martinis.

Library of Congress Control Number:		2016914404
ISBN:	Hardcover	978-1-5245-3994-8
	Softcover	978-1-5245-3993-1
	eBook	978-1-5245-3992-4

All rights reserved. No part of this book may be reproduced or transmitted in any form or by any means, electronic or mechanical, including photocopying, recording, or by any information storage and retrieval system, without permission in writing from the copyright owner.

This is a work of fiction. Names, characters, places and incidents either are the product of the author's imagination or are used fictitiously, and any resemblance to any actual persons, living or dead, events, or locales is entirely coincidental.

Any people depicted in stock imagery provided by Thinkstock are models, and such images are being used for illustrative purposes only.
Certain stock imagery © Thinkstock.

Print information available on the last page.

Rev. date: 09/06/2016

To order additional copies of this book, contact:
Xlibris
1-888-795-4274
www.Xlibris.com
Orders@Xlibris.com
747723

TROUBLE 2

Chapter 1

The red jump light came on!

How the hell did I ever get into this mess? Jim thought to himself. *I hate airplanes, and, most of all, I hate to jump out of airplanes. If God wanted us to fly, he would have given us wings.* He couldn't believe that he even thought of that trite cliché.

The tough-looking Special Forces sergeant grabbed his shoulder, exerting enough pressure to ensure that he was awake and that, under no uncertain terms, he was in charge and this passenger was going to jump when the green light came on.

"Time to hook up, sir," the sergeant bellowed over the roar of the old DC-3's laboring engines.

Jim opened his eyes and looked up at the sergeant. *He probably thought I was asleep,* Jim thought to himself. He kept his eyes closed to try and make all that was happening disappear, giving him hope that when he opened them, he would be back home in Virginia. *Besides, if my eyes are closed, that behemoth with the stripes wouldn't be able to see the fear in them.*

He forced his eyes opened and gave the sergeant a halfhearted grunt to convince both of them that he was tough, and a half a smile so as not to get him mad. *After all, he is going to push me out of this plane because I don't think I can do it on my own.* A shudder went through his body at the thought of the impending jump.

"Thanks, Sarge," he said as he stood on shaky legs, hoping the sergeant wouldn't notice the sway in his legs as he stood, the rocking of the old DC-3 was great cover for that. The old plane was really rocking and rolling as the turbulence was tossing it around like a cork in the ocean. They used these old tubs because they fly under the radar, and it wouldn't give Saddam's people heartburn if they did see it. After all, no self-respecting spoiled American would be caught dead in one; that is, except for a foreign agent.

Jim grabbed his camouflaged helmet and strapped it tightly under his chin. He checked his straps; first, the backpack, which contained all of his equipment and disguises and included the weapons and the special grenades that were guaranteed by the experts to do the job quickly and efficiently. He tugged at the line that attached it to his harness and then checked his chute for the tenth time. He finally hooked the metal clasp over the guy-wire, which ran along the ceiling of the plane and terminated at the door. The door was open and prepared for his jump to hell. *I'll never make it,* he thought to himself. *How in the heck did I ever end up . . . up here?*

The sergeant was listening intently to the earphones he was wearing. He kept pressing them against his ears with both his beefy hands while managing to balance himself as the plane continued to be jostled in the foreboding sky. The yellow light came on. The sergeant then motioned for Jim to go to the door.

Jim stumbled forward toward the door like a drunken sailor. He grabbed each side of the door and crouched down a little in the standard jump position, just as he had done before, each time, in doing so, hating it and fearing it all the more . . . if that were possible. He gallantly fought back the urge to upchuck. *At least it's not raining,* he thought. He no sooner finished the thought than a lightning bolt zigzagged its way across the sky, startling him and causing him to push back from the door.

He looked around at the sergeant and smiled at him. As if to read his mind, the sergeant said, "Don't worry, sir, it's only heat lightning. It doesn't rain in the desert." Jim once again grabbed each side of the door, swearing to himself that if he survives this, he will never jump from a plane again. In fact, he thought, fantasizing, *I will never fly in anything but the most luxurious airlines and in first class.*

"Give my regards to Saddam," the sergeant said. Jim looked to his left at the sergeant, who was so close, he could smell the coffee on his breath.

"OK," Jim said as the green light came on, and he felt himself being hurled through space. He wasn't sure whether he had jumped or the beefy sergeant threw him out of the plane.

His chute opened. *Look at that,* he thought as the roar of the DC-3's engines became faint. *It's blue. They even gave me a dark-blue chute so that it would blend in with the sky. They thought of everything, I sure hope so. Anyway, I'm going to need all the help I can get to pull this one off.*

He drifted toward the earth and forced himself to open is eyes and look down. The moon shone brightly on the desert floor and for a minute struck fear into his heart as he mistakenly thought it might be water. *If there's one thing I hate worse than jumping . . . it's jumping into water,* he thought to himself.

Then he saw the light. It was a very narrow beam of light shining up toward him from the ground. *I hope it's the contact and not some camel jockey with a Rayovac,* Jim cursed to himself. He tugged on the left line on his parachute to drift closer to the beam. One problem . . . the signal was supposed to be three sets of two flashes, and this was one steady beam. He wanted to reach down and unhook the strap on the automatic that was attached to his belt at his side but decided against it. He didn't want to let go of the lines, which gave him a small modicum of security. All of a sudden, the beam of light went out. *I'm dead*, he thought to himself. *The SOB is going to shoot me, and me dangling up here like a monkey in a tree.*

As he neared the earth, he pulled on the cords, which slowed his fall and almost leveled him with the ground. He landed with hardly a bump. He immediately tugged at his parachute and released it from his body as quickly as he could. He gathered it up and lay on it. He pulled on the tether that attached the backpack to the parachute harness, dragging the backpack to him. He reached into it and removed a small Uzi-type machine gun, which had a silencer attached. He lay there sweating profusely, waiting for the stranger to show himself.

It didn't take long. Over the sand dune and to his left came the unmistakable thumps of camels crunching their huge paws on the dry sand. Jim squirmed as quietly as he could, turning his body on the ground to face them. They were only twenty yards away. Two camels were being led by what looked like a camel jockey. *Looks good,* Jim thought. *Two camels, one jockey. Either he was sent to pick me up or he's dead meat and I have two camels.*

They almost walked by him as he lay quietly on the ground. "Stop! Put up your hands," Jim called out in Farsi. They stopped, and the camel jockey turned to face him. He had something in his hand. Jim pulled the trigger on his weapon and sent a few rounds into the air, whizzing past the camel jockey' ear.

"Please, sir, see I have camels to bring us back. Please, sir."

Jim smiled to himself as he noticed that the camel jockey had a flashlight, probably a Rayovac in his hand. "Dammit, man. Don't ever do that again if you want to live," Jim said, motioning toward the flashlight in his hand.

"Do what, sir?" he answered.

"Carry a flashlight like a gun," Jim retorted.

"Well, sir, I will remember that. Thank you, sir, but pardon, sir. How do you carry a flashlight?" the jockey responded.

Jim wasn't sure whether he was being mocked. "Never mind, I don't have time for a training lecture now. Why didn't Russell come to pick me up?" Jim asked.

"Pardon me, sir, but Mr. Russell was hurt. Not seriously. I am happy to report, sir, that he will be fine. Come, sir, I will take you to him."

This could be a trap, Jim thought. *Why would Russell send a camel jockey? Either he trusts him with the keys to the kingdom or he had no other choice. Either way, I'm stuck. Well, at least it's better than sitting in the middle of the desert, slowly dying of thirst.*

"What's your name?" Jim asked.

"What makes a difference, my name, sir?" he responded. "The good gentleman, Mr. Russell, calls me sergeant. He put me in charge of the camels, sir. My family name I will keep to myself, sir. I like the name Sergeant, sir."

Jim thought there was something about this man that made him much sharper than the run-of-the-mill camel jockey.

"OK, OK, I'll call you Sarge. Now, Sarge, bury the chute and let's get outta here."

"Yes, sir. Yes, sir," Sarge responded as he began digging into the sand with his cupped hands. "Sir, begging your pardon, my given name by the good Mr. Russell was Sergeant, not Sarge." Jim ignored his remark but thought there was something about the way he said it. He was sure this was no camel jockey.

Chapter 2

The ride was long and bumpy. Camels are not like horses. They bounced in the most ridiculous way, and Jim was getting a rash on his inner thigh from it rubbing against the saddle. It reminded him of the time when he was a boy of about eight in Queens, New York. He and his friends used to go to an old riding stable that was just off the Belt Parkway. The last time he inquired, the stable was still there, but Jim was told that it had gone modern and no kids were allowed to hang around anymore, at least not like he and his friends did. In those days, as was typical, they never had any money; but if they cleaned out the stables and did odd chores around the barns, the owner would let them have free rides. Jim didn't like riding that much, but it was something to do during summer vacation from PS 63. It seemed like ancient history. He was bright and a good student, although he never studied and did get into minor trouble from time to time.

I wonder what happened to all of those wonderful teachers whom I never appreciated at the time. I still remember them, Mrs. Hannon, Mrs. Young, and, yes, Mrs. Hathaway, who gave me an appreciation of classical music that has never waned. I can still see her in the classroom playing a small excerpt from a classical piece and then all of us raising our hands when we could identify the name of the piece and the composer.

And the girls and puppy love. He was in love with a different girl in his class every week. Not that he was girl crazy; he much preferred sports and hanging around with his boyfriends, but the girls always fascinated him. Jim was embarrassed as he thought of how he would moon after them, taking his bicycle and hanging around their neighborhood for a chance to bump into them. When he did, the chances were that they went steady for at least a week or two until one of them fell in love again with someone else. In those days, it was all a big dream being played on a live screen.

His mother had died when he was very young, and his father remarried. His stepmother was from Iraq, and that's how he learned to speak Farsi. She was very nice and took a genuine interest in him. She treated him well, but he would never go to her for advice and wouldn't confide in her. She spoke with a thick accent, and he, not knowing any better, was ashamed of her and never had her take part in any activities at school. He didn't want his friends to visit and so he would always make excuses and would meet at their homes. His stepmother did, on the rare occasions that he had friends over, treat them very well. Thinking about how shabbily he treated her embarrassed him. He was grateful he had made it up to her after they both survived his terrible teens.

In his teen years, he had become a real wise guy. Things never moved fast enough for him. He was always on the go and didn't care much for high school. Then he met Susan. Jim was only sixteen at the time, and Susan was thirteen. They met through a mutual friend at a party. Jim liked her immediately, but Susan ignored him. He found out later that Susan's girlfriend, Barbara, had a crush on him, and out of loyalty to her friend, she pretended not to like him. Many people to this day say that the only reason Jim didn't end up in jail was because of Susan. She was all any man could want in a woman—intelligent, good looking, always smiling and finding the good in everything and everybody; whereas Jim would always be looking for the dark side of things. Jim loved her from the start. The beautiful thing about it was how their love developed and grew stronger and stronger through the years. Finally, five years later, they were married. A few years after that, Ken was born, and everything seemed to be going their way. Jim became a cop. It was a steady job. It didn't pay that much money but had a good potential for advancement. He could make detective or perhaps study and attain some rank. Although he would tell everyone that he took the job for the security that it offered—after all, he was a father—but he really loved what he was doing. Susan worked in a law office as a paralegal until Ken was born. She decided to devote her life to raising their son, and Jim was all for it. Everything was going well until that fatal day of the accident. Susan was driving Ken home from school when an out-of-control truck T-boned them, killing them instantly. It took Jim years to recover, and the truth be told, he probably never did. That is why today he can kill without emotion and he took the job with the "Group" that he knew involved doing assassinations when necessary.

Chapter 3

Finally, they came to a small desert town. It consisted of some small hovels that looked like they were dug out of the sand and barely above ground level. *Probably half buried by sandstorms,* Jim thought. He felt uneasy. Things were too quiet. Even though it was about four in the morning, Jim felt that there should be some movement. *After all,* he thought, *they should be expecting me, and Sarge, there was something about him . . . He acted as if a beggar, uneducated, but his movements were sharp, and so was his speech. Not what you would expect.*

After they dismounted, he grabbed Sarge from the rear, clamping his left arm around his neck from behind and shoving his 9 mm automatic into his side hard enough to inflict pain.

"Where is Russell?" he whispered, holding his startled escort.

"He is in there, sir, probably sleeping, sir," Sarge answered, sweat visible on his brow as Jim forced his head back.

"Where is your flashlight?" Jim asked.

"In my right pocket, sir," Sarge answered, both his hands on Jim's arm, trying to relieve the tension against his throat.

"Take it out slowly and shine it in front of you until I tell you differently," Jim ordered as he jabbed the gun into Sarge's ribs to emphasize his order.

Sarge took out the flashlight and did as he had been told. Jim pushed him forward, using him for a shield

"We are coming in, Mr. Russell. Please don't shoot. It's Sergeant," he spoke to the darkened opening of the hovel. He was forced forward by Jim.

"Shine your light around the room," he ordered Sarge. The light caught something shiny to Jim's left. Then he heard the sickening sound of an automatic weapon and three quick flashes. Sarge's body was thrown back into Jim. Jim was trying to get his balance as Sarge was falling backward onto him. The flashlight fell from the Sarge's hand to the floor, and two more shots from inside the hovel spat at it.

Jim was finally able to get out from under Sarge and rolled to one side. He fired four quick rounds at the point where he saw the bullet flashes. The noise was unmistakable as another body flew backward and an audible groan filled the room. The light came on in the room, and Jim bolted out before anyone had a chance to adjust the brightness. He ran as fast as he could and leaped over a small dune about twenty yards from the entrance to the hovel. In a matter of seconds, three people came out of the building, all armed. They looked around, and one of them, obviously the leader, gave whispered commands. At that, one of the others moved away from the front of the hovel and went behind the building. Jim reached into his backpack and pulled out a hand grenade and placed it on the ground next to him. He also took out an extra clip for the Uzi, which he now held at the ready, its sights pointed at the two remaining figures. Just then, he heard the roar of an engine. A jeep-type vehicle came out from behind the building and stopped in front of the doorway. The two men that were standing there backed into the hovel, all the while keeping a watchful eye on the terrain around them. In a few seconds, they came out each holding the arm of a limp body and dragging it toward the vehicle. Jim knew he had to make a decision. If that was Russell, he could not let them take him away. On the other hand, it could be their compatriot whom Jim had just shot. *No way,* Jim thought to himself, *they would leave their wounded or dead behind. That had to be Russell.* He sprang into action. First, he fired a few rounds, peppering the jeep. This caused the men to drop the limp body and take cover behind the vehicle. Jim quickly rolled to his left as a quick succession of bullets threw sand in the area where he had been. He moved farther to his left and cautiously peeked over the dune. He was going to throw the hand grenade but decided against it because Russell, if that was him, was lying too close to the vehicle. He circled the area and came to the dunes to the rear of the jeep. Again, he felt his adversaries were too close to Russell to chance a shot. He was a marksman and a deadly accurate shot, but the angle was all wrong, and the weapon he had was made for close combat and not accuracy. He did not want to take a chance that a ricochet would hit Russell. He slowly crawled toward the vehicle and could clearly see the right sides of two of the people and a limp body lying on the ground slightly behind them. This was a good shot, but where was the third person? *Perhaps he is circling around and is coming up on my rear,* Jim thought to himself. He involuntarily looked behind him and saw nothing. He may have gone back inside or is circling in the wrong direction. At any rate, Jim decided that it was now or never. He lay flat and took careful aim. Two quick bursts dispatched both the men. Jim immediately removed the clip from his Uzi and replaced it with a fresh one. Just then, the third figure came out of the hovel, quickly assessed the situation, and fired his weapon into the head of the figure lying on the ground, causing it to jump with the impact of the bullets. Jim quickly fired at him, killing him instantly, but too late to save the motionless figure on the ground.

Jim leaped over the dune and ran as fast as he could toward the jeep. His adversaries were lying on the ground around the jeep and were dressed in the uniform of the Iraqi army. He turned over the body of the one that was executed to identify him. It was no good. His whole face was blown away by the shot. *The bastards must use explosive rounds,* Jim thought to himself.

Just then, he heard a moan from the doorway. He spun quickly and was about to fire when he realized it was Sarge.

"Help me," Sarge said, looking up at him. *How could he have survived?* Jim thought to himself as he pulled at the clothing to survey the wounds. Then he felt it. Sarge had a bulletproof vest on.

"Where did you get this?" Jim asked. Before he could answer, they heard the faint roar of engines coming their way. Jim spun around. He reached into the backpack he had brought with him and pulled out a pair of small night vision goggles. He looked in the direction of the noise and, to his dismay, saw four army trucks, which appeared to be loaded with soldiers, heading in their direction. Jim tossed the goggles back into the backpack and then took the backpack off and laid it on the ground next to him. He took out a few clips of ammunition and placed them on the ground next to him. He decided that he would use the jeep for cover for the upcoming battle, probably his last.

The trucks stopped, and heavily armed men quickly jumped out of them. They spread out and were encircling his position. *This is one heck of a place to die,* Jim thought to himself. He slammed a fresh magazine into the Uzi, took a deep breath, and started to sight in on the closest group of soldiers who were approaching directly in front of him. They were crouching low as they approached. He was about to pull the trigger when he felt something hit him sharply on the back of his head. First, he saw stars, and then the blackness closed in on him.

Chapter 4

Jim tried to open his eyes. His head ached. His vision was blurry. He realized he was on the floor of a truck, which was speeding across the sand. His hands were tightly tied behind him and he was lying face down, the hot metal floor of the truck burning his face. He lifted his head slightly and could barely make out the silhouettes of men sitting on the wooden bench seats that lined both sides of the truck bed on either side of him. They were obviously soldiers, each sitting in a row on the wooden seats. Some were leisurely carrying on conversations, while others, heads bobbing, were lazily dozing. Each soldier with a rifle, its butt resting on the floor cradled between their legs.

"So you're awake," one of the soldiers said, looking down at him. The next thing Jim saw was a rifle butt coming toward him. He didn't have the strength or the ability to get out of its way. Again, he was enveloped in pain and then darkness.

His head was buzzing. He slowly opened his eyes. He cautiously tried to focus on his surroundings, not opening his eyes too widely, fearing another rifle butt to the head. It was quiet. He was sitting . . . in a chair. He tried to move his hands but he couldn't. An uncontrollable shiver racked his body.

Think, he said to himself. He closed his eyes and tried to figure out what had happened. He remembered the soldiers coming toward him, and that was all until he was hit while lying on the floor of the truck. Then the pain in the back of his head jarred his memory. Someone must have hit me in the back of the head. *Sarge!* It came to him. Sarge must be one of them. *But why did he lead me back to Russell?* The thought of Russell's body lying in the sand without a face sent another shiver through him. *Sarge could have killed me when I was parachuting from the DC-3. It must have been a plan to capture me. They knew about my mission and they want me alive! Why?* Jim's head was filled with half events that gave him more questions than he could answer. Then things went dark again.

He opened his eyes again. This time he could focus. He was in a dark room with just a sliver of light coming from around what appeared to be a loose-fitting door, which was to his right. His hands were tied behind him, and he was sitting in a chair in the center of what seemed to be a small basement room. His legs were tightly tied to the chair legs, allowing no room to move them. He was bare from the waist up. He suddenly realized that the soldiers must have undressed him to search him . . . or perhaps . . . inject him. He tried to look at his arms but couldn't see anything. The room was too dark. He tried mentally to locate any point of pain in his arms, but because of the overpowering pain in his head, he could not. *They probably drugged me,* he thought to himself. *Why? Why didn't they just kill me?*

Noise! He heard some shuffling. Someone was outside the door, probably a guard. Maybe only one . . . There was no talk. If there were more than one, they probably would be talking to each other, unless one of them went to the bathroom or was taking a smoke or doing something else.

He tried to manipulate the ropes in a vain attempt to free his hands. It was no use. The ropes were too tight, and he still felt exhausted and disoriented. He tried to move his legs but with the same results. He could, by extending his foot, put his toes on the floor. He tried to move using his toes but couldn't. He could not get enough leverage. He figured if he lunged to one side, he could fall to the ground, but that would make noise and probably get him another bang on the head. Or worse, shot. He heard what sounded like some men walking down a hallway outside and approaching his tiny prison. They stopped outside the door and started talking in Farsi. One asked if there had been any trouble, and the other answered no.

The door swung open, and some men entered. He kept his eyes closed, pretending to still be unconscious, figuring that it was his only option.

One of the men leaned over him and slapped him hard across the face. "Wake up, Mr. James Vara," he said in very broken English. Jim opened his eyes, not wanting to receive another slap. He could taste the blood in his mouth.

The room was lit with a bare bulb hanging from the ceiling. It caused Jim to squint to protect his eyes from the harsh glare of the lone bright bulb.

"Very good, Mr. James Vara," the gruff accented voice responded.

"Where am I? Who is Vara?" Jim bluffed, surprised at how weak he sounded.

The gruff voiced man smiled an uneven smile at him. He was a huge behemoth of a man. He had two front teeth missing, and the rest looked like they hadn't seen a toothbrush in a long, long time. He sported a dirty beard and mustache and needed a shave and trim. He looked like something from a bad children's cartoon.

"We know all about you. You are Mr. James Vara, American pig."

"In that case, I demand you call the American embassy immediately," Jim bluffed again.

"Certainly, Mr. Vara, you know that there is no Americana embassy here. We threw you out. Right now, I think, first, we have to have some fun with you. You Americans like fun, don't you, Mr. James Vara?" The sarcasm oozed from his ugly face; his breath was bad enough to wilt flowers.

His voice was full of hate as he spat out the words in broken English.

He grabbed a handful of Jim's hair and yanked as if to lift him off the chair. "Oh, my sincere apologies, Mr. Vara, American pig, I did not realize you were all tied up." The behemoth laughed, causing the other soldiers in the room to laugh, although they seemed to laugh uneasily and more out of fear of the behemoth than at what was happening.

Then, without warning, he punched Jim hard in the chest, causing him to fall over backward onto the hard concrete floor, hitting the back of his already sore head, his feet in the air, still tied to the chair legs.

Jim gasped for air. He felt dizzy. The room started to spin around him. The behemoth grabbed another handful of Jim's hair and picked him up until his chair was sitting on all fours again. He had blood on his hands from the wound on the back of Jim's head. He wiped his hand on Jim's trouser leg and then raised his hand again, ready to slap Jim across the face, when shouting voices came from the hallway outside the cell. He turned his head in the direction of the voices. *Whoever they are, they are shouting in Farsi and are obviously looking for me,* Jim thought. The interrogator and the others in the room immediately snapped to attention as a colonel entered.

"Is this the American?" the officer asked in Farsi.

"Yes, sir," the soldier answered. The officer slowly walked around Jim as if to survey him. He looked him up and down and looked Jim in the face.

"My apologies for the way you were treated, Mr. Vara," he said in almost perfect English with only the very slightest accent.

"My name is Colonel Safir. I will take care of you from now on. You will be my guest during your stay with us."

"Untie him," he snapped at the soldier in Farsi. The behemoth almost tripped over himself trying to comply with the colonel's order as swiftly as he could. Jim felt instant relief as the bonds were cut loose. He rubbed his wrists, which were red with rope burns. He then rubbed the back of his head with his hand and felt the moist blood. One of the men with the colonel handed Jim a clean handkerchief, which Jim placed on the wound.

"We will have a doctor take a look at that for you, Mr. Vara. It looks like just a superficial wound, but we wouldn't want to take any chances." The colonel smiled at Jim. Jim was thoroughly confused, just as he had been since he started this mission.

They stood Jim on his feet and allowed him to stand there for a few minutes until his circulation returned and he was able to walk. Then they handed him his shirt, which was on the floor, and motioned to him to put it on. He struggled with the buttons, having difficulty manipulating them. He silently hoped he did not have a concussion.

After he finally finished buttoning the shirt, the colonel and his entourage escorted him out of his tiny basement prison and into the hallway, which had a narrow staircase at the end. Jim, still walking on wobbly legs, tried to take in as much of his surroundings as he could without being obvious. At the top of the stairway, the entire atmosphere changed. They entered a hallway, which was decorated with pictures of still life and had expensive white opaque wallpaper. At the end of the hallway was a door. One of his escorts went ahead through the door, while the other, Jim, and Colonel Safir waited. The escort came back and told the others in Farsi that it was clear. They then went through the door, which led into a huge open foyer with a large crystal chandelier hanging from the ceiling, which was about four stories high. At the opposite end from where they had entered was the front door, which was made of ornate carved wood and glass. On either side of the room were stairways forming a semicircle and leading to a large open second-floor balcony. Both the stairs and balcony had finely worked wooden balusters. The walls were decorated with what appeared to be fine art work. They were obviously in a grand residential house or palace.

Jim was hustled into another hallway, which was to the right and next to the one they just exited. There appeared to be a few hallways like spokes on a wheel with the main room acting as a hub. The hallway they entered was wider and contained an elevator. *This is probably where servants entered and exited,* Jim thought, although he could not see any external exit. They entered the elevator and went to the top, the fifth floor. When they exited the elevator, they were in a hallway, which resembled a Holiday Inn. The floors were carpeted with dark durable-looking carpet. The walls were covered with a dull brown-colored paper. The hallway branched in either direction from the elevator, and there were doors every twelve feet or so. *Probably for sleep-in servants or bodyguards,* Jim thought.

Jim was taken halfway down the hallway, and then one of the men accompanying them opened one of the doors. They entered a small furnished room.

"This will be your accommodations during your stay with us, Mr. Vara. I hope you will find everything you need. If not, don't hesitate to call us," the colonel said, motioning toward the telephone.

"Please do make yourself comfortable, and I will send a doctor up to see you as soon as one is available. If you don't require anything else, I will leave you now. I must attend to some urgent business, but I will be up to see you later. I do suggest you rest, though, and please do not bother yourself with thoughts of, er . . . er, leaving us unexpectedly." The colonel was struggling for the right diplomatic words that would appease and warn at the same time.

"I will have two men outside your door to, er . . . er, see that you are not disturbed." The colonel smiled, proud of his discourse and his mastery of the English language.

"So then, Mr. Vara, if there is nothing else, I will leave you."

"Thank you," Jim said, wanting to ask questions but realizing that he was in no position, either mentally or strategically, and fearing it may antagonize what was the most pleasant surprise thus far, and above all, he did not want another session with the behemoth. They smiled at each other, and the colonel and his entourage left. Jim could hear the door being locked behind them.

Chapter 5

Jim surveyed the room. There was a typical mirror over the dresser, which was probably two way and from which they were watching him. He quickly glanced at the ceiling to see if there were any obvious pinhole camera lenses but saw none. He knew he would have to make an inch-by-inch search before making any moves to escape. A double bed took up most of the room. He leaned on it and found it to be fairly soft. He then went to the window and pulled back the heavy drapes. The windows were split in the middle with a metal bar and a large twist lock in the center and each side opening out from the room. He opened one side and immediately felt a hot breeze engulf him. He looked out and saw that there was no balcony or any other vantage point from which to climb out. He looked back at his bed and quickly calculated that there were probably two sheets and a light blanket on it, not enough to use to climb down, even if they were strong enough to hold his weight, which he seriously doubted. He closed the window and the drapes that were used to keep the sun out. He went back into the room and opened a closet door. Hanging from a pole on a metal hanger was a robe and a light-colored old-fashioned suit with wide lapels. A pair of very thin laced shoes and a cheap pair of slippers were on the floor. He went into the bathroom and was surprised to see that it looked to be a typical hotel-type bathroom. It was small and compact but had all the essentials. He tried to open what appeared to be a medicine cabinet but quickly learned that it was just a mirror and probably two way, like the one in the bedroom from which they could watch him. He turned the water on in the shower and was pleasantly surprised that it worked. He went back into the room, retrieved the bathrobe and the slippers, and got into the shower. He soaked himself. The water was hard and felt a little cold but brought welcome relief to the aches and pains from the recent beatings he had received. After the shower, he climbed into bed, and exhausted, he immediately fell asleep.

He had no idea how long he had slept. He could hear knocking. Someone was at the door. He struggled to get out of bed and make his way to the door. He opened it and was greeted by Colonel Safir, followed by a waiter who was pushing a tea cart containing two covered silver trays, a large coffee urn, and cups and saucers.

"Good morning, Mr. Vara. I trust you slept well?" The colonel smiled.

"Yes, thank you," Jim responded.

"I hope you don't mind, but I thought we might have breakfast together," Colonel Safir said, motioning toward the cart that was being wheeled into the room. Jim smelled the strong coffee.

"It would be my pleasure," he said as he motioned toward the bathroom and took his leave. Jim splashed water on his face and ran a comb that he found on the countertop through his hair. He immediately felt pain from the nasty head wound when he was knocked to the floor by the behemoth.

What is the colonel up to? Why the royal treatment? He is setting me up for something. Jim splashed more water on his face, dried himself, and smiled in the mirror and waved good morning to the person he was sure was watching him on the other side.

When he came out, everything was set up and the waiter was leaving. Colonel Safir was sitting in a chair at the small round table that was next to the window. He motioned Jim to sit in the other chair. The coffee had already been poured, and Jim lifted his cup, motioned toward Colonel Safir as if making a toast, and took a sip. Just as he suspected, it was hot and thick and strong.

"I thought so," the colonel said, smiling at Jim. "You Americans have the reputation for loving coffee." Jim nodded in the affirmative. He decided that the direct approach may give him an edge with the colonel, as they usually are steeped in tradition that requires long multiple niceties during the greeting process.

"Shall we get down to business?" Jim said. "I appreciate this royal treatment, but I am afraid of the bill."

"You Westerners, always in a rush," Colonel Safir responded, a smile on his face. "Let us eat and enjoy the good food that my people have prepared especially for you." Colonel Safir's smile broadened.

They sat for about a half hour, eating their breakfast and drinking coffee. They made a lot of small talk, each trying to obtain from the other even the slightest bit of information that might be useful. Colonel Safir insisted that Jim call him Ali, which was an English aberration of his real name, and Jim responded in kind.

They were both pros, and neither gave up any information. Jim had to admit to himself that he enjoyed the bantering and positioning. If this meeting were taking place under different circumstances, he might even be able to enjoy Colonel Safir's company. He knew better, though. He cautioned himself that the man sitting opposite him, making small talk, would probably cut his heart out with a carving knife and think nothing of it.

"Well, Jim," the colonel said, "shall we get down to business?"

Here it comes, Jim thought to himself. He felt a slight relief. *At least now I'll know what these people want.*

"I work for one of our leader's sons," the colonel started. "Which one is not important. I tell you this so that you know what I have to say comes from the very top of the government. I have been authorized to make you a proposition, which I am sure you will find most generous. I ask that you not respond without thinking over very carefully what we propose and weighing all of the pros and cons before you give me an answer. You may take your time. However, I would expect a decision by tomorrow.

"As you know, our country has been kept under extremely heavy sanctions by the United Nations. They, of course, are just a front and are lackeys for the United States in order that they may legitimize their world domination. These sanctions have been instigated by some very high level corporate executives who have manipulated both your government and in turn the UN. These executives are in control of the oil industry in many countries, including yours. They want these sanctions kept in place so that they can artificially inflate oil prices from certain parts of the world and deflate prices in other parts, as they see fit. If my country were to produce oil at the levels prior to the, er . . . er, the conflict, they would lose a great deal of power and control and, of course, money.

"As you well know, Jim, these sanctions are hurting the poor people of this country and are not having the effect on the government of this country that the great American media is trying to portray. Your government has a misconception that these sanctions will bring about a revolution to overthrow our government. They have completely misjudged us. We are very loyal people and we would put up with starvation for our leaders and our country. We are much like your patriots during your revolution. They also starved and died for their ideals, and so will we, if we must."

Jim felt uneasy. He felt like shouting, "How dare you compare our revolution for freedom with your revolution to keep a few despots in power! Yours only serves the dictators that are running your country. Ours was for freedom from that kind of oppression." Jim knew, however, that if he said this out loud, he might get a few minutes of gratification, but it would probably end the conversation, and lord knows what else would happen. He fought back the urge to respond and kept his silence while feigning interest in what the colonel was saying.

"We wish to employ you, Jim," the colonel said, staring into Jim's eyes for a reaction.

"Oh." Jim was thinking quickly, trying to maintain his poker face while searching his mind for the proper response. He forced himself to stare back into his adversary's eyes.

"In what capacity?" Jim responded as he studied the colonel's face.

"We wish you to keep us informed regarding the oil cartels. You know, information like who is running them from behind the scenes, when and if they are going to raise or lower the price of oil, things like that." The colonel lied.

The classic setup, Jim thought. *They tell you all they want is to give you a simple task, and once they suck you in, they will have you giving them the secrets of your country.*

"We are prepared to pay you handsomely. We would give you a $100,000 retainer, deposited in a Swiss bank or anywhere else you wish. Then we will pay you a monthly stipend plus a bonus for each piece of information you provide."

Yes, sir, Jim thought. *It's the same classic pitch we used to recruit double agents.*

"And all I have to do is get you information on the oil cartels?" Jim asked, feigning interest.

"Yes, that is all. This information would assist us a great deal with our deliberations with the UN and the cartels and, in the long run, help the poor people of our country," the colonel continued, lying.

Does he really think I would fall for this sophomoric rationale? Jim thought to himself, his opinion of Colonel Safir diminishing.

"The kind of information you want can be obtained from CNN faster than I could get it to you." Jim toyed with the colonel.

"No, no," the colonel continued, "you could get us the inside information before it becomes public. We have certain contacts that you can use to penetrate the upper levels of the cartels. We will provide bribe money, women, cars, whatever it takes to compromise . . . or should I say . . . win them over. Once you have ingratiated yourself into their midst, there is no end to what information you may be privy to."

"Why don't you send your own people to do the job?" Jim inquired.

"We would immediately arouse suspicion. They watch us like hawks. Ah, but an American can move around in that circle, and nobody would think anything of it. Especially an American with your credentials and working where you do."

"And you would not ask me to give up any secrets of my own government?" Jim continued, toying with the colonel, already knowing his answer, and that it would be a lie.

"No, no, we would not ask you to compromise your position or country," the colonel answered.

"It sounds very interesting, but for the sake of argument, what if I decided I didn't want the job? What then?"

"Let's not talk nonsense, Jim. You would probably be turned over to the corporal I rescued you from. Those were his men you killed. I don't think you would want that, Jim," the colonel responded with a feigned look of concern on his face.

"No, I don't have a death wish. But what if I say I'll take the job and when I get back to the States, I change my mind?" Jim smiled, probing his adversary.

"I hate to sound trite, Jim, but we have ways."

"What will you do, send a hit team? After all, I would be under my country's protection, and you said yourself that your people are being watched like hawks," Jim pushed.

"We have others. You would not be the only one working for us." There it was—the colonel's first slip. Jim had heard rumors that they were recruiting people in the United States, but this was the first verification that they were successful, or . . . *was he lying to impress me?*

"Besides, we could put out the word through various channels that you are working for us. Your own people would probably take care of you, or at least isolate you. You would be finished, Jim. Neither one of us wants that," the colonel said smugly, smiling and satisfied that he raised enough concern with this American to bring him over to their side.

"What if I get caught or have to get away? What then?" Jim asked as if he was really considering the deal.

"Don't worry, Jim, we would take care of you. You would live here or any country of your choice and would never have to worry."

Sure, Jim thought. *My address would be the local cemetery.*

"Well, Colonel, I must admit you are pretty thorough. However, I would like to take advantage of your generous offer and think about it for a while," Jim said, stalling for time to think.

"But of course! We can pick up where we left off tomorrow morning. We can have breakfast again. You can give me your answer then," the colonel responded, fairly certain he had won the American over.

"In the meantime, rest, and if you need anything at all, don't hesitate to pick up the phone and ask. By the way, it is the son's birthday today, and there will be a huge celebration this evening. His people love him so much. If you hear the music and merriment, it will be the people celebrating with the son. I think I will send you up some entertainment so that you won't feel left out," the colonel winked, smiled broadly, and stood.

"One question if I may, Colonel," Jim hesitated. "How does everyone know my name?"

"I told you, Jim, we have ways," the colonel smiled, feeling very smug.

"Thank you, Colonel. You certainly have given me a lot to think about," Jim said, shaking the colonel's hand as they walked toward the door.

"One more thing, Jim, as a gesture of good faith on your part, we wish you to confirm what your mission was," the colonel said in a matter-of-fact tone of voice. "Of course, we already know, but we seek confirmation that you are being truthful and fully cooperative." The colonel smiled.

Very shrewd, Jim thought. *If I thought they knew and they didn't, I would be giving them what they want. I would have no way of knowing what they knew, so I couldn't bluff.*

"Until tomorrow morning then," the colonel nodded and opened the door. "I will look forward to our breakfast."

Chapter 6

Jim spent most of the day studying his room and formulating plans for his escape. He knew there was probably no way he could get out the window, so that left the door with at least two guards. First, he would have to blind the people on the other side of the mirror who were probably constantly watching him. Then he would have to lure the guards into the room and somehow either overpower them, which he doubted he could do, or create a diversion that lasted long enough for him to get out of this palace . . . fortress, or whatever it was that he was in. Perhaps he could smash through the mirror and get out through that room. The problem was that he didn't know who or how many people were in there. He could listen intently and maybe learn their routines, when they entered and when they left or went to the bathroom, etc. Jim knew that the idea was implausible because he only had until tomorrow morning, not nearly enough time for lengthy surveillance.

He was becoming frustrated. He did not even know what city he was in, if in fact he was in a city. He mulled over and over what the colonel had said to him, looking for clues. *A birthday party tonight*—that would probably provide the best opportunity. *The leader's son's birthday*—it must mean they are more than likely in a city, probably Baghdad.

I will send up some entertainment, probably a hooker, to compromise him, Jim thought.

After hours of reflecting on the recent events, Jim came to the conclusion that the only way out was to bluff by pretending to accept the deal. Once he was out of their country, it would be easier to escape their clutches. Even if they put out the word that he turned, he could overcome that by taking lie detector tests, and, besides, his compatriots back in the States would never believe it. But would anyone ever trust him again? He remembered when rumors would circulate about someone who may have been compromised. Even when they didn't believe it and they were cleared, they were never treated the same, not by his friends or the agency. He would have to face that, when and if it came, he thought, right now, he knew he had to escape to survive.

Several hours had passed, and Jim was no closer to a plan for escape than when he first entered the room. All he had accomplished up to that point was to eliminate possible escape routes. He did have an idea of how he could get by the two-way mirror, but that was about all. He needed a break, some fluke that was not planned.

He heard the noise, music. The party must have started. Jim wondered what time it was. He picked up the telephone.

"May I help you?" the heavily accented, stern, businesslike voice said on the other end.

"Yes. Can you tell me what time it is?"

"Yes. It is 8:45 p.m." It was obvious, even over the telephone, that the person on the other end did not like him.

"I would like something to eat and drink, please?" Jim asked in as pleasant a voice as he could muster

"Yes. I will have something brought to your room" was the response, and then the phone was abruptly hung up.

Jim went back to thinking about his immediate problem and how he was going to escape this palatial fortress. An hour had passed when his thoughts were interrupted by the sound of a key in the door. A guard entered and held the door open for a waiter, pushing a service cart that contained his dinner. To Jim's surprise, it was followed by a beautiful young woman.

"Hello, my name Fatima," she said in a broken English, smiling at Jim, her eyes flashing. "Colonel Safir requested that we have dinner together." Again, her eyes flashed as she conveyed the message that it was more than dinner she was directed to provide. *She is beautiful,* Jim thought. Long dark hair, round face with a pleasing smile, and beautiful oval-shaped dark eyes. She was dressed in a black evening dress with a very low cut front, revealing much of her ample breasts. She was slightly on the heavy side, but it was more than made up for it in curves and femininity.

"It will be my pleasure to dine with you." Jim returned her smile.

She sauntered into the room without hesitation, indicating to Jim that she probably had done this many times before. The heavy perfume she wore immediately filled the room. It was sweet smelling and sexy.

The waiter set up the small area used by Jim and the colonel that morning. He uncovered the dishes to reveal a generous portion of leg of lamb, potatoes garnished with parsley, and some sort of greens that Jim didn't recognize. The waiter then poured wine into their glasses, nodded, and made a hasty retreat out the door.

"You very handsome man, you like Fatima?" she said in a heavily accented voice.

"Yes. You are a very beautiful woman." Jim smiled as he started on his lamb. He hadn't realized how hungry he was.

As they ate, they made small talk about the weather, her family, and her love of the country and the dictator who ran it. Jim figured it was well rehearsed and said for those listening from behind the mirror. He was able to get out of her that they were in a small suburb of Baghdad. He also sensed a nervousness about her that was out of character for a palace whore who was sure of herself and in her ability to perform. *They may figure that sex was my weakness and that she could break down my resistance in a way that the colonel couldn't.* Jim was well aware that most of the turncoats and traitors were compromised using sex, but even if he were inclined to have her, there was no way she could get to him. Sometimes they are just looking for a slip of the tongue while the male ego tries to impress the female with their stories of power or position. More often than not, photographs are taken with the subject shown in a compromising position. *We're probably being photographed right now from behind the mirrored wall,* Jim thought.

After dinner, they relaxed over coffee and sweet drinks. *I could get used to this,* Jim thought. *Better be careful and not let my guard down.*

"You want to make bang-bang now?" Fatima said, rising from her chair.

Jim, startled by the abrupt offer, had all he could do not to laugh at the primitive manner in which it was delivered.

"No. You are a very pretty and desirable woman, Fatima, but I am tired and don't think I have the energy." Jim lied.

"That's OK, I help you," she said with a smile as she leaned over toward him, exposing more of her ample breasts. *You play dirty,* Jim thought, enjoying the view and feeling a yearning developing inside him.

"No, no, maybe tomorrow night," Jim said to put her off and let their listening friends behind the mirror think he made up his mind to come over to their side.

"I help you, you see, we make good bang-bang," she said as she fumbled with the tie on his bathrobe.

"No," Jim said, purposely sounding annoyed. He had detected something in her voice again. It was a sense of urgency. Was she going to be shot if she was not successful in seducing him? *They couldn't be that bad, could they?* he wondered. She tried to get him to the bed, her eyes pleading, not in a sexy way but . . . yes, it was fear!

"We make nice, you see. You will like Fatima," she said, this time unzipping the back of her dress and letting it fall to the floor, revealing beautiful bare breasts and just the briefest of bikini panties.

"No," Jim said emphatically. "Not now." He grabbed her arms as she tried to hug him.

"Please," she pleaded. "I have something for you," she whispered, her lips scarcely an inch from his ear.

Jim looked into her eyes and decided to go along with her. It was obvious that there was another agenda taking place that he didn't understand.

"One minute," he said as he walked to the dresser with the mirror. He tilted the lamp shade and angled it so that it shown directly into the mirror. He took the lamp off the desk and also put it on the dresser and did the same thing with the shade. *This ought to blind them,* he thought. Then he turned back to Fatima. She immediately threw her arms about him, kissing him full on the mouth and pressing her body tightly to his. Jim felt himself being aroused. The perfume, her body, and those breasts against his bare chest were extremely hard to resist. He wanted her but knew he couldn't have her. His life depended on it. She then gently took one of his fingers and placed it inside the side of her panties, where he felt a small piece of paper. She looked directly into his eyes and moved her head ever so little as she nodded yes. He fingered the paper, removed it, and held it in the palm of his hand. He opened the note and read it as she feigned pleasure, as if he were sexually pleasing her.

"We will get you out at 1:00 a.m. Be ready," it read. She then took the note from his hand, and he saw that she was chewing it and finally swallowed it. They then went to the table and poured themselves drinks from the decanter. He handed her the drink and bent over her as if to kiss her cheek and whispered into her ear, "Who is coming?"

She shrugged her shoulders as if to say, "I don't know."

She then kissed his cheek and hugged him and whispered, "I don't know anything. I was just told to give you the message."

After they finished their drinks, she got up to leave. She started to dress, and he asked her what time it was. She looked at her wristwatch and responded, "Twelve thirty." When Jim heard the hour, he almost panicked. He realized he only had thirty minutes to be prepared for whatever was going to happen.

Fatima gulped the remainder of her drink and headed for the door. Jim grasped her hand, looked into her eyes, and said, "Thank you very much. You are wonderful." He winked at her as she knocked on the door. One of the guards opened the door and looked in and smiled at Jim. Jim followed her closely to try to get a peek out of the room, but the burley guard's smile turned into a sneer as he unceremoniously put a hand on Jim's chest and shoved him back into the room and closed and locked the door.

Chapter 7

Jim went to the closet and took out an old-fashioned suit. He quickly dressed and put on the shoes, which were very pointed and black and looked like they were polished with pure grease.

He checked the mirror and was satisfied that the bare bulbs would blind anyone trying to look in on him. He decided to obscure the vision in the bathroom mirror, just in case, and smeared a combination of toothpaste and shaving cream on it. Then he waited for someone to come in and make him move the lights, but it didn't happen.

He sat on the edge of his bed for a few minutes when he heard the voice. "Take the lights from the mirror and step away." The gruff order came from the other side.

Jim hesitated a minute, mulling over the idea of not obeying to see what would happen, but realized it would probably be futile and end in his getting a beating. He removed the lights and stepped back as directed. He was not prepared for what happened next. The sound of a sharp instrument against the mirror, and within seconds, most of it was removed and carried into the adjoining room. It surprised Jim, and he moved back, away from the dresser. Then the most incredible sight of all; there was Sarge. He was wearing a very chic and expensive-looking suit and gave the appearance of being a diplomat.

Sarge couldn't help but smile when he saw the look on Jim's face. "Quickly, put this on," he said, handing Jim a garment bag.

"How did you escape?" Jim asked as he quickly removed the suit he had just put on and took a burka out of the bag. By then, two more men, who were dressed to look like the body guards, entered the room through the mirror, which made the small room feel crowded and added to Jim's confusion. The men helped Jim dress.

"I will answer all of your questions later. As for now, you will act as one of my women, Jim," Sarge explained. "The burka will cover your face and hide those cuts and bumps. I hope to get you out right through the party. Acting as one of my many women, you should not be questioned. The other guards will be around you to try to hide you as much as possible. Do not say or do anything but just follow along behind me with your eyes always on me. I have two more men waiting in the other room. They will also protect you in case of any inquisitive advances on you. When we get downstairs, we don't mingle but make our way straight to the door, without being noticed if possible. This has to work, Jim, because I doubt we can shoot our way out of this place. So you are going to have to play your role to the hilt."

"What about the guards outside my door?" Jim whispered as one of the other guards straightened Jim's burka.

"They have been taken care of, replaced with two of my men," Sarge responded.

Jim noticed that Sarge had lost his accent and was speaking almost perfect English with just a hint of a Middle Eastern accent.

"I feel a little foolish in this outfit," Jim quipped.

"Better a live fool than a dead eunuch," Sarge responded. "I have two cars waiting outside the front door," Sarge continued. "The first is a jeep for my men, the second is a limousine. I will get into the limousine first, and you will follow me and get in after me. Any questions?"

Jim had a lot of questions but none that had to be answered immediately. He knew the most important thing at this time was to get the hell out of there. He nodded his head no. "No? In that case, let's do it," Sarge said as if to spur his men on.

The two men unceremoniously lifted Jim and almost threw him through the hole where the mirror had been. He noticed two men waiting in the small hotel-type room. On the floor were two other men, either unconscious or dead. Obviously, the guards from his door, Jim thought. Sarge followed and walked directly to the door. He knocked softly twice and waited. Jim could feel the sweat forming on his forehead. The door opened slowly, and a uniformed arm came through the small opening, motioning to them to come ahead.

Sarge signaled two of his men to lead the way. He followed them and motioned Jim to stay close to him. The last two men fell in place, and the entourage made its way down the hall to the elevator.

The elevator seemed to take forever. While they waited, a door toward the end of the hall opened, and two uniformed officers, who apparently were in a heated argument, started walking down the hall toward them. When they reached the room where Jim had been held, they stopped short in front of the guards.

"Who are you? What outfit did you come from?" the first officer to reach them asked in an authoritative and inquisitive tone. The situation was tense. The guards looked down the hall toward the group waiting for the elevator.

"Perhaps I can explain," Sarge said as he turned to walk toward them, distracting the officers momentarily. That was all the time the guards needed. In a split second, they had bayonets in their hands and they plunged them into the officers as they held their victims about the neck to stifle any screams. Sarge quickly ran down the hall and opened the door to the room they had just left, and the guards dragged their victims into the room. Just then the elevator door opened. A man who was dressed as a waiter was inside the elevator. He looked at the entourage waiting outside the elevator door and smiled at them. Sarge was still down the hall, and Jim did not want to enter the elevator without him. The man, seeing what appeared to him to be guards, probably for royalty of some kind, he thought, immediately bowed and tried to exit the elevator to make room for the party to enter. As he bent over, one of the guards hit him on the head with the butt of his revolver, and the poor waiter sank to his knees, not knowing what had happened. The two guards, one on each arm, immediately grabbed him and dragged him down the hall at a run to the room, which was now starting to get crowded with bodies. Sarge, who had seen what had happened, held the door open as the guards unceremoniously threw the limp waiter into the room. They closed the door behind them and once again headed for the elevator, which was being held open by Jim.

They rode the tiny elevator shoulder to shoulder until at last it arrived at the first floor. No one spoke until the elevator came to a stop. "Remember," Sarge admonished Jim, "keep your eyes on me and follow close behind." Then turning to the other men, he said, "You know what to do." A couple nodded yes, and the others stared straight ahead. The tension of what was about to come was obviously building inside them.

The door opened. The noise level of the party, which had been muffled in the elevator, increased dramatically. It added to the tension felt by the small party of men exiting the lift. They were in a hallway just off the main foyer where the party was in full bloom. Sarge nodded his head toward the door leading to the foyer.

As they entered, they saw a room full of people drinking and making small talk. Some circulating the room, others in small groups were chatting, and all the while a small orchestra playing a subdued tune from under one of the stairwells that had been converted to a temporary bandstand.

The small group led by Sarge entered the room and headed almost directly for the front door. They maneuvered around some of the groups, and Sarge nodded to those in response to some of them looking in his direction. *So far, so good,* Jim thought to himself. Then he saw the colonel. He was standing by the front door almost directly in the path they were on. Jim wanted to warn Sarge, but there was no way without being obvious and giving themselves away. As they got closer to the front door and the colonel, Jim realized that there was no way to avoid being seen by him. He had to keep cadence with the others or he would become obvious. He was within ten feet of the colonel when their eyes made contact. Colonel Safir looked directly at Jim, a glint of recognition in his eyes. Jim tried to turn his face, but it was too late. Safir had recognized him.

Chapter 8

Jim stared defiantly into Colonel Safir's eyes. Their eyes locked for a second, and then a weird thing happened. Safir turned and walked away further into the room as if he hadn't recognized him. *Impossible,* Jim thought to himself. *Safir was a sharp cookie. I don't think much gets by him, especially someone like me.*

Jim couldn't believe what happened but just kept pace with Sarge, who by this time had reached the front door. He walked through the open door, which was being held by a smartly dressed soldier who gave a sharp salute as Sarge and his entourage passed. The group quickly walked to the curb, which was about fifty feet from the door. A jeep with two men sat at the curb along with a Mercedes limousine, which was parked behind it. One of the men in the group walked rapidly ahead and opened the door for Sarge, who immediately entered, and Jim followed closely behind. The man who held the car door slammed it shut as soon as Jim had entered and walked around and sat behind the wheel. The jeep pulled away from the curb with the limo following closely behind. The driver looked closely at Jim through the rearview mirror, making Jim feel uneasy.

Jim turned to Sarge and started to speak, but Sarge placed his finger across his lips in a motion telling Jim to be quiet. He leaned close to Jim and whispered, "I know you have a lot of questions and I will answer them all later, but not now. Just do as I tell you and trust me."

Sarge reached into a trunk that was sitting on the floor of the limo in front of them. He pulled out a set of military-type camouflage fatigues and Jim's backpack, the one he had taken with him from the plane. He motioned to Jim to put them on. Sarge then pulled out a set for himself and changed clothes.

Jim pondered his situation and for a minute was considering making a break for it then; realizing that he hadn't the foggiest idea where he was, he figured he had better go along with Sarge. He felt at this time he had no choice, and, besides, Sarge could have killed him many times in the past if that was his intent.

Chapter 9

They had driven for about twenty minutes, and it was clear to Jim, who was staring out the window in an attempt to find out where he was, that they were leaving the city and were now in a sparsely populated suburb.

After driving for another ten minutes, the jeep in front suddenly pulled off of the road into an abandoned gas station. "Follow me," Sarge said as he opened the limo door and jogged to the jeep. Jim wanted to ask where they were going but felt that it would be better just to follow Sarge, at least for now. He grabbed his backpack and trotted after Sarge.

The two men got into the back of the open jeep, which immediately sped off, leaving the limo in a cloud of dust. Jim turned and looked at the limo, which was making a U-turn and heading back in the direction they had come.

The wind from the open jeep was annoying and loud. Jim wondered where they were going and how long they were going to be subjected to this rough riding crowded vehicle. He was glad, however, that, from what he could tell, they were apparently heading away from his luxurious prison.

"My name is Lev," Sarge said above the roar of the wind, startling Jim. "I am Israeli. I was here on assignment when I was ordered to rescue you."

"Can we start at the beginning?" Jim shouted. "What happened at the drop site, where is Colonel Russell, and why did you knock me out and let me be captured?" Jim inquired, asking questions in rapid succession.

"First," Lev began, "I was playing the role of a local nomad to carry out my original assignment, which will remain my business for now. Then you Americans come on the scene and screwed up everything." Lev was obviously annoyed. "I was ordered to meet Colonel Russell and obtain a package from him and smuggle it out of the country and turn it over to a contact. I was told that I was to drop my assignment, which I considered vital to the existence of Israel, and become a delivery boy for you Americans."

"What was the package?" Jim interjected.

"I don't know. I never got it. Colonel Russell was waiting for it when you arrived."

"What happened to . . . Was he killed at the hovel?" Jim asked.

"I don't know that either. I think so. Let me go back. When I recovered from your using me for a shield," Lev said sarcastically, "I saw Colonel Russell lying on the floor in the hovel, or at least I think it was him. As you know, it was very dark in there. At any rate, I calculated that there were at least fifty soldiers coming at us and you were preparing to play Rambo. I figured the best course would be for you to be taken prisoner and then your government could work on getting you out. I never thought that you were so important that they would assign me to rescue you."

"But I'm not," Jim interrupted.

"At any rate, there was a small tunnel that connects the two hovels, so when the troops were closing in, I knocked you out and hid in the tunnel until they left."

"In other words, you used me as bait. You knew that if no one was found, they would search the place until they found us, so you sacrificed me," Jim shot back at Lev.

Lev smiled and started to develop a respect for Jim's quick mind and his grasp of the situation.

The road gradually disappeared, and the jeep was traveling on compacted earth ruts that were obviously made by numerous vehicles that traversed it in the past. It was still pitch black, and except for the vehicle's headlights, which cut a swath into the darkness, Jim could see nothing. Lev leaned forward and said something to the driver, who stopped the vehicle. All four men got out and stretched, trying to relieve the kinks that they had developed riding in the cramped jeep. Lev spoke to the others in Hebrew, and all got back into the jeep. The driver put on night vision goggles and proceeded to drive without headlights. At first, it was scary. The jeep was hurling along at a rapid rate on a rutted road in the pitch black. Jim held tight to the side of the jeep, knowing that at any moment, they would hit something and they would be killed.

"How did you manage the rescue?" Jim asked, partly to get his mind off the driving.

"It was a big bluff," Lev continued.

Jim could pick up, even above the roar of the wind, a sense of satisfaction in Lev's voice.

"You must realize that there are many disgruntled people in this country. It was easy for us to compromise some of them. We use money or sex where they will work—that is the easiest. Sometimes even patriotism. Many of them wanted a new regime in power that could provide for the masses that are starving, thanks to this present despot. Sometimes we right out blackmail some of them. We use whatever works."

"Did they know you were Israeli?" Jim asked, finding it hard to believe that many Arab citizens could be compromised if they knew it was by Israelis.

"No, of course not. They thought that we were from different Arab countries with a grudge against their political regime."

"Then Safir must be on your payroll?" Jim queried.

Lev did not answer, but his smile confirmed Jim's statement.

They drove for a couple of hours when the sun started to rise. "They will be after us now," Lev said, showing no emotion in his voice.

"Where are we going?" Jim inquired.

"We are going to try to make it to the mountains and meet up with some friendly Kurds," Lev responded.

Jim noticed that the flat plain that they were riding on had become hilly. They were obviously entering the foothills of a mountain chain.

As the sun rose higher, Jim could see the mountains more clearly, but it was still difficult to estimate their distance.

After another hour's travel, the jeep started to struggle, and the driver had to gear down to ascend the mountain. After a few more minutes, they stopped, and the driver went to the side of the jeep and started to remove a gas can, which was tightly strapped to it.

Chapter 10

They all heard it at once. It was the unmistakable sound of a helicopter heading in their direction. Lev quickly motioned to the men to take cover behind some boulders near the jeep. The thump, thump of the helicopter's engine became louder and louder until it was visible coming over a mountain to their right.

"Maybe they'll miss it," one of Lev's men said, motioning toward the jeep and without much hope in his voice.

The helicopter slowly came over the mountain and headed in their direction. It was a huge machine, the type used for carrying men and equipment. It slowly lumbered toward the jeep and then began to circle. There was no doubt they had spotted it. The men hugged the rocks in an attempt to keep from being seen. After a few minutes of slowly flying in a circle, it descended and landed in a clearing about 525 yards from the jeep in the opposite direction of where the men were huddled. As soon as the helicopter touched down, about six men and an officer jumped out and cautiously headed for the jeep. They looked it over, and the officer pulled a walkie-talkie from his belt and began to speak. About a dozen or more soldiers jumped from the helicopter and headed in the direction of the jeep.

Lev motioned for the men to move back further up the mountain. He knew that the soldiers would start looking for the former occupants of the jeep and they probably knew that they were looking for armed spies. They had to run across a small clearing. They waited until all of the soldiers were around the officer who was obviously giving orders and waving his arms while dispatching men in small groups of three and four, in different directions.

Suddenly, they were spotted. The helicopter pilot noticed the movement and immediately informed the officer. The helicopter then took flight and headed in the direction of the men, while the soldiers who had been dispatched in different directions immediately ran back toward the officer near the jeep.

The helicopter sprayed the area where the small band of men huddled against the rocks with machine gun fire. They were trapped, not being able to move because they were pinned down by the helicopter firing. Bullets were splattering off the rocks and ricocheting all around them, and the soldiers were advancing toward them.

"We have to make a break for it!" Lev shouted.

"We'll go in different directions. Maybe some of us can make it," Lev ordered.

He motioned to his two men, signaling one to go in one direction toward some boulders further up the mountain, and another in a different direction.

"I'm going to head up there," he said to Jim, pointing to some rocks about fifty yards northwest of their position. "I suggest you head in that direction, toward that outcropping." He pointed.

"That's insane. You'll never make it," Jim said to Lev, not for one minute thinking he could dissuade him but having no ideas for an alternative.

Lev ignored Jim's admonition.

"On the count of three!" he shouted above the roar of the helicopter engines. "One, two, three!"

The four men scrambled and headed in different directions and for a minute confused the helicopter pilot as well as the soldiers, who did not expect the move. They had been moving slowly toward the position of the four men, scrambling from covered positions behind rocks, hedgehopping closer with each move, not knowing what firepower, if any, the four had.

It only took the helicopter pilot a minute to realize what was happening. He quickly maneuvered his ship and, with a burst of machine gun fire, quickly hit one of the men running in the clearing. A third man was heading for some rocks and was almost behind them when the pilot let go with cannon fire, shattering the ground and sending the man flying through the air.

Chapter 11

Salek was leading his band of men over the rugged terrain. He was very proud of them. They had fought together for many years. Many of them had survived with him from the almost constant wars since their childhood. These were strong men who endured many hardships. They fought the Turks to the west, the Iranians to the south, and even fellow Kurds from different tribes to the east. Even the lack of food and clothing, the cold of the mountains in winter, and the fact that they were always outgunned by the enemy could not deter them from their quest to free their people and to obtain a country for their fellow Kurds.

They survived because they knew every nook and cranny in these mountains. To them this was literally mother earth. She provided shelter from the many different storms and gave them water to drink food to eat and a place to rest.

Things had gotten better, though. The Americans attacking the Iraqis had taken a great deal of pressure from them, at least for a little while. And now the Americans were supplying them with sophisticated weapons and clothing and much of the material necessary to carry on a war. Salek could see the Americans fly overhead. He and his men would wave at the vapor trails of the jets. They kept the Iraqis from bombing their villages and camps and gassing their families. If only the Americans would finish the job.

Salek's thoughts were interrupted by the sounds of a helicopter. He was not too concerned, as he and his men were sheltered by the tall trees, although he knew that on the other side of this mountain, there was very little foliage to protect them.

It sounded like the helicopter had stopped and was circling in one place. He decided to take a look and signaled his men to spread out and head for the crest of the mountain.

When they reached the top of the mountain, Salek heard machine gun fire. He cautiously peered over the mountain and saw the helicopter in front of him at eye level and only about three hundred yards away. It was definitely Iraqi. He signaled his men to prepare the ground-to-air missile, the one the Americans recently provided. As the men readied the missile, Salek could see that the helicopter was firing at some men on the ground and there were Iraqi soldiers nearby. The helicopter let go with a burst of cannon fire as Salek signaled his men to fire.

The missile streaked forward, leaving a thin trail of smoke. It slammed into the helicopter, causing a huge explosion. Pieces flew everywhere, and for a minute, Salek's men stood in awe of what had just happened. They had fired the ground-to-air missiles before but were never successful, always either misfiring or missing their target altogether.

Chapter 12

Jim ran for all he was worth. The roar of the helicopter and the machine gun fire was all the incentive he needed. He leaped over a large boulder, only to find that it fell away on the other side, causing him to fall about six feet before his feet hit the earth. His forward momentum caused him to fall on his face. He quickly scrambled to his feet, realizing that he had not been shot at. *The others must have taken the brunt of it,* he thought. He hoisted himself up and peered over the large boulder. There were two men still in the clearing and lying very still. He quickly looked for the third but did not see him. Jim hoped that it was Lev and that he had made it to cover. He looked up at the helicopter and saw that it seemed to be slowly turning and heading in his direction. Jim rubbed his eyes, but there was no doubt about it. He braced his back against the boulder facing the crest of the hill and waited for the cannon explosion he thought was sure to come.

Jim couldn't believe his eyes. A thick wisp of smoke came from the direction he was facing. In a split second, Jim heard a huge explosion, and the ground was peppered with shrapnel. He wasn't sure whether that was the helicopter's cannon firing at him. Then he realized that he did not hear the helicopter engine anymore. Before he could peer over the boulder again, men came running over the crest, firing their weapons. Two of them ran past Jim and were chasing the soldiers who, after realizing what had transpired, were in full retreat running down the mountain. Jim stood up and raised his hands in the air to show them he had no hostile intentions.

In a matter of minutes, Salek mounted his horse slowly and led it down the hill toward Jim.

"Good day," Salek said to Jim. "You can put your hands down."

"Thank you," Jim responded. "Do you mind if I go over there and check on the others?" Jim said, motioning with his head toward his fallen rescuers.

"Not so fast," Salek responded. "What is your name, and where did you come from?"

"My name is Jim Vara, and they rescued me from prison," Jim responded.

"Ah, yes, Mr. Vara. We have been waiting for you. Go ahead, check on your comrades."

Jim climbed around the large boulder that had served as his refuge. He braced himself for what was ahead. He knew that he had not been shot at until it was almost over, so that meant that Lev and the others took the brunt of it.

His worst thoughts were realized. Lying on the ground in from of him was two of Lev's men. They were about five yards from each other and had not made much progress from their original cover before they were gunned down. Both had numerous bloody spots on their backs, obviously entry wounds.

Jim looked around for Lev but did not see him. He headed in the direction of the rocks where Lev had said he would go. Jim jumped over a hole that was obviously made by the helicopter's cannon. He went around the tall rocks to the other side and saw Lev lying in a pool of blood. His right leg was at an abnormal angle to the rest of his body, which meant that it was either severed or at least broken. Jim immediately went to him and bent down and put his head close to Lev's face. He wasn't breathing.

Jim put his finger in Lev's mouth to see if anything was blocking his air passage. His tongue was back into his throat. Jim pulled out Lev's tongue until it was in its proper position. He then placed his mouth on Lev's, pinched his nose closed, and started CPR. In a matter of seconds, Lev's eyes opened and he gasped for air, taking in deep gulps, his chest heaving.

Salek, who was still on horseback, followed Jim and was towering over him, taking in the entire scene. "You do good work," he said, a broad smile on his face. "Perhaps you should join us as a medic," he kidded.

"You do good work too," Jim responded. "You really knocked the hell out of that helicopter."

Salek's smile broadened. He instantly liked the American.

Jim supported the back of Lev's head as he tried to sit up, his gasps subsiding. Lev let out a groan as the pain from his leg finally started to register. Jim reached into his backpack and took out a rugged-looking knife. He slowly cut Lev's trouser leg until he came to the huge wound just above the knee.

Salek shouted commands to some of his men, and almost immediately, a first aid kit was handed to Jim. *American*, he thought as he opened it, hoping it contained morphine. Lev was in luck. Jim tore open the package and was about to give the injection when Lev grabbed his hand to stop him.

"First," Lev began painfully, "where are my men?"

"I'm sorry," Jim began. "The helicopter got them."

"Are they both dead?" Lev asked.

"Yes."

"Then I must tell you before you inject me."

"What?" Jim inquired.

Lev looked toward Salek, who was riding off to check on his men and Iraqi soldiers.

"You can trust him only so far," Lev began. "He is honest, but he has some men that we are not sure of. You must get to Kirkuk."

Jim knew that that was the town where the CIA was secretly stationed, working as staff in a makeshift embassy.

"Salek can get you there," Lev continued. His pain was getting unbearable; he hesitated longer between labored words.

"I know," Jim began, but Lev stopped him.

"My mission, you have to carry out my mission first." Lev motioned to his collar and began to struggle with it. "Tear it," Lev directed.

Jim reached for the collar and realized that Lev was trying to tell him that there was something in it. Jim took his knife and cut a hole in the collar. He saw that a small piece of film was lodged in it.

"Whatever you do, Jim, get this to Manachem Zula in Rome. Promise me, Jim. The fate of my country now rests with you." Lev then collapsed unconscious from the pain.

Jim tried to ask Lev more questions, but he was not responding. He palmed the film, looked at it, and decided to put it in his shirt pocket for now.

He injected the morphine into Lev. He stood up and looked around for something he could use to splint Lev's leg. He found a branch that was bent, but it would have to do. He took bandages out of the first aid kit and was going to cover the wound when he decided that he had to try to straighten Lev's leg. It would probably have to be amputated by the time they got to a doctor. He motioned to one of Salek's men—a group had formed, curiously watching the American—to hold Lev down. Jim tried to sterilize his hands using alcohol rubs from the first aid kit. He took a deep breath and pulled slightly on Lev's leg. He could feel the bone was not setting properly. He placed one hand on the wound, at the point where it had shattered, and tried to align the leg. Lev let out moans of pain. Jim finally felt that it was as straight as he could get it. He asked the men for some water and washed the blood from his hands. He dressed the wound using a wound spray and sterile gauze pads from the first aid kit. He then tied the leg to the branch, which would have to serve as a splint.

In the meantime, Salek had some of his men bring a stretcher. They lifted Lev as gently as they could, and two men started carrying him toward the crest of the mountain. They then straddled the stretcher between two mules and led the makeshift ambulance through the rugged mountainous terrain.

"I have a truck about two miles from here. We can take him to the village in that," Salek volunteered.

"Is there a doctor in the village?" Jim inquired.

"We don't have a schooled doctor, but we have one that is better. He has fixed up more people in a week than your doctors do in a year," Salek said as he motioned to a horse, indicating Jim should mount. "Hurry. We must get out of here in case the soldiers called for reinforcements," Salek continued.

Chapter 13

They rode a short distance through woods on the opposite side of the mountain from where the brief battle had taken place. They exited onto a dirt path, which served as a road, then took the road for a while when one of Salek's men who was riding point signaled to halt. A few men dismounted and began pulling branches from the side of the road, revealing an old World War II truck. The truck had been a troop carrier that had, at one time, a canvas top. Now all it contained on the bed was the strapping where the canvas used to be tied. They loaded Lev's stretcher onto it, and Jim climbed up and sat next to him. Lev did not move but would groan each time the truck hit a groove or hole in the road. *It must be causing him excruciating pain,* Jim thought. He hoped the morphine had kicked in.

Before long, they arrived in a small village that consisted of small mud houses and several tents, all camouflaged. Jim helped the men carry Lev into one of the houses. They had to go through two doors. The first was a large room with a dirt floor. Bunk beds lined the walls with injured men lying on them. When they entered the second room, Jim saw that it was surprisingly clean. It had wood flooring and three tables that were used for the wounded. There were a couple of cabinets along the far wall that contained medical supplies, a small table in the corner with a bucket on it, and a desk that looked like it dated back to the 1800s.

The doctor [sic] was waiting for them and signaled them to put Lev down on the table nearest him. He glanced at Lev and looked at his leg for a few minutes. He walked away and washed his hands in a bucket of water that was on a corner table. Just then, a young woman, obviously his assistant, entered the room. The doctor returned to his patient and began to take off the makeshift splint and bandages. He looked up and, as if as an afterthought, signaled for everyone to leave the room.

Jim reluctantly went into the outer room and sat on the floor next to the door. He was exhausted. He hadn't slept the night before because of the escape and the harrowing jeep ride. He put his backpack on the dirt floor, laid his head on it, and closed his eyes.

He awoke to the sound of voices whispering around him. Jim opened his eyes to see three men talking in low tones. He sat up, rubbed his eyes, and looked around the room. On one of the cots lay Lev. *I must have slept for hours,* he thought to himself. The three men looked at Jim and then left the room.

Jim got up and walked over to where Lev was lying. He had a coarse blanket over him and appeared to be resting comfortably. He was tempted to lift the blanket to look at Lev's wound but decided against it for fear he would wake him. He could clearly see the outline of two legs through the blanket and felt somewhat relieved that at least the doctor hadn't amputated the leg.

Jim heard the door open, and Salek entered the room. He was carrying a bowl and a large spoon. He looked at Jim and smiled. "How are you feeling today?" he said.

"Fine," answered Jim.

"I brought you something to eat."

"Thank you," Jim responded, taking the bowl. He looked in it and saw what appeared to be chunks of meat on top of yellow rice. The two men sat on the dirt floor, and Jim began to eat his breakfast.

"How is Mojah?" Salek asked, looking over at Lev.

"I don't know. He seems to be resting well," Jim responded, not letting on that his name was Lev. Or at least he thought the name was Lev, *or Sarge,* Jim mused to himself.

"I will check with the doctor," Salek said as he rose and went into the inner office.

The meat was salty, but Jim ate it. He was hungrier than he knew. He wished for a nice hot shower but realized it probably would be a long time before he got one.

Salek reentered the room followed by the doctor, who smiled at Jim.

"He said that Mojah will be fine," Salek said. "Do you have any questions? I will be your interpreter."

"Will he be able to use that leg, and how long will he be laid up?" Jim inquired.

Salek turned to the doctor and repeated Jim's questions. The doctor answered, and Salek translated for Jim, who had not let on that he spoke Farsi. "He said he thinks that he will get some use of the leg, but not 100 percent. He should be able to get around on a crutch in a couple of days, but he will probably be laid up for two or three weeks to a month."

Jim thanked the doctor, who then went back into the rear room.

"Well, Jim, now we must get you to Kirkuk," Salek said.

"I know, but I want to make sure Mojah will be OK."

"He will be fine. You heard the doctor. He'll be up and around in a couple of weeks. Don't worry, you have my word. I will see that he is well taken care of." Salek tried to assure Jim.

43

"You will leave tonight. I have made arrangements. I have a car to take you part of the way, and then you will travel by horseback over the mountains to Samaria, where another car will be waiting to take you to a lake that must be crossed. It will be like American Pony Express." Salek laughed. Jim didn't want to go without Lev but knew that he had to.

"OK, I'll be ready," Jim responded.

"Good. In the meantime, if you need anything, ask anyone. We are all brothers here," Salek said as he exited the house.

Jim looked over at Lev, who was still sleeping soundly. He decided to find a bathroom and see if he could get washed up. He opened the door and stepped out. A cold camp breeze wafted against his face, and chill shook his body. He was about to walk down the dirt path when he noticed two men down a path to his left. *Perhaps they are just curious onlookers,* Jim thought to himself. But something in his gut told him differently. He had learned long ago in the NYPD to trust his gut. He walked to his right up the path a short way and turned right again behind the building, heading toward what might be an outhouse. As soon as he made the turn, he stopped and peeked around the corner. The two men were heading toward the house. All doubts were erased when they opened the door and entered. Jim raced back to the house, taking out his pistol from its holster as he ran. He swung open the door and saw the two men standing over Lev, one with his hand over his head. The shine of a large knife in that hand was unmistakable. Jim fired several shots into both men, who were thrown to the side by the impact of the bullets. They both fell to the earthen floor, blood oozing from their bodies. Jim ran quickly to Lev, who was still in a deep sleep.

Within minutes, men came running through the front door, pointing semiautomatic weapons at him. He quickly dropped his pistol and raised his hands. The doctor entered from his office, quickly surveyed the scene, and bent over to examine the two bodies on the floor.

Salek also heard the shots and came running into the room.

"What happened?" he inquired as he watched the doctor examine the bodies of the two men.

'They were going to kill Mojah," Jim answered.

The doctor moved away and told Salek that they were both dead. Salek took the knife, which had fallen to the floor, and nodded at Jim. He looked worried, which made Jim feel uneasy. He shouted orders to his men, who quickly removed the two bodies.

"Who are they, and why would they want to kill Mojah?" Jim inquired.

"I don't know, Jim. They are not my men. They must have somehow infiltrated our ranks. Perhaps they were waiting here for us to get back."

"But why would they come after Mojah? How would they know he would be here?" Jim pressed.

"I don't know that either, Jim," Salek responded deep in thought. "I guess it means I can't leave here tonight."

"Yes, you can. I will have Mojah removed to my house and keep him under guard. I guarantee he will be well taken care of," Salek continued. "I will institute a very strict security system. I cannot afford to have traitors in our midst. This is really unbelievable, Jim."

Chapter 14

After asking several men, Jim was finally able to locate a stream where he could bathe. It was ice cold in the mountains, so he could not submerge himself in the icy water. He took off his backpack, stripped off his shirt, and, with a handkerchief for a facecloth, managed to clean at least the upper part of his body. Shivering, he put his shirt back on. He wished he had a jacket, but landing in the desert as he did, did not really call for one. As he was buttoning his shirt, he thought of the film. He reached into the pocket and was relieved to find it still there. He wondered what it contained. Lev placed a lot of importance on it. Jim figured he must get to Kirkuk, contact the CIA, and then make arrangements to get to Rome and find this Manachem Zula.

Jim's thoughts were interrupted. Someone was coming down the path toward him and the stream. He quickly put the film back in his shirt pocket. Still being very wary, he took out his pistol. He wished that he had reloaded it before he put it in its holster back at the house.

The sounds of feet on the path came closer and closer. Jim crouched low behind a large tree, pistol at the ready. And then he saw her. It was a young woman carrying a basket of clothing. She passed within a few feet of him, but he decided not to say anything for fear that he would scare her. She went to the edge of the stream and walked up the bank a bit and passed the tree where Jim was hiding. She walked another fifteen yards and finally stopped in an area where stones jutted out into the stream, forming a small pier. She put the basket down, and Jim could see that they contained bloody clothing. She bent over and began to wash her hands and face. Then Jim realized she was the nurse. She then turned her attention to the bloody clothing, extracting one piece at a time and scrubbing it using a bar of brown-looking soap and then pounding the piece on a stone. She then twisted the clothing to get as much water out as possible. Jim sat there for a while, resting and fascinated by the scene.

When she finished, she wiped her hands on her apron, bent over, and picked up the basket. She turned, but instead of walking back toward the path, she stepped into the woods, which lined the banks on both sides of the stream. She stopped and looked around as if to see if anyone was around. It appeared to Jim, who could barely see her because of the brush, that she extracted something from her pocket and bent over. She then came out of the woods, looked up and down the stream, and, satisfied that no one was there, walked back along the stream bank and up the path.

Jim waited until he was sure she was far enough away from the area so that she would not see him. He went along the stream bank to the area where the nurse had been. He retraced her steps into the woods but saw nothing. He searched around the area a little further, widening his circle.

It reminded him of the time when he was a rookie doing plainclothes work. He would tail a subject, and when they spotted him, the chase would be on. When he started to gain on the subject, they would invariably throw away the narcotics. At that point, Jim would have to make a decision. If you stop to pick up the evidence, the subject could get away. But if you catch the subject and return to the area, the evidence would probably have disappeared. Probably a junkie looking to get high would have picked it up, and all you would have is an irate citizen crying injustice at the hands of the honky cop, at the same time attracting a crowd and you would have to let him go. That was bad enough, but the curses regarding his mother that inevitably followed were hard for him to take. He learned quickly that you never let the evidence get away. He was frustrated the few times that he turned in evidence without a suspect, but it was all part of the job.

Jim's attention was drawn to a tree with a small hole on its trunk. He peeked inside, but it was too dark to see anything. He hesitated for a minute. He didn't want to stick his hand into the unknown, visualizing all sorts of snakes and rodents residing inside. The hole was small, barely big enough to put his hand in. Jim took a breath and cautiously put his hand into the hole. Once inside, it flared out a bit, making the inside of the hole larger than the opening. He felt something. Hard metal . . . a gun. He slowly extracted it and studied it for a minute. It was an old-fashioned revolver. *Nothing extraordinary,* he thought. He put his hand into the hole again and felt what could be leaves or papers. He grasped them and pulled them out. It was two pieces of paper with a symbol on the top and writing that he did not understand. *Very interesting,* he thought. *I'd better show it to Salek.*

He headed straight back to Salek's house. Upon entering, he was met by a mean-looking guard. The guard recognized Jim and let him pass. He knocked on the inner door and was greeted by another guard.

"Salek," Jim said.

The guard looked him over and closed the door in his face. A minute passed, and Salek opened the door and welcomed Jim, inviting him in.

"You're here to see Mojah," he said as Jim entered, a warm smile on his face.

"Yes, and to show you something you may find interesting." Jim took out the papers and the gun and handed them to Salek as he explained what had happened

47

at the stream. Salek's smile quickly turned into a frown. He disregarded the gun, laying it on a table. He studied the papers intently. He then called the guard and gave him instructions. The guard immediately rushed out of the house.

"Very bad, Jim," Salek said as he contemplated the papers. "It says you are here in the village and are leaving tonight. The second paper says that Mojah lives and that his assassins were killed by you."

"That means the nurse must be a spy, but whom is she working for?" Jim asked.

"Yes," Salek responded. "You see the symbol? It is of our Kurdish enemies from the west, the Syrians. They work with the Iranians and are devils."

Shouting could be heard from outside. In a moment, the door swung open, and two men entered and spoke rapidly to Salek. Salek nodded to Jim to follow him to the outer room. When he entered, Jim saw two other men, one on each side holding the nurse practically off the floor. Two other women were being held back by other guards and were uncontrollably sobbing.

Salek approached the nurse. His face turned red as he started shouting at her and waving the papers in her face. She said nothing but looked as though she was resigned to what was going to happen to her. The other two women stopped their sobbing long enough to hear what Salek was saying to the nurse and then they began screaming. Salek shouted something to the guards that were keeping the women back, and they quickly removed them from the house, followed by the nurse and her guards. Salek looked at Jim and motioned him to follow.

They all entered what appeared to be a small town square. In the center was a pole. The nurse was stripped of her clothing and tied to the pole, hands high above her. Splinters from the pole were cutting into her soft stomach and breasts. She was still defiant, showing no emotion. The two women who had been with her were then placed in front of her and each shot in the backs of their heads by the guards. The nurse lurched, but the ropes held her fast. The whole town seemed to be entering the square as word rapidly spread from house to house.

Jim was startled. He never expected the shootings and in fact didn't realize what had happened until it was over. He looked to Salek, who was busy arguing with the doctor, who had also come into the square. Then Salek raised his voice and apparently ordered the doctor away. The doctor turned and, with head bowed, left.

Jim was getting mad. He knew this was not his business, but he felt responsible, as he had turned in the notes, and couldn't stand by and do nothing. He approached Salek.

"What the hell is going on!" he shouted to Salek.

"If you want to be my friend, you mind your business and do not shout at me in front of my people, or I will do something we will both regret," Salek responded in an agitated voice. Jim could see that Salek was mad and did not want to lose face in front of the crowd in the square. He also realized he had blundered by shouting at Salek in front of everyone and decided that the best course of action would be to defer to Salek, so he backed away, made a small head bow, and left the square.

Jim went back to Salek's house. The town was deserted with everyone in or near the square. He entered Salek's house and went to the back room, where, to his surprise, a guard was still standing watch. Jim nodded to the guard and walked over to the cot where Lev/Mojah was lying. Lev opened his eyes.

"What are you doing here? I thought you would be in Kirkuk by now," Lev spoke slowly, showing pain in speaking. Jim quickly explained the events of the day, including his run-in with the nurse. He explained that he was leaving at dusk, which would be soon.

"Whatever you do, Jim," Lev admonished, "get that film to Zula."

"I will, I promise," Jim responded.

"What is on it?" Jim regretted asking because he knew that Lev would either be forced to lie not to insult Jim or evade the question.

"It is very important to the survival of my country," Lev answered.

"I also want to tell you, Jim, that you must have been betrayed. Everyone knew about you and your movements. Someone in your organization must have revealed your entire mission."

"I know," Jim answered. "It seems like they were waiting for me."

"Be very careful and trust no one," Lev admonished. "When you get to Kirkuk, call the Canadian embassy—they can help you. But be careful not to reveal who you are. Ask for Trigvey. He is a friend of mine and he can steer you in the right direction."

Lev then gave Jim detailed instructions on how and where he was to deliver the film.

Lev's eyes closed as he started falling into a drug-induced sleep. Jim got up and started for the door.

"Thanks," Lev said, his voice getting faint.

"For what?" Jim asked.

"For saving my life, twice," Lev said, his arm falling to his side as he fell fast asleep

Chapter 15

Jim sat down in the outer room for what seemed only a few minutes. He dozed off only to be awakened by a short round-faced man nudging him. "Mister, mister, wake up . . . we go," the round figure said in Farsi.

"Who are you?" Jim asked, still a little groggy.

"I your driver," the round man responded as he pointed to the door.

Jim got up, stretched, bent over, and grabbed his backpack. He swung it over his shoulders. He hefted it a few times until he had it in a comfortable position and then tightened the straps. He signaled the driver to wait. He went into the next room to see if Lev was awake but found him sound asleep. He looked around for Salek but didn't see him either, so he left the room, signaled the driver to lead the way, and followed him out into the street.

The cold air woke Jim up. He wished he had a hot cup of coffee. In front of the house was a very small old French car. It was pathetically small. When he first saw them in France, he thought that the drivers were sitting in the backseat. Jim marveled at how the round man managed to get in behind the wheel. Jim walked around and, after taking off his backpack, got into the passenger's seat. He held the backpack on his lap as the car started with a chug and a backfire. The ride was bumpy and tedious. The roads soon became nonexistent. As darkness fell, the only thing visible was the small headlights carving a hole in the blackness. Jim felt a little relaxed. The driver seemed to know the road and where he was going.

They hit several bumps, and Jim thought he heard something but chalked it off as the groans of the old car. He felt very uncomfortable and decided to throw his backpack into the ready. He decided to remove the Uzi, just in case they ran into trouble. He lifted the backpack over his head and was facing the rear while unfastening the strap to get at the Uzi. He heard it again. This time he was sure. There was something in the back of the car. He sat back in his seat, drew his automatic, and pointed it at the driver.

"Pull over, now," he ordered in Farsi.

The driver slowly pulled the car over the side of the road. Jim motioned to the driver to get out of the car as he pointed his automatic at him. Jim motioned the driver toward the back of the car and opened the back overhead door. On the floor of the car, partially covered in a canvas tarp, was the nurse. She had bruises all over her body. The driver reached in and cradled her in his arms. He looked back at Jim and said in Farsi, "Please, sir, this is my daughter."

Jim looked at the two of them and felt very sad. He realized that it was his fault that the women had been beaten. He was surprised that she had not been killed as were the other two in the plaza.

The driver pleaded with Jim, saying, "Sir, let me take her to my brother's house, where she can be taken care of. It will only take a half hour and will not delay our meeting with the next part of your trip. I can make up the time by driving a little faster."

Jim looked at the driver cradling his daughter in his arms and pondered what he should do. He wanted to help the driver and his daughter but was concerned that if Salek ever found out, it would be the end of their cooperation and friendship. On the other hand, he could not, in good conscience, leave the suffering woman in this condition or take her back to Salek, who would probably kill her. He decided to let the driver take his daughter to his brother.

"How did you save her?" Jim inquired.

"They left her tied to a pole in the plaza, and when no one was around, I took her. I had nowhere to take her in that town, so I put her in the car."

Jim found some rags at the back of the car and covered the woman as best as he could. He then took her in his arms and returned to the passenger's seat. The driver got behind the wheel of the car and thanked Jim profusely as they drove off.

In about twenty minutes, they arrived at the driver's brother's house. The driver came around the car and took his daughter from Jim and disappeared into the house. In about ten minutes, the driver returned and thanked Jim profusely for allowing him to take care of his daughter.

They immediately left at a high rate of speed into the night. They drove for about two hours, then arrived at the next meeting point of the trip. A thin bearded man was waiting for them with two horses. Jim took his backpack from behind his seat and got out of the car. The driver came out of the car and again thanked Jim, kissing the back of his hand. Jim was embarrassed and pulled his hand away. He turned to the bearded man, who motioned for Jim to get on one of the horses. As they rode away, Jim turned back and waved at the driver, who was getting back into the car.

They rode over mountains for more than three hours. Jim tried to communicate with his guide, but each time he tried to say something, the bearded man would just put his finger over his lips, indicating silence.

Finally, they arrived at the place where they were to meet the next driver. Jim marveled at the way the trip had been set up and coordinated in this primitive part of the world. The driver had been waiting for them and offered Jim some food, which consisted of dried figs and dates. Jim ate them rapidly, realizing that he was hungry and hadn't eaten for a while. He thanked the driver as they drove off on dusty dirt roads.

The trip only took about a half hour when the driver suddenly stopped and motioned to Jim that this is where he was to meet his next guide. Jim saw nothing but woods, and the driver got out and led Jim about fifty feet into the woods to a path where he told Jim in Farsi that he should continue on the path until he came to a lake where men would be waiting to take him across in a boat. Jim thanked the driver and began his trek through the woods.

After about an hour's walk, Jim heard voices. He paused and wondered to himself if these were the people he was to meet. He removed his Uzi from his backpack and slowly made his way toward the voices. The men were speaking in Farsi, and Jim could barely make out what they were saying. There were three of them and they were huddled around a small campfire. Then what Jim heard sent a chill up his spine. They were discussing what to do with Jim's body after they killed him. One of the men was objecting to killing Jim and he tried to persuade the others that if Salek ever found out what they did, he would skin them alive. The other two were adamant and insisted that it was their Muslim duty to kill the infidel, and, besides, he was worth more dead than alive.

Jim heard enough. He entered the camp area, Uzi at the ready. When the startled men saw him, they reached for their rifles, which were lying on the ground next to them. They didn't stand a chance. Jim shot the two of them closest to him and motioned for the third to put his hands up. The frightened man raised his hands and stood up. Jim examined the bodies and, satisfied that they were dead, turned his attention to the remaining man. He motioned to him to turn around and put his hands against the tree and then he patted him down, removing a large knife from his belt. Jim told the man in Farsi to sit on the ground after he removed his rifle and knife. He then interrogated the man, asking him what his plans were to get him to Kirkuk. The man explained that he had a small boat on the lake and that the town was on the other side of the lake. He further reiterated that it would take about a half hour to get to Kirkuk. The man further stated that it was his duty to bury his comrades before he could leave. Jim didn't see how it would be possible because it was a heavily wooded area and they had no equipment to dig with. It would be impossible with the huge trees and roots covering the ground. The man said he would use stones to cover the bodies. Jim motioned him to go ahead but kept a very leery eye on him. The job took about two hours before it was complete, and the man was satisfied that he had done all he could to put the bodies to rest. Jim told the man to go ahead in front of him to the boat. He walked about twenty-five yards, and they came to the lake with a small motor boat anchored in a couple of feet of water. Jim waded into the water and got into the boat. He told the man to follow him, pull up the anchor, and push the boat out into the water until it could float on its own. He then jumped into the boat, while Jim kept an eye on him, Uzi at the ready. The man immediately tugged at the starting rope and, after three vigorous tries, got the motor to run. They slowly crossed the lake, and Jim pondered what he was going to do with the man after they arrived on the other side of the island. He devised a plan and took a hand grenade from his backpack and made sure the man saw all that he was doing. He placed the grenade in the point of the bow of the boat. He explained to the man that this grenade could be detonated by remote control and that after he left Jim off, he was to return to the campsite where they left. If, however, he tried anything funny while on the lake, Jim would detonate the grenade, killing him. This was all a big bluff on Jim's part, as he had no way of detonating the grenade. His only hope was that the man didn't know any better and believed him. When he got out of the boat, he motioned for the man to go back across the lake and pointed toward the grenade. The man immediately turned the boat around and started back to the other side of the lake. Jim put his Uzi back into his backpack, got out of the boat, and started walking toward the town, which was about one hundred yards away. He entered the town and felt that he was standing out, as he did not look like any of the people who were there. He was still wearing a camouflage outfit, which had been given to him, and he felt uneasy.

Chapter 16

He took out the cell phone Lev had given him and dialed the number to the Canadian embassy. The telephone was answered by a professional-sounding secretary. Jim asked for Trigvey and was put on hold while the call was transferred.

Trigvey got on the line and asked, "Who is this?"

Jim responded with "I was told to call you by Mojah." Trigvey told Jim that he would call him back in five minutes. Jim assumed that Trigvey was going to use a scrambled phone to call so that their conversation could not be intercepted. When Trigvey called back, he asked Jim where he was. Jim told him that he had no idea because there were no street signs that he could relate to Trigvey. Jim looked around and said that up the street was a restaurant called the Dragon House. Trigvey told him that he knew where it was and that he would send Americans to meet him. He told Jim to go into the restaurant and order a meal and be as inconspicuous as he could while waiting. Jim thought to himself that this was not going to be easy. He hung up the phone and slowly headed toward the restaurant. He entered what appeared to be a fairly dark and dingy eatery. There were only a few people present who were eating even though it was dinnertime. Jim walked to a table where his back would be against the wall and he would be able to see the front door. A man with a dirty apron came toward him and looked at Jim with a suspicious eye. He spoke to Jim in Farsi, telling him that today they had yellow rice and chicken. He could have tea with the meal to drink for four rials. Jim told the man that that would be fine and asked him where the bathroom was. The man gave Jim a funny look and pointed to the back door. Jim got up and walked through the back door and found himself outside. A few feet away was a small structure, which was obviously an outhouse. Jim entered the outhouse and was immediately taken back by the strong odor of human waste. He reached into his backpack and took out his automatic and placed it into his belt. He got out of the outhouse as quickly as he could and reentered the restaurant. He sat back down at his table and kept an eye on the front door.

About five minutes later, the waiter served him a bowl of the yellow rice with pieces of chicken. He also placed a paper napkin and utensils consisting of a dirty-looking spoon and knife next to the plate. He then placed a cup of tea, which appeared to be very hot, next to the plate. Then the waiter turned and left without saying anything. Jim perused the food and made up his mind that there was no way he was going to eat it, even though he was very hungry. The last thing he needed was a case of dysentery.

Jim sat there for another fifteen minutes when the door to the restaurant opened, and two men, obviously not natives, entered and looked around the restaurant. One was about six feet two inches tall, while the other was a little shorter.

Their eyes immediately locked onto Jim, and they slowly walked to his table. Both men were grim faced, looking Jim up and down. Jim motioned them to sit down opposite him as he reached under the table and placed his hand on the automatic in his belt.

"Jim Vara, I presume," one of the men said, breaking the tense silence.

"Yes, and you are?" Jim inquired.

"It's not necessary to know our names. You will understand in a minute," the tall one said.

"Let's get right down to business," the shorter man said. "We were sent here to kill you."

Jim tensed and pulled the automatic a few inches out of his belt so that he could release it quickly if necessary.

"No need for that," the shorter man said, obviously aware of what Jim had in mind. "If we were going to kill you, you would be dead already."

"I don't understand. What is going on?" Jim asked with as strong a voice as he could muster.

The taller man looked at Jim and grinned. "There is a contract out on you in every consulate in the world. The word is that you turned and betrayed your . . . our country. We are supposed to take you out before you can do any damage."

"Then why haven't you?" Jim asked, his hand still holding the grip on the automatic.

"We have a mutual friend who vouched for you."

"Who?" Jim inquired.

"Tony Chapman. We worked a couple of cases with him in the past, and so when we saw the contract on you, we knew you had also worked with him. We called him, and he said you would be the last person on earth to turn on your country. He said he would bet his life on it and that you had saved his life in the past and is his hero."

Jim relaxed his grip on the automatic. "Yes, I worked many cases with Tony, and he is one of the best."

"How did you save his life?" the shorter man asked.

Jim smiled and relaxed. He loved telling the story and relished the opportunity to tell it again.

"When Tony and I worked in the NYPD, we were planting a bug in a midtown restaurant in Manhattan. We were almost finished when the bad guys walked in, guns out. They had us cold. Tony was half under a table, tapping the bug, when he saw what was happening and reached for his badge. The bad guys thought he was going for a gun and fired. The first shot missed, and Tony fell backward behind me. The second shot hit me in the chest, but I had my bulletproof vest on. The velocity of the bullet knocked me backward over Tony. By that time, Tony had his badge out and yelled, 'Police!' The bad guys panicked and ran for it. When we finally got up from the floor, we started laughing and couldn't stop. I guess we were releasing the tension and then we realized we must have looked like Keystone cops lying on the floor in a heap. At any rate, it took two weeks for the pain of the bullet to stop, but I was lucky it didn't break a rib. Ever since then, Tony and I became brothers."

Both men smiled as they visualized the scene in the restaurant.

"OK, we understand now," the tall one said, still smiling.

His demeanor suddenly changed. "Here's the deal. We will say we never saw you and you didn't show up at the meeting," he said. "You have to get out of here—I mean, out of this country. It's much too hot for you here. I suggest you get to the airport, which is about a twenty-minute ride from here. You should fly to Moscow, since that will not arouse any suspicions, and then go where you have to from there. If you walk up three blocks in that direction," he said, pointing over his shoulder, "you should be able to grab a cab. Good luck." With that, both men got up and walked out of the restaurant without looking back.

Jim sat there for a few minutes to absorb all that was said. Finally, he reached in his pocket and put ten dinars on the table and headed for the door, not having touched his food or drink.

When he got outside, he headed in the direction the agents had indicated and looked for a cab but saw none. After about twenty minutes, a small car appeared, which could be a cab. Jim waved at it, and it pulled up in front of him. He got in and told the driver he wanted to go to a haberdashery and then to the airport. The driver eyed Jim and decided that he was a good fare.

Chapter 17

At the haberdashery, Jim purchased a new set of clothing and discarded his old clothes. The trip to the airport was quiet, as neither Jim nor the driver spoke. Jim looked out the window and watched the town go by as he contemplated what he could do with his backpack, which contained weapons, money from different countries, and four passports all with his picture. If he threw the backpack in the trash and someone found it, it would cause an alarm, and if he didn't get into the air quick enough he would be detained. He doubted the airport would have lockers that he could rent and would give him time enough to get away.

Before long, they arrived at the airport, and Jim paid the cabbie and entered the airport. It was dirty and smoke filled just as Jim suspected. He looked for the bathroom, and when he spotted it, he made a beeline for it. The bathroom was as dirty as the rest of the airport, and Jim entered a stall and quickly removed the money and passports from the backpack. He placed two hundred dinars in the passport and put the rest in his pockets and, after leaving the stall, looked around for a place to dump the backpack. Seeing none, he reentered the main part of the airport and headed for the nearest ticket counter. He marveled that there were no lines and he was the first to speak to the ticket agent. He asked when the next flight for Moscow was leaving and was told that one was scheduled in about three hours. He could tell by the look on her face that she didn't think that was viable. He asked for a ticket and paid the women the fare. She asked to see his passport, and Jim handed her one with Italian origin. She perused the passport picture and looked at Jim and, satisfied, gave him a small ticket, which she perforated with a hole punch. She asked if he had luggage, which gave Jim pause. He hadn't thought about that and feared he would stand out and give extra scrutiny traveling one way to Moscow without luggage. Thinking quickly, he told the woman that his luggage was still outside at the curb and that he would check it in as soon as he retrieved it. She looked at him, suspicious of his explanation, but smiled and told him to bring it to her as soon as he gets it. She then asked about the backpack, and Jim lied that it was business material and he would carry it on the plane.

He left the counter and started looking for a luggage store. He noticed in the reflection of the glass storefronts that he had a tail. A salt-and-pepper-haired middle-aged man was very interested in what Jim was doing. Jim realized that he could not buy luggage without his tail noticing it. He looked around and observed the airport too small to lose a tail, so he headed for the bathroom again. He entered the bathroom and immediately went to the sink and ran water over his hands, looking into the mirror. He waited, but his tail did not enter. He dried his hands, picked up the backpack, and walked out. He immediately saw that his tail was waiting for him. Thinking quickly, Jim headed for the door and the cab stand. He walked out to the curb and observed a couple of cabs pull up and place suitcases on the sidewalk. He approached one cab as the driver was unloading the suitcases and began to speak with its passenger. This was distraction enough for Jim, who flung his backpack into the open trunk of the cab. When the cab driver finished speaking to his passenger, he closed the trunk of the cab without looking in, got into the cab, and drove away. Jim hoped this would buy him enough time to get out of Iraq.

He turned and noticed his tail was observing him from just inside the door of the airport. Jim nonchalantly walked where luggage had been piled up and grabbed a suitcase, which looked as if it could belong to him. He walked back into the airport, passed his tail without looking at him, and headed for the ticket counter. He approached the same ticket agent and handed her the suitcase. She asked Jim for his ticket and wrote out a ticket, which she tore in half, placing half on the suitcase and giving the other half to Jim. She then placed the suitcase behind the counter and nodded at Jim. Jim went to a row of seats where he sat down and could observe the ticket counter. His tail sat down about three rows behind him. Jim picked up a paper that was on the empty seat next to him and feigned that he was interested in the news printed on the page before him. He looked at the clock, knowing it was 1:00 p.m. and hoping that the plane would take off on time.

Time went by slowly, and Jim once again walked around the airport, looking in the few stores and trying to fill his time. He was hungry but did not want to eat, as he feared the poor sanitation he had encountered all along his route. Finally, he saw large pretzels on a counter and could not hold out any longer. He bought the pretzels and a magazine and returned to the place where he had been sitting. He began eating the pretzel and looked up at the clock and realized only a half hour had passed. He glanced back at his tail, who had no expression on his face and seemed to be bored with the whole situation. Jim finished his pretzels and thumbed through the magazine and waited. Minutes went by slowly, and, finally, it was three fifteen when he decided to approach the agent and ask if the flight was going to be on time. She responded that it was going to be fifteen minutes late and that they would begin boarding at three thirty. Once again, he glanced at the clock.

He mindlessly thumbed through the pages of the magazine as time once again weighed heavily on him. Without warning, a voice came over the loudspeaker and in Farsi announced that the plane for Moscow would begin boarding and that all passengers should report to gate 3. Jim got up and walked toward the gate area. He noted that there was no security in the main part of the airport. As he approached gate 3, he also noticed that people were being interrogated and searched prior to boarding. It seemed each gate had its own security. He entered the gate and approached the security desk. He turned his head and noted that his tail was waiting outside the gate area and had his eye on him. The man behind the counter asked Jim why he was going to Moscow. Jim lied and told him he was going on business. The officer asked him where he was staying in Moscow, and Jim bluffed and told him he was staying in a hotel near the airport where he was going to meet his associates. The guard asked him if he had anything to declare or any weapons on his person. Jim said no. The guard came from around the desk and told Jim to raise his arms. He scanned Jim with an electronic wand, paying close attention to his pockets. When he came to the money and passports, he just kept going, and Jim was grateful that the guard had missed discovering them.

Jim was glad he had put two hundred dinars in his passport because when the passport was returned to him, the money was missing, and it probably helped with his cursory search and easy questioning. The guard motioned Jim to proceed to the tarmac, where he climbed the stairs and entered the plane. As he entered, he looked back to see if his tail was still following him. He was relieved to see him walking away from the entry ramp, obviously satisfied that Jim was legitimate.

He boarded the plane, which looked like something left over from World War II. There were about thirty people on board; no stewardesses or any amenities at all.

The flight was slow and tedious and very loud as the two propeller-driven engines struggled to keep the craft airborne.

Chapter 18

When they finally landed in Moscow, Jim prepared himself for the inevitable questioning by the Russian immigration authorities. He decided to stick with the Italian passport and try to bluff his way into the country. The passport was genuine, and his picture was original, so that should not arouse any suspicions.

When it was his turn to identify himself to the officer, he tried to approach with an air of confidence and boredom. The Russian inspector asked him questions in Russian, which Jim did not understand. Jim in turn spoke in Farsi, which annoyed the inspector. After perusing the passport, the inspector gave Jim a look of disdain and stamped his passport and motioned him to move on.

Jim entered the main portion of the airport and immediately looked at a bulletin board for the next flight to Rome. There were no flights until the following day. This concerned Jim, as he did not want to spend the day and night in the airport but did not know where to go. He retrieved his bag from a pile that was placed haphazardly along a wall with many others. He still had no idea what was in it, but it provided legitimacy to his travels. The airport in Moscow was just the opposite of the one he left in Iraq. It was large and clean and looked very modern. He went to the ticket counter and inquired about buying a ticket to Rome. He managed to communicate with the young but very stern-looking woman behind the counter and was told that a plane would be leaving the following day at three o'clock in the afternoon and he could not buy a ticket using dinar.

He asked where he could change the money, and the clerk motioned toward a hallway to his rear. Jim turned and walked in the direction of the money changer. To his surprise, it was an official-looking kiosk with the different currencies listed on a bulletin board. He cashed in all the dinars he had left, getting enough rubles to buy the ticket to Rome and pay for a hotel and meals, and changed the rest in euros. He returned to the ticket counter, bought the ticket to Rome, and checked in the black suitcase.

He left the airport and looked around for a hotel or some form of lodging that he could use for the night. To his surprise, there were several modern-looking hotels in the immediate area of the airport. He walked to the nearest one and entered into a fairly large foyer. He went to the front desk, where he was greeted by a young clerk, who actually smiled at him. Jim tried to converse with him, but it was no use, as either of them could speak the other's language. Jim pointed to the wall behind the clerk that contained the room keys, and the clerk immediately provided a form for him to make out. Jim did the best he could, as the captions were all in Russian. The clerk was obviously used to this and helped Jim wherever he could. The clerk then asked Jim for his passport, which is normal in this part of the world. Jim handed him the Italian passport, and the clerk handed him a key with number 202 written on it. Jim paid for the room and climbed the stairs to the second floor.

His room was adequate with the bed being soft enough to sleep on. He was happy to see his own bathroom and immediately undressed and took a shower. Feeling refreshed, he got dressed and decided to go downstairs and look for something to eat.

The smiling clerk was behind the desk and motioned Jim to the rear of the building when Jim made an eating motion with his hands to his mouth.

Jim went to where the clerk had motioned and, to his surprise, found a nice, albeit small, dining room with about eight tables. Two of the tables were occupied by couples. A waitress motioned Jim to one of the empty tables and handed him what appeared to be a one-page menu written entirely in Russian. Not understanding any of it, he waited for the waitress to return and shrugged his shoulders, indicating he did not understand. The waitress obviously had dealt with this type of situation before and took the menu from Jim and turned and left. Jim wondered if he was going to get something to eat that would, in fact, be edible. To his surprise, the waitress returned almost immediately with a bowl of hot soup. Jim tasted it, and it was delicious. This was followed by a meat course, which was also very tasty. When he finished, he returned to his room and fell asleep. When he woke, he went down to the desk clerk to retrieve his passport. The clerk appeared nervous and motioned Jim back into the dining room for breakfast. He once again was seated at a table and was immediately given a hot cup of coffee, black, and some toast. He started to eat when he noticed two men enter the hotel, one carrying what looked like his borrowed black suitcase. The men approached the desk clerk, who handed them a passport, which Jim figured was probably his, and motioned toward the dining room where Jim was sitting. They approached Jim, and one speaking in Farsi asked him to return to his room with them. Jim immediately acquiesced, and they headed for the stairs. As they climbed up the stairs, Jim assessed the two men and thought to himself that he could take them both if he had to. But then he thought, where would he go? He is in a foreign country, doesn't speak the language, and could not go to the embassy for fear of what would happen to him.

They entered the room, and the Farsi speaker placed the suitcase on the bed. All sorts of thoughts went through Jim's head, and he wondered if the suitcase had precipitated this meeting. The Farsi speaker opened the suitcase to reveal women's undergarments. At that point, Jim didn't know whether to laugh or cry. The Farsi-speaking Russian asked him why he was carrying women's underwear. Jim, thinking rapidly, said that he was an underwear salesman and that he sold women's underwear to major stores in Baghdad.

The Farsi speaker then turned to his partner and spoke to him in Russian, obviously telling him Jim's answer. His partner looked at him with distrust and spoke to him in Russian. The Farsi speaker then asked Jim how come some of the clothes were worn. Jim, again thinking on his feet, answered that they were worn on mannequins and he replaced them every so often. Once again, this was relayed to the Russian partner, who then asked another question. The Farsi speaker then asked him where the order forms were. Jim responded that order forms get you in trouble because they can be stolen and duplicated. He therefore memorized orders. As an example, he told them that he orders in lots of twelve, and he named a fictitious store in Baghdad and said they would take four lots of 32A, two of 32B, and one of 32C as an example. To make light of it, Jim said that women in Baghdad had small chests. This seemed to satisfy both the Russians, who smiled and rose from their chairs. Jim motioned to them to take whatever samples they would like as a gesture of friendship. They looked at each other, and one took a couple of pieces of the underwear and stuffed them into his jacket pocket. They handed Jim his passport and, without further conversation, left the room. Jim almost burst out laughing after the confrontation, not sure whether it was due to the relief of tension or the comical way the whole scenario took place.

Jim quickly left for the airport and rechecked his borrowed bag and settled down to wait for the flight to Rome. He went through security again, which was no problem, and entered an aircraft, which this time was a jet and fairly modern. When they took off, Jim finally relaxed and realized how tense he had been.

Chapter 19

The flight to Rome was uneventful, as was the landing. When Jim exited the plane, he followed the crowd until they reached immigration checkpoint. The line for inspection was about a block long and had several lanes. Jim decided he was probably better off using his American passport but, first, had to ascertain if anyone on the line had come in from that country. He asked a few people where they were from, and finding a few had just landed from New York, he headed for the bathroom, where he took out his American passport and hid his Italian passport.

It took about a half hour to get through passport inspections and finally to the carousels containing the luggage. He did not want to leave the black suitcase behind in case, as it could be traceable.

When he retrieved the suitcase, he immediately headed for the exit and the cab stand, where he found another line of waiting passengers. When he finally got a cab, he asked the driver to take him to a good hotel in Rome. The driver was only too happy to accommodate Jim and, after a forty-five minute trip, delivered him to a nice-looking hotel in downtown Rome.

After Jim checked in, he went to his room and showered. For the first time in quite a while, he felt a sense of freedom and relaxation. After he was done dressing, he took the black suitcase, which served so well, removed all the tags, and left the hotel. Looking for a Dumpster, which he found behind the hotel, he unceremoniously heaved the suitcase into it. At last, he was free from the ladies' undergarments.

Jim found what looked to be an upscale restaurant and settled in for a five-course meal that the Italians were famous for. He was not disappointed.

After eating, he decided he had better buy some new clothes. The clothes he was wearing that he had purchased in Iraq were out of style and could bring attention to him. They were obviously old fashioned and out of date. He spotted a haberdashery just a few stores from the restaurant. It was obviously upscale, but all Jim had in mind was to buy one outfit. He was able to purchase the entire ensemble, including shirt, tie, and shoes along with a pair of socks. He was a little taken aback when he received a bill of over eight hundred euros. This left him with a little over two thousand euros, which should be enough to get the film delivered and get back to the States.

He decided to get back to the hotel and get a good night's sleep and start on his mission to deliver the film first thing in the morning. He mulled over in his mind the instructions Lev gave him. "Go to Via Arturri, which is just off Piazza Navona, look for a shop selling tiles by the name of Perfetta, and ask for a special tile with a printing of a lion and a lamb. The person you give the film will answer that he has no such tile but can get one of two zebras. Tell him you are interested in zebras and will take the tile. As part of the payment, slip the film in with the money. Take the tile and go. Make sure you are not followed in your comings and goings or it could be fatal."

Jim woke up refreshed and felt better than he had since he started this mission. He showered dressed in his new clothes, put the film in his pants pocket, went downstairs to the hotel restaurant, and had a light breakfast of eggs, toast, and three cups of American coffee.

After breakfast, he exited the hotel, stepping into a hot sunny day. He wished he had sunglasses and made a mental note to buy some at his first opportunity. He motioned to the doorman for a cab. The doorman raised his hand, and before he could put it down, a cab pulled to the curb. The doorman opened the door for Jim, who was impressed with the service. He wanted to tip the doorman but had no small bills.

He told the cab driver to take him to Piazza Navona, figuring he could walk the Piazza and find Via Arturri and this would give him the opportunity to make sure he was not followed, although he couldn't imagine being followed after all his travels. He was certain he wasn't but nonetheless opted to mind Lev's warning and err on the side of caution.

It was a beautiful day, and there were only a few people in the piazza, most of whom were enjoying their morning cappuccino in the cafés that bordered the outer rim of the piazza. Some artists were setting up their easels, ready to paint the beautiful scenery and hoping that some tourists would like their portraits painted. Jim thought to himself that he could get used to this and made a mental note to return someday. He walked about a hundred feet and turned to see if any other cars came up the street he just left. There weren't any, and he was satisfied that he was not being tailed.

He walked the rim of the piazza until he came to Via Arturri. He decided to pass the street and then double back as a precaution. Once again, he was satisfied that he was alone, so he headed up Via Arturri and looked for the tile shop. He had walked about three blocks when he saw the plain-looking store by the name of Perfetta. Once again, Jim looked back and noticed a man about a half block behind him. He didn't like the look of the man, so he decided to keep walking.

AN AMERICAN ASSASSIN

He turned the next corner to his right and waited. He watched as the man passed, walking straight up Via Arturri. Jim waited a few minutes and then walked to the corner where he observed the man still walking casually up the street. Satisfied, he walked back to the shop and, after taking one more look around, entered. It was a small shop with murals made of marble and stacks of tiles lined up on tables along the walls and down the center of the store. The place was covered with dust, probably from cutting marble and stone. Behind the counter was a young-looking thin male, who smiled at Jim and spoke to him in Italian. Jim figured he was asking him if he could help him. The young man behind the counter looked too young to be his contact, but he figured he had to try, so he asked for a tile with a lion and lamb on it. The young man didn't understand Jim and motioned him to wait. He went to the rear of the shop and returned with a gray-haired man who was about sixty years old and slightly stoop shouldered. The man looked Jim over and again in Italian asked Jim if he could help him. Jim asked him if he could speak English, and the man replied that he could speak a little English. Jim once again asked for a tile with a lion and lamb on it. The man turned to the younger man and told him he would take care of the customer and to finish his work in the back of the shop. When the older man turned to Jim, he responded in broken English that he didn't have the tile he wanted but has one with two zebras on it that he thought Jim would like. The man retrieved a tile from under the counter, and Jim said he would take it. Jim reached into his pocket to retrieve a twenty-euro note with the film tucked inside the folds. The man took the twenty, carefully placing it under a tray in the small cash register, and gave Jim a ten-euro note as change. He placed the tile in a small bag and handed to Jim. As he did so, he took Jim's hand and squeezed it as if to say, "Thank you." He looked deep into Jim's eyes and nodded. Jim took the bag turned and left the shop.

When he was back onto the sidewalk, once again he felt relieved that his promise to Lev was fulfilled and that he had gotten rid of the film. The next issue was to find out who betrayed him and why, and for that, he will need help.

Chapter 20

On his way back to the hotel, he stopped in a cell phone store and purchased a phone he could use to call Washington and then throw away. He dialed the tech office, hoping Tony would answer. When he did, Jim said "Ten thirteen." Tony responded that he would get back to him and immediately hung up.

To any NYPD officer, "ten thirteen" meant officer in trouble and in need of assistance. All officers receiving this call would drop whatever they are doing and respond to the scene. Jim knew that Tony would understand and was probably going to a "safe" telephone to call him back.

It only took a few minutes before his new cell phone rang.

"Where the hell are you, and how did you get into such a mess?" Tony said.

"I'm coming in and I need help," Jim responded. "I need money and a throwaway." To an officer, that meant an untraceable gun.

"You got it," Tony answered. "Where do you want it delivered?"

"When I'm in town, I'll call you back," Jim answered.

"Call me on 882-7184, it's a safe phone" was Tony's response.

"OK. See you soon . . . I hope," Jim responded as he hung up the phone.

Jim took the back off the cell phone and removed the SIM card. He bent the card and tried to break it into two pieces but could not. Satisfied that it was unusable and therefore untraceable, he dropped the SIM card into a sewer. He then threw the cell phone into a trash receptacle that was on the street.

When he returned to the hotel, he used their computer to check on flights to Dulles Airport in Washington. Since he knew he could not use a credit card, he took a taxi to Fiumicino, the airport in Rome, and purchased a ticket for the next day. This left him without much money. He calculated that he could just about get by with meals and taxi to the airport. It was a funny feeling being low on funds. He hadn't felt that way since he was a rookie officer and had a family to support.

The next day, Jim rose, showered, dressed, and had a light breakfast in the hotel. He took a taxi to the airport and, after going through a strenuous security check, probably due to him not having luggage, enjoyed a cappuccino while waiting for his flight to board. He was concerned that using his American passport might get someone's attention if he was in the lookout book but felt he had to take the chance.

The flight to Washington was uneventful except for a bump or two. He whiled away the time watching an old movie to try to keep his mind off what was lying ahead for him. He knew he had to stay out of sight, which would not be too difficult in a city as large as Washington, but how to find out who and why the word was put out that he was a traitor and a contract placed on his head was going to be difficult. One good thing, he thought, only the CIA and the Group probably have the contract on him. He doubted that the FBI or other agencies would be notified, as they would probably discover the Group, which would not be in their best interest.

Chapter 21

As the flight continued, Jim reminisced about how he became involved in such high-level intrigue. He recalled years ago being contacted by a friend of his who was formerly an assistant district attorney in New York and who was now an assistant U.S. attorney for the Department of Justice. His friend told him about this group that was being formed and that he thought Jim could significantly add to it and become part of a hush-hush federal enclave. Jim, who had lost his family, thought that a change in his direction would probably be good for him and get him out of New York, where he had too many memories. He was then contacted by someone in the U.S. Attorney's Office, who asked him to come in for an interview. The meeting took place on a Sunday morning when the Department of Justice building was practically empty. Jim gave his name to the security person at the door, who looked on a piece of paper, gave Jim a pass, and gave him directions to the office where he was to be interviewed. He entered the office and was surprised to see a desk and a middle-aged man sitting behind it, beckoning him to come in and take a seat in front of the desk. Jim looked around the room and realized that there was a camera hidden in the corner of the ceiling and surmised that he was being recorded. He was asked very basic questions, which he answered forthrightly, and again was surprised to be summarily dismissed without having been introduced to his questioner or even given a handshake.

Approximately a week later, he was asked to return to the same location for a further interview. This time there were three people, including the original interviewer, a woman, and another man, whom he assumed were assistant attorney generals. Their questions came at him in rapid succession, basically about his background and experiences. Jim fielded the questions without a problem and in fact enjoyed the exchange. Again, he was summarily dismissed and figured he would not see them again as he left. During the following week, he was contacted once more, and it was requested that he come back to the same location. He was beginning to think that this was silly but complied because he had nothing else to do. When he entered the office, the woman who had been there before began to question him. This time the questions regarded what he was willing to do for his country and if he was patriotic. Of course, Jim responded that he was and that he loved his country. He added that his service in the Marine Corps proved it. The woman then asked him if he was willing to kill for his country to save the lives of his countrymen. Jim answered that it would depend on the situation and that hypotheticals don't mean much. He stated that when he was in the Marine Corps, he did kill his country's enemies without reservation, and that if the situation were the same, he would do it again. The woman asked him what if it was not in a combat situation but was just as important, if not more so, for his country. Jim responded that if the situation were that grave, he probably could do it. The woman started to write a few notes on a pad that was on the desk in front of her, and Jim, for the first time, noticed that she was an attractive female and, in some strange way, appealed to him. The woman again dismissed Jim but this time stood up, called him by name, and shook his hand. He noticed her handshake was warm and firm. She told him that he would be contacted. Jim then left the office, and the interview was ended.

Three days later, Jim was contacted by the same woman, who asked him to come to a residence in Falls Church, Virginia. He rented a car and drove out to the location, which was fairly remote. He entered a long circular driveway, which was surrounded by woods that hid the house. About a quarter mile down the driveway, he came upon a three-story home with four tall columns in the front. It was obviously a replicate of an anti-Belem home. Stopping in front of the home, he was approached by two men, one requesting the keys to his car, the other asking him to follow. As they climbed the steps to the home, Jim noticed that his car was being moved toward the rear of the house. The man escorted Jim into the building and to an office, where he knocked on the door. A feminine voice told him to enter. The same woman who had interviewed him a few days before was standing behind a desk. This time she smiled at Jim and reached out to shake his hand. Jim's escort immediately turned and left the room. The woman smiled at Jim, for the first time, and said, "Hello. My name is Doris. We prefer not to use last names here. I am going to offer you a position that may seem shocking at first, but I ask you to take your time and consider carefully what I am about to say. We are a small organization who has a mission of eliminating those who cause this country harm. I do mean eliminate. I want you to consider that we are not averse to killing those who would kill us and are now working for the destruction of America. We do not know each other by other than the first name, with the exception of one or two of us who are in administrative positions. Should you accept the position, you will be compensated at the rate of $500,000 a year. You will be paid that for the rest of your life." Jim was taken aback by the figure but tried to act coolly. "Of course, you would be expected to pay minor expenses out of that money. Should you need additional funds to carry out your mission, they will be made available to you."

Jim asked, "Who will I work with, and what is the chain of command?"

Doris answered, "You will work alone unless otherwise necessary. You will not know who your counterparts are, as we are a highly secretive organization, as you can imagine. You will report to me. By report, I mean an occasional phone call in case you need anything. As far as the chain of command, I am it. We receive special funding to cover compensation from the vice president, and that is all I am going to tell you. I want you to consider everything I have told you, and especially that you will be serving your country without fanfare or credit except that you will know in your heart that your service is invaluable." Jim asked the name of the organization. Doris smiled and said, "We do not have a name. We are so secretive, we do not even have a name. We are just a group of patriotic men and women. You may leave now, but I will expect your answer within twenty-four hours." He was handed a blank card with a typewritten telephone number written on it. "I will expect to hear from you," she said. She stood, shook his hand, and smiled.

Jim looked at her and, with a twinkle in his eye, said, "Do I call you *boss?*"

She smiled again and responded, "No, you call me Doris and I call you Jim."

With that, Jim turned and left the office and was escorted by the same man who had brought him in. This time they exited through the rear of the building, where his car had been parked.

Jim had restless night thinking about Doris's conversation and what it would mean for his future. He certainly couldn't complain about the money, but the whole idea of an agency so secretive that it did not even have a name bothered him, and, besides, the money for the rest of his life could mean that they didn't expect him to live that long. He was looking for some excitement—not that the NYPD wasn't exciting enough—but a total change of environment was probably what he needed.

The next morning, the phone rang. Jim picked up the phone and was surprised to hear a man's voice. The voice stated matter-of-factly, "Just say yes or no."

Jim responded yes and was told to go to the same place he was yesterday at 11:00 a.m.

He was again escorted to Doris's office. After the good morning niceties, he noted that there was a gun on Doris's desk. She smiled and told him it was his along with an ID card and badge. Jim took the gun and holster and threaded it through his belt. He then perused the ID, which indicated he was a U.S. Marshal. He was then told by Doris to go down the hall and ask for Tom, who would give him more paperwork showing that he was an investigator for Homeland Security along with a badge. Doris explained that that was in case he was stopped by local authorities and questioned about carrying a firearm. Jim noted that the picture on the ID was probably taken by a hidden camera during one of his interviews.

Jim jokingly asked Doris if she was the firearms officer for the group, and she responded that they did not have a tech/firearms person yet. Jim then proceeded to tell her about Tony Chapman, who was the best tech man he ever worked with. He explained that Tony was the undisputed best tech person in NYPD. He was unsurpassed when it came to electronics and the use of eavesdropping equipment and could do a myriad of others jobs. He was a "pick expert" and could open practically any lock as well as open safes without having a combination. Doris was intrigued and told Jim she would look at Tony for the position. It turned out that they hired Tony almost immediately. In the meantime, she told Jim to go down the hall to room 207 and ask for Tom, who will give him an orientation regarding his assignments. Jim asked if he were to sign for the weapon or a pledge of secrecy or anything, and Doris smiled and told him that it would not be necessary. This made Jim feel uneasy. Things were just not kosher, he thought. They work on nothing but your word, not the way federal authorities usually function.

Jim was bored with the orientation. He was obviously more experienced than his instructor. The only thing he came away with was how to set up a bank account to receive his annual pay. And that he should park in the rear of the building when he has to "come in." He was given a cell phone and told to call 7 from that phone at least once a week if he does not hear from anyone. This made Jim all the more uneasy. How can they pay all this money to have me hanging around doing nothing? Perhaps I won't be hanging around and they will keep me busy . . . he hoped.

When he left the building, he started out on his self-made tasks by severing his connections in New York and looking for a place to rent and setting up his bank account per instructions.

He found a nice small ranch house in Burke, Virginia, which was not too far from Falls Church. He paid six months' rent in advance and hoped it did not create any suspicions with the landlord. He settled into his house and made it as comfortable as possible buying whatever furniture he needed. He made his first "phone-in" and was told to call again next week.

He found a nice little local pub close to his house where he passed the first few nights making friends and passing the time. He was certain that most of the people in the pub were federal employees, so he limited his drinking to make sure he had his wits about him at all times. On the fourth day, his cell phone rang, and he was told to "come in" and go to room 207 again. He hoped that he would see Doris again but thought he would have been told to report to her office.

He parked in the rear of the building as instructed and noted that there were several other cars parked. When he got to room 207, a different person he had never seen before was waiting for him. He smiled, shook Jim's hand, but never introduced himself. He handed Jim an eighty-by-ten picture of an Oriental man and some documents. He was told to follow the man and report his whereabouts by pressing 7 on his cell phone and dictating the person's actions.

Pretty sophisticated, Jim thought as he was summarily dismissed and returned to his car.

When he got home, he studied the documents he had been given, which contained a dossier on the Oriental man. His name was David Lee and he lived in Arlington, which was a suburb of Washington DC. The cell phone that was given to him had a GPS on it, so Jim decided to plug in the address and go to the house, which turned out to be an apartment in a six-story building. Jim entered the foyer and looked for the name of Lee, which did not show on the rows of mailboxes. He checked to see if there were any Oriental-sounding names but found none. He returned to his car, which he parked across the street from the building, and pressed 7 on his cell phone and dictated what he had found, or in this case not found, at the residence. Jim checked his watch and noted that it was 4:15 p.m. and decided to wait to see if Lee would show up. He figured that in another hour or so, many workers would be ending their shift and hopefully coming home along with Mr. Lee.

When Lee did not show up, he pressed 7 on the phone and reported it. He was surprised when the phone rang almost immediately after he had called and was told to report to Falls Church the next morning. To this day, he still wonders who Lee was or if he even existed.

His thoughts were interrupted by the captain, who announced that they would land in thirty minutes.

Chapter 22

He exited the plane at Dulles after a smooth landing and headed for customs/immigration. The officer behind the desk took Jim's passport and looked at Jim and his picture. Being satisfied, he placed the passport into a reader and said to Jim, "Welcome home," as he handed Jim back his passport.

Jim felt good being welcomed home and never realized that he missed his country so much. On the other hand, he was worried that when the passport was put into the reader, the Group would know he was back in country. As soon as he left the customs area, he went directly to the money exchange kiosk and exchanged his euros for American money. It turned out that the exchange rate was in his favor, and after fees, he received almost $300.

He exited the airport to find a driveway in a semicircle in front of the airport, which held many cabs waiting for fares.

He opened the door to the nearest cab and got in. The driver, a foreign-looking male wearing a turban, said in a heavily accented voice, "Where to, sir?"

"Take me to a hotel in Springfield," Jim answered.

"Which one, sir?" the cabbie asked.

"The one by the mall," Jim bluffed.

"Oh, you mean the Hilton."

"Yes, that's it," Jim responded, happy that his bluff paid off.

When they arrived at the hotel, Jim was concerned that the fare was $100 and, with the tip, left him with very little money.

He watched as the cab pull away and pondered what to do to get a room in the hotel. He could not give the desk clerk a credit card, as that would tip off everyone at the Group as to where he was, and he only had about $150 to his name.

He entered the hotel and walked to the front desk, where there was a young-looking man behind the desk. The man looked up from the computer he was peering into and gave Jim the once-over.

"Can I help you, sir?" the young man said while looking to see if Jim had any luggage.

"I'd like a room, please," Jim responded.

"Yes, sir, and how long will you be staying with us?" was his reply. It was clear that the young man was suspicious of Jim.

"Just a few days," Jim answered.

"And what credit card will you be using, sir?"

"I'll pay cash. My wallet was stolen, and all my cards were in it," Jim replied, hoping the desk clerk would buy his story.

"I'm sorry to hear that. Was your luggage stolen also?" the clerk responded, clearly a sarcastic tone in his voice.

"No, the airline will deliver my bags in the morning." Jim lied.

"Very well, sir. That will be $150, please."

Jim took out his money and counted out the $150 and noted that he had only a few singles left.

The clerk took the money and handed Jim a keycard.

"That's room 250, just at the head of the stairs," the clerk said with a stiff smile on his face.

Jim thanked the clerk and headed for the stairs.

The room was typical hotel room and would be adequate for the night, Jim thought. He immediately went to the telephone and called the number Tony had given him.

Tony answered after three rings with the usual smile in his voice.

"Tony . . . Jim. I'm in the Hilton in Springfield and I need what we discussed before, along with a set of picks." "Picks" was the term they used to mean small thin metal devices that were used to pick open locks. "How about meeting me here for breakfast around seven?"

"Fine, see you then." Tony hung up his phone. They always kept their telephone conversations brief and to the point, a habit most people in their business had.

Jim admired Tony. He was the kind of person that most people took a liking to right away. He had a smile that was warm and infectious. The women especially liked Tony. He prided himself on his ability to bed any of them he wanted. He had a wife and two children from whom he was separated and who were living in New York. He loved his kids but didn't let them interfere with his work, and he was good at what he did. An expert in wiretapping, electronic surveillance, and all the many and various requirements and equipment needed in undercover work. He was a con man par excellence and could usually talk his way into or out of sticky situations. Most importantly, he was loyal to Jim and could be trusted, and that counted heavily in this kind of work.

Jim showered and went to bed, exhausted after the flight from Rome. He woke up at four in the morning, his body still working on European time. He tossed and turned for the next few hours until it was time to meet Tony. He dressed quickly and studied his face in the mirror. He desperately needed a shave, and his hair was a mess. Not having shaving equipment or a comb, he did the best he could and then headed for the dining room in the hotel.

Tony was waiting for him, sitting at a table at the far end of the dining room, where he could keep his back to a wall and monitor everyone who entered the room. When he spotted Jim, he broke out in a big smile that said he was genuinely happy to see him.

Jim shook Tony's hand and sat down next to him so that he could also see the entry to the dining room.

"How are you doing, pal?" Jim said.

"I'm great . . . but you look like crap," Tony responded. "How did you get yourself in such a mess?"

"Someone set me up, and I intend to find out who it was."

"Why would anyone do that?" Tony asked.

"That's the million-dollar question."

Just then, the waitress approached, and they ordered a breakfast of eggs, toast, and coffee.

"OK. What can I do to help? I have everything you asked for in there," Tony said, nodding toward a briefcase that was sitting on the floor next to him.

"Great. I'm going to start with Doris and work up the chain of command until I find out who put the word out that I was a traitor and why they did it. I want you to nosey around the secretaries at the office and find out who is above Doris and anything else you think I may need. I'll follow Doris from the office and find out where she lives and see what she knows. Also, I want to get into my house, and I assume you have it bugged."

"I'm sure it's bugged, but I didn't do it. They sent out a different team to do it probably because of our relationship. Don't worry. It'll be a piece of cake to clear it. I'll let you know when it's done. As far as the secretaries go, I'll give up my body in the line of duty for you, Lou," Tony said with a grin on his face.

Tony still slipped every so often and called Jim Lou, as he did when Jim was his lieutenant in the NYPD. Back then, all lieutenants were addressed as Lou.

The breakfast arrived, and Jim devoured it and downed his coffee. It tasted great to him, as it has been a while since he had good American food.

Tony watched Jim eat and couldn't help but smile at his companion's voracious appetite.

"I can't get near the office, so I'll need you to tip me off when Doris leaves so I can pick up a tail on her. She probably leaves between five and seven, so I'll be in the area. You can get me as much background on her and anyone else in the chain you discover. Be careful—these people can't be trusted."

"In the briefcase, there is a safe cell phone, which is connected to mine. We can talk, and it will be scrambled to anyone trying to listen in. We'll use that from now on."

"Agreed," Jim responded as he picked up the briefcase.

"*Ciao,*" Tony said. "Take care of yourself."

"Will do," Jim responded and headed for the door.

Jim went up to his room and opened the briefcase. He removed several hundred dollars and put it in his pocket. He examined the gun and made sure it was loaded. Everything else was there that he and Tony had discussed, including a false driver's license and other forms of identification.

He left the hotel and headed for the mall, where he luxuriated with a haircut and a shave. He then went to a clothing store and purchased a suit, shirts, and some slacks along with shoes and socks. Upon his return to the hotel, he changed and retrieved more money from the briefcase, as he had spent quite a bit on his wardrobe. He went downstairs to the front desk, where he was happy to see a different clerk behind the counter, and he paid for two more nights. He then asked the clerk where he could rent a car and was told that one would be provided for him at the hotel. He requested a car with a V8 engine and was medium size or larger. The clerk informed that that would not be a problem and he could have it in a half hour as soon as he filled out the rental form.

Jim perused the form and took out the false driver's license and proceeded to fill out the form. Upon completion, he brought it back to the desk and was asked for a credit card, which he provided, thanks to Tony again.

When the car arrived, Jim was very satisfied because it was unremarkable. It was a bland tan-colored Chevy, which would not stand out on the street.

He whiled away the rest of the day window-shopping in the mall and at 4:00 p.m. headed for Falls Church. He found a parking place four blocks from the Group's headquarters and contacted Tony to let him know he was in place.

Tony monitored the camera that was in the hallway that Doris would take to leave the building.

Chapter 23

Jim was bored. He always got bored on stakeouts when he had to patiently wait and there was no action. He forced himself to stay alert and passed the time by trying to guess the make and model of passing cars. Finally, the phone rang, and Tony told him that Doris was leaving the building and was driving a green Mustang. Jim started his car and slowly headed toward the headquarters building, trying to time his speed to coincide with the length of time it would take Doris to enter the street. He was off, as the green Mustang was about three cars ahead of him. It was difficult tailing someone in rush-hour traffic, but Jim was very experienced at it.

It took about thirty minutes before Doris entered the underground garage that was in her apartment house. Jim found a parking place about a half block away. He got out of the car and walked to the entrance of the building. He observed a doorman who was opening the door for the tenants as they arrived by cab or were being dropped off. There was no way he could check the names or apartment numbers of the tenants with the doorman staying near the front door. Jim had to come up with a better plan to find out which apartment was Doris's.

The next day, Jim went to a florist near Doris's apartment and bought a bouquet of flowers. He approached the doorman and told him he had a bouquet for Doris Bucanon and had to deliver them personally, as he had a message to deliver with the flowers. The doorman told Jim that there was no Doris Bucanon in the living in the building and that he must have the wrong address. Jim protested and said the person who ordered the flowers was very explicit and needed the flowers delivered today. The doorman apologized and told Jim that there was a mistake and he was wrong. Jim asked if there were any Dorises in the building, as the last name may be wrong. The doorman told Jim that the only Doris was Doris Macon and that she never received flowers. Jim told the doorman that he had better check with his boss and left.

Jim dumped the flowers in a trash barrel and went into the parking garage under Doris's apartment. He noted the security cameras in the garage and made sure he avoided them. He picked the lock on the entrance door and entered a hallway where the elevators were. On the side of the elevator door was a ledger with the last names of the tenants and their apartment and telephone numbers. *Probably there for delivery people,* Jim thought. He scanned the listing and found Macon in apartment 11A. He entered the elevator and pressed 11. He took out a handkerchief and pretended to blow his nose for the benefit of anyone who may be monitoring and photographing him from the camera that was placed in the upper corner of the small cubicle. He doubted anyone was watching the pictures but knew that the tape would be kept to provide the police or anyone else that required it in the future.

He exited the elevator and noted that there were only two apartments on the floor and the first one was 11A. He sent the elevator back down and listened for any noise coming from either apartment. When he heard none, he quickly moved to apartment 11A and removed the lock picks Tony had provided for him. The lock was not new, and the pins were sloppy, causing him to make several attempts before the lock finally clicked and the barrel moved, indicating that the door was unlocked. His next worry was that the apartment may have an alarm that would be triggered if the right code would not be entered on a keypad, letting the alarm monitor know that it was the tenant who belonged in the apartment. Jim took a deep breath and opened the door. He was relieved to see that the apartment was not alarmed and he breathed a sigh of relief.

The apartment had an odor of perfume that Jim found pleasant. He looked around and observed a picture on a credenza. He picked up the picture and saw Doris standing with a man and a boy who looked to be about eleven years old. He thought that he had seen it before, probably in Doris's office. He returned the picture and went to the bedroom. He observed a very feminine-looking room with lace curtains, a bed made up with at least ten pillows, and a jewelry box, which was opened and contained many necklaces, rings, and a verity of brooches. He opened the drawer in the nightstand next to the bed, where he found a .25-caliber automatic. He examined the gun and removed the clip from the handle. It was fully loaded. One by one, he removed the bullets and put them in his pocket. Then he pulled back the ejector, and a bullet bounced on the bed. *She had it loaded and ready to go,* he thought to himself.

He went to the dresser and opened the top drawer. Everything was neatly folded and stacked just as he expected. He then went to the second drawer, which contained her lingerie. Jim's experience taught him that women kept things that were important to them in that drawer. He was disappointed when he found only an envelope containing cash. He finished going through the drawers and headed for the kitchen. It was small, containing the usual appliances on one wall and a small table with two chairs on the other.

He was hungry and wanted to see what was available in the refrigerator. To his surprise, the refrigerator contained only butter and milk and some containers with unidentifiable substances in them. As he closed the door, his phone vibrated. It was Tony, who told him that Doris had just left the building and that he had dismantled the bugging devices in Jim's home. Jim thanked him and resumed his search for food. Looking in a pantry, he spotted some crackers and settled for them while he waited for Doris. He looked at his watch. It was six fifteen, and he estimated she would arrive between six forty-five and seven.

He went into the living room and finished off what remained in the cracker box, which did not satisfy him and only made him thirsty.

Time went by slowly. Finally, he heard a key rattle in the door lock and he quickly moved to the back of the door as it opened. Doris entered the room and placed her pocketbook on a small table next to the door and a briefcase on the floor. Jim moved quickly and grabbed her from behind and put his hand over her mouth. She struggled and grabbed his hand, but he was too strong for her. He pushed the door closed with his hip and pushed her back against it.

"It's me—Jim," he said in a hushed tone. "I will not hurt you. I just want to talk to you. If I let go you, promise not to scream?"

She nodded yes and relaxed slightly.

"What are you doing here? You're supposed to be, er . . . er."

"In Iraq," he finished her sentence.

"Yes, yes," she said as she straightened her blouse, a shiver convulsing her body.

Jim felt strange. He watched her as she fixed her clothing and was sorry he had manhandled her. She looked so vulnerable. He had brushed against her breasts when he grabbed her and felt an inner excitement. He had not felt that way about a woman in a long time, and to top it off, she smelled so good. He realized he was turned on by her and that he had to fight the feeling. He was there on business and he couldn't let whatever his feelings were to get in the way. But . . .

Why was he here? Doesn't he know he's in danger? I wonder how much he really knows? If I were a man, I'd punch him in the nose. He has some nerve grabbing me like that. He is strong and rather handsome, but he scared the hell out of me. How am I going to get him out of here?

"I'm sorry. I only want to ask you a few questions and then I'll leave," Jim said. "I just didn't know how to keep you from screaming. In the meantime, do you have anything to eat? I haven't eaten since this morning."

Typical man—all they think about is their stomach and sex. They are so shallow.

"Today is Thursday, and I usually send for Chinese food." She lied.

"That will do fine. Would you mind if I join you? We could have an Oriental feast. I think I could eat a dragon," Jim said with a smile, hoping to break the ice.

"OK, if you promise to leave after we eat."

"I promise that if you want me to go . . . I will," Jim responded.

"I have a menu in the kitchen drawer. I'll get it, and you can see what appeals to you."

"Fine," Jim responded, thinking, *Right now, lady, you appeal to me.*

She went to the kitchen drawer and opened it. On top of the counter, no more than six inches away, were the kitchen knives. She hesitated for a second and then thought better of it. *After all, he seems to be friendly enough and he could have hurt me if that was his goal.*

They ordered the food, and while waiting, Jim thought it would be a good time to question her. He wanted to move slowly and not alarm her but by the same token needed answers, as his neck was on the line. He had to find out who set him up and why.

"Whose idea was it to send me to Iraq?" he inquired.

"I don't know, and if I did, I couldn't tell you, you know that, Jim," she answered. "Our work is so hush-hush that the right hand doesn't know what the left hand is doing. I'll tell you this—you are the perfect choice, and if it were up to me, I would have sent you. How many people speak native Farsi? And by the way, I did sanction your selection when it came across my desk."

"Well, then someone sent it to your desk, so you must know who that was."

"Again, you know I can't tell you, but use your head and figure it out for yourself."

She is cagey, and, of course, it has to be her boss, but who is her boss?

"Who do you report to?" Jim asked.

"Let me think about it before I answer you. I'm not sure if I would be violating the rules if I tell you."

"Don't be naive. You're an attorney. You know you're not violating any trust," Jim responded and hoped he didn't come on too strong. The last thing he wanted to do was turn her off. He needed her if he was going to get to the bottom of his problem.

Jim thought it was time to ease up, as he felt the conversation was getting tense. He felt he would come back at her later.

"I was looking at the picture on the credenza," he said. "Is that your husband and son?"

"Yes," she said, offering no further information.

"Are they are living in New York?" he inquired, hoping to draw her out and that she was divorced.

"My husband and I are divorced, and my son died."

"I'm so sorry," Jim responded, feeling sorry he asked the question and realizing why she was not forthcoming in the first place.

Why is he asking so many questions? Doris wondered. *I wish he'd leave me alone.*

Thankfully, the doorbell rang just in time to break the tension.

Doris answered the door and paid the deliverer. Jim stood behind the door and accepted the food as Doris passed it to him while he stayed out of view.

Jim brought the food into the kitchen, and Doris spread it out over the counter, while Jim opened the boxes. Doris retrieved two dishes from a corner cabinet, and when she reached up, Jim sneaked a peek at her body. *She is beautiful and sexy,* he thought to himself while opening drawers looking for utensils.

They sat at the small table and began to eat. Jim tried to eat slowly. He was still very hungry.

They made small talk while they ate. They talked about the weather, the traffic conditions, and the quality and tastiness of the food they were consuming.

He is cute. Look how he eats. I haven't had dinner with a man in this kitchen ever. It's kind of nice. If we had met under different circumstances . . . well, who knows?

Jim got up from the table to get some more food. Doris tried to scoop some rice onto his plate when their hands touched. It was electricity for Jim. He would have taken her right then and there if she was willing. But, alas, this is business, and as they say, you should not mix business with pleasure.

What was that! Wow! She quickly composed herself. *I'm not a schoolgirl. This man is dangerous. I've got to get him out of here.* But she had to admit she did like the thrill.

They finished eating in silence. Jim was thinking about the feel of her hand touching his and what his next move would be. He was brought back to reality immediately when Doris got up and said, "I'd like you to leave now. You promised you would leave when you finished eating," she reminded him.

Jim was flustered and did not expect her reaction. "I have some more questions I would like to ask you." He quickly tried recoup.

"Not tonight. I am tired and have work to do for tomorrow." She lied. "Please leave."

He looked at her in disbelief. He thought he was making headway with her and already had plans for the night. He reluctantly walked toward the door.

"OK, but I still want to know whom you work for. Maybe I'll come back tomorrow evening and we can resume where we left off."

"I'm afraid that's impossible. I won't be here," she offered without further explanation.

"OK," Jim said, feeling the chill she was emitting. "But I'll be back."

He mulled over in his mind what had just happened as he made his way to the service elevator. At first, she was frightened and then she seemed to warm up and then ice. *Did I say something to trigger that reaction?* He tried to remember their conversations, but that did not help. He hurried to the street and his car in case she called someone to pick him up . . . or do worse.

He got into his car and watched the front of the building, but there was no action. No one he had to be concerned about went into the building. *Oh, well,* he thought, *at least that's a small victory for my side.*

Chapter 24

He looked at his watch. It was 9:30 p.m., so he decided to go to his house and look things over.

He was at his house in less than twenty minutes. He decided to go around the block a couple of times to see if anyone was watching. When he was satisfied no one was there, he parked about a block away and walked the rest of the way. He went to the rear of the house to a shed, where he removed a key that he had hidden there. He went to the back door and opened it. Nothing, all was quiet. Not that he expected an alarm. He knew that the planted transmitters would send a silent signal to whoever was monitoring the system. He put the key in his pocket and entered the house.

He waited for a second for his eyes to adjust to the darkness. He did not want to turn on any lights because his neighbors might think he was a burglar and call the police, and, besides, there was enough light coming through the windows from a nearby streetlight. He walked from the back porch to the kitchen. Nothing was out of place there. He headed for the living room when something on the floor caught his eye. The light from outside glittered on something that was on the floor. He cautiously approached it and discovered it was a wire. He instinctively knew it was a trip wire probably tied to a hand grenade. He was going to trace it but decided it might be too dangerous in the dark. He stepped over it and proceeded to the bedrooms. He slowly entered his bedroom and went through to the bathroom. He opened the medicine cabinet and then removed the middle shelf that revealed a small door. He opened the door and removed a stack of money he had placed there for emergencies. He left the 9 mm automatic, since Tony had provided him with one. He closed the door, replaced the shelf, and shut the cabinet door. He decided that was enough for the night, so he cautiously retraced his steps, making sure he stepped over the wire, and left for the hotel.

As he lay in bed, he thought about the events of the evening. It was bad enough that he was given a cold shoulder by Doris, but the booby trap in the house really bothered him. Tony had said the place was cleared, but it wasn't. He trusted Tony, so what happened? He called Tony, and they agreed to meet for breakfast again.

Jim spent a restless night, tossing and turning and, worst of all, thinking.

Chapter 25

The next morning, Jim got up and showered, dressed, and went downstairs for breakfast, still thinking about the events of last evening.

Tony showed up with the usual smile on his face and greeted Jim warmly. After they ordered, Jim told Tony the events of the evening regarding his home. Tony was perplexed and embarrassed. He explained to Jim that he disconnected all the electronic surveillance bugs from the office and never dreamed that such a device would be planted in the home; besides, a booby trap is designed to kill and not capture. He was certain that no one from his office would do such a thing. He promised Jim he would look into it and let him know if he found anything. Jim told Tony that he didn't think Doris had anything to do with his betrayal, so he implored Tony to find out who was next in the chain of command as quickly as possible. Tony agreed and left.

Jim headed for his room and, as he passed the front desk of the hotel, noticed a small stack of newspapers. He picked one up and was startled by the large headline. "Israel Bombs Iraq," the headline read. Jim perused the article, which contained what he expected. "UN Condemns Israel and Calls for Sanctions." He read on, and the article contained more of the same. No mention of why they did it. Jim couldn't help but wonder if the message he had delivered had anything to do with it.

He went up to his room and put the TV on, looking for more news. Finally, one reporter, who was quoting unnamed sources, reported that Israel had photographic proof that Iraq had long-range missiles that were being prepared to fire and were pointed at them. They stated that they had to take action to protect their country. Iraq, of course, denied the missiles were for aggression and stated that they were for peaceful exploration of the space.

The reporter droned on, and Jim started to get bored. He was startled when his secure phone rang. It was Tony.

"Did you see the papers this morning?" Tony asked with a smile in his voice.

"Yes, I did. Are we getting ready for World War III?" Jim asked jokingly.

"I don't think so, but guess whom I heard from . . . Lev. He wanted to make sure you got the news and told me to tell you 'thank you.'"

Well, I'll be, Jim thought to himself. *That message must have been about those missiles.*

"I don't know what for," Jim responded cagily. "How is he, and where is he?" Jim asked.

"I don't know, and even if I asked, you know he wouldn't tell me," Tony answered.

"Right," Jim answered and, changing the subject, asked, "Do you have anything else for me?"

"Yes, I have quite a bit, some you're not going to like. First, John Corcoran is the next in line above Doris. He works in the Department of Justice as some sort of liaison officer. Liaison to what, I don't know yet, probably the CIA. He works out of the Justice building on Independence and Tenth Street. It seems Doris is the only supervisor who works in our building. All the rest are scattered through the government."

"That's not bad news. What else?" Jim asked.

"I'm not sure, but the scuttlebutt is that there is a loose cannon on deck, some kind of nutjob. He got an assignment, and no one can reel him in. He has tunnel vision, and it seems no one can deter him from finishing his assignment."

"What has that got to do with me?" Jim asked.

"From what I hear, and I have not verified it, his assignment was to assassinate you."

Jim felt the blood drain from his head. *There is a nut who can't be stopped coming after me, and I know nothing about him. Who he is? What's his name? What does he look like?*

"Tony, you have to find out more for me. Verify the info and get everything you can on him."

"I intend to," Tony answered. "But I thought I should tell you . . . just in case. At any rate, everyone still thinks you're on assignment overseas, so I doubt he will be looking for you around here."

"Yes, but my questioning the hierarchy may just change that."

"Hmm, I hadn't thought about that, but everything is so hush-hush in this place that I doubt word about that would get out," Tony responded.

"Unless I hit on the culprit who tried to do me in . . . in the first place."

"I guess so." Tony's voice had a worried tone to it. "I'll dig up all the info I can on Corcoran and nutjob and get back to you. It may take some time. These secretaries are tight-lipped, and I have to open the safes at night after they're gone. I hate to admit it, but the safes are easier than their legs."

"Don't tell me that lover boy Tony is losing his touch," Jim kidded.

"No way," Tony responded with an exaggerated tone of hurt. "It's just that they believe strongly in that oath they took and think that everyone is a spy or trying to get information out of them."

"Well, aren't we?" Jim answered, chuckling.

"That's beside the point." Tony was trying to justify what he was doing. "This is for the good of the country. There are some bad people out there, and we are the only ones who know it."

"Right, Tony. Get me that info as soon as you can, and if you hear from Lev again, tell him I said hello. In the meantime, I'm going to work on Doris," Jim said as he pressed the button to end the call.

The next day, Tony had more information for Jim. He told him that he had found more on John Corcoran. He was a male, white, five feet nine inches tall, and had graying blond hair. The most important information was that he drove a new blue Chevrolet Camaro convertible. Jim figured that Tony must have been able to access the Motor Vehicle Bureau because federal employees who had high-level clearances were not in the public domain.

Jim went to the Justice building and watched the parking exit to see if he could pick up on Corcoran. He watched the exit and saw car after car leave, but no blue convertible. He waited until 7:00 p.m., and no more cars were exiting, and decided to give Doris a call.

"Hello," she answered. He felt a rush when he heard her voice.

"Hi, this is Jim. I'd like to come by and finish our conversation."

"Well, I'm kind of busy," she responded.

"It will only take a few minutes."

"OK," she answered. "How about in an hour?"

"Fine. Will you tell the doorman you are expecting me? I'll use the name Joe Daniels."

"OK," she said and promptly hung up, disappointing Jim, who would have liked to have continued the conversation.

Jim decided to head to her apartment and keep an eye on it just in case it was a setup. As usual, no one who would pose a danger to him was around. He parked his car two blocks away, as it was the nearest legal parking place he could find. He got out of his car and started for the apartment house. When he was close to the apartment, he had a sense that he was being followed. He stepped into a doorway and looked around. He saw nothing suspicious, so he continued to the apartment house. When he entered, he told the doorman he was Joe Daniels and was told that he was expected.

When he exited the elevator, he went straight to her door and rang the bell. When the door was opened, Doris stood there dressed in black slacks and a silk blouse that put emphasis on her bosom. Jim noted that she had fresh makeup on and her hair was done up. He felt himself melting.

"Hi," he said with a warm smile.

"Hi." She motioned him to enter.

"I'm Joe Daniels," he said in an attempt to make her smile and to break the ice.

"I know," she responded with the hint of a smile.

Jim noted that she didn't seem as cold as she was during their last meeting. It made him hopeful that he could . . .

"Would you like a drink?" She interrupted his thoughts.

A great sign, a drink. "I sure could use one. Thanks."

"All I have is scotch. Will that be OK?"

"That will be fine," Jim answered. He did not like scotch, but he was willing to try anything to keep the conversation and the meeting going. "On the rocks would be great." He lied.

He watched her as she moved across the room and retrieved two glasses and a bottle of scotch from a cabinet. He noted that the bottle was almost full. She looked very sexy as she crossed in front of him and went to the refrigerator to get some ice cubes. She put the ice cubes in the glasses and poured a soda in one glass and returned to the cabinet and put scotch in the second glass for Jim. She extended her arm and handed Jim the glass. It was an obvious move to keep distance between them.

Why did I offer him a drink? she asked herself. *What am I doing? He's handsome and seems to be very nice, but not for me. Still, it's been a long time since I had a man put his arms around me and show me some attention. I do miss it. He does seem interested in me. Careful, girl, I can really be hurt.*

Jim sipped the scotch and sat back in the overstuffed chair. He was going to ask Doris questions but thought better of it. He was enjoying being with her and didn't want to spoil it with business, and after all, he already knew the identity of her supervisor.

"How long have you lived here?" Jim asked, feigning interest.

"I guess it's about two and a half years. Why do you ask?"

"Nothing. It has nothing to do with our business. I was just curious. It seems like a nice place."

"It is. Everyone that I've met in the building is very nice and they keep the place immaculate."

"That's nice. I often thought I would like to live in an apartment house, but I usually opt for a private house or a room somewhere. Right now, I don't even have a country to call my own." Jim lied, looking for some sympathy.

"I don't think it's as bad as that . . . is it?" Doris had a concerned look on her face.

"Yes, it is. I have to keep looking over my shoulder waiting for the ax to fall, and I don't even know why."

AN AMERICAN ASSASSIN

"You must have some idea, don't you?" Doris asked, probing Jim and showing interest in his plight.

"None whatever," Jim responded. "One minute I'm being interviewed by you. The next minute I'm sent overseas, and then, wham." Jim motioned with his hand to in a downward fashion as if being struck by an ax to lend emphasis.

"But why would anyone call you a traitor? What did you do to earn that reputation?"

"That's it—I have no idea at all. That's why I have to find out who branded me a traitor and why. It's very frustrating, to put it mildly, and now I understand some nut is coming after me and for no good reason, and I haven't the foggiest idea who it is." Jim regretted giving Doris the information that he knew about the assassin. She probably could figure out that it was Tony who gave it to him. She had to know that Tony was working with Jim.

Jim got up from his chair and headed to for the cabinet to freshen his drink. Doris also got up in an effort to help him. They met face-to-face in front of the cabinet. They looked into each other's eyes, and Jim put his hands on her shoulders and pulled her toward him. Before she could object, he kissed her. For a second, it was great and it felt so right for him. Doris repelled and slapped him hard on the face. She stepped back and looked into his eyes again, regretting the slap. Then in spite of everything and all the cautious admonitions she had given herself, and knowing that she shouldn't do it, she let herself go and kissed him. This time it was soft and warm and with a great deal of feeling.

She felt her body tremble and she knew that she wanted him. It would be so easy to take him to bed and feel the warmth of his body next to hers and make love. Even if it was a passing thing, it would be worth it. It had been so long since . . .

Jim felt the sting on his face. The slap dampened any expectations that he had. But then she took the lead and kissed him. It was more than he expected. He wanted her and now he was certain that they would end up in bed, making love all night.

"You have to leave now," Doris said, breaking the mood. "I'm sorry if I gave you any ideas, but I'm not ready for any kind of relationship now." She lied. It took all her strength to step away from him.

"I, I don't understand. I have nothing but the best of intentions."

"Please give me some time. I'm afraid I'm moving too quickly. I have to think about this . . . us."

As he left her apartment and walked toward his car, his mind was on what just happened, and he tried to reconcile the fact that she slapped him and kissed him all at once. He could not understand it. She was a woman and had been married before and surely knew she set him on fire, and then to back off the way she did was a total puzzle. All he knew was that he wanted her more than ever. He never noticed the man sitting in the car watching his every move.

Chapter 26

John Crowe watched as Jim left the apartment house. *What an idiot he is. Who does he think he is? Does he really think he can betray his country and get away with it? He'll pay for it, and I'm just the person to make him pay. I'd like to tie him up and watch him as he slowly dies. Let him think about all this country did for him as his life slowly ebbs and look into his eyes and see the fear as the realization of his impending death sets in. That's the best part. What a wonderful country. I would do this for nothing, but to get paid for it is icing on the cake. It would be so easy to shoot him now as he walks down the street, oblivious of his pending death, but there are too many people around. No, that would be too easy. He deserves a traitor's death, and he's going to get it, and I'm the one to see that he does.*

She poured herself a scotch. *What have I done, what am I doing?* She sipped the scotch and was repelled by the strong burning taste. *How do people drink this stuff anyway?* she thought. *Am I going to take him on as a lover, a quick roll in the hay, or just as a friend? It's too late for the latter. He already is way beyond that. Why do I feel so much for him? Why do I want him so? I can't, I can't. It's crazy.*

Jim got into his car and headed for the hotel. His thoughts were never far from Doris. *She's driving me crazy. What do I have to do to convince her that I'm serious, or is that the problem . . . she's not ready for a serious relationship? I'd take a quick roll in the hay.* He smiled at that thought.

He was so intent on what was going on with Doris that he did not notice the car following him. That would never happen under normal circumstances. He was always acutely aware of all that was happening around him.

Crowe tailed the car carrying the traitor to the hotel. He watched as Jim exited the car and walked toward the front door. He removed the .44 Magnum from its holster and screwed on a silencer on the end of the barrel. It would muffle some of the sound, he thought, and give him enough time to get away before anyone spotted him. He lowered the car door window. Resting his left elbow on the door armrest, he formed a V with his thumb and forefinger and then rested his right wrist in the V to steady his shot. He took aim at Jim. As he started to squeeze the trigger, he heard laughter coming from behind him. Two couples were heading for the front door and were passing his car on the passenger's side. He quickly hid the weapon as they passed. *You're a lucky SOB,* he thought to himself as he watched Jim enter the hotel lobby.

Jim entered the hotel and decided to head to the bar and have a nightcap. He took a stool at the bar and ordered his usual vodka martini. At the bar were two women who looked like ladies of the night. Both were dressed with low-cut tops, and their makeup was extremely overdone. *Much too much,* Jim thought. *It made them look very cheap. Perhaps this was the look they wanted.* On the other side of Jim was a man about fifty who wore glasses and appeared to be the business type, probably a salesman. He obviously had been drinking and was eyeing the two women. *A perfect mark for the women,* Jim thought. *He soon will be relieved of his money.* Just then, two couples entered the bar and sat at a table. They probably had been at a wedding and were dressed formerly and were a little giddy.

As Jim sipped the drink, he mulled over the events of the day but could not get Doris out of his thoughts. He decided to call Tony and see if he made any progress regarding the nutcase that may be after him and the hierarchy of the Group.

Tony answered on the second ring.

"Hi, Jim, what's up?" Tony answered.

"I thought maybe you could tell me," Jim responded. "Any news on that loose cannon?"

"No, I didn't find anything on him. He must be a private contractor who is used on an as-needed basis. No record here at all. It's as if he didn't exist, paperwise, but people heard of him. They call him the Phantom."

"Wonderful," Jim answered sarcastically. "That's just what I need, a phantom trying to kill me."

"I wouldn't worry too much about him. After all, people still think you're in Iraq."

"How about the chain of command? Any news on that front?" Jim asked.

"No, not yet, but I'm working on it. I finally have made, er . . . er . . . friends with one of the secretaries. It may take me a day, or should I say a night or two to get the info."

"Keep up the good work." Jim laughed. "I'll call you tomorrow. Ciao."

"Ciao," Tony responded as he hung up.

Jim finished his drink and went upstairs to bed. He had a rough night, tossing and turning, feeling frustrated sexually with the thought of not having Doris alongside him in bed. It had been a long time since he had those kinds of feelings. For a minute, he thought about going back to the bar and picking up a hooker to satisfy his urgings but then thought better of it and decided to tough it out. And tough it out he did.

Chapter 27

The next morning, Jim whiled away the time watching TV and reading the papers. He decided to wait until evening to watch the Department of Justice building and try to spot Corcoran. The day went by slowly. He wanted to call Doris but would not dare contact her at the office. *She probably doesn't want to hear from me anyway,* he thought. *But then again, the second kiss. I just can't figure her out.*

At around four, he headed to the Department of Justice. Traffic was light in his direction with all the cars heading in the other direction toward Virginia.

When he arrived, he drove around the Justice building and realized there were two entrances to the parking garage, each on the opposite street to the other. He decided to watch the entrance opposite the one he was at the night before. He parked about a half block away in a no-parking zone but figured, as long as he stayed in the car, he could pretend to be waiting for someone. As he surveyed the building, he made a mental note that there was a camera mounted on the top of the building facing in his direction. He estimated that the camera could easily see his car, but as long as he leaned back in his seat, they could not see him. Jim was so intent on watching the entrance to the garage, he did not notice the car that stopped a few hundred yards behind him.

Look at the bastard, Crowe thought. *He's surveilling the Justice building. He's probably taking photos to give to his jihadi friends. He's showing the entrance to the garage. What better place to plant a bomb to take down the building?*

Crowe decided that he had to take action. He put his car in gear and slowly drove toward Jim as he removed his revolver from its holster. Just then, Jim's car started to move. Crowe had no choice but to fall in behind him.

Jim spotted the Chevy convertible exit the garage and make a right turn headed for Constitution Avenue. He slowly followed, leaving a large space between them. When the Chevy made a right turn on Constitution, Jim had to go through a red light to keep up with it. He was lucky in that he could fit in between the traffic without causing an accident or bringing unwanted attention to himself.

"Damn," Crowe muttered as he had to stop at the light at Constitution because the rush-hour traffic had stopped in the intersection and did not allow him enough room to pull out. He watched Jim drive further and further away. Frustrated, he banged his hands on the steering wheel to let out his anger. "I'll get you, I'll get you," he kept repeating.

Jim followed Corcoran for several miles as he headed for home. When Corcoran stopped at a beautiful home with a manicured lawn, Jim parked down the street, on the opposite side, where he could see the front of the house. Corcoran pulled into the driveway and exited the car, carrying a briefcase, and headed for the front door. Suddenly, the door opened, and two children, ages about three and five, came running down the front steps and gleefully greeted their father, who bent over and was smothered with kisses and hugs from the happy children; even a dog came running out of the house and jumped up and down, excited to see him. Corcoran, holding on to his briefcase, took the children one under each arm and continued toward the front door where a woman was waiting. He put the children down and kissed the woman as they entered the house. *American Pie,* Jim thought to himself. He had to smile and feel a little envious as he drove away. He decided that he would confront Corcoran somewhere away from his house. He had to devise a plan that would not create suspicion or alarm Corcoran. That was going to be a problem.

His thoughts once again were on Doris. He decided to call her. He hoped her phone was not tapped and decided it shouldn't be. If it were, Tony would have told him by now, unless another agency was doing it. *Now I'm being paranoid,* he thought to himself.

"Hello." Her voice was businesslike.

"Hi," Jim said as warmly as he could.

"Oh, it's you," she said, a nicer tone in her voice.

"Yes. I was wondering if I could see you. How about going out to dinner? I could meet you at a restaurant if you like."

"I don't know. I'm not sure."

"What's to be sure of? We would be in a public restaurant, and I would be a perfect gentleman," Jim said with a smile in his voice. "How about tomorrow night, at around seven? You name the place."

There was silence on the other end of the phone, and, finally, she said, "I thought you were afraid that someone was after you."

"Let me worry about that," Jim answered. "It's just two people dining and hopefully enjoying each other's company. Seriously, I would love to see you."

"OK, but just dinner and no dessert," she kidded.

Jim's heart jumped at her warm response, even though he was hoping for dessert.

"I'll meet you at seven at Dino's restaurant. Do you know where it is?"

LOUIS DE MARTINIS

"I'll find it," Jim said.

"OK. I'll see you tomorrow evening. Bye," Doris said as she hung up.

Jim was excited. *At last, I'm making a little headway with her. I can't wait to see her. Corcoran will have to wait.*

Chapter 28

The next day went by slowly. Jim spoke with Tony, who had no further news for him. Just as well, Jim thought, his interest being on Doris. He looked up the location of Dino's restaurant, showered, shaved, and put on a suit. On his way to Dino's, he stopped at a florist and purchased one long-stemmed yellow rose.

He arrived at the restaurant a little early and asked for a table for two, motioning toward a table that was a darker corner. He was escorted to the table and sat down facing the entrance. The restaurant was small, containing only about twelve tables, and had a distinct odor of garlic. *A good omen,* Jim thought.

The waiter asked Jim if he would like a drink while he waited. Jim wanted one but thought better of it. He would wait and let Doris lead the way regarding the drinks. The waiter made a small bow and retreated toward the front of the restaurant.

Ten minutes passed very slowly for Jim. Finally, Doris entered the restaurant and was greeted by the waiter. She looked beautiful. Her hair was done up, and she had makeup on. This was the first time Jim saw her made up, and she looked more stunning than ever. Her clothes were tight fitting, accenting every curve of her body.

Jim smiled as the waiter escorted her to his table. He stood and took her hand in his as she sat down. They didn't speak but only nodded to each other as Jim handed her the yellow rose.

"It's beautiful. Thank you. This is very thoughtful of you," Doris said as she pressed the rose to her nose to inhale its fragrance.

"You make it look even more beautiful. It becomes you." Jim wanted to say much more but controlled himself. *The night is young,* he told himself, and he did not want to come on too strong, even though he felt like it.

"Have you eaten here before?" he asked.

"Yes, a few times. The food is excellent."

"Good. I'm hungry and I love Italian. Do you care for a drink?"

"I think I would like some wine with my dinner," she responded.

"Good. White or red?" he asked as the waiter, who was only standing a few feet away, approached.

"I like red, especially with Italian food."

"Great. How about a Pinot Noir?" he asked.

"That will be fine."

She looks beautiful, he thought.

Jim perused the wine list and came to a bottle of Louis Latour Pinot Noir.

"Waiter, we'll have a bottle of Louis Latour Pinot Noir."

"Very good, sir," the waiter said as he retrieved the wine list and left.

"How was your day? And you look beautiful," Jim said with a smile.

"Not a bad day," she said, "and you don't look so bad yourself."

They both chuckled.

"I have been looking forward to this evening all day," he said.

"I shouldn't tell you this, but so have I."

"You mean the Italian food," Jim teased.

"Of course, what did you think I meant?" she teased back.

And so it went. The evening was full of small talk and teasing, and both thoroughly enjoying each other's company.

Many people entered the restaurant, ate, and left, but neither Doris nor Jim paid any attention. They ate and kept up the talk that seemed to come so easy to the two of them. They were comfortable with each other with just the right amount of sexual tension to intensify their conversation and feelings for each other.

Reluctantly, Doris looked at her watch. It was eleven thirty. They had been in the restaurant for four and a half hours, but it felt like only one. She looked around and saw that they were the only people there. The waiter was leaning against a podium near the entrance, reading a newspaper. He looked up and smiled at Doris with an expression that indicated he knew what was happening. *They are lovers,* he thought.

"We have to go, it's late," she said to Jim.

"Must we?"

"Yes. I have to go to work tomorrow, and I need my beauty rest."

"No, you don't. You're already beautiful."

"Flattery will get you everything." She smiled.

"Everything?" he said with a grin.

"Well, maybe not everything," she teased.

She stood up and picked up the rose. Jim quickly stood and took her hand, and they smiled at the waiter as they passed him and walked out the door.

"I don't want this evening to end," he whispered in her ear.

"Neither do I," she said and laid her head on his shoulder as they walked to her car. He put his arm around her shoulder, and they snuggled into each other as they walked.

"Can I come to your place, or shall we go to mine?" Jim asked, hoping.

"No, Jim, not yet."

"Why?" Jim asked, feeling disappointed.

"Please, Jim," she pleaded, "try to understand, I need a little more time. I'll make it up to you, I promise."

"OK, but not much longer. You're driving me crazy."

They arrived at her car and stood there looking into each other's eyes. Jim leaned forward and kissed her. He felt her body melting into his and desperately wanted to make love to her. He was certain that she felt the same way as she kissed him passionately, holding him tightly. She suddenly let go and turned toward her car. She unlocked it and got in. She let down the window and as she started the car and said to Jim, "Thanks for a truly wonderful evening."

"Thank you. Let's do it again, and soon."

He watched as she drove away, already missing her.

Chapter 29

The next day, Jim couldn't get Doris out of his mind. *Am I in love?* he asked himself. *I don't know. All I know is that I want to be with her all the time. She makes me feel so good. When I'm away from her, I feel terrible. It must be love. Maybe after I sleep with her, if I ever get to sleep with her, I'll feel differently. Could it be just the chase, as some of the books claim, and after I catch her, I won't feel this way? I doubt it.*

Doris rose as usual at 7:30 a.m. and started her daily routine. Something was different this morning. It was Jim. She couldn't stop thinking about him. *What a wonderful evening it was last night. I haven't felt that way in a very long time.* She glanced over to her dresser where the yellow rose stood in a tall thin vase. A warm feeling came over her. *I must stop this,* she thought to herself. *This is not right. How can I feel this way about a man I only know for such a short period and who is wanted and has a price on his head? I'm a mature woman and I can handle this.* She looked in the mirror and said aloud, "Who am I kidding? I want him. He makes me feel like a real woman again. I feel so alive when I'm with him. I hope he calls tonight."

Jim decided to sit at the Justice building to try to pick up Corcoran again just in case he made a stop where he could approach him. As he sat there, his thoughts were never far from Doris. *I have to stop this,* he thought to himself. *I have business to take care of. I have to clear my name. But I want her so badly.* Just then, he spotted the Camaro exit the garage and make the right turn heading for Independence. He followed the Camaro, hoping he would not be seen by Corcoran. As usual, the traffic was heavy, and Jim was boxed in by a bus and a line of cars, causing him to lose sight of Corcoran. He broke off the tail and decided to call Doris. He was unaware that he was also being followed.

"Hi," she said, answering on the second ring.

"Hi," Jim responded, feeling a pang at hearing her voice. "I thought maybe we could get together this evening for a drink or something."

"I would love to, but I just took a shower and washed my hair."

"Then maybe I could come up and see you," Jim answered.

She laughed and said, "I don't think you would want to see me looking like this."

"I do want to see you and I think you would look beautiful no matter how many times you wash your hair."

"Careful now," she kidded, "you may give me a swollen head."

"I want to give you more than that," he said, sounding like a lovesick child.

"Not tonight, Jim, but maybe we can get together Friday night. That way I won't have to worry about getting to work the next day."

"But it's only Wednesday," Jim responded, sounding disappointed. "How about tomorrow night?"

"I can't. I have a conference at the Justice Department and I don't know how late I'll be there."

"Why do you guys have conferences at night . . . as if I didn't know?"

"Sorry, Jim."

"What time and where Friday night? Want to go Italian again?"

"That sounds great. I'll meet you there at seven, if that's OK with you."

"It's not all right because I have to wait. I really would like to see you before that."

"I'm sorry, but I can't! But you know what they say . . . Absence makes the heart grow fonder."

"My heart is already fonder," Jim responded with a laugh.

"See you Friday," she said as she hung up the phone.

Jim pushed the end call button on his phone, feeling very disappointed. *Is she playing me?* he wondered. *I guess I'm coming on too strong. Perhaps I'm scaring her. Maybe I should back off a little, but she seems to like it. I wonder why I'm like a babbling teenager when I talk to her on the phone. I think maybe I'll try to use a little more self-control. Play it cool. But I really don't want to.*

Doris hung up the phone and smiled to herself. *He really likes me,* she thought. *I can't wait until Friday night. I wonder what I should wear. If only I could tell him that the meeting I'm going to tomorrow night is about him. I'd better be careful. If anyone sees us together, it will be the end of me and my job.*

Thursday went by slowly. Jim decided not to go to the Department of Justice building and wait on Corcoran again for fear that Doris may spot him when she goes to her meeting. He spent the time eating a leisurely lunch and watching TV. At dinnertime, he went downstairs and ate in the hotel dining room. After that, he decided to spend a few hours in the bar. While at the bar, he had a conversation with a man seated on a stool near him. The man was a salesman from Michigan and wanted to talk sports. Since Jim was out of the country, he was not up to date with the sports world and found the conversation dull. After two drinks, he said good night to the salesman and the bartender and headed for his room.

He called Tony, who told him that he heard from Lev and all was well in the Middle East. Tony also told him that he learned that Doris was going to a meeting at the Department of Justice, but the subject was hush-hush and he hadn't been able to find out any particulars. Jim told Tony that he was going to check out of the hotel and move to another one as soon as he could. He told Tony that he was in this one too long and he felt it was time to move. Tony agreed and asked Jim to let him know where he decides to settle. They said good-bye, and Jim decided to go to bed early and get up early so that he may pick up Corcoran on his way to work in case he makes stops where Jim could possibly confront him. He set the radio alarm for 5:00 a.m. and went to sleep.

He woke up to the sound of the harsh alarm and quickly showered and dressed. He went down to his car and drove to Corcoran's residence. On the way, he stopped at a gas station, filled the car, and got a coffee and bun, which he quickly devoured.

When he arrived at Corcoran's home, he parked down the block and settled down to wait for him to leave. He waited for a couple of hours and there was no sign of Corcoran. He then decided since there was a meeting scheduled for this evening at the Department of Justice, Corcoran would probably be going to work late. Having lost his patience, Jim decided to leave.

He returned to the hotel, quickly packed, and checked out. He scouted out a hotel nearer Doris's and checked in. He called Tony and told him of his new quarters and was informed by Tony that nothing was new and he was still working on the subject of the meeting tonight. He told Jim that if he found anything of interest, he would let him know right away.

Jim unpacked and spent the remainder of the day walking around his new hotel to see what was in the area that might be of interest to him.

Crowe sat in his car at the Hilton, waiting for Jim to come out. After a couple of hours, he grew impatient and drove through the parking lot to see if he could spot Jim's car. He didn't find it and decided that Jim must have left earlier and he would pick him up at his usual parking spot at the Department of Justice this afternoon. This time, he would push it and take action as soon as he spotted him. *Enough with the cat-and-mouse game,* he thought. *This guy has to go.*

Chapter 30

At last, Friday evening came, and Jim once again went to the florist and bought a long-stemmed yellow rose. He drove to the restaurant and asked and received the same table.

Doris arrived and looked as beautiful as ever. He stood as she approached and gave her the rose. She smiled and was delighted with his gift and the attention he showered on her. Once again, they ate and drank and had wonderful conversations learning about each other. This time, however, their sexual tensions were rising to a fever pitch. Neither one of them could wait until the end of the meal. They ate quickly and decided to leave. They walked to Doris's car and both got in and drove to her apartment. They barely got the door closed before they started to remove each other's clothes.

They spent the night in bed, making love and enjoying each other's body. It was more than Jim had imagined. It was perfect.

Saturday morning came with a lazy feeling of contentment for Doris. She had thoroughly enjoyed herself and felt completely relaxed and happy for the first time in many years. She slowly rose from the bed and looked at Jim, who was still asleep. *I could really love this man,* she thought to herself. *Why must it be so complicated? Why did I have to do what I did before I got to know him? I wish we could run away from reality and spend the rest of our lives together. Maybe I'm getting ahead of myself. Maybe all he wanted was a roll in the hay, and now that he got it, he'll leave me. I'd feel crushed if he did that.*

Jim awoke to the smell of coffee perking. He slowly opened his eyes and smiled at the thought of last night. He felt happy and relaxed. She was great, and he hoped that this was just the beginning and that she felt the same way. *I am not going to live without her,* he thought. *I will make her happy.*

And so the weekend went. They laughed and made love and ate and slept and thoroughly enjoyed themselves. When Sunday night came, Doris was adamant that they should not see each other until the next weekend. She felt that seeing him during the week would get her mind off her work, and that could be disastrous. Jim reluctantly agreed and figured that he could work on Corcoran and he would have the coming weekend to look forward to. They parted with kisses and hugs as though he were going off to war.

Jim took a cab to Dino's, where he had left his car Friday night. He drove to the hotel still feeling warm and fuzzy from the weekend's love fest. He realized that he wanted Doris and felt confident that she wanted him and that, in a matter of time, they would work things out so that they could always be together without the interference of her job and his problem. That made him all the more determined to confront Corcoran and settle things.

The next evening, he sat outside the Department of Justice, waiting for Corcoran.

Crowe saw Jim park at his usual spot and decided that he would take action immediately.

Harry and Jane Hopkins were sightseeing and enjoying the Capitol along with their two children. The children, tired from the day's events, began to fight with each other over every little thing, annoying their father, who was driving and had just turned onto Tenth Street. Harry scolded them and told them to be quiet or they would not get the ice cream promised them.

Crowe took out his pistol and drove his car next to Jim's as if to double park, where he stopped and let down his window and took aim at Jim's head.

Jim saw the car that had pulled next to him and realized that a gun was pointed at him. He tried to duck down, but the car seat belt prevented him from moving too much. The sound of the shot resounded in his ears, and a burning sensation caused his right shoulder to convulse.

Crowe took aim again and was about to fire another round.

Harry took his eyes off the road for a second and looked into the rearview mirror to again chastise his children when he felt the sickening feeling that his car hit something.

Crowe's car was hit from behind before he could get off the next shot. He looked in the rearview mirror and saw the vehicle that hit him and immediately hit the gas pedal and took off.

Harry stopped his car and got out to peruse the damage. He was puzzled why the car he hit took off because there was no major damage, just a small scratch on his front bumper. Jane also exited the car and looked in the direction of Jim's car and saw blood on the inside windshield and saw Jim holding his shoulder. He then slumped over and was apparently unconscious. She let out a scream and told Harry to call 911 right away as she pointed out Jim to him. Harry complied, and within minutes, two police cars arrived at the scene. They examined Jim and called for an ambulance that took Jim to the hospital.

Jim woke up and saw a young doctor who looked like a teenager standing over him.

"Hello, I'm Dr. Kravitz. How are you feeling?"

Jim felt the pain in his shoulder and was not able to move it. He was relieved to feel and see the bandages that were holding it in place.

"I guess I've been better." He tried to smile at the doctor, but the pain when he moved made him grimace. "How long have I been here?" he asked.

"You've only been here an hour. We kept you under while we worked on that shoulder. Nasty wound. How did it happen?"

"It's a long story, doc," Jim answered.

"Well, there are police and people from the marshal's office that want to hear that story. They're waiting outside. When you feel up to it, I'll let them in.

"Give me a little while, will you, doc? I'm a little fuzzy yet." Jim lied.

"OK. Let me know when you're ready." The doctor smiled and walked out of the room.

As soon as he left, Jim looked around the room. His jacket was lying on the floor and was torn where they probably cut it off him to get at the wound. He had no shirt on. He had a sling over his shoulder holding his right arm at a ninety-degree angle. At least he still had his pants on but needed something to cover his chest. The best he could do was put on a hospital gown and tuck it in his trousers. His wallet and phony credentials were on a small table next to him. When he bent forward to retrieve them, he felt a little dizzy and had to hold on to the table to steady himself. He straightened up and called Doris. After explaining to Doris what happened, he asked her to pick him up at the emergency room entrance to the hospital. In much pain, he exited his room and was surprised to be ignored by the police and marshals, who were having a heated argument over who would interview him first. One officer looked at him but decided that he must be headed for the bathroom and returned to the argument. After all, why wouldn't a marshal want to cooperate and catch the person who shot him?

Jim painfully walked down a hallway and followed the signs to the exit. He was astonished to see that he barely had enough strength to open the exit door. A blast of hot air hit him as he took the steps to the ambulance driveway. He made his way to the street and found a spot where he could partially conceal himself and lean on a wall while he waited for Doris.

Doris entered the emergency room driveway and looked around for Jim. She spotted him leaning against a wall and pulled her car as close to him as she could get. She put the car in park and put the emergency brake on and got out of the car and walked around to where Jim was standing. She took hold of Jim, who seemed very weak and barely able to walk. She opened the passenger's side door and helped Jim into the car. He was obviously in pain and let out a dull moan as he sat. She got back into the driver's seat and drove to her apartment. She entered the underground garage and asked Jim if he could make it to the service elevator. He said he thought he could, and she slowly helped him get out of the car and into the elevator. At last, they entered her apartment, and she helped him get into bed.

He was exhausted, so she thought better of asking him any questions at that time. Jim immediately fell asleep. She slowly and very carefully undressed him, trying not to move him too much.

The next morning, Jim woke up and for a while had no idea where he was. He tried to sit up but felt dizzy and decided the best course of action was to lie still. Then he noticed the odor of perfume and the roses in the vase on the dresser and he relaxed.

Doris came into the bedroom and sat on the edge of the bed. She held his hand and asked how he felt.

"I feel like I was run over by a Mack truck," he answered.

"What happened?"

"I think the loose cannon caught up to me. I was sitting in my car. Then the next thing I knew was that I was being shot at from a car that pulled up next to me."

"Oh my god, I'm so sorry."

"What time is it? Shouldn't you be at work?"

"I took the week off. Somebody has to take care of you. I'm so sorry," she repeated.

"Do you have anything to eat?"

"Typical man, you've just been shot and you're worried about your stomach," she said with a smile as she headed for the kitchen.

"That's nothing. If I didn't hurt so much, I'd be thinking of other things to do."

Jim tried to roll over on his side so that he could watch her, but the pain was too much.

Doris brought Jim food and fed him, treating him like a baby. Truth be told, she enjoyed it, and so did he.

Jim relished all the attention Doris bestowed on him. He slowly recovered as the week progressed and was able to move his arm a bit, albeit with a great deal of pain. He still did not have full movement and couldn't raise his arm above his head. Doris fashioned another sling for him, and that helped keep his arm still and lessened the pain. She insisted he go to a doctor, but Jim refused. He was worried that the police were now after him along with the shooter and the marshals. He had to lie low for a while. He kept in touch with Tony, and they made plans for the time that Jim would have to leave Doris's apartment.

Chapter 31

The week went by quickly. Jim tried to do small exercises with his shoulder but could not get much more movement out of it without experiencing excruciating pain. Although they slept together, Jim could barely move, negating any intimacy. It was a frustrating time for both of them, although Jim liked the attention showered on him by Doris, and Doris enjoyed nursing him.

Before they knew it, it was Sunday evening, and they dreaded the thought that in the morning, Doris would have to go to work. She did not want to leave Jim, but she knew she had to. Jim, for his part, wanted to stay with Doris but felt more than ever that he had to find out who was behind all that happened especially before his nemesis takes another shot at him with more accuracy.

Monday morning came around, and Jim watched as Doris prepared for work. He loved watching her get dressed and put on her makeup. They kissed and promised that they would not be away from each other and would get together as soon as they could.

Jim had made arrangements for Tony to pick him up at the apartment. They decided that Jim would stay at Tony's apartment until he could function well enough to be on his own. Tony's apartment was a two-bedroom, but one of the bedrooms did not contain a bed. Tony brought a cot that he offered to sleep on it, but Jim insisted on using it, since he did not want to inconvenience Tony more than he already had. That day, Tony went to Jim's hotel and removed Jim's clothing and checked out for him.

Crowe was waiting outside the hotel for Jim to appear. He had been watching the hotel for a week. He knew he shot Jim but was not sure whether his shot did any damage. When Tony exited the hotel carrying Jim's suitcase, he recognized him and knew that he had seen him before but wasn't sure where. He decided to follow Tony, just in case, feeling that all the time he spent at the hotel was not paying off, so he had nothing to lose.

Tony almost immediately picked up that he was being tailed and pulled into an underground garage. He pulled his car around to face the exit and waited, and, sure enough, the car tailing him entered the garage. Tony took out his camera and snapped picture after picture of the unsuspecting Crowe as he drove past him. He was also able to photograph Crowe's license plate.

He put his car in gear and raced out of the garage, leaving Crowe trying to maneuver his car to get back on Tony's tail.

Crowe realized that he was spotted but thought that he had nothing to lose and this was the best lead he had as to Jim's location. He would try to follow Tony from a greater distance and maybe get lucky and Tony would lead him to Jim.

Tony kept a close eye on his rearview mirror to see if his tail picked him up again. He thought he saw the car again but wasn't sure, so he made an illegal turn and went the wrong way down a one-way street. If anyone was following him, he would have to be obvious to keep up with him.

Crowe saw Tony make the turns and decided to break off the tail. He had gotten Tony's license plate number and figured he could find out who he was and where he lived using that information.

When Tony returned to his apartment, he showed the pictures to Jim. "Do you know this guy?" Tony asked.

"No. Don't forget, all I saw was a flash when he shot me. I have no idea who he is."

"I'll head to the office and run a DMV on his car and see if anyone recognizes him. In the meantime, you had better get some rest and stay in. I'm sure he didn't follow me here, but until we can nail him, keep a very low profile," Tony admonished.

"I'm too tired to go anywhere. Right now, that cot looks like paradise to me," Jim responded.

Tony left Jim and headed for his office. He kept a wary eye in his rearview mirror and made some illegal U-turns just to make sure he wasn't being followed.

Jim hit the cot and almost immediately fell asleep. Even the thoughts of the loose cannon and Doris could not keep him awake. The sound of his cell phone woke him. He looked at his watch and realized he had slept for six hours. It was Tony.

"I got news for you, both good and bad. Which one do you want first?" Tony asked.

"Give me the bad," Jim answered.

"The car our shooter was in was rented. The renter's name is William Smith. How about that for being original? At any rate, it was turned in this afternoon, and, of course, our guy left a fictitious address and phone number. No one around the office recognized him, so I think we hit a temporary dead end."

"Great," a disappointed Jim responded. "How about the good news, or is there more bad stuff?"

"No more bad stuff. Lev is in town and wants to get together. He called earlier, and I brought him up to date on your exploits."

"Great. I'd love to see him. Maybe between my shoulder and his leg, we could make one whole man," Jim kidded.

"You two guys together would make ten men," Tony answered.

"Thanks, but how and where do we meet?"

"He said he had some business to take care of and will call me back. Would you like me to bring home something special for dinner?"

"Not really, whatever looks good."

"I'm in the mood for hamburgers and french fries. What do you think about that?"

"Sounds good. See you later," Jim responded as he hung up.

Lev called Tony on his safe cell phone the next day, and they decided to meet in a local pub that evening. Tony picked up Jim after work, and they drove to the pub.

It was like a family reunion for Jim and Lev. Although they did not know each other for a very long time, when you experience combat together, you become very close.

"How long were you with Salek?" Jim asked.

"It took me over a month to heal enough so that I could walk alone without help. Salek was great. He made sure I had everything I needed. Even though his hospital was primitive, I managed to survive with only a little limp. How about you? How did you make out getting out of country? I know you made it to Italy, and I can never repay you enough for that."

"Piece of cake," Jim responded. He then went on to tell of his experiences leaving the country, and they had a laugh about Jim's underwear suitcase.

The night went by quickly, and before they knew it, the bar was closing. They said their good-byes and promised to see each other very soon, although they all realized that it was probably the last time they would see Lev. Jim felt sad as he watched Lev use a cane and limp out of the bar.

"There goes a great man," Jim said to Tony. "I only wish we had more patriots like him in this country."

"We have some," Tony responded. "Aren't we patriots?"

"I guess so. I never thought about it that way."

They fell silent in thought as they drove to Tony's apartment.

Chapter 32

The next day, it was decided that Tony would rent a car in his name for Jim to use. Jim was in a hurry to get back to business and, most of all, to get the person who shot him. He felt that if he came up with the person who betrayed him, he would solve both problems at once.

Because he was shot near the Department of Justice, he decided the safest way to meet up with Corcoran was to follow him from his house. It was a little difficult driving with the pain from his right shoulder occasionally shooting down his arm.

He sat down the block from Corcoran's home. Corcoran came out and headed for the driveway and got into his car. He backed down the driveway and headed down the street with Jim following. Corcoran was a careful driver, which made it easier for Jim to keep up. Then it happened! Corcoran pulled into the parking lot of a diner and exited his vehicle. Jim followed at a discreet distance and parked in the diner's parking lot as far from Corcoran's car as he could. He watched as Corcoran entered the diner, and after looking around to make sure the shooter wasn't there, he entered the diner himself. Corcoran was seated in a booth about five rows from the front door. Jim decided this would be the time to confront him. He walked past the greeter and told him that he was with the man in the booth, pointing at Corcoran. The greeter smiled and offered to walk Jim to the seat, but Jim took the menu from his hand and proceeded to Corcoran's table.

"Excuse me, but this table is taken," Corcoran said with a puzzled look on his face.

"My name is Jim Vara. We need to talk."

"Oh, you're the one," Corcoran blurted out.

"Yes, I'm the one who has been betrayed and shot for no good reason."

"We spoke about you at our conference. You have a friend who was trying to clear your name."

"I'm glad to hear that, but I want to know here and now if you were the one that betrayed me and why?" Jim asked sternly.

"No, and I don't know anything about you except what was discussed at the meeting, and I cannot divulge that."

"Don't give me that cock-and-bull story. My life is in danger, and I've been beaten and shot and I want answers now or I'll end your career and your life right now," Jim bluffed and made a motion toward his belt as if he had a gun, sending a sharp pain from his shoulder to his hand.

Corcoran noticed the pain in Jim's face.

"I think you're bluffing, but for what it's worth, I had nothing to do with you. I approved you're going to Iraq when the paperwork came up from Doris, but that was it. The next I heard of you was at the conference when Doris tried to clear you."

"You're saying the paperwork on me came from Doris and not the other way around?" Jim asked.

"Yes. Why do you ask?" Corcoran responded.

"Never mind that. I find it hard to believe that you had nothing to do with putting the word out that I was a traitor."

"Believe what you want, but that's the truth. What would I gain by doing that? I don't even know you or anything about you."

Jim had a problem. He believed Corcoran. He seemed forthcoming and honest. But then, who could it have been? Why was the shooter waiting at the Department of Justice? What was the outcome of the conference about him at the Department of Justice? Who is Corcoran's boss?

"What was discussed about me at that conference?" Jim asked.

"I will tell you this much," Corcoran stated. "Doris explained what happened to you in Iraq and wanted to get the word out that you were clean."

"So what was decided?"

"It was decided that the word would be put out and that you should be cleared."

"Then why was I shot?"

"I have no knowledge that you were shot or why or who would do it," Corcoran responded. "This is all new to me. Are you sure that it had to do with your mission and not something from your past?"

"It had to be the mission. I have nothing in the past to cause anyone to want to kill me, and, besides, I have information that the shooter works for your—our organization."

"I'm sorry, but I can't help you. I wish I could."

"You can tell me if you hired the shooter and who he is so that I would have half a chance of getting him before he gets me again and who your boss is."

"I don't know anything about him. I will try to find out who he is because we don't need this happening in our organization. We are not the Mafia. We do some horrible things that must be done for the good of our country but not this to one of our own. If you were a traitor, I would have you legally hung."

"You couldn't do that. We are too secretive, and putting someone on trial would reveal the work that we do and would probably give the ACLU enough fodder to bring down the whole administration," Jim answered.

"True, but we could ship you off to Guantanamo and give you a military trial."

"I see you thought this out. Have you done it before?"

"No, but it's just an idea. As for my boss, you know full well that I can't tell you who it is. I will give you this—I will keep my eyes open, and if I come up with anything I think may help you, I'll let you know. I will also look into this shooter character and if he does work for us. I guarantee you it will not be for long and heads will roll."

Jim liked Corcoran's response and was building a great deal of respect for him.

"How do I get in touch with you if I do come up with something?" Corcoran asked.

"I move around a lot, so I don't have a good number. If you come up with something, call Tony—he works in the office. I will call him every couple of days to check in." Jim lied.

"OK. I have to go to work now," Corcoran responded. "Good luck," he said to Jim as he rose to leave.

"But you didn't eat anything." Jim motioned toward the menu.

"I'm late and I'll grab something at the office."

With that, Corcoran was out the door.

Jim was tempted to eat at the diner but decided against it. He left the diner and headed for his car. He opened the door and got in and suddenly realized he didn't need the key to enter; it was unlocked. He quickly turned to look in the backseat, but it was too late. He felt a sharp blow to the back of his head, and although he tried to fight it, he drifted off into unconsciousness.

Chapter 33

The horrendous pain in his shoulder woke him up. He opened his eyes and realized he was in a dark building that smelled of mold. He was tied to a chair with his arms behind him, causing agonizing pain in his right shoulder and arm. He tried to move to ease the pain, but it was no use; the chair back held him in place. His legs were tied to the chair legs, and he seemed to have little feeling in them and knew they must be numb from the tight rope that encircled them.

"Ah, so you're awake." It was a voice from behind him. It sounded raspy and sinister, like something out of an old horror movie.

"Where am I? Who are you? What do you want with me?"

"Never mind that, you rotten bastard. Just think of me as the American avenger. I'm the guy who is going to make you pay for being a traitor."

He sounded like he was insane. It was surreal. All of a sudden, blows came raining down on him. First, to his head with what felt like a club of some sort and then to his left shoulder. The latter blows knocked him over onto the floor. Then the kicks came to his head, chest, and stomach. Jim felt like he was going to heave and black out. He fought the feeling as best he could, but he was lying on his right shoulder, which only intensified the pain. Crow picked him up, chair and all, and smacked him two more times, this time with an open hand.

"I've got something special for you."

Crowe took out a small black box from a bag that was sitting in the corner of the room. Jim tried to focus but was having trouble. His left eye was swollen shut, and the vision in his right eye was very blurry. He could barely make out what was happening.

"You see this baby? With a little injection, you will be in agonizing pain for about eight hours, after which, you will die. Death will be a relief, and during the eight hours, you'll be praying for it."

Jim could see the hypodermic syringe in Crowe's hand. He had to think fast or do something, but he could not move.

"You're making a big mistake," Jim blurted out along with blood. "You don't understand. I'm a double agent. I was called a traitor so I could infiltrate the Iraqi regime. You kill me and you'll go down in history as the man who killed a patriot."

Crowe stopped and looked at Jim. "A likely story," he snorted.

"It's true. Call someone in headquarters and verify it. Call Tony or Doris, they'll tell you."

"Who is Tony?" Crow hesitated.

Jim thought that he had a chance.

"He works at the house in Virginia. He's the tech man."

Crowe studied Jim's face. He was no longer sure of himself and what he was doing. He began to have doubts. *If I kill him and he's telling the truth, I'll be a marked man for the rest of my life,* he thought.

"OK. You bought some time," Crowe said as he took out his cell phone. He dialed a number and had a conversation with someone.

"She said it's true. She backed your story. If I find out differently, I'll be back."

Crowe untied Jim, who fell to the floor.

"Who backed my story?" Jim asked.

"The one who hired me . . . Doris."

Jim couldn't believe what he heard.

"You mean Doris was the one who sent you after me?"

Crowe did not bother to answer him but just walked out.

Jim lay on the floor for a while and passed out. When he came to, he got up on his knees but could not stand. Then he heard the door open. He thought that Crowe was coming back. He had to do something but didn't have the strength. He inched himself toward the wall, thinking he could use it for support and help him stand. Then he smelled the perfume. Not any perfume . . . but her perfume.

"Darling, are you all right? Let me help you," Doris said.

"You, it was you all the while. Why, why?" Jim could taste the blood in his mouth.

"We can talk about it later. Let me help you."

"No. We can talk about it now. Why did you want me dead? I loved you." Jim pushed her hand away when she reached to help him. He wedged himself against the wall and was finally able to stand up. He leaned back on the wall and caught his breath. It was hard to breath. He had serious pain in his chest.

"I love you," she said. "Please try to understand."

"Understand what—that you wanted to kill me?"

"I didn't know, I didn't know," she repeated.

"Didn't know what?" Jim was getting frustrated and was afraid he was going to pass out again.

"I didn't know what a good man you are. When my son hanged himself, I blamed you. I guess I had to blame someone to justify it and not blame myself."

"Now I'm thoroughly confused. What did I have to do with your son hanging himself?"

"You were the arresting officer in New York."

"I don't even remember him. Why was he arrested?"

"You arrested him and six others on a narcotics charge. He hanged himself while being held in detention. I blamed you for it happening. At the time, I thought that if you hadn't arrested him, he would be alive today. I now realize it wasn't your fault. You were just doing your job, and I was just trying to justify what happened to him. After I met you and fell in love with you, I realized how wrong I was. I tried to stop what was happening to you, but it was too late."

Doris tried to put her arm around Jim to help him, but he moved away.

"Let me take you to a doctor. You need medical attention," she said.

"Get away from me," Jim spat out. "I don't want anything from you. If I never see you again, it will be too soon." He struggled with the pain and headed for the door.

"I'm so sorry, Jim. I love you. Please, please try to forgive me," she called after him.

Jim did not respond. The pain was making him light-headed. How he got to Tony's apartment, he still can't remember to this day.

Chapter 34

One year later

It had taken Jim months to heal and move back into his home.

He dated very little, as every woman he went out with did or said something that reminded him of Doris. It could have been their perfume or the way they pushed their hair from their face, the way they dressed, anything.

He became friendly with John Corcoran, going to his home a few times for dinner and even attending some of his son's soccer games.

Doris quit her job and took a job with a law firm in New York. She wanted to leave Washington and tried to forget all that happened. She occasionally went out with a man usually on a double date at the urging of a friend. She really wasn't interested in men anymore and would rather stay at home with a good book than go out. She was lonely but figured that it was the price she had to pay for what she had done to Jim. She desperately missed him.

One day, Jim received a call from Corcoran to come to his office. He knew it was business by Corcoran's tone and that it was a Sunday meeting at the Department of Justice. When he arrived after going through security, he was escorted to Corcoran's office.

"Hi, Jim." As usual, his demeanor was warm and friendly. "I have a job for you. No more sitting at home and collecting the big dollars for doing nothing."

"Gee, I was just getting used to it," Jim kidded.

"Let's get down to business. My kid has a game tonight, and I don't want to miss it. Remember all those pictures and the hullabaloo of Saddam being hanged?"

"Yes. Why?" Jim asked.

"Remember how they ceremoniously walked up to the gallows with a hood over his head and then hanged him for the entire world to see?"

"As a matter of fact, I do remember. How could I forget after all that I went through?"

"Well, guess what?" Corcoran stated. "That wasn't him under the hood."

AN AMERICAN ASSASSIN

Jim fell back in his chair in disbelief. "You gotta be kidding."

"I wish I was. I hate to tell you this, Jim, but your job is to go back and finish the job quietly and without any fanfare. It shouldn't be that difficult in that our troops control the area at this time."

Corcoran handed him a folder. "This contains everything you need, all our intelligence as well as tickets for your flight. You leave from Dulles Airport tomorrow and arrive in Baghdad the next day. General McAllister will meet you at the airport and help you to get to where we think Saddam is hiding. Good luck. Keep me informed as to how it is going over there. Don't forget, you have to get back in time for my son's championship game."

With that, Corcoran stood, smiled, and shook Jim's hand. Jim turned and left for home to pack and take care of last-minute details before he left.

The next day, he arrived at Dulles Airport and checked on his flight. It was due to leave in fifteen minutes. He took out his cell phone and looked at it. He hesitated but decided to go ahead and dial her number. He had to hear her voice before he left. *I guess I still love her,* he thought to himself. The phone rang, and a receptionist answered.

"May I speak to Doris Macon?" he said.

"May I ask what this is about?" the receptionist asked.

"It's a personal call," Jim responded.

"Whom should I say is calling?"

"An old friend," Jim responded.

"One moment, please." The receptionist was putting him through.

"Call for you on line two," the receptionist informed.

"Who is it?" Doris asked.

"I don't know. He only said he was an old friend and it was personal."

She suddenly felt a rush. *Could it be him? Could it be Jim after all this time? I guess I still love him. Oh, God, please let it be him.*

"Hello," she spoke into the telephone.

"Hello," she tried again.

When Jim heard her voice, he weakened. He wanted to answer but told himself it would not be fair to her or him. He just wanted to have some connection with her. He was about to get on a plane and he may never come back. *Oh, why do I still love her, it hurts so much?*

Doris hung up the phone after four tries to get an answer. *I know it was him. It hurts so much to think about him and what I did.*

Her thoughts were interrupted by the intercom. The receptionist told Doris that there was a messenger here for her.

"Send him in," she said, trying to get Jim out of her mind.

A scruffy-looking young man entered and asked, "Are you Doris Macon?"

"Yes," she answered, whereupon he handed her a long-stemmed yellow rose.

115

BOOK TWO

TROUBLE 3

Chapter 1

The plane landed gently on the concrete runway at the air base just outside of Baghdad, Iraq. Jim was glad to have arrived, as military planes are not noted for their comfort. He was anxious to get his assignment over with so he could get back to the States.

When the plane's door was opened, a blast of hot air hit him and caught him by surprise. He felt as if he couldn't breathe without burning his lungs. He stood at the doorway of the plane for a few seconds to catch his breath and then proceeded down the stairs to the tarmac. Two soldiers were waiting for him at the bottom of the stairs.

"Mr. Vara?" one asked.

"Yes," Jim responded.

"General McAllister is waiting for you. If you follow me, sir, we will take you to him."

"Thank you," Jim responded as they got into a jeep.

On the way to the general's office, Jim noticed men playing soccer and marveled at their ability to run in this stifling heat. He noticed that each time they ran or kicked the ball, dust would spiral up from the ground. *This place is close to hell,* he thought to himself.

They arrived at a Quonset hut, and the jeep came to a halt. The two soldiers quickly exited the jeep and held the hut's door open for Jim, who nodded a thank-you as he entered the building.

Inside the hut, an air conditioner was pumping cool air into the room, which felt like heaven. A soldier was sitting behind a desk and looked up at Jim and his escorts. One of the soldiers informed the clerk that this was Mr. Vara and that General McAllister was expecting him. The clerk nodded and spoke into an intercom, advising the general that Jim was here. Jim could not hear the general's response but was told to go right in and that the general was expecting him.

When Jim entered the general's office, he was surprised to see a tall man who looked a little like John Wayne. The general smiled at Jim.

"Welcome aboard," the general said, reaching for Jim's hand.

"Thank you, sir," Jim responded, noting that the handshake was firm, just as he expected.

"Please sit down. May I offer you a drink, ice tea or perhaps something stronger?" the general inquired.

"Ice tea would be fine. This is some place. How do you put up with the heat?"

"Believe it or not, this is not a hot day. It's only about 105. We have been known to get to 130 for a summertime average. They say its dry heat, but that's BS. It's still hot as hell," the general said and then spoke into the intercom, ordering two ice teas.

"Please call me Ken when not in public," he went on. "I'm not the type to go with formalities. If it's OK with you, I'll call you Jim."

"That will be fine," Jim responded, already taking a liking to the general.

Just then, there was a knock on the door, and the general said, "Come in."

The soldier from the front desk entered with a tray on which sat two tall glasses obviously containing the ice tea. He sat them down on the desk and made a quick about-face and left the room without saying anything.

The general handed Jim a glass and said, "Cheers."

The tea tasted great and went down easy even though it was very cold.

"I'll have one of my men show you around and take you to your billet where you can get some sleep. I know you must be tired after that trip. We can have dinner tonight and then we can get down to business." The general was a no-nonsense type of man who got to the point without dallying.

"Sounds great, Ken. I look forward to dinner."

The general once again spoke into the intercom, and within a few minutes, one of the soldiers who escorted Jim from the plane entered the room.

They said their good-byes, and Jim followed the soldier, who took him on a quick tour of the base, highlighting places he thought Jim might be interested in. He then took Jim to a barracks-type building, which contained a walled-off section that would serve as Jim's bedroom. Jim was elated that it was air conditioned. After thanking the soldier, he fell onto the bed and immediately fell asleep.

When he woke, he looked at his watch and saw that it was five o'clock. He had slept for six hours and felt refreshed. He made his way to the bathroom and splashed water on his face to wake up. He looked around and saw that this must be an officers' quarters, as those in the area were all lieutenants and above. He went back to his cubicle and retrieved his toilet kit and took a shower, shaved, and changed his clothes. He had nothing else to do but wait for the general's call.

At six thirty, a soldier knocked on his door and took him back to the general's office, where a dinner was set up on a sideboard table.

"Normally I eat in the officers' mess, but tonight I thought we could use some privacy," the general said as he poured two glasses of red wine. "You do drink wine, don't you?" he inquired.

"Yes, I do, and red is my favorite," Jim responded.

They made small talk as they ate, discussing weather, conditions in the United States, population problems in different parts of the world, and migration. Finally, the meal was consumed, and the general poured two glasses of brandy and moved to a comfortable seat and motioned Jim to join him.

"Well, let's get down to brass tacks, shall we? All I was told that I was to provide you with whatever you need and get you up-country. Is there anything else you would like to tell me?" the general asked, knowing full well that Jim wouldn't tell him any more than he had to.

"No, Ken, that about sums it up. I would like to spend a couple of days here and work on my tan. I need to get a little darker for my mission."

"You're going undercover then?"

"I guess I can tell you that I am."

"I will send two of my best men with to keep an eye on you."

"I don't know about that—they may cramp my style."

"These guys are pros. You won't even know that they are there. They will stay out of town but within reach if you need them. They can also extricate you immediately if necessary. They are tough and can hold off a platoon if need be."

"They sound great, and I'll give it some thought."

"OK. You can let me know during one of your tanning sessions." The general smiled. "By the way, who do you work for? I know you're not CIA. So where do you fit in?"

"Sorry, Ken, but that's need-to-know stuff, and right now, you have all the info you need."

"Just thought I'd try," the general quipped. "See you tomorrow, Jim. My men will take you back to your billet now."

With that, the general rose and shook Jim's hand.

The next day, Jim got up at 5:00 a.m. because of the noise the men in the barracks were making. He washed, dressed, and went to the mess hall for breakfast. It worried him seeing local people serve the food and was afraid they may give him away if they were not friendlies.

After breakfast, he found a lounging chair near the barracks and started working on his tan. He timed himself and used suntan lotion so that he didn't burn. This process went on for three days, and finally he was satisfied that he could pass for a native Iraqi. While he was tanning, he pondered the idea of taking the two men the general had offered with him and decided it would be all right as long as they did not enter the village where he was going.

He went to the general's hut and was ushered into his office by the soldier/clerk.

"Ken, I will need a 9 mm automatic with a silencer and a jeep. If the offer still holds, I will take the two men with me. I'll need some form of communication with them after we separate."

"Well," the general responded, "you sure do get down to business, don't you?"

"Sorry, sir, but I decided to leave tonight."

"Very well. I'll see that my men meet with you this afternoon, and if in the meantime you think of anything else you need, they can let me know."

"Thanks, Ken. You've been very helpful."

"Good luck with your mission, whatever it is, and there's a dinner waiting for you when you return."

The two men shook hands, and Jim left the office and headed for his billet.

Later that afternoon, two soldiers approached Jim, who was sitting outside, trying to get the final touches on his tan.

"Hi, my name is Tim, and this is my partner, John," the taller of the two said. "We understand that you need a ride up-country tonight."

"Yes, I do," Jim responded. "I assume you are the two General McAllister sent to take me there."

"Yes, we are, and I think we should set out some rules of engagement before we leave," Tim said.

"Good idea," Jim responded. "I assume you both have top-secret clearances for this job."

"Yes, we are Special Forces and we have gone on secret missions like this before."

"OK. I need a ride to Tirkut. I would like you to stay out of town nearby in case I have to make a fast getaway or have to be extricated in case I am made. In any event, how do I make contact with you after we separate?"

"We thought of that," John answered. "We have two devices. One is a cell phone that you could call us on, and the other is this small button that inserts into your belt. All you have to do is press it, and it will signal us that you want out. A special feature it has is that it sends us a signal that allows us to zero in on your location."

"Sounds good," Jim said while looking over the devices that John held in his hand.

"What time do we leave, sir?" Tim inquired.

"We'll leave at sunset, and please call me Jim."

"OK," John said. "We will see you at seven, and that will give me some time to put a last-minute charge on our toys."

The soldiers left, and Jim got back to his tanning.

Chapter 2

At 6:30 p.m., Jim got dressed into clothes he had brought with him for the assignment. He left the billet and waited out front for John and Tim. At exactly 7:00 p.m., the soldiers arrived in a jeep and had with them what looked to be some heavy weapons. They said their hellos, and Jim entered the jeep, and they were off to Tirkut.

They drove for five and a half hours and finally arrived at the outskirts of the town. John handed Jim the cell phone and helped Jim place the signaling device on the inside of his belt. John then gave Jim the 9 mm after ensuring it was loaded along with two extra clips of ammunition. It was decided that the two soldiers would find a spot hidden from the road but close enough to Tirkut so that they could respond immediately in case Jim was in trouble. They said their good-byes, and Jim started up the road toward the town.

By the time Jim got into town, it was three thirty in the morning, and the town appeared to be deserted. Jim found an empty bench in a park and sat closing his eyes and dozing on and off. He awoke at the sound of the Muslim chanter calling for prayer. Dawn was just coming over the horizon, and daylight was breaking. About a half hour later, the town seemed to come to life with people scurrying about, performing their daily routines. Jim slowly walked into town and entered what appeared to be a restaurant. Inside there were four tables with chairs and a long bench on the side wall where men were sitting and chatting. Jim sat at one of the tables, and the men stopped talking and looked at him. It was obvious to Jim that they knew that he did not belong. A scruffy-looking man came toward him from behind a low counter and asked what Jim wanted. Jim asked for a cup of tea, which would be what the natives would drink. He noted that the men appeared to be suspicious of him. He quickly drank the tea and left. Jim walked down the street and, as he looked at the passersby, felt that he was dressed appropriately and should have fit in. He walked a few more blocks and decided to try another restaurant. As he entered, he heard a man shouting, "There you are . . . How are you? I haven't seen you in a long time." To Jim's surprise, it was Lev, the Mossad agent. Lev shouted so everyone could hear him greeting Jim as though he belonged in the area. After Jim got over the shock, he also yelled in a loud voice, acknowledging his long-lost friend. Jim went to Lev's table and sat with him.

"What the hell are you doing here?" Jim asked. "I can't believe you also speak Farsi."

Lev smiled at Jim and said, "I speak several languages, you son of a gun. How are you? I think," Lev said, "we must have the same assignment."

Jim said, "I don't know about you, but I am here to kill an old friend."

"You mean our buddy Saddam?"

"Yes," Jim responded, "and what are you doing here?"

Lev said, "Our buddy is responsible for the deaths of many of my countrymen, and I am here to bring him back to Israel."

"What do we do now?" Jim asked.

Lev responded, "I don't care one way or another. If he is dead, he is dead. If not, I am taking him back with me." Lev raised his voice again for the benefit of those in the restaurant and asked Jim how his family was, how his mother was doing, and many questions of that nature. Jim responded in a loud voice, saying that everyone in his family was well, that they missed him and hoped that he could visit soon. They then lowered their voices, and Jim asked Lev, "Do you have any idea where our friend is?"

Lev responded, "Yes. It is my understanding that he is trying to put together a small army to take back the country. He pretty well rules this town, and you have to be very careful. It took me a month before I was accepted here."

Jim inquired, "Well, do we work together, or do we go off on our own?"

Lev answered, "He is in that building at the end of the next block. He is protected, so you must be careful. I will give you one opportunity to carry out your mission. If you fail, I will try to take him during the time that will follow."

Jim agreed stood and said, "I hope we will meet again soon."

For the benefit of those in the restaurant, they parted as they hugged each other and in loud voices proclaimed their friendship.

Jim left the restaurant and started walking toward the building Lev had indicated. He was still in shock at seeing Lev. The last time they had met was in Washington, and it was a very happy occasion. Jim walked past the building that Lev had indicated that Saddam was in. He saw nothing unusual—no guards outside—and decided to double back and enter the building. Upon opening the huge wooden door, he entered and observed two men sitting in chairs, one on each side of a door, which was about twelve feet, in front of him. The men had rifles on their laps and alerted to Jim's presence. Before they could react, Jim took out his automatic and fired, hitting each man and knocking the men back and onto the ground. The silencer on the automatic muffled any sounds that would alert anyone on the other side of the door. Jim ran to the door, opened it, and observed a large room with ample furniture and at the opposite end a desk with a man sitting behind it. The man appeared to be Saddam. Jim raised his weapon, and the man reacted, leaping to his right side onto the floor. Jim fired twice, splintering the top of the desk. To Jim's surprise, a hand came over the top of the desk, holding a machine gun. The machine gun was blindly fired, slamming into pictures and furniture in the room. Jim fell to the floor and rolled toward the door, keeping very low. When he passed the door, he got up, put his weapon away, and ran out the front door. By that time, a crowd was gathering, since they had been alerted by the sound of the machine gun fire. Jim quickly pointed toward the building and yelled in Farsi, "Quick, inside! Quick, inside!" The people reacted to Jim and were heading into the building. Jim walked down the street as fast as he could without drawing too much attention to himself. He noticed a small, old black car sitting at the curb. He approached it and peered in. He saw that the ignition switch was missing. He got into the car, grounded the bare wire that was where the ignition should be, and started the car. He headed out of town toward the place where Tim and John were waiting. He activated the cell phone and told them he was in the black car heading toward their position and that there might be people following him.

After a short distance, he peered into the rearview mirror and saw two trucks and a jeep gaining on him. On the bed of each truck were men waving rifles. The jeep contained three men and what looked like a small cannon or a mounted machine gun.

The car started to stall. Jim pressed the accelerator to the floor only to watch the speedometer go slower and slower. Suddenly, the engine compartment seemed to explode, and a cloud of steam rose into the air. The car came to a halt, and Jim looked into the rearview mirror as he exited to see that the vehicles that were chasing him were only a few hundred yards away. He ran to the front of the car to use it as cover and took out his automatic. He braced himself for the battle that was about to take place.

As Tim and John drew closer to the black car, they saw the steam gushing from its engine, and Jim crouched behind it. John decided to take immediate action and fired a missile at the truck nearest the black car. The truck exploded and ran off the road, scattering bodies as it broke into pieces. The driver of the second truck, seeing the first explode, jerked his wheel to the right, causing the truck to leave the road and flip on its side in a gully, throwing its passengers onto the ground. At the sight of the melee, the jeep came to a screeching halt and quickly turned around and headed back in the direction it came from.

As the jeep with Tim and John drew closer, Jim jumped in, and they were off to another five-and-a-half-hour ride back to the base. When they arrived, they let Jim off at his billet and reported to General McAllister.

Chapter 3

Jim showered and immediately fell asleep. He slept for about six hours when a knock on his door woke him. It was a young soldier who informed that the general was waiting for Jim to have dinner. Jim quickly dressed and got into the waiting jeep, and they left for the general's quarters. When they arrived, Jim was ushered into his office, where the general was waiting. The general was not as friendly as before and had a stern look on his face. He motioned Jim to sit down, and they began to eat in silence. After the meal was over, the general poured a couple of brandies and once again motioned Jim to take a seat in an easy chair.

"Let's get to it, shall we, Jim?" the general started. "I heard about the skirmish and I want to know exactly what went on and what caused it. I know I will probably have to make a report to Washington, so I need the facts."

"Ken, I don't know what to say. If I tell you what happened and more to the point what caused the skirmish, you won't be able to use it in your report."

"Well, in that case, why don't you tell me and let me make the decision as to what I can and can't report?"

"I will let you in on the secret, but, first, I need your word that you won't publish it until I get the OK from my boss."

"OK," the general agreed.

Jim started, "Do you remember all of those pictures of Saddam Hussein being hanged in Baghdad?"

The general nodded in the affirmative.

"If you recall, Ken, he was hooded when he was hung. We know that that was not Saddam under the hood."

The general looked at Ken in disbelief.

"You mean to tell me that that SOB is still alive and kicking?"

"Yes, and what's more, he is still dangerous. I know it is hard to believe, but it's true, and I proved it. My mission was to find Saddam and eliminate him. He was in Tirkut when I came upon him. I discovered that he was trying to put together a small army to take back his power. I entered his building and fired a couple of shots at him but missed. He came up with a machine gun and sprayed the room, causing me to retreat and get out of there. His followers heard the machine gun fire and came running to the building. I managed to escape taking a car and driving to the location where Tim and John were. Saddam's group took up chase and almost had me until your men fired on them, causing them to break off. And that is the whole story, Ken."

The general looked closely at Jim and asked again, "Who do you work for?"

Jim responded, "I can't tell you that. All I will say is that we do go all the way into the White House."

The general said, "How can I write this report if I can't tell them that Saddam was involved? I know what I can do." The general perked up. "I will put together a raid on Tirkut using the intelligence that an army of insurrection was being formed, and, if necessary, I will say the intelligence came from you through a backdoor source."

"That sounds good to me," Jim responded.

"OK, Jim, get out of here. I have a lot of planning to do. We will leave tonight and hit them the first thing in the morning."

Jim swallowed his brandy, stood, shook the general's hand, and left.

That night, Jim was woken several times due to the movement of men and machinery. He knew that that was the American forces on their way to Tirkut.

The next morning, Jim entered the general's quarters and left a note with his clerk soldier that he had to get back to Washington. The clerk arranged for a flight that was leaving in a few hours for the air force base just outside of Washington.

Chapter 4

The following morning, Jim headed into the Department of Justice building, where he met with his boss, John Corcoran. He informed Corcoran of all that had taken place and apologized for not getting Saddam. Corcoran responded that he was surprised that Jim could do so much in the matter of a few days. Jim answered that he will get Saddam one way or another.

After he left Corcoran's office and on his drive back to Virginia, once again, the thought of Doris filled his head. He wondered, since it had been a year, if she had married or if she would even speak to him after the way they parted. He wanted desperately to call her but fought the urge and decided to sleep on it before making a rash judgment.

Once again, he had sleepless night thinking about Doris and the wonderful albeit short time they had spent together. He realized that he had loved her and probably still did. He feared that during the course of the past year, she had forgotten about him or, even worse, had found someone else.

After breakfast, he made the decision to call her and let the chips fall where they may. He understood that he did not want to go through life without her and felt that whatever happens, he would have at least tried. As he dialed her office number, he realized that he was sweating. He thought it ironic that he had been shot at and had gone through all kinds of hell, but this was a more challenging time for him than that. When the phone rang on the other end, he almost hung up, but then the receptionist answered, "Doris Macon's office. Can I help you?"

He responded, "I would like to speak to Ms. Macon, please."

She asked, "May I ask who is calling please, and what is the topic you wish to discuss?"

"It is a personal call. Please tell her that it is an old friend."

The receptionist told Jim to please hold while she buzzed Doris on the other line.

"There is a call for you, Ms. Macon, and the man on the other end says it is personal and that he is an old friend. He did not give me his name."

Doris looked at the intercom and thought to herself, *Could it be? Could it really be Jim?*

"Put the call through, please." She felt a tremor in her voice as she responded.

"Hello, this is Doris Macon. May I help you?"

Jim felt a shiver go through his back when he heard her voice.

"Doris, this is Jim." There was silence on the line at both ends as both of them felt the excitement of the moment.

"Jim? Is this Jim Vara?"

"Yes, Doris, it's me. How have you been?"

"I have been OK. Where are you? What are you up to?"

"As you know, I am in the same line of work and I miss our little get-togethers and was wondering, if you are free, if we can go out to dinner sometime?"

"Of course, Jim. I miss our little get-togethers too."

"I am in Washington now. If you let me know when you're available, I can catch a shuttle and be up there in an hour or so."

"How about tomorrow night, say, around seven?"

"That will be great. Where shall we meet?" Jim asked.

"Can you meet me at my office? I work at 656 Eighth Avenue."

"Fine, I'll meet you at seven. I'll be the one with bells on," Jim kidded.

"No more than me," she responded.

"Do you think we can pick up where we left off?" Jim asked.

"Let's save that for an in-person conversation. See you tomorrow," Doris responded as she hung up.

When Jim hung up the phone, he couldn't believe how he felt. He was excited again, just as he had been before. After all she put him through, he still had feelings for her. He realized that he missed her terribly and wanted nothing more than to be with her.

Doris sat there staring at the phone that she just hung up. *Could this be really happening after all this time of praying for it? Does he really forgive me? He sure sounds like he does. He sounds so wonderful. Please, God, help me make it up to him. I still love him so much*

Chapter 5

The next morning, Jim rose from his sleep still feeling excited as he did the night before when he spoke to Doris. He called the airlines and booked a late afternoon flight to New York. The airline desk clerk warned him that due to storms out west, his flight may be delayed.

After breakfast, he received a call from his boss, Corcoran, who told him to come to his office right away. Jim jumped into his car and hurried to the Department of Justice building.

After being examined by security, he went immediately to Corcoran's office, where a secretary ushered him into the main office. Corcoran rose from behind his desk and greeted Jim warmly.

"How are you doing, Jim?"

"Fine, I'm doing just fine, John," Jim responded. "What's up? Why the hurry call?"

"I want you to get on the phone and call General McAllister right away. There have been some worrisome developments over there. Dial 0 and my secretary will put you through."

Jim didn't like the tone of Corcoran's voice. He dialed the 0 and asked the secretary to put him through to General McAllister.

"General McAllister's office," the clerk answered.

"This is Jim Vara. Can I speak with the general, please?"

"Yes, sir. I'll put you through right away," the clerk answered.

Jim didn't like that response either. It was like they were waiting for him.

"Ken, this is Jim. How are you?"

"I've been better," the general responded. "It seems like we have a situation on our hands."

"What's the matter, Ken?"

"Well, as you know," the general began, "we went into Tirkut the night before you left. Well, I have to hand it to them—the place was clean as a whistle. There was no sign of our friend and not even a poster calling for rebellion. The only thing we found was the desk with two bullet holes in it as you described, and therein lies the problem."

"I don't understand," Jim interrupted. "Why would that be a problem?"

"Well, they filed a serious complaint of harassment against us."

"I would think that you would be used to that by now, Ken. I would think you've had plenty of them. It's all nonsense and just a smoke screen."

"Yes, Jim, you're right, but this time, my hands are tied, and I have to send it on to Washington."

"Why?" Jim asked.

"The gist of their complaint was that they were trying to apprehend a person who stole a car when they were fired upon by my troops. One of them was killed, and they had fifteen casualties."

"So," Jim answered, "we know who that was."

"Yes, and therein lies the problem. They have the perfect case of a violation of rules of engagement and are demanding heads on the chopping block."

"That's BS, and you know it, Ken. Tim and John saved my cookies. If it weren't for them, we would not be having this conversation."

"I agree," the general responded, "but think about it, Jim—to a political who wants to embarrass the military or the administration, or just make a name for himself, this is perfect fodder."

Jim was floored. "What can I do, Ken? I can't let them throw Tim and John under the bus."

"There's nothing you can do now. I'm just giving you a heads up. I can foresee you testifying in front of a Congressional Committee in the near future, so you had better clear it with whomever you work for. They will probably be out for blood, and it will be yours, Tim's, and John's along with some of mine. I heard the Inspector General's Office is already on its way to investigate. They're not wasting any time."

"Thanks for the heads up, Ken. I'm going to have to give this some serious thought. I can't let Tim and John or you swing for this. I have to do something."

Jim hung up the phone and looked over at Corcoran, who was obviously also giving it some thought.

"You know about this?" Jim inquired.

"Yes, I heard about it earlier," Corcoran responded. "I would normally fix you up with an attorney from this department, but they probably will be the ones prosecuting the case."

Jim was floored. "What do you mean *prosecute?* Do you think it's that serious?"

"You never know about something like this. It could go away, or it could end up in court or at a military tribunal. My guess is the latter. I suggest you get a good attorney to look out for your interest. I can provide you with some names of lawyers who have some experience in these things."

"What about Tim and John?" Jim inquired

"They will be provided with a military attorney who will defend them."

"This is BS." Jim was turning red. "We have to defend a case where we did the right thing, and that SOB Saddam is still out there, probably laughing his head off."

"Such is American politics today, Jim."

"What if I nail Saddam? Can we then come out in the open and end all this?"

"No guarantees, Jim, but probably," Corcoran responded.

"I'm out of here. I'm going to get him if it's the last thing I do." Jim was getting furious.

"Make sure it's not the last thing you do—I'd miss you. Good luck, Jim. And bring me back a scalp."

Jim left the office and still couldn't believe what had just transpired. He knew he had to do something, and hiring a lawyer was not it. He drove to Falls Church, where the Group's headquarters are. On the way, he called his former partner, Tony, and asked him to meet him there. He figured he would probably need Tony's expertise with electronics.

When he arrived, he went immediately to the tech room and waited for Tony. When Tony arrived, he explained all that transpired and asked him if he knew how to contact Lev. Tony went to his computer, and Jim watched in awe as his fingers flew over the keys. In a few seconds, Tony reported that he had a phone number that may be Lev's. He dialed the number and handed the phone to Jim, telling him it was on a secure line. Jim was elated when he heard Lev's voice on the other end. He explained the predicament he was in and asked him if he could help and if he knew the whereabouts of "our mutual friend."

"Yes, I do," Lev answered to Jim's delight. "Come to Paris right away and I'll meet you at the base of the Eiffel Tower tomorrow morning at ten, French time."

"I'm on my way," Jim responded as he ended the call. He looked at his watch and realized he had very little time to get a flight and make it to the airport, as it was rush hour and getting to Dulles Airport would take an inordinate amount of time. He asked Tony to book him a flight to Paris, and once he arrived at the airport, he would call him for the particulars. He had no time to go home and pack anything. He called a cab company and asked them to meet him in ten minutes a few blocks from where they were.

While waiting for the cab, Jim tried to call Doris. The secretary informed that Doris was not in her office and was not expected for the rest of the day. Jim asked for her home phone number and was told that she could not give it to him. He tried to explain that it was an emergency, but the secretary would not budge on the matter. Frustrated, he finally decided to leave Doris a message. He explained that he was called out of the country on a matter from her former employer, knowing that she would understand what that meant. He only hoped that she would believe him and would not read anything into it that was not meant.

At last, the cab arrived, and Jim told the driver to get him to Dulles Airport as fast as possible and that there would be a large tip in it for him if he did it in an hour or less. Jim did not have any confidence that he could do it, since they hadn't gone very far and were already in bumper-to-bumper rush-hour traffic.

On the way to the airport, Jim tried to call Corcoran but was told that he was not in his office. He then called Tony and asked him to call Corcoran and explain the situation. Tony then informed him that he had a few flights to Paris lined up. The first left in twenty minutes, so that was out of the question. Jim chose one that was leaving in two hours but would get him into Paris at 10:00 a.m., the time he was supposed to meet Lev. He asked Tony to contact Lev and explain the situation and ask him to postpone their meeting until noon.

It took an hour and a half to get to the airport, and Jim had just enough time to purchase a ticket and get through security. He boarded the flight and settled in to try to get some sleep. Unfortunately, a small child was sitting in front of him and basically kept him up most of the night.

When he landed at Charles De Gaulle Airport, he hailed a cab and headed for the Eiffel Tower.

Chapter 6

Doris returned to her office with butterflies dancing in her stomach at the thought of her meeting Jim again after all this time. When she read the message left by Jim, she was heartbroken. At first, she thought that this was Jim's way of getting out of their meeting, but as she analyzed the note, she realized that it was possible that he was on assignment, especially knowing the type of work he was doing, as she had worked for the same Group until she resigned right after the horrible happenings with Jim. *Time will tell,* she thought, *and in the meantime, I have my hopes to keep me going, and I hope nothing happens to him and he is safe.*

Jim arrived at the Eiffel Tower at eleven thirty, exhausted from lack of sleep. As soon as he walked under the tower, Lev arrived. They shook hands, and Lev motioned to Jim to follow him. They arrived at Lev's car and got in. Lev told Jim that they were going to a safe house where Jim could get some rest and then they will catch up.

They arrived at a nondescript four-story building, where Lev unlocked the front door, and they walked up two flights of stairs. The stairwells were dirty and filled with graffiti. When they arrived on the third floor, Lev unlocked a door and bade Jim to enter. He entered what looked to be a living room with a sofa and two large overstuffed chairs. Jim was surprised to see two men in undershirts sitting in the chairs. They casually looked at Jim and nodded. They obviously had been expecting him. Jim nodded a greeting in return and followed Lev into a small kitchen and then to a bedroom. Lev told Jim he could sleep there and he would wake him in six hours and then they could talk.

Jim fell asleep as soon as his head hit the pillow. He didn't even take off his clothes but just lay down and was out cold. The six hours felt like ten minutes, and before he knew it, Lev was shaking him and telling him to get up. He rose and entered the kitchen, where a steaming hot cup of coffee and a croissant were waiting for him. He smiled at Lev for the reception.

"Thanks, Lev. I can really use this," he said, nodding toward the light repast.

"You're welcome. After you finish, we can talk and I can find out what you're up to these days."

Jim drank the coffee and ate the croissant as Lev watched with a smile on his face.

Jim then explained all that happened, from his missing Saddam to the chase and the pending court battles.

Lev shook his head in disbelief. "You Americans are nuts. You're always looking to blame something on someone when it's politically expedient. I think you have all lost your common sense."

"In this case, I have to agree with you," Jim answered.

"Can't you go to a closed committee and testify so that things can be kept secret?"

"No, I can't because of Tim and John. I can't let them swing for saving me, and their plight is already public."

Lev shook his head and motioned Jim to follow him into the living room. The two men who had been there previously were gone, so Jim sat in one of the seats, while Lev opted for the sofa.

"So can I assume you're here to finish the job you started in Iraq?" Lev inquired.

"Yes. I have to get him to save many good people."

"Yes, I understand," Lev said, nodding his head as if to say "I agree."

"May I ask why we are here in France?"

"We have been able to establish that he is here. After your little escapade in Iraq, he fled to this country. I guess he figures he can ferment his revolution from a distance."

"That's interesting, but do you have any idea where in this country he could be?" Jim asked.

"Yes, he is in Marseille. Marseille is a very interesting city. It has a port and has a 40 percent Muslim population. Most of them are Shiites, who are trying to establish Sharia law in the city. A smaller number are Sunni, and that is where our friend is. To top this off, the port, as I mentioned, is a transit point for narcotics, so we have the Mafia present. As I said, it is a very interesting city."

"What about the French government? Why aren't they doing something about it?" Jim asked.

"As in your country, they want to be politically correct and do not want to appear to be picking on a minority group. Until things get way out of hand, I don't envision them doing anything. Unfortunately, it may be too late then."

"That is very interesting," Jim responded. "But how do I get into the city without arousing suspicion?"

"That's easy. People from the Middle East are arriving every day with virtually no inspection from the government. We just ride in."

"We, you said *we?*" Jim questioned.

"Yes, I'm going with you. I know the territory, as my agents have already infiltrated it while on a different assignment and they will be very helpful. They do not know you and will only deal with me."

"Are you sure you're not tagging along to make sure I finish the job this time?" Jim kidded with a smile on his face.

"Well, someone has to take care of you. Look at the mess you're in," Lev kidded in return.

"OK. When do we start?"

"I'm waiting for my agents to get back to me with some more information, hopefully with our friend's whereabouts. As soon as I get it, we'll leave. In the meantime, let's go out and get some of that famous French food."

They left the apartment and went to a French restaurant that Lev recommended, where they enjoyed a great five-course meal.

Chapter 7

Two days went by without any word. Then Lev received a call with the information they needed. They immediately went downstairs and got into a car and started the drive to Marseille.

The drive was long, but the countryside was beautiful with lush vegetation on both sides of the road. *France is a beautiful place,* Jim thought. *Someday, I would like to bring Doris here.* Thoughts of Doris immediately flooded his mind, and he hoped she got his message and understood his situation. He made a mental note that he would have to explain it all to her when they were together again.

As they approached Marseille, they could see what appeared to be a barrier further up the road ahead, and Lev stopped the car and pulled to the side of the road.

"Blockade!" Lev exclaimed. "Probably one of those Shiite checkpoints I heard about. They check everyone and go through the car to check for contraband or anything that does not conform to their religion. I've heard rumors that they will summarily execute anyone on the spot if their caught with narcotics."

"What's the problem?" Jim asked. "We're not carrying anything, are we?"

"Jim," Lev answered, "we have weapons in the trunk, including your favorite 9 mm automatic with a silencer attached."

"Oh," Jim responded. "What will we do now?"

"We'll find another way in. There are dozens of ways to get into Marseille including going through the woods."

Lev turned the car around and drove for about two miles where he pulled into a gas station. He took out his phone and called someone. *Probably one of his agents,* Jim thought.

After a few minutes, Lev's phone buzzed. It was one of his agents who instructed Lev on a route to take to get into Marseille without being stopped. Lev put the car in gear and once again drove for about a half mile where Lev was obviously satisfied and headed toward the city again.

As they drove through the city, Jim could not believe what he saw. The streets were lined with garbage and all sorts of filth and debris. He had always heard what a beautiful city Marseille was, but this was a disaster. He thought he was in a Third World country. There were street vendors hawking things, and all the women wore burkas.

"Why doesn't the government do something about this?"

"Who knows? I think they must have lost complete control over it," Lev responded. "It seems to be run by its own Shiite form of government."

"Unbelievable," Jim responded.

They drove around, while Lev seemed to be looking for a specific address. When he found it, they parked in front of a three-story stucco home that looked like it was in good shape at one time but now it was dirty and in need of a good power washing. When they entered the building, they found it to be one of considerable wealth in its time. The stairway had a banister made of hardwood that still had a bright sheen on parts of it. The doors were all hardwood and thick, as was appropriate in its day, probably fifty or so years ago.

Lev removed a key from his pocket, and they entered a first-floor apartment. It looked the same as the house they left in Paris on the inside with the living room as you enter followed by a kitchen, which was off to one side, and the bedrooms probably in the rear of the apartment.

"We stay here tonight and tomorrow we start out on our quest," Lev said.

"Do we have any ideas as to where our friend is?" Jim asked.

"Yes, we have, and I have two men working to verify it right now. You can't recruit people for a revolution and hide at the same time." Lev smiled.

"I just want to let you know that I must bring back some DNA to prove that it was our friend and not another hooded stand-in," Jim said.

"Yes, I realize that and have told my men that in the unlikely event they had to take him out, that if it were humanly possible, they were to bring back samples."

"Thanks, Lev," Jim responded. "How can I ever repay you?"

"I'm repaying you for saving me when we were in Iraq. Besides, we are friends and we are working for the same ideals."

"Yes, but sometimes I think were the only ones."

"Don't lose faith, my friend. There are many good patriots out there." Lev tried to reassure Jim.

"I know, but they seem to be well hidden." Jim tried to lighten the conversation.

Just then, Lev's phone buzzed. He answered and looked at Jim, smiled, and nodded yes as he spoke into the phone.

After the call ended, he said to Jim, "We located him, but there is a complication."

"What is it?" Jim asked.

"There is a Shiite hit squad after him, and they are closing in, so we had better hurry if you want to do the job."

Jim thought that Lev must have either infiltrated or had an informant in the Shiite community.

"OK. Where to?" Jim asked.

"First, I must get some toys out of the car and then we can go."

Lev left the apartment and came back in minutes carrying a backpack. He placed it on a table in the kitchen and took out a couple of hand grenades and two automatic pistols, one with a silencer attached. He handed the latter to Jim, who placed it in his waistband. He also gave Jim one of the grenades, which he put in his jacket pocket.

Chapter 8

The four men entered a car that was so small, they could barely fit their heavy weapons in it. They were on a mission of jihad and had sworn an oath to give their lives to carry it out. They were soldiers of God and were fearless in their mission. They would kill Saddam Hussein and behead him for all the hurt and suffering he caused their people.

Jim and Lev drove through the streets of Marseille, looking for the address given to them over the phone. As they approached the area, a small car carrying four men turned the corner and fell in behind them. Lev looked into his rearview mirror, saw the small car, but thought nothing of it, just another group of men on their way to who knows where.

As they approached the area, there was no place to park, so Lev decided to go around the block once in case one would open up.

The small car double parked, and the four men exited the vehicle. With their heavy weapons exposed, two of the men took positions outside the building, their weapons at the ready. The other two men entered the building, and almost immediately, heavy weapons fire could be heard. They sprayed the entire area with gunfire, causing people to run for cover. They entered the inner part of the building and shot several people who were unlucky enough to be inside. They then entered an office complex, and standing behind a desk was Saddam. He knew what was happening and accepted his fate, standing defiantly and looking straight at his executioners as they sprayed him with bullets. One of the assailants took out a large knife and decapitated his dead body.

In the meantime, the two men outside were coming under fire from buildings across the street. The two men sprayed the building with gunfire, causing huge pockmarks in the face of the structures.

Meanwhile, Lev and Jim saw what was happening and left their car at the corner and proceeded to slowly move up the street toward the two men who were outside the building, spraying the houses across the street with gunfire. They slowly moved forward using the cars that were parked along the curb for cover. One of the men caught a glimpse of them and was turning toward them to fire at them when a bullet from across the street struck him in the chest. The assailant was wearing a suicide vest, and when the bullet hit him, it exploded. It blew him to smithereens and also blew up the steps of the building they were in front of, killed his fellow assassin, and took out the car at the curb and his own small car that they arrived in.

In the meantime, the two men from inside were exiting, carrying the head of Saddam. When they arrived at the front steps, they were also killed by the explosion. Lev and Jim, seeing what happened, ran toward the demolished steps. Jim was removing an envelope and a knife as he moved forward. When they got to where the steps were, Jim proceeded to cut some of the hair off the decapitated head and put it in the envelope. For good measure, he let some blood from Saddam's severed head drip into the envelope.

At this time, the men who had been firing at the assailants from across the street recovered from the blast and saw Lev and Jim with the severed head. Thinking they were part of the assassin team, they started to open fire at them. Lev returned the fire as they ran up the street toward their car, once again using the cars along the curb for cover. Then it happened; Jim was hit with a bullet in his left calf. He tumbled over onto the ground in excruciating pain. Lev, who was in front of Jim, saw what happened and returned to help Jim. He threw a grenade toward the house where most of the fire was coming from and helped Jim to his feet. They hobbled to their car and started to drive away when a barrage of gunfire sprayed the vehicle. Lev was hit in his left thigh but managed to get the car in gear and started to drive away. He was not able to shift the manual transmission, so their progress was slow. Lev fought the feeling that he was going to pass out and pressed on using all his remaining strength. Finally, he gave in and lost control of the car and crashed into a car that was parked at the curb.

Jim, seeing what happened, got out of the car and, with much pain, came around to the driver's side and opened the door. He helped Lev out of the car and looked around for a place to take cover. Seeing an alleyway, he helped Lev, who was in a great deal of pain, hobble into the darkened areaway. He sat Lev down against a brick wall and looked for a place where they could hide. There was a doorway further down the alley, and Jim knew that he had to use it to find cover.

"Leave me, Jim," Lev said with pain in his voice.

"No way," Jim replied. "We got into this mess together and we'll get out of it together."

Jim removed his handkerchief and tried to cover Lev's wound. He applied pressure to try to stop the bleeding, but it was a futile attempt.

It started to rain. Not just a shower but a downpour. Jim knew that the rain would provide some cover for them.

Men were running up and down the street outside the alleyway, and Jim knew it was only a matter of time before they were discovered. He lifted Lev up and half carried him and half dragged him further into the alleyway, hopping on his good leg toward the door. When they reached the door, it was unlocked, and then Jim realized that it was an abandoned building. They entered through the door, and to the right, Jim saw a stairway, and to the left was another door presumably to an apartment. Jim dragged Lev toward the stairs when he noted a door under the stairs probably used for storage at one time. He pushed open the door and peered in. There was nothing inside but some debris and wood lying on the floor. He heard voices getting closer and decided that the underside of the stairwell would have to do to get out of the way of their pursuers. He helped Lev in through the door and entered, closing the door behind him. He sat Lev down with his back to the wall and found a piece of wood that he wedged between the wall and the door holding it closed. It was crude but would have to do. Satisfied the door was sufficiently secure, he turned his attention to Lev. It was dark under the stairwell, and Jim could not see adequately enough to tend to Lev's or his own wound.

The voices got louder, and Jim knew that their pursuers were searching the building. He reached down and took Lev's gun with his left hand and held his gun in his right hand and pointed them both toward the door. He heard footsteps outside the door and braced himself for whatever was about to happen. The stairwell door rattled as one of the searchers tried to open it to look inside. Frustrated that the door would not open, he walked away and left. Jim breathed a sigh of relief as the footsteps sounded further and further away.

Chapter 9

They sat there for hours. Finally, Lev seemed to recover a bit, and Jim thought that the time was right for them to leave. He removed the piece of wood that was holding the door shut and peeked out. He could not see anyone, so he crawled out of their hiding place and saw that all seemed to be clear. The rain had stopped. There was no running or scrambling of feet on the street that he had heard earlier. He slowly moved through the alley and to the sidewalk in front, leaning against a wall for support. All seemed quiet. He returned to the stairwell and spoke to Lev, telling him all seemed to be clear. He asked Lev if he thought he could walk, and Lev told him he didn't think so, but he could call for help from the agents that Jim had met in Paris. Jim helped him get his cell phone out and watched as Lev made the call.

"They are not far away and could be here in a half hour," Lev told Jim. "I told them the route we took and to look for our crashed car and then the alley."

"OK. I'll try to wait outside in the alley and signal them when they come," Jim said. "In the meantime, can I do anything for you?" Jim asked.

"Do you have any morphine on you?" Lev said, trying to make light of their situation.

"If I did, I would be using it myself," Jim retorted.

The time went by slowly. Finally, when Jim saw that twenty minutes had passed, he decided to head out the alley and hopefully flag down Lev's agents. He stood on the sidewalk, leaning against a wall for support, and waited. Only a few people passed by, and they ignored Jim, which was a good thing.

Finally, a car slowly approached, and Jim recognized the agents. He slowly hopped off the curb and into the street and gestured it to stop. The car pulled to the curb, and the agents helped Jim to the stairwell where they extracted Lev and carried him into the car. One of the agents got into the back of the car with Lev, while Jim sat in the front. The agent in the back told the agent in front that the wound looked serious and Lev had to be taken to a hospital. Since they did not want to go to a local hospital, they decided to drive all the way to Paris.

The drive was torturous for Jim and especially for Lev, who every so often moaned in pain. Finally, they arrived at a hospital in Paris and brought both Jim and Lev to the emergency room.

Jim questioned the doctor on duty who was working on him as to Lev's condition, but the doctor just frowned and ignored him. One of the agents told Jim that they had called a doctor who worked with them in the past and who will arrive shortly and probably take over. Jim felt a little better after hearing that.

Jim was bandaged, given a cane and some pain pills, and released, his wound being only superficial. He hobbled to the waiting room and sat down. He looked at his clothes and realized he was covered with blood. One of the agents offered to take Jim to the safe house, but he refused until their doctor arrived. Once the doctor arrived and ensured them that Lev will be OK, they left for the safe house.

When he arrived at the safe house, he took off his clothes, washed up, and got into bed and fell asleep. When he awoke, he asked the agents if they heard anything about Lev. They told him that they knew no more than what the doctor told them last night, and that was that Lev had a fighting chance. Jim was perplexed with the response because the doctor told him that Lev would be OK. He decided to head to the hospital and asked the agents if they would give him a lift. They said they couldn't because they had an assignment that they must carry out that morning but that Jim could catch a cab down the block. They did, however, provide him with a set of clothes from one of the agents who were about Jim's size. Jim changed his clothes, making sure he retained the envelope containing Saddam's DNA.

On the way to the hospital in the cab, Jim called Tony and advised him that he was coming in. He asked Tony to contact Corcoran and to tell him to stand by because he was bringing back what they had been after.

When Jim arrived at the hospital, he went directly to the emergency room only to be told that Lev was upstairs in a private room. He took the elevator to the third floor and found Lev's room. Lev was asleep and had all sorts of tubes attached to him that were pumping fluids into his arm. He looked fairly good having some color returned to his face. Jim did not want to wake him, so he went to the nurses' station and inquired as to his condition. The nurse told him that he had to speak with the doctor, but when Jim explained that he had to leave the country that day, she told him that Lev's condition was good and that he was stable. Jim thanked her and headed down the elevator and hailed a cab to take him to the airport.

When he arrived at the airport, he discovered that he had to wait two hours for the next flight to Dulles Airport. He whiled away the hour prior to boarding looking at magazines and trying to ignore the throbbing pain in his leg. Finally, his flight was called, and he boarded the plane, found his seat, and settled in for the nine-hour flight to Washington.

After he landed at Dulles Airport, he took a cab to the Department of Justice building and went directly to Corcoran's office after being cleared through security. Corcoran had been waiting for Jim having received a call from Tony alerting him. He warmly greeted Jim, shaking his hand and practically hugging him.

"I understand your trip was successful," Corcoran said, smiling at Jim.

"Yes, but it was expensive."

"What do you mean?" Corcoran asked.

"An agent I was with was shot and is in the hospital."

"I didn't know you took another agent with you?" Corcoran said with a question in his voice.

"I didn't. He is an Israeli who provided me with the information I needed to get our friend."

Jim then told Corcoran the whole story from the meeting with Lev to the shootout and his being able to get some DNA samples. Corcoran took the samples from Jim and promised he'd get the DNA samples to the FBI lab for verification that they did belong to Saddam.

Jim's leg was throbbing again, and when he grimaced in pain, Corcoran noticed and asked what the problem was. Jim told him his leg was hurting. Corcoran suggested that Jim go to the doctor's and have it checked out. Jim promised that he would and left Corcoran's office and headed for his home. He was exhausted from the flight and his inability to get any sleep because of the pain in his leg. He felt like he was getting a fever but chalked it off to jet lag. He decided to get it checked out before he called Doris because he did not want to frighten her in case the pain was noticeable when he spoke.

On his way home, he spotted a walk-in clinic and decided he needed to get the leg checked out, since even the pain pills given to him Paris were not working. He entered the clinic and, after filling out several pages of information, was able to see a doctor. The doctor removed the bandages to reveal that Jim's leg was infected. He told Jim he had to get to a hospital right away to receive intravenous transfusions of antibiotics, as the infection was so bad that he could lose his leg.

Jim didn't like the sound of the doctor's prognosis and decided to head to the nearest hospital, which was about ten miles away. When he arrived, he went to the emergency room, where he was examined again and admitted. He was taken to a room, and intravenous transfusions of antibiotics were started immediately. He finally fell asleep, and even though he was being prodded and poked by doctors and nurses, he was able to get some well-needed shut-eye.

After two days in the hospital, he was discharged and sent home with an admonishment that he should keep an eye on his wound to make sure it does not become infected and to rest and take the prescription drugs ordered for him. Jim was very happy to leave the hospital and go home.

At home, Jim slept some more, and when he woke, he felt like his old self again.

He finally called Doris.

"Hi, it's me—Jim."

"Hello, how are you? I was worried when I didn't hear from you."

"I was on a job for the Group and got delayed."

"I was beginning to think you were avoiding me," Doris said.

"No, not a chance. As I said, I was delayed, but I'm home now and ready to take up where we left off."

"Well, so am I, but just where did we leave off?"

"I was going to meet you for dinner. Don't tell me you've forgotten already?" Jim answered.

"No, not a chance. I never forget when there is a possibility of getting a free meal," Doris teased.

"How about I meet you tonight and I'll buy you that dinner?" Jim kidded.

"Wonderful. Say, around seven? Why don't we meet at my apartment this time?" Doris suggested. "I live at 222 West Seventy-Second Street."

"Sounds good. I'm looking forward to it."

"So am I. See you at seven," Doris said as she hung up.

She was excited again. She loved hearing his voice and kidding with him like in the old days. She would leave work early, she thought, and buy a new sexy dress for tonight. She couldn't wait.

Chapter 10

He no sooner hung up the phone than it rang. He picked it up, and it was Corcoran on the other end.

"Jim, I got news for you. They decided to put Tim and John in front of a military tribunal. You will most likely be called as a witness, so you had better lawyer up. Remember what you say at that trial can and probably will be used against you."

Jim couldn't believe what he was hearing.

"Won't the fact that we got Saddam prove that we were justified in what we did?" Jim asked.

"I don't know what impact that will have, but it certainly will be a mitigating circumstance," Corcoran responded.

"I've drawn up a list of a few attorneys that I know are good at this, so you may want to take a look at it and see if you want to engage one of them."

"How about Doris? Is she qualified?" Jim asked.

"I really don't know. Why do you ask?"

"Because I know her and I thought she may be good at defending me, since she was part of the Group at one time and knows what we do and why."

"Good point, Jim, but I don't know if she is qualified and if she has done any criminal work of this sort. I will look her up."

Jim was devastated when he heard the word "criminal."

"I'm no criminal, and you know that. I've been on the good guys' side for all my life."

"I know that, Jim, but it's not me you have to convince—it's a jury."

"I can't believe this, I just can't believe it," Jim repeated.

"And what about the Group? What role will they play in this?"

"Of course, they'll pay your legal expenses, but remember, you signed an agreement not to disclose that they exist or what they do for that matter."

"From here it sounds like they're going to hang me out to dry," Jim said, anger creeping into his voice.

"I'm sure this will all go away, but I just wanted to prepare you and see that you are protected by having good legal advice."

"Thanks, but when the truth comes out about Saddam, I'm sure I'll be OK."

"Why don't you drop by the office tomorrow and I'll give you the list? In the meantime, try not to worry," Corcoran said as he hung up.

That evening, Jim caught a flight to New York to see Doris. He landed at LaGuardia Airport and took a cab to her apartment. The doorman greeted Jim and, after identifying him, told him where the elevators where.

Jim took the elevator and got off on Doris's floor. He felt a great deal of excitement but was a little apprehensive, as this would be their first meeting in a long time, and when they last saw each other, it was a brutal parting. Jim tried to forget that she had set him up to be killed and caused him a great deal of pain, but every so often, the memories would flood back into his brain. When this happened, he tried to concentrate on their love affair and how great it was and the feelings he had for her.

She was getting dressed and hoped that Jim would like the blue dress she bought just for him. She hoped it wasn't too sexy, as she did not want to give him the impression that she was ready to jump into the sack with him, yet she wanted him to forget the bad parts of their past and concentrate on the here and now. She almost jumped out of her skin when the doorbell rang. *Why am I so nervous?* she thought as she walked to the door.

As he rang the bell at her apartment door, he noted that his hand shook a little. The door opened, and there she was, as beautiful as he remembered. She was wearing a beautiful blue dress and her makeup was perfect and her perfume was the same as he remembered. He wanted to kiss her right then and there and pretend that they were still back a year ago when things between them had been beautiful but thought that he had better slow down until he was certain she felt the same way about him.

"Hi, remember me?" Jim smiled.

"How can I forget you?" she answered.

He handed her the long-stemmed yellow rose he had bought on his way to her apartment.

When she saw the rose, she almost broke out in tears.

"This is getting to be your calling card, isn't it?" she said, trying to act cool.

"If you don't like them, I can easily stop bringing them," he said.

"I love them. I can't pass a flower shop without thinking of you."

"Good. I don't ever want you to forget me."

"I don't think that's possible," she said, beckoning him in from the hallway.

That did it for Jim. He took her in his arms and passionately kissed her on the lips.

She melted in his arms. It had been so long, and she missed him so much. *Oh god,* she thought, *I still love him.*

She forced herself to pull away from him feeling that it was too much too soon.

"I thought I was going to get a free meal tonight," she said, trying to cool down.

"I guess I'll buy you that meal, but it might cost you . . . us a lot."

"Let's see, shall we?" she said as she motioned for him to head to the door.

They exited the apartment and took the elevator down. She told him of a good restaurant only a few blocks away. She noted Jim's limp but did not question it, feeling that he would tell when and if he wanted to. She asked the doorman to call a cab. They held hands in the back of the cab and both felt young and excited again.

The restaurant was a small place, and the food was excellent, but neither of them really paid too much attention to it. They made small talk but both knew that there was an eight-hundred-pound gorilla in the room that had to be addressed if their relationship was going to be as it was before. They finished their meals and headed back to Doris's apartment.

When they arrived, Jim sat on an easy chair, trying to find the right words to explain his dilemma.

"How about a drink?" she offered. "You like scotch, don't you?"

"Truth be known, I hate scotch. I only drank it to keep us going," Jim confessed.

She laughed. "I bought you a bottle of the stuff because I thought it was your favorite."

They both laughed, and Doris settled on the sofa near Jim.

"How are you doing?" Jim asked. "What's happened in your life since we last met?"

"I'm doing very well. I concentrated on work since we, err . . . err . . . parted and I became a partner in the law firm I'm with and managed to get some really big law suits. I've made millions."

Jim was flabbergasted. "Well, as you can see, our parting did have some positive effects."

"Jim, I would give it all up in a heartbeat if I could take back the hurt I caused you."

"I guess we had better talk about it and get it all out so that it won't fester or interfere with our relationship," Jim said. "I want you to know that I think I understand and I do forgive you."

"I know I was wrong to think you had anything to do with my son's death. When I read you were the arresting officer, I guess I zeroed in on you so that I could justify his being an addict and hanging himself. I didn't know you. You were just a name on an arrest form. Then when I got to know you, I realized you are a good and decent man and that you meant no harm to my son. But it was too late—I had already put the contract out on you and couldn't rescind it, although I tried. Can you really forgive me?" Doris asked, with tears welling in her eyes.

"As I said, I forgive . . . and what is a little pain among friends?" Jim tried to lighten the conversation. He felt sad for her and got up and sat on the sofa and cuddled her in his arms as she sobbed.

They sat there holding each other and feeling a closeness that only lovers can feel.

Chapter 11

Jim woke the next morning to the smell of fresh coffee perking in the kitchen. He smiled to himself when he thought of the night before and their making love. *This is paradise,* he thought. *I don't want it ever to end.* Then realism struck him like a ton of bricks. He had to get back to Washington. He hadn't told Doris about his dilemma and the trouble he was in. He decided to tell her after breakfast.

"Do you eat breakfast?" Doris asked.

"As a matter of fact, I do," Jim responded.

"Well, we'll have to go out. I have a stove only so that my maid has something to dust," she kidded.

"Do you have to work today?" Jim asked.

"I do have a few things I have to do, but I already told my secretary that I'll be in late."

"Good. Let's go back to bed," Jim said.

"But what happened to the breakfast eater?" she kidded.

"He can wait. Right now, he has better things he can do," Jim responded.

After they got up and dressed, they went out to a local restaurant and had breakfast. Even Doris ate.

"I think sex gives me an appetite." She smiled.

"In that case, you're going to be putting on a lot of weight," Jim kidded.

She smiled, and they ate breakfast while in a state of euphoria. They gazed into each other's eyes, held hands, and kissed between bites.

They walked back to her apartment with their arms around each other, enjoying the closeness of each other's bodies.

When they arrived, they sat on the sofa together, still entwined.

"I'm sorry we lost all that time because of me," she said, sadness in her voice.

"Don't go there—it's past and done with."

"I know, but when I think of all we missed . . ."

"Listen, Doris," Jim started, "I'm afraid I have some more bad news for you."

He explained the situation he was in from the meeting with General McAllister to getting the DNA from Saddam.

She listened intently and in disbelief.

"You mean they are going to put those two soldiers on trial?" she said.

"Unfortunately, that's exactly what's happening."

"I can't believe it. We are going to hold two soldiers responsible for something that happened in a foreign land when they were defending an American?" Doris said with utter disbelief.

"Yes, I'm afraid so. The kicker is I'm going to have to testify and I am very limited in what I can say."

"That's not your only problem. They can then charge you in criminal court using your own words against you."

"What about taking the Fifth? Can I use that?" Jim asked.

"Not if you want to defend the soldiers. You can't testify and then take the Fifth. Once you say something, you're all in. You can't have it both ways."

"What should I do?" Jim asked.

"If it were up to me, I'd tell you to walk away."

"And leave Tim and John to swing? No way, I can't do that."

"I know. I was just thinking selfishly."

"I know what I have to do," Doris went on as though thinking out loud. "I'll take a leave of absence and ask the court to put me on as an assistant to the defense council."

"Would you do that?"

"Yes, darling, I will," Doris answered.

They parted with kisses and hugs, and Jim promised to keep Doris up to date as things progressed. Doris promised to clear up matters she had to attend to and meet Jim in Washington as soon as she could.

On the way to the airport, Jim called the hospital in Paris to check on Lev. When the operator answered, they wanted the name of the person to whom he wished to speak, and Jim did not know what name Lev was using. Finally, he asked to be put through room 312, which was where Lev was the last time he checked on him.

"Hello." Jim was surprised to hear Lev's voice.

"Lev, this is Jim. How are you?"

"Jim, I'm doing well except for these damn tubes they have in me. I want to get out of here, but they won't let me go. I guess it's my winning personality."

"Gee, I would think the opposite," Jim kidded. "I would think they would pay you to leave."

"That's very funny, my friend. By the way, did I save you, or did you save me?" Lev asked.

"What do you think? You're the one in the hospital."

"I was hoping I saved you this time so that we're even from Iraq," Lev said.

"No way, buddy. You owe me big time," Jim jibbed.

"So you saved my life again. That means I owe you a beer."

"And I intend to collect," Jim answered. "Call me when you get out."

With that, Jim hung up. He was glad to hear Lev in such great spirits. Their friendship had developed way beyond a working relationship, and they had a great deal of respect for each other.

Jim caught the shuttle to Washington and called Corcoran, who told him to come and get the list of attorneys from him.

Jim headed for the Department of Justice building and tried to enter but was stopped at security. The guard apologized but said he was on a list of persons not to be admitted. Annoyed, Jim left the building and called Corcoran again.

"I'm surprised they have you on that list already," Corcoran told him. "Meet me in the little restaurant on Tenth. I'll be about ten minutes."

Jim found the restaurant, ordered a cup of coffee, and sat at a small table and waited for Corcoran.

"Hi, sorry about that," Corcoran said as he entered.

"What's going on?" Jim inquired.

"Since you are a possible witness in a case that may impact the department, they automatically put you on a do-not-enter list. I'm surprised. It usually takes as long as a week to get on that list. Security must be on the ball, at least in your case."

"Oh, great, I can't even get into the Department of Justice building anymore," Jim lamented.

"Here's the list of attorneys I promised. I would personally opt for the top name, Gregg Burke, but that's strictly up to you."

"I spoke with Doris Macon, and she said she was willing to help."

"Great. The more legal brains on this case, the better," Corcoran offered as he rose to leave. "I'll keep in touch and let you know the latest, but in the meantime, I strongly suggest you get in touch with a lawyer."

"OK, I will," Jim promised as he left the restaurant.

Jim went home and spent a restless night thinking about all that transpired between him and Doris and the battles he was certain he would have to fight in the near future.

The next day, after he got up from a fitful night, he dialed the number next to Gregg Burke's name from the list Corcoran had provided. After a brief hold and explaining to the secretary that he was from Corcoran's office, he was put through. He briefly spoke to Gregg and made an appointment to see him the following morning.

The next morning, Jim went to Gregg Burke's office. He explained the entire matter to Gregg, who took copious notes. He did not tell Gregg about his mission and why he escaped the town, taking the black car. This left Gregg perplexed and not totally believing Jim's story. Jim explained that it was all he could say until he got clearance from his superiors. He further explained how Doris was willing to help and could explain his situation after she talked to Corcoran. Gregg said he would call her and discuss the situation with her. In the meantime, he cautioned Jim not to speak to anyone about the case without consulting him first. Jim left Gregg's office feeling a little better about his dilemma, having confidence in his new attorney. He went home and called Corcoran to tell him he retained Burke. His next call was to Doris, and he explained all that transpired and that she would probably be hearing from Gregg shortly. They spent the next hour on the phone making plans for their future. Doris told Jim she would come down to Washington in about two days. Jim said he couldn't wait and that he would straighten out his house in preparation for her arrival.

Jim called his cleaning service and asked them to come the following day to prepare for Doris. He pondered whether to stock up on food but decided that since neither of them cooked, it would be a waste of time. He would, however, buy snacks and drinks for their evenings at home.

Chapter 12

As the days passed, he became more and more excited thinking about Doris's arrival. He hadn't lived with a woman since his wife and child were killed in an accident and wondered how he would feel having a woman present all the time. He considered whether her feelings for him would wane or get worse if she got tired of him over time.

Finally, he received the call he was waiting for. Doris was flying in and would arrive at Reagan Airport at 7:00 p.m. He tried to stay calm at the thought of seeing her again, but no matter how busy he kept himself, the thought of her was never very far. Time seemed to pass very slowly, and watching the clock only made it go even slower.

He left for the airport early just in case of the unlikely event that her flight might arrive ahead of time. He thought that at least at the airport, he would feel closer to her, and people watching would help him pass the time.

At last, the arrivals screen posted that her flight had landed. He waited by the arrivals gate to catch a glimpse of her as she exited and to make sure he didn't miss her. It took an agonizing thirty minutes before she arrived, looking as beautiful as ever even though she just flew down from New York.

She spotted Jim and smiled. She hurried to him, and they embraced and kissed as if she had just arrived from an extended absence. They held each other tightly, enjoying the feel of each other's body.

After they gathered Doris's luggage—she had three large suitcases—they headed for Jim's house. When they arrived, they unloaded the luggage from the car, and Doris surveyed her new surroundings. Jim could see that in her mind, she was already moving furniture and redecorating. He smiled to himself and thought that it would be fun helping her change things, as long as the home did not become too feminine. He never was interested in decorating and was happy as long as things were functional, but now he knew that things were going to change, especially with a woman around.

Doris immediately asked Jim where she could work and set up her computer. They decided on a side room that could be closed off from the rest of the house utilizing two French doors. They then checked to determine how strong the signal from the Wi-Fi was in the house and found that her computer received a strong signal. They agreed that the first thing in the morning, they would go shopping and buy whatever she needed. In the meantime, they would go out for dinner and enjoy each other's company, as Doris knew that there would be much work and long hours ahead, especially since she did not have a paralegal to help her and she would have to do all the research herself.

They went out for dinner to a nice Italian restaurant that Jim frequented. They were warmly greeted, and everyone wanted to meet Doris, the woman Jim spoke so much of during his nightly dinners. The owner brought out a unique bottle of wine that he reserved for special occasions, and they turned the dinner into a mini party. They were seated at a table that contained the dozen yellow roses in the center, which Jim had prearranged. The evening was full of laughter and music and special delicacies along with winks from servers who waited their table. Doris thoroughly enjoyed the evening, and her heart was full at the thought that this was the beginning of her new life with Jim.

The next morning, reality set in. Doris's demeanor seemed to change. She was all business and hurried Jim so they could get to the store where they purchased a desk, chair, and a four-drawer file cabinet, and she insisted on immediate delivery. Jim was taken aback by Doris's attitude. He was still overwhelmed by her presence and did not want his mood to change, but there it was, the attorney in her was taking over. She was obviously worried about what lay ahead for Jim and the upcoming trials.

That afternoon, boxes arrived at Jim's house, and Doris explained that it was material she had gathered in New York that she felt may be useful in a military hearing. As soon as Jim brought the boxes into her new office, Doris immediately closed the doors and started poring over the material.

Jim felt left out and, after a time, knocked on the door and entered Doris's new office. He was shocked to see the amount of paper strewn about the room and Doris sitting on the floor in the middle of a pile of papers.

"I just thought I'd drop in to see how things were going and if you needed me for any reason. After all, I am the subject of this mess," Jim said, waving his arm around the room.

"No, darling," Doris responded. "These are all legal papers containing precedents set by the courts regarding military trials. I thought I'd bone up on it in preparation for my meeting with Gregg Burke on Thursday."

"I didn't know we had a meeting on Thursday—no one told me."

"It's a lawyer thing," she said. "You don't have to be there because we're just going over some of these precedents in preparation for the hearing coming up next week."

Jim was surprised. "What about me? Am I going to have to testify?"

"No. It's just a meeting with the judge to set some ground rules."

"What about Corcoran? Did you speak to him?" Jim asked.

"Yes, but he had no news regarding the lab and Saddam. I assume that's what you're asking."

"Yes. It is I wonder what's taking them such a long time."

"They have to be sure. They can't make any mistakes with that," Doris answered.

"Maybe I'll give him a call, and while I'm at it, I'll call Lev and see how he's doing."

"How about some dinner?" Jim asked, changing the subject.

"I'm too busy. Why don't you send out for a pizza or something, darling?" Doris responded.

"I thought we would go out for dinner—after all, this is only your second day here."

"Sorry, darling, but we can do that tomorrow. Right now, I don't want to lose my train of thought."

"OK," Jim answered, very disappointed with Doris's demeanor. "I'll call for a pizza."

Jim left the room, closing the door behind him, and headed for the kitchen. He looked around but couldn't find a menu from any pizza shops, so he looked in the phone book and came up with one nearby. He called and ordered a large pizza, and when he was asked about the toppings, he had no idea what Doris liked, so he just ordered a plain cheese, without asking, as he didn't want to bother her.

He realized that he was feeling lonely even though she was in the next room. *Stop being an idiot,* he told himself; after all, she was doing this for him. But still . . . he didn't like the lawyer in her.

He left the house to pick up the pizza and stopped at a florist and bought a long-stemmed yellow rose. *This will make her smile,* he thought to himself, *and maybe it'll get her out of her lawyer mood and into the bedroom.*

When he returned home, he put the pizza on the kitchen counter and looked for a vase for the rose. Finding none, he took out three tall beer glasses, placed one on each side of the table where they would be sitting, and used the third as a vase, which he carefully placed in the center of the table. He took two cans of beer out of the refrigerator and poured them into the empty glasses. Satisfied that all looked well, he went to the office and tapped on the door.

"Pizza man," he called.

"Thanks, darling. Could you just bring a slice in here for me?"

"I have the kitchen set up and I poured a couple of beers. Why don't you take a break and enjoy the pizza and my company?" Jim said hopefully.

"I can't right now, sweetheart. I'm in the middle of something. Just bring me a slice."

Jim returned to the kitchen fuming. He took out a plate and placed a slice of pizza on it and returned to the office.

"Pizza coming right up," he tried to make light of the situation and not let Doris know how he really felt.

"Thanks, sweetheart. Just put it on the desk. I'll eat it later. Please close the door behind you. I need to concentrate."

Jim left the room and wanted to throw something. He was very upset at Doris's attitude. *What the hell!* he thought. *She's only here a day and already ignoring me. I know that she's doing all this research for me, but I can't help feeling mad.*

He decided to go out and have a drink at the local pub and cool off. He didn't bother to tell Doris where he was going for fear of interrupting her. *And, besides, she probably wouldn't even know I'm gone,* he thought to himself.

The pub was fairly crowded, but he found a place at the bar and ordered a Jack Daniels on the rocks. When the drink came, he sipped it slowly and looked around the room. He spotted three women sitting at a table deep in conversation. One of the women had dark-red hair, and he was sure he knew her from somewhere. He decided to walk to the table and find out.

"Pardon me," he said, "but don't I know you from somewhere? I'm sure we met before."

Before the redhead could answer, one of the other women at the table turned to Jim and snarled, "Listen, buster, just because three women are sitting without a man doesn't mean we need your attention. Why don't you be a nice little boy and go back to the bar and mind your own damn business?"

Jim felt his face flush as he pivoted and returned to the bar. He sat there sipping his drink and hoping no one else in the bar heard the exchange. He decided to finish his drink and get out of there before he lost his temper and gave the women a piece of his mind. As he was removing his change from the bar, he felt a tug on his sleeve. He turned to see the redhead smiling at him.

"I'm sorry for my friend," she said. "She's a flight attendant and just got off a long trip. Even so, she had no right to speak to you that way. We do know each other. I was a detective in NYPD, and even though we did not work together, our paths crossed several times."

Jim smiled and said, "I thought so. You worked in the robbery squad, didn't you?"

He couldn't help but look over at the women sitting at the table who had embarrassed him. The women turned away as soon as she noticed that Jim was looking at them.

"Yes, and you were in the District Attorney's Squad, weren't you? I think we were looking at the same crew who were steeling valuable paintings the last time we crossed paths."

"That's right, I remember. Did you ever collar Nat Crossland? Wasn't he the one behind the whole thing?"

"Yes, we did. He's doing ten to twenty. By the way, my name is Helen, Helen Morrow." She held out her hand.

Jim shook her hand and said, "Jim, Jim Vara. It's a pleasure to see you again, Helen. What are you doing in Virginia?"

"I'm here working for the Inspector Generals' Office at Homeland Security. I landed a job as an investigator after I left NYPD. How about you? What are you doing down here?"

"I'm working over at the Department of Justice." Jim lied. "Can I buy you a drink?"

"No, no, thanks. I got to get back to the girls before tongues start to wag. Maybe some other time. I'd love to talk about old times on the job. Sorry to be so frank, but are you married?"

"Typical detective, don't beat around the bush." Jim laughed. "No, I'm not married, but I am seeing someone."

"OK, then I'm not sure if we can get together . . . for a drink . . . can we?"

"I don't see why not. I'd love to talk about the job with you," Jim responded. "Are you married?"

"No, don't have the time for it. By the way, whatever happened to Tony, your wire man?"

Another one of his conquests, Jim thought to himself. "He's fine. He's working with me at the department." Jim lied again.

"Well, great. I look forward to getting together with the two of you and chewing the fat. Here's my number." She handed Jim a business card.

"Fine, I'm looking forward to it," Jim said as he watched her walk back to her table.

She still has a great figure, he thought to himself.

He finished his drink and headed for home. He looked at his watch and saw that it was eleven thirty. Where did the time go? He quietly entered the house and walked to the kitchen and turned on the light. The pizza box was gone, and so were the beers and the rose. She must have cleaned up and gone to bed. The thought of her in bed excited him. He went to the bedroom but did not turn on the light. He could feel her presence in the room and hear her deep breathing. He quietly undressed and got into bed. There she was sound asleep. He put his arm around her and tried to snuggle up closer to her, but she moved away, letting out a deep breath as she turned her back to him. Frustrated again, he had a tough time falling asleep.

Chapter 13

The next morning, Jim woke to the rattle of dishes. He got out of bed and went to the bathroom and splashed some water on his face. He slowly moved to the kitchen where Doris was sitting at the table, drinking coffee and perusing a white paper.

"Good morning, darling," Doris said upon seeing him.

"Good morning, dear," Jim said in reply as he moved to her and kissed her on the forehead.

Jim noticed she was dressed in a business suit and looked very professional.

"How come you're dressed so early?" he said.

"The meeting with Gregg was moved up to this morning, so I have to run. There's coffee in the pot," she said as she rose and straightened out her skirt. "Hopefully it won't take too long and I'll be back before you know it."

"How are you getting to town?" Jim inquired. "Do you want me to take you?"

"No, thanks, darling, I called a cab."

As if on cue, a horn was sounded in front of the house, indicating the cab had arrived.

"See you later, honey," Doris said without looking at Jim as she grabbed her briefcase and walked out the door.

"Bye," Jim said to her back.

Jim whiled away the morning drinking coffee and watching the news on TV. At around eleven thirty, he decided to call Tony and tell him about Helen. Tony was excited to hear that Helen was in town and pushed Jim to call her and set up a meeting so that they could get together soon and talk "the job," as NYPD is commonly referred to by its present and retired members. Jim promised Tony that he would and hung up.

After a while, he looked at the clock and decided to call Corcoran to see if he was available for lunch. When Corcoran got on the phone, he told Jim he was available and wanted to speak with Jim, and lunch would be an ideal time. They decided to meet at a restaurant Corcoran recommended in Washington in about an hour.

Jim dressed and got into his car for the drive to DC. On the way, he thought about Corcoran saying he wanted to speak with him and wondered if he had news regarding the lab and Saddam. *It is about time,* he mused.

The restaurant was crowded, but Corcoran, who beat Jim there, was able to get a table in the corner where there was a modicum of privacy. After they greeted each other, Jim sat down and noted that Corcoran had a serious look on his face.

"Well, what's the good news?" Jim said.

"Why don't we eat first, then we can get down to business?" Corcoran said.

"No way," Jim retorted. "You have me worried now."

"I'm sorry if I worried you, but I have bad news."

"I haven't been getting much good news lately, so let me have it."

"The lab results came back, and it was definitely Saddam's DNA."

"Great," Jim said, smiling broadly. "So what's so bad about that? It proves everything I said was true and should clear us once and for all."

"Not so fast, Jim. I also got a call from the White House, and they do not want to make it public. They want to keep it under wraps and they were adamant about that. They fear that if it goes public, it will open a can of worms and place doubt on the whole Iraq War."

Jim was flabbergasted. He sat back in his chair and tried to process what Corcoran said.

"You mean I can't use it at Tim and John's trial? Do they intend to throw all of us under the bus?" Jim was getting madder by the moment.

Corcoran shrugged his shoulders and looked embarrassed.

"I'm afraid so," he said. "I did get a promise from them that if you do not mention Saddam, and if you're convicted, whatever sentence you receive will be commuted by them."

"Great, I can't believe it. How do they expect us to stand trial and not have a defense? Do they expect us to plead guilty? I'm as patriotic as anyone, but I don't know if I can do that. If not for me, what about Tim and John? How can they defend themselves?"

"I'm sure I can get the same deal for them," Corcoran responded.

"They're young. Their whole future will be ruined not only in the military but also in civilian life." Jim was getting angrier. "Go back and tell them they will have to do better," Jim snorted.

"Jim, I'm on your side and I'll see what I can do, but I can't speak for them or guarantee anything."

"Do the best you can and get back to me." Jim rose from his seat and said, "I'm sorry, but I lost my appetite." He turned and left the restaurant, leaving Corcoran alone.

Jim was fuming on his ride back to his house. *How can they expect me to do this to the general and to Tim and John?* he thought. *I can't do it. It's bad enough that they are hanging me out to dry, but I can't do it to the others.*

He waited at home for Doris, who didn't arrive until almost 5:00 p.m. As soon as she walked into the house, Jim hugged her and blurted out what happened with Corcoran. She kissed him and tried to calm him.

"That explains a few things," she said, a pensive look on her face.

"What do you mean?" he asked.

"While I was working with Gregg, he got a call from the advocate's office offering a deal."

"What kind of deal?"

"He offered the general a discharge without prejudice due to his exemplarily thirty-two years of service. As far as Tim and John, they want them to plead guilty and face a lesser charge of failing to follow the rules of engagement. If they don't plead out, they will face murder charges."

"What are they charged with now?" Jim asked.

"They are facing second-degree murder charges due to the death of an Iraqi civilian, as well as failing to follow the rules of engagement. The government puts forth that they were not fired upon, so they should not have fired their weapons."

"That's BS," Jim responded. "They were military out to get my scalp and they were firing at me. If it wasn't for Tim and John, I wouldn't be here now."

"You could testify to that, but then you would be opened to questions as to why they were firing at you and what you were doing there in the first place. I'm afraid we're in a catch-22 situation, darling. Without bringing Saddam into it, you can't really testify for the soldiers without incriminating yourself, and I'm sure they will then put you on trial. As your attorney, I would advise you to take the Fifth."

"I can't do that."

"I know, darling. We have to figure something out. Gregg and I are working on it."

"I told Corcoran that he has to come up with a better deal from the White House or I'll splash Saddam's name all over the newspapers."

"Careful, sweetheart. Don't forget who they are and what they can do. You should know you are in the killing business with them. If you back them to the wall, you may be their next target."

"I know, I know," Jim responded, "but I'm so damn frustrated."

"I understand, darling, but don't lose heart. We'll beat this thing together."

As frustrated as Jim was, he felt much better at her words of togetherness. They kissed and hugged and made love that afternoon.

Chapter 14

Days passed with Doris plodding through papers and meeting with Gregg. Finally, she was told by Gregg that the military judge wanted to meet with them.

When she told Jim of the meeting, he was irritated and wanted to go with her, but she told him he couldn't because it was just for the attorneys involved and was for setting up ground rules and to see if there was any movement regarding a possible plea or a proffer by the prosecution.

The next morning, Doris left early for Gregg's office, where they would prepare for and then go to the Pentagon to meet with the judge.

Jim stayed home and was happy to receive a call from Lev, whom he had been trying to contact for the past several days. Lev had been discharged from the hospital and was almost completely recovered. Jim brought him up to date as to the pending trial and his inability to use what they did in France on the stand. Lev was incensed and asked if it would do any good for him to testify on Jim's behalf. Jim explained that he would ask Doris but that he was pretty sure it would only complicate matters.

Lev promised Jim that he would be there for him even if it meant breaking him out of jail. They ended the call laughing at the thought of Lev breaking Jim out of jail.

Later, Jim received a call from Tony, who wanted to know if Jim set up the meeting with Helen yet. He told him he hadn't but promised he would call her that day. It was obvious to Jim that Tony was very interested in Helen.

Jim paced the floor, waiting for Doris to come home or call. When it got to be about three in the afternoon, he decided to call Doris's cell phone. Receiving the answering service, he left a short message and asked her to call him. He wasn't worried for himself because he felt he could handle anything they could throw at him, but he was anxious for Tim and John.

While waiting for Doris to call, he called Helen and made a date for the next night. He then called Tony and told him they would meet in the Red Bird Lounge at eight the following evening. Tony thanked Jim and said he would meet them tomorrow night.

Finally, Jim heard a car door close, and after a minute, the front door opened. Doris entered looking tired. Jim kissed her, and they hugged.

"You look like you can use a drink. Can I get you one?" Jim asked.

"No, thanks, darling," she responded as she dropped her briefcase and sat on the couch.

"How did it go?"

"It went OK. We are set for trial next Tuesday for Tim and John. The prosecutor is a young lieutenant who looks like he is trying to make reputation of being tough. Don't worry about it. Gregg can handle him. Lieutenant Marconi will be the defense attorney, and I will be sitting with the defense and will assist him. The bad news is that the General McAllister took the offer and resigned. I know they will make him testify against you if you have to go to trial. As far as for Tim and John, all the general can say is that he ordered them to accompany you at your request. They will ask him about the rules of engagement, and he will give them boilerplate answers for the prosecution to build on. If the court believes Tim and John didn't follow the rules, they will be convicted."

"What are they facing?" Jim asked.

"I can't really tell. I'm sure our government is getting a lot of pressure from Iraq, and if the pressure finds its way into the court, they can get life. Don't forget, the court is made up of military personnel who would like to advance in rank and may be afraid that if Washington wants to pacify Iraq, and they are not tough on our guys, they can be looked on with disfavor when their promotions come up. We will watch them very closely, and if there is any inkling of that, we will make a motion for a mistrial."

Jim was shaking his head in disbelief. "This can't be happening," he said. "If they do anything to those guys, I swear I'll spill the beans, and they can come after me."

"Careful, Jim. Don't lose your temper. Cool heads will prevail," Doris said as she got up and gave him a hug.

"I know, I know," Jim repeated, looking angry. "It's just so damn wrong and frustrating."

"I know, darling, but try to take it easy. I believe that in the end, justice will prevail," Doris said, trying to reassure Jim but not fully believing it herself.

The following day, Doris busied herself going through all the paperwork she had accumulated in the past couple of days. Jim told her about his meeting Helen and the date that was set up for that evening. He asked her if she wanted to come along but told her that they would be talking job and it might get boring for her. She assured Jim that it would not. After all, she had been an assistant district attorney and worked many criminal cases with many police officers. She told Jim that if it weren't for all the papers to go through before Tuesday's trial, she would love to tag along. Jim made the decision not to go and called Tony and told him he was tied up and Tony would have to meet Helen by himself. Jim could hear in Tony's voice a great sigh of approval. He thanked Jim and hung up the phone. Jim smiled to himself, knowing full well what Tony had in mind, and Jim would have only been in the way.

Chapter 15

Tuesday finally came. Jim and Doris rode in the heavy traffic, heading for downtown Washington. Doris tried to make small talk, but Jim wasn't biting. He was obviously worried about Tim and John and didn't want to be bothered with small talk.

When they arrived at the Pentagon, Doris informed Jim that he would have to wait in an outer office, as he was a witness and could not be present in the courtroom during the testimony of others who were called. Jim already knew that, as he had done it many times in New York during the trials of persons he locked up or other cases he was involved with. This time, it seemed to bother him.

Doris entered the courtroom and said hello to Gregg Burke and Lt. Dom Marconi, who was the defense attorney assigned to the case. She looked at the prosecutor's table and nodded hello to the Lt. Mark Ingram, the prosecutor in the case. She discussed last-minute details with Gregg and waited for the three-judge panel to arrive. She was startled as the side door opened, and Tim and John were escorted in by three military policemen. Tom and John were dressed in their military uniforms and looked very professional. Doris moved to the first row behind the small fence that was separating the business end of the court, which was reserved for those who will participate in the proceeding. She took out a pencil and a legal pad and was prepared to take notes. She noted that there were a few people sitting in the courtroom who were doing the same. She thought she recognized one man whom she thought worked for the Department of Justice. This worried her, as it could mean that he was there to take in testimony that could be used in the trial against Jim. She tapped Gregg on the shoulder and told him of her concern. Gregg looked at the man and then turned his attention back toward the bench when the bailiff called, "All rise," as the judges entered the courtroom.

After sitting, the judge in charge, who was sitting in the center of the other two, looked over at the prosecutor's table and said,

"Good morning. Are we ready to proceed today?"

"Yes, Colonel," the prosecutor responded.

The judge then looked at Lieutenant Marconi and said, "Is the defense ready?"

"Yes, sir," the young lieutenant responded.

"Very well, Lieutenant. You may call your first witness."

Lieutenant Ingram stood and, in a loud voice, said, "We call Kenneth McAllister to the stand."

Doris noted that he did not use the general rank.

The general walked in wearing civilian clothes. He took the stand after being sworn and sat down.

"General," the prosecutor started, "I would like you to tell the court what transpired on March 4 of last year with regard to your meeting with a James Vara."

"I had received a call from Ops headquarters, telling me that Mr. Vara was arriving at my command and I was to render to him any assistance he might need."

"Did Mr. Vara arrive, and what did you provide him?"

"Yes, he did, and I provided him with weaponry and two men to give him assistance with his mission."

"What was his mission, General?"

"I'm afraid I was sworn to secrecy and cannot reveal that at this time."

"You mean to tell me, sir, that you gave him weapons and two of your men and you did not know why?" the prosecutor probed.

"Yes, that was what I was ordered to do."

"Are the men you assigned to aid Mr. Vara in this courtroom?"

"Yes. They are sitting over there, Cpl. Tim Mussige and Pvt. John Talmidge. They are . . . were two of my best men."

"And what were your orders to these men, General?"

"I told them to give Mr. Vara any assistance he might need to carry out his mission."

"A mission, I might add, that you knew nothing about," the prosecutor added.

"In a war zone, that is not that uncommon."

"Did, in fact, the two men assist Mr. Vara with his . . . who knows what?"

Lieutenant Marconi jumped to his feet and objected to the characterizations used by the prosecutor. "Objection, Your Honor. Lieutenant Ingram is casting aspersions regarding a mission he knows nothing about."

"Exactly, Your Honor. How can a general send men into harm's way and not know what they are doing?"

"The general is not on trial here, Lieutenant, and may I remind you that General McAllister has served his country honorably for thirty-two years," the colonel answered. "However, the objection is overruled."

"Thank you, Your Honor," the prosecutor responded.

The prosecutor continued. "General, did your men report to you when they completed their mission?"

"Yes," the general answered.

"Please tell the court what they reported."

"They said they took Mr. Vara to a location he requested and waited outside of town for his return."

"And then what happened?"

"After a few hours, they said they received a call from Mr. Vara, who explained that hostile forces were after him and that he was heading toward them in an old blue car."

"What did they say happened next?" the prosecutor probed.

"They said they observed the car heading toward them, and then the car seemed to explode, and Mr. Vara got out and appeared to be using the car as cover because two trucks and a jeep that were filled with armed people were coming after him."

"And what did they do then?"

"They fired at the lead truck, causing it to leave the road, and the chase was halted."

"Did they say whose car it was that Mr. Vara was driving?"

"No."

"Did you give them orders to fire at the vehicles allegedly following Mr. Vara?"

"No."

"Isn't true that under the rules of engagement, they are not to fire their weapons unless they are fired upon?"

"Yes, but they can fire their weapons to protect someone in their presence who are in eminent danger and are in fear for their lives," the general stated.

"I have no further questions," the prosecutor said, looking over at the defense table.

"We have no questions, Colonel," Lieutenant Marconi responded.

"Very well. You may step down, General, and thank you," the colonel said, dismissing the general, who got up and left the room.

"The prosecution calls Mr. Abdullah Kasim to the stand," Lieutenant Ingram announced.

A man entered the courtroom dressed in a dark-blue suit and moved toward the stand.

"Mr. Kasim, raise your right hand and place your left on the Bible," the bailiff said.

"I do not swear on that book," Kasim said.

"Very well. Please take the stand," the colonel said. "Do you swear to tell the truth?"

"I always tell the truth," Mr. Kasim said as he sat down.

"Mr. Kasim, were you in Tirkut on March 4 of this year?" the prosecutor asked.

"Yes, I was."

"Will you tell the court what happened that day with regard to a blue car?"

"We saw a man stealing my car and trying to take it out of town."

"What did you do then?" Lieutenant Ingram asked.

"My friends and I gave chase to try to catch him. We wanted to arrest him and bring him back to court and get my car back."

"And then what happened?" the prosecutor continued.

"People started shooting at us and they killed my cousin."

"Do you know why they were shooting at you, Mr. Kasim?"

"No. We were just trying to get my car back."

"Do you know who was shooting at you?"

"No."

"No further questions. Your witness," the prosecutor said, looking over at the defense table.

Lieutenant Marconi rose and walked to the witness stand.

"Mr. Kasim, you say that the car was yours, is that correct?"

"Yes," he responded.

"Do you have the registration for the car?"

The witness hesitated and said, "We don't register cars in Iraq."

"I see. Can you tell me about the car? How old is it, and what shape was it in?"

Lieutenant Ingram was on his feet. "Objection. The age of the car and its shape have nothing to do with this case. The defense is only trying to confuse the court."

"I am not confused. Overruled," the colonel responded.

"Answer the question, please, Mr. Kasim," Lieutenant Marconi said while leaning close to the witness.

"It was a good car and not too old," Kasim answered.

"Don't you know what year it was built?" Marconi shot back.

"What difference does it make? I do not bother myself with years."

"Was there anything wrong with the car? For instance, were the tires in good shape? Was the ignition in good working order?"

"Yes, yes, it was a good car," Kasim answered.

"Can you explain to the court how the ignition switch was missing?" Marconi shot back.

"Objection, Your Honor." Lieutenant Ingram was on his feet again. "What possible difference does the condition of the car make?"

"Your Honor, we intend to prove that the car does not belong to Mr. Kasim and that the ignition was missing from the car."

"Will you both come forward to the bench, please?" the colonel said.

Both lieutenants advanced to the bench, where the colonel leaned forward and addressed them.

Marconi spoke first. "Colonel, the car was not his, and he had no business going after it, and if he's lying about this, I think all his testimony should be thrown out."

Ingram countered. "Colonel, what difference does it make whose car it is? It was stolen, and he had every right to pursue it."

Lieutenant Marconi responded, "It's not so much whose car it is but that he's lying."

"I will take it under advisement," the colonel responded. "Now, gentlemen, I intend to break for lunch."

The lieutenants returned to their desks, and the colonel announced in a loud voice, "We will break for lunch now and reconvene at two o'clock."

Both lieutenants, along with Gregg and Doris, gathered their papers, placed them in their briefcases, and left the courtroom.

Jim was in the hall, waiting for Doris.

"Darling," Doris started, "I can't go to lunch with you. We have to review what happened this morning and plan our strategy for this afternoon. Sorry, dear. Why don't you grab something to eat and meet me here at one forty-five?"

"Damn," Jim said without thinking. "I wanted to spend some time with you."

"I know. I feel the same way, but until this trial is over, we are going to have to make sacrifices for the good of Tim and John."

"OK," Jim said reluctantly. "I'll see you at quarter to two."

They kissed, and Jim turned and walked away, feeling disappointed. He took out his phone and called Corcoran. He explained that he was in court, waiting to testify, and that Tim and John did not have a chance. He warned Corcoran that if they get convicted, he was going to tell the truth and reveal all that happened with Saddam and why Tim and John were justified in protecting him. Corcoran responded that he would call the White House and see what he could do.

Jim had lunch in one of the fast-food restaurants that cater to local businesspeople who are in a hurry to eat and return to work. After lunch, he returned to the court and waited in the hallway for Doris. About ten minutes later, she arrived with Lieutenant Marconi and Gregg.

"Hello, did you guys have a good lunch?" Jim said to no one in particular.

"We sent out for sandwiches while we worked through some of the problems we see coming our way this afternoon," Doris said. She motioned to Jim to come further down the hall so they could speak privately.

"Darling, I want you to listen to what I have to say very carefully and try to understand," she cautioned Jim.

Jim was getting upset, as he did not like her warning or what he was afraid was coming his way.

"We feel that you should not testify this afternoon."

"Why?" he said, trying to remain calm.

"We feel, and it's unanimous, that your testimony can only hurt Tim and John. I understand how you feel, but if you can't tell about your mission and Saddam, it will only hurt them."

Jim was shocked.

"We are going to tell them to plead guilty and we'll try to get them the best deal possible."

Jim slammed his fist into the marble wall, causing pain in his hand and arm. "No way. I'll blow the whistle on the whole operation and the Group if they get hurt." Jim's face was getting beet red.

"Calm down, Jim," Doris said in a quiet voice, trying to soothe him.

"Think of the greater good for our country. I'm sure Tim and John will."

"What kind of country do we have if two decent men have to go to jail and lose their future for doing something that was right and honorable?"

"I know how you feel, darling, but we can stall and appeal, and maybe by then, the truth will come out," Doris said without much conviction in her voice.

"In the meantime, they will be rotting in jail . . . won't they?"

"We'll try to get them bail while awaiting sentencing."

"Have you talked to them? How do they feel about this?" Jim asked.

"We haven't spoken to them yet, but we will ask for a postponement and then we'll lay it all out to them this afternoon."

"I'll never be able to face them," Jim said dejectedly.

Doris smiled at him and walked back to where the others were standing. They then reentered the courtroom.

When the colonel entered the courtroom, he had a very stern look on his face. He looked over at the prosecutor's table and then the defense and said, "Will Lieutenants Marconi and Ingram please come to the chambers now?" With that, he walked to the side of the courtroom behind the bench and was followed by the two lieutenants.

After about thirty minutes, they returned to the courtroom, and Lieutenant Marconi had a smile on his face as he walked to the defense's table.

"Due to circumstances beyond my control, I am going to postpone this trial indefinitely. The defendants will return to their commands until further orders." The colonel then rose from his seat and left the courtroom.

You could hear a pin drop. The courtroom was stunned into silence.

"What just happened?" Doris asked Lieutenant Marconi.

"This is not for publication, but the colonel told us that he got orders from the Pentagon to postpone the case. One of these guys"—he motioned toward Tim and John —"must have connections in very high places."

Doris smiled and walked to the side room to get Jim.

After she told Jim what happened, they returned to the courtroom to say good-bye to the defense team and Tim and John. Doris told them that she wanted to be notified if ever they tried to bring the case to trial again.

After they left the courthouse, Doris and Jim laughed and hugged.

"They think Tim or John have friends in high places." She winked at Jim.

"Yes. I better call Corcoran and thank him. I hope I didn't get anyone mad at him or me for applying too much pressure. We shall see."

When they returned home, Doris literally threw her briefcase into the room she had used for her office.

"Let's go get something to eat," she said, smiling broadly. "I'm in the mood for that great Italian restaurant."

"I'm in the mood for something else," Jim countered. "We can eat later."

They made love for the next couple of hours, and all was well with the world.

Chapter 16

The next day, Jim finally called Corcoran to thank him.

"I owe you one, buddy." Jim laughed over the telephone.

"In that case, you had better get in here. I have some work for you," Corcoran answered. "I'll call security and get you off the watch list so you can come up to my office."

"It will be my pleasure," Jim answered with a smile in his voice. "When do you want to see me?"

"How about meeting this afternoon, around two?"

"I'll be there. See you then," Jim said as he hung up the phone.

That afternoon, Jim took a ride into Washington. He went to the Department of Justice security entrance. He was a little apprehensive as he entered the area. When he showed his identification to the security guard, he was relieved to be allowed to enter. He went to Corcoran's office, where the secretary ushered him in. Corcoran came out from behind his desk and greeted Jim with a smile and a warm handshake.

"How are you, Jim?" Corcoran warmly greeted him.

"I'm doing fine now that I'm no longer a felon."

"I'm glad to hear that and I'm sorry that you had to put up with all that, but to quote an old cliché, all is well that ends well. Have a seat. I have a case I want to discuss with you. I think it is right up your alley. You will probably like this one for a change."

"Well, I like it already. I hope it's not too far from here, as I would love to go home at night," Jim said.

"I'm afraid it is back in your old stomping grounds. It is in Iraq. But I am sure you will like to know that you have been requested personally for this job."

"Now you have my attention," Jim said. "Who did ask for me personally?"

"It is your old friend Lev," Corcoran said.

"Lev? Where in the world is he?"

"He is in Iraq. He's in a small town near the Syrian border. There have been some problems there. It seems like our government along with Israel had a listening post in Iraq near the Syrian border. A bunker, which was manned by an American and an Israeli, was providing intelligence for both our countries. It seems that in this enclosed secure bunker, both an American and an Israeli were killed. Lev has been dispatched to look into the matter. He requested you, since you do speak Farsi, and as a former homicide detective, it makes sense for you to help in the investigation. The FBI looked into the case but did not make any headway. A disc was removed from the computer, which I believe contained information vital to our countries. I want you to jump on a plane tomorrow morning and get over there and help Lev solve this crime and, most importantly, retrieve the disc. The FBI will meet you in Baghdad and bring you up to speed. From there, you will have to travel overland and through the desert to the secure area near the Syrian border."

"I was hoping that it would be a job here in the States. I think you know that Doris and I have a thing going. I would hate to leave her at this time," Jim said.

"I heard that you two were together. I wish you both all the happiness. However, as you know, we have very important work to do here, and, unfortunately, that has to take precedence over our personal lives."

"I know," Jim said. "I was just dreaming, I guess. I'll make arrangements and leave first thing in the morning. Where will I meet Lev?"

"As soon as you know what time you will arrive in Baghdad, I will notify him, and I am sure he will meet you at the airport."

"OK. I'll see you when I finish the job. Keep the home fires burning," Jim kidded as he rose and left the office.

When he got out into the street, he called Tony at the office. He briefed him on what was happening and asked him to make arrangements for him to catch a flight to Baghdad early in the morning. Tony said that he would call him back later with the information. He asked if he could come along on the investigation, but Jim told him not at this time. However, if he should need him, he will let him know right away.

On the way home to Virginia, Jim mulled over in his mind how he would break the news to Doris. He knew that it would upset her, but he also knew that she was aware of the type of work he does and that she would have to accept the situation.

When he arrived home, he entered the house and saw that Doris was waiting for him, and she had a look on her face as if to say that she knew what was going to happen.

"Hi, darling," she said as he entered.

"I am sorry, honey, but I have some bad news. Corcoran has just ordered me back to Iraq. There was a breach of intelligence in one of our bases, and he wants me to look into it."

"When will you have to leave? Do we have any time?" Doris said, hoping that they could spend some time together before he left.

"I'm sorry, honey. I have to leave first thing in the morning. Let's go to our favorite Italian restaurant for dinner and then we can come home and spend the rest of the night together."

"I was hoping we would have more time than that. We have to talk. As you know, I am not the type of woman to sit around the house and wait for you to come back God knows when from Iraq."

"I know, dear. Let's discuss this over a bottle of Chianti."

They left for the restaurant and enjoyed the usual Italian delicacies along with some strong wine. They held hands and gazed into each other's eyes, knowing full well that this could be the end of their relationship.

"I don't want you to leave. Isn't there anything you could do?" Doris said.

"You know that if there were a way to stay, I would. But you know the business I'm in, since you were in the same business years ago. I will miss you terribly, but I have to do it."

"I know. It's just wishful thinking on my part."

That night, they stayed awake, cuddling each other, and from time to time, Doris would sob. Jim felt terrible but he knew he had to go on with the mission even though he realized that Doris would return to New York and not be there when he got back.

Chapter 17

The next morning, Jim threw a few things in the suitcase, called a taxi, and said good-bye to Doris. As he was getting into the cab, he looked back at Doris, who tried to smile as she waved good-bye. He hoped in his heart that this was not the end of their affair.

At the airport, Jim went to the counter and picked up the ticket that Tony had arranged the night before. As he boarded the plane, a feeling of despair came over him. He tried to shake it off, but the sadness of leaving Doris would not go away.

When he got off the plane in Baghdad and walked to the terminal, he looked around for Lev. He spotted him by a coffee shop. When they met, they embraced each other and began walking toward the exit. After Jim retrieved his luggage, they exited the terminal and hailed a taxicab. Lev told Jim that he was going to take him to his hotel, where he could get some rest, and that the next morning, they will meet with two FBI agents who were working the case.

After Jim checked into the hotel, he and Lev went up to the room, where Jim tried to get some sleep. He tossed and turned due to his suffering from jet lag. After a few hours, he finally fell asleep.

In the morning, he was awakened by Lev, who had coffee ready for him. Jim drank the hot brew and thanked Lev for being so considerate. They went down into the hotel's restaurant and ate a light breakfast.

After they finished eating, they hailed a cab and went to the American embassy. Upon identifying themselves and stating their business, they were ushered into a third-floor office. Five minutes later, two FBI agents entered the room. After introducing themselves, the agents opened a briefcase and removed documents. Showing the documents to Lev and Jim, they explained that the area in which the employees worked and were murdered was heavily secured and extremely difficult to enter if you did not know the combination to the lock. Only three people had that combination, two of whom work here in Baghdad, and the other was the commanding officer, a major who lived in the building. They then showed pictures of the inside of the secure bunker showing the two men slumped over desks, obviously shot in the back of the head. The agents told them that they had interrogated those who worked in and around the bunker as well as the two individuals who had the combination to the lock who were in the embassy without shedding any light on the matter. They left Lev and Jim a copy of their investigation along with a map indicating where the building was and directions to get there. Jim thanked the agents and requested information on how to obtain a vehicle to proceed to the bunker.

After they obtained a vehicle provided by the embassy staff, they headed west toward their objective. The drive was slow and tedious especially when they drove through the desert. As they arrived, Jim observed that there was nothing in the area of the bunker. It was just a low-level building that looked like it was two stories high with half of the first story buried in the ground. There were no windows on the first floor, and it was painted a tan color so that it blended into the desert.

They exited their vehicle and walked to the door. There was a button that activated a bell inside. A voice called out to them over a speaker that was obviously hidden above the door.

"Identify yourselves, please." The voice was strong and the command clear.

"Jim Vara," he answered. "We are here from Baghdad."

They heard a loud click, and the door opened.

"We've been expecting you," a young-looking marine major said. "I'm Maj. Bert Finch. I'm in charge of this building. CO Ops notified us you were coming. Welcome aboard."

"Thank you, Major. I'm Jim, and this is Lev, and I guess you know what we're here for."

"Yes, I do. I don't understand why the FBI turned the investigation over to you, but you can expect my full cooperation. If we have a mole here, I want them caught. If you, gentlemen, will follow me, we can go to my office, and I can bring you up to speed."

They walked through a gray austere hallway and then up a flight of stairs. It reminded Jim of an old elementary school he attended.

At the top of the stairs, the major opened a door and ushered Jim and Lev into his office. It was also painted gray with no pictures or anything that even remotely made it look like a civilian office. The walls were cement block, and Jim realized why it was referred to as a bunker.

"Please have seat, gentlemen. I would offer you a drink, but the best I can do is either coffee or a soft drink."

"Coffee would be fine," Jim answered.

"I'll take a Coke if you have one."

The major poured coffee from a coffeepot that was obviously always on. He then bent over a small college-type refrigerator and retrieved a Coke for Lev.

"Milk or sugar?" he asked Jim.

"No. I'll take it the way it is," Jim responded.

"OK. Before we get into specifics, I'll give you a breakdown of our facility. As you know, we intercept transmissions between Syria and the rebels. We gather that information and send it on to our embassy in Baghdad, who I assume share it with Israel," the major said, looking at Lev. "We have a contingent of four Marines and ten civilians whose job it is to translate incoming intercepts. Four of the translators are women. Of course, they have a separate sleeping area, which is out of bounds to all other personnel. Later, I'll have one of my men show you around. Any questions, gentlemen?"

"Yes," Lev answered. "How do the people intercepting the communications enter the area they use? I understand you are the only one here with the combination."

"That is correct. I open the door for them at the beginning and end of each shift. They work twelve-hour shifts, so it only requires that I open the door twice a day. They have bathroom facilities in that area and bring in their own food from our kitchen. In my opinion, it is a terrible job, but they don't seem to mind. I am told that they are very well compensated."

"And no one else has the combination?" Jim inquired.

"No," the major answered. "I guess that makes me a suspect."

"Until we get to the bottom of this, everyone is a suspect," Jim answered.

They took a tour of the facility. First, they went to the women's quarters and peeked into a room that contained six beds, some sparse furniture, and a couple of chairs. They then went to the translation room, where the women sat at tables and were busy transcribing material. After that, they went to a kitchen facility, which contained only two large tables. They then asked the major to take them to the room where the homicides were committed. Standing outside the room, Jim asked if they could enter and see the area for themselves. The major acquiesced and opened the door. They entered a fairly large office area. Two men were sitting at computers and appeared to be surprised at Jim and Lev entering. The room contained six computers like machines that were monitoring the situation in Syria. There were also two laptop computers and various electronic machineries that Jim could not identify. They asked the major where the computer disc that was taken would have been placed. He pointed to one of the machines, and the operator opened a small door, which then ejected a disc. Replacing the disc immediately, he returned to his computer.

They exited the room, and Jim and Lev examined the combination lock on the door and the outer walls of the office. They then checked the ceiling. The major informed them that there was strong mesh wiring circling the ceiling around the upper part of the office, so no one could get in or out using that areaway.

The major then took Jim and Lev to the area where they would be staying. It was a small room, smaller than the office they had just left. The room contained a couch, a desk, and two small cots along with a cabinet. They said their goodbyes, and the major informed them that dinner would be served at 1800 hours in the dining area.

After the major left, Jim and Lev sat and began discussing the situation. Jim asked Lev if he had noticed the indentation on the corner of the ceiling tile. Lev said that he had, and that would have been a perfect place to set a pinhole camera so that when the major uses the combination on the door, it could be recorded. They decided that that was probably the way the perpetrator obtained the combination to the door.

That evening, Jim and Lev went to the dining area and ate a fairly delicious meal. Prior to eating, they were introduced to all the personnel present, who consisted of the six translators, two technicians, two Marines, and the major. The two missing Marines and the two men who were working in the tiny office were the only ones missing.

Jim and Lev ate at the table with the major and the two Marines. During the course of the meal, Jim inquired as to how the food was transported to the building. The major informed that a truck and two Marines would deliver the food daily and take back the translations in a sealed pouch once a day. Lev asked the major when they could start interviewing the personnel. The major said he would make arrangements so that they could start the interview process the next morning. Lev said that would be all right and asked what area could be used to conduct the interviews. The major volunteered his office and said that they could start with the Marines at 0800, after which he would send in the translators one at a time. They all agreed that that would be the best way to handle it.

After the meal, Jim and Lev returned to their room, where they formulated questions and wrote them on a pad that was in the desk. Because there was no TV or any form of recreation in their room, they wondered how the personnel whiled away their leisure time. It was no wonder that the men worked twelve-hour shifts in the office, since there seemed to be nothing else to do. They retired for the day and looked forward to the morning interviews.

They were awakened the next morning by a bugle call over a loudspeaker. Getting to their feet, they noted that it was 6:00 a.m. They took turns going down the hall and using the bathroom facilities to wash, etc.

At 7:00 a.m., they went to the kitchen area for breakfast. They appeared to be the last ones to enter, as everyone was already sitting and eating. The major greeted them and said that he had made arrangements for the interviews.

After breakfast was finished, the major escorted Jim and Lev to his office, where they sat and enjoyed a cup of coffee while waiting for the first Marine to enter. After ten minutes, at exactly 0800, there was a knock on the door. The major open the door and introduced the first Marine to Jim and Lev. The Marine explained his duties and could not add anything to the investigation. Likewise, the other three Marines who were interviewed knew or observed nothing that could help in the investigation.

After the last Marine left, the first of the translators entered. She was obviously a Muslim woman who wore a head scarf. She stated that she neither saw nor heard anything regarding the shootings.

The second translator was very petite and pretty. She, like the others, said she didn't see or hear anything about the shooting. She did say, however, that she saw Naaz, another translator, be very chummy with one of the technicians who was killed. She also said that she thought it odd that she did not have any reaction when told about the slayings. When asked if she told this to the FBI, she said she didn't think it important enough to mention it.

Jim and Lev decided to stop the rest of the interviews and asked the Major if they could search Naaz's area in the sleeping quarters. Since all the translators were busy in their work area, the major said he would escort them. They meticulously went through all her meager belongings but found nothing.

Disappointed, they returned to the major's office, where he received a call from the technicians. Jim could tell something was wrong by the concerned look on the major's face. After he hung up, he explained to Jim and Lev that a large group of hostiles left southern Syria and were headed in their direction. He didn't want to alarm them but explained that if they get within ten miles, their orders were to pull out and head back to Baghdad. He said that they were about sixty miles away and that the odds were that they were just checking out the area, or were lost, and would most likely return to their base in Syria before long. He further stated that the techs would monitor their movements and he would be kept informed. However, he asked Lev and Jim to forego their use of his office until the matter was clarified. They agreed and they decided to return to their quarters until they could use the major's office again.

About forty-five minutes later, a Marine came to their door and told them that the major would like to see them. Jim figured the concern over the movement of the hostiles was over and they could use his office again. He realized he was very wrong the minute he stepped into the office. Three Marines were already present and they were studying a map, which was placed across the major's desk. The major looked up and bid Jim and Lev to enter.

"This is the latest information we have," he said, looking at the duo. "The hostiles have already covered twenty miles at a very fast pace with no deviation in their direction, which happens to be straight for us. At that speed, they can be here in less than an hour. For the life of me, I can't figure out what they are doing unless we are their target. Therefore, I am ordering the translators to pack up and head back to Baghdad. When and if the hostiles get within twenty miles, all other personnel will be ordered to leave. The Marines and I will remain back until they get within ten miles, and if attacked, we will destroy our listening post and then we'll head for Baghdad. You, gentlemen, can leave with the translators or stay behind for a while to see how it all plays out. Let me caution you, though, we only have a few vehicles, so some of us may have to walk out of here."

"If it's OK with you, Major, Lev and I would like to stay for a while. We're just getting used to the scenery," Jim said with a smile.

"Very well, suit yourselves. Two doors down on the right of the hallway is a closet that contains weapons in the unlikely event we'll need them. I have ordered it unlocked."

"Thank you, sir," Jim responded, noting that the Marines were already carrying M16s.

The translators were loaded into a van and started on their way to Baghdad. Jim and Lev were disappointed in that they wanted to question the translators again.

Jim requested permission from the major to go up to the roof with binoculars to see when the hostiles got close to their facility. Jim and Lev were surprised when they entered the roof as to how hot it was. They walked to the end of the building, which had a three-foot wall, which was higher than the roof, encircling the structure. They peered over the cement block wall using powerful binoculars they had borrowed from the major; however, they could see nothing. They decided to return to the major's office, and on the way, they armed themselves with the weapons from the closet. Jim retrieved an automatic weapon with the large bullet canister attached. Lev took out an M16 with a sitting telescope. They both strapped on holsters containing 9 mm automatics. When they entered the major's office, they realized that the situation was rapidly getting serious. The major told them that he felt that the hostiles were using pickup trucks or some form of rapid transportation, as they were closing in on them quickly. He ordered remaining personnel to leave as soon as possible and ordered the Marines up on the roof to provide covering fire in case the hostiles got there quicker than they expected. The Marines quickly left and headed for the roof, with Jim and Lev following.

The remaining personnel from the building quickly gathered personal items and entered two vehicles, which were parked in the rear of the structure, which left one Humvee for the Marines and Jim and Lev to use for their escape to Baghdad.

The Marines, Lev, and Jim entered the roof and went to the forward wall, with Jim using the binoculars and Lev sighting through the telescope that was mounted on his M16. They didn't have to wait long before they could see dust rising in the distance. It was obviously the hostiles coming toward them.

A few minutes later, a helicopter could be heard heading in their direction. The Marines, Jim, and Lev lay flat against the wall to provide cover in case the helicopter was with the hostiles. Within a few minutes, the helicopter was over them and spraying them with machine gun fire. They were very vulnerable in that there was no cover to protect them from above. One of the Marines rolled out from the side of the abutment, lay flat on his back, raised his weapon, and fired at the helicopter. The machine gun blast from the helicopter sprayed him, and he was hit in both legs. He continued firing, and the helicopter began to sputter, and black smoke exited the engine. The helicopter immediately turned and headed back in the direction it came from spewing black smoke as it went. Another Marine quickly ran out and surveyed the wounds of the Marine who had fired on the helicopter. He tore the pants legs from the Marine using a knife and, from a kit, removed bandages and wrapped his legs. At that point, the major entered the roof, surveyed what had taken place, and ordered one of the Marines to carry his wounded comrade down into the Humvee below. The major told Jim that he had completed wiring the building with explosives and had a remote device with which he could detonate the explosives. Peering over the cement wall, Jim observed a pickup truck with a weapon mounted in its bed heading their way. He motioned to the others pointing in the direction of the truck. The major ordered them to hold fire until the truck was closer and then to provide covering fire until the wounded Marine was in the Humvee. The truck slowed down as it approached the building, obviously wary that there was no activity that they could see. As that truck closed in on them, the major ordered them to fire. The truck was sprayed with bullets and swerved off to the left side with its driver and the gunner in the truck bed obviously wounded or killed. Within a few minutes, three more trucks came into view. Surveying what had happened to their compatriots, the gunners in the trucks immediately started firing upon the building. Bullets started chattering the cement blocks on the side of the building, including the roof area that the Marines, Jim, and Lev were using for cover. They returned fire, and the truck stopped and backed up. They backed far enough away until the light firearms of the contingent on the roof were out of range, but the heavier weapons on the beds of the truck could still reach the building. They continued firing forcing the Marines, Jim, and Lev to back away from the outer wall. The major ordered them to leave the building and get into the Humvee. They made their way down the stairs and out the door and into the Humvee without being observed by the people in the pickup truck. A Marine jumped behind the wheel and started the vehicle, while the major sat beside him. One of the other Marines was in the backseat, tending to his wounded comrade. Lev was sitting next to them with Jim standing on the running board and a Marine on the opposite side running board.

When they were about one hundred yards away from the building, the major told the driver to stop. He got out of the Humvee, took a device out of his pocket, and activated it and pressed a button. Within seconds, the building shook, with flames bursting out of the windows. The major got back into the vehicle and ordered the driver to proceed.

The advancing hostiles in the pickup trucks were taken by surprise by the massive explosion. It took them a few minutes to recover and then head to the structure. In the meantime, the Humvee was traveling as fast as it could toward Baghdad.

They weren't gone more than ten minutes when they saw in a distance that two of the pickup trucks were heading toward them. They pushed the Humvee as fast as they could, but the trucks were obviously gaining on them. The major ordered the Marines to prepare for battle and to put their wounded comrade on the floor in the rear of the vehicle. The wounded Marine protested and told the major that he can fight if they prop him up on the seat. The major looked at him and then the Marine who was caring for him and nodded OK. They sat him up, causing him much pain, but he refused to show it. He removed a pistol from his holster, as the M16 was left on the roof after he was wounded.

The trucks steadily gained on them. One of the trucks fired a shot from the small cannon that was mounted on its bed. The shell fell short by about fifty feet, and the occupants in the Humvee realized that it was only a matter of minutes before they would be in range. The major ordered the driver to zigzag so as not to give the trucks an easy target. He knew that it would allow the trucks to catch up quicker but felt they did not have a choice. The trucks had to turn perpendicular to the Humvee to get a shot at them, and that would slow them down.

Finally, a truck caught up with them and was pulling even with them and was about a hundred yards to their side. The Marines and Lev opened up, firing their weapons. The truck fired at them and struck them in the front wheel. The hit caused the Humvee to veer sharply to the left and then slowly started to turn over on its side. The forward motion of the vehicle gouged a deep rut in the sand and slowed it to a crawl. The Marines, Lev, and Jim all jumped clear of the teetering vehicle, which came to rest, lying on its side. The wounded Marine managed to get out on his own.

They used the Humvee for cover but knew that it was only a matter of time before the other truck came around and they would be almost totally exposed to their fire. Lev sighted the gunner in the truck that had shot them and managed to shoot the person firing the small cannon, who then fell over and out of the bed and onto the ground. The driver, seeing what happened, stopped the truck and got out the opposite side, away from the Humvee, to take the gunner's place, where he could fire at will at the turned over vehicle. As soon as the driver got out of the truck, one of the Marines got up and started running toward the truck. Lev and Jim, realizing what was happening, opened fire on the truck, causing the driver to stay behind the truck for cover.

The second truck made a wide circle and was bearing down on the disabled Humvee that the men were using for cover. The major ordered the remaining Marines to fire at the second truck, while Lev and Jim kept the driver of the first truck pinned down.

LOUIS DE MARTINIS

The Marine reached the first truck and entered it, getting behind the wheel. He put the idling truck in gear and drove toward the Humvee. The driver, who was hiding behind the truck for cover, was startled by the truck moving and leaving him exposed to the gunfire coming from the Humvee. He started to run to try to catch up with the vehicle, and then realizing what had happened, he fell flat onto the ground, trying to make him as small a target as possible.

The major ordered everyone to change sides of the overturned Humvee to use it for cover. The second truck rained fire at the Humvee, causing bullets to slam into it. In the meantime, the Marine drove the first truck up to the Humvee, and one of the Marines jumped onto its bed and manned the small cannon that was mounted on it. He immediately fired at the other truck, causing sand to sprout up all around it. The second truck then turned about and headed back toward the abandoned building as fast as it could.

Jim, Lev, and the other Marines sat on the ground, perspiring from the heat of the sun and the rigors of the battle. They stayed there for a few minutes and then started a search for water. Finding none, they decided that they had better head to Baghdad as quickly as possible, since the sun was overhead, and without water, they would not last long. They put the wounded Marine in the front seat with the driver, while the major and the others sat in the bed of the truck. They covered their heads with shirts, handkerchiefs, and any other material that they could use for cover.

The trip to Baghdad was long and hot, but at last, they were at the edge of the city. The major ordered the Marine driver to head to their base, where they could get medical help for their comrade. When they arrived at the aid station, they gently carried their comrade into the Quonset hut, where he was immediately looked after. After seeing that he was being cared for, they headed for the mess hall, where they consumed large quantities of water and food.

After feeling sated, the major told Jim and Lev that he had to report to the commanding officer and questioned where they would go. Jim said they would head for a hotel and then the consulate and asked for transportation, which the major provided for them.

Chapter 18

When they got to the hotel, they checked in and headed for the shower. After cleaning the desert from themselves, they decided to buy some new clothes, as everything they had brought with them was blown up in the desert building. They headed for the street and were astonished to see so much activity. The word of the invasion of hostiles had reached the civilian population in Baghdad and was causing a mini panic. People were running back and forth and appeared to be going nowhere. They were arguing over what the invasion would mean to them and if it would impact Baghdad.

Jim and Lev found a clothing store where they could purchase American-made jeans and T-shirts. They returned to the hotel, changed, and then headed for the American embassy. When they arrived, they were shocked to be ushered into the ambassador's office. The ambassador questioned them about the hostiles and wanted to know the size of the force, their sophistication, and the weapons they had. Jim and Lev could only give him a thumbnail sketch of the force, since what they saw was limited to the skirmishes they endured. The ambassador thanked them, and they were ushered out of his office.

They requested to see the two FBI agents that they had dealt with before going into the field and the bunker. They were put in a small office, where they waited for the agents. About ten minutes later, one of the agents walked into the office. He explained that the other agent was out in the field and would not be back until tonight. Jim explained to the agent what had happened at the bunker and requested another copy of their investigation into the homicides. The agent told them that he would speak to his supervisor and get back to them. Jim opined that since he had given him a copy of the investigation in the past, he did not see any reason for the agent to have to check with his supervisor. The agent insisted, so Lev told him that they would wait. The agent then told them that the supervisor was in the field with the other agent. Frustrated, Lev gave the agent their phone number at the hotel and asked that he get back to them as soon as possible.

They stopped on their way to the hotel and had a meal. When they returned to their room, they turned on the television and searched for the news. They were surprised to learn that a full-scale invasion of Iraq was in progress and they had been in the forefront of it. They wondered what effect it would have on their investigation.

The next day, not having heard from the FBI, they decided to call the agent. Once again, they were surprised to learn that the FBI along with other members of the government from the embassy had been removed and sent to other locations out of the country. They were told, however, that a package had been left for them and they had to come to the embassy to sign for it.

They took a taxi to the embassy and retrieved the package. It was a copy of the FBI's investigations into the two deaths at the bunker. They used the small office that they had waited for the agents the previous day to study the information. They were looking for the address of the women who worked in the bunker and were hoping that personal information including addresses was in the package. They especially wanted to locate Naaz, as she was their leading suspect. There were no background checks on individuals, only cursory information. The reports did have current addresses for the civilian employees who had worked in the bunker. While they were studying, the major walked in on them.

"I heard you guys were here. How are you doing?" the major said.

"We're fine. How is your buddy who was shot on the roof?" Jim inquired.

"He's coming along fine. The medics bandaged him up, and he's on his way to a hospital in Germany. As a matter of fact, he probably is already there," the major said, looking at his watch.

"I have a question for you, if you don't mind," Jim said.

"Shoot," the major responded.

"What are you guys doing here? I heard all American troops had been sent home months ago."

"Well, they were. We are here to guard the embassy."

"The embassy doesn't stretch all the way to the bunker, does it?" Jim answered with a grin on his face.

"Let's just say that some of us have extra duty." The major smiled and winked at Jim.

"I see," Lev chimed in.

"What are you fellows up to? I thought all nonessential personnel were evacuated."

"Well, that just goes to show you how important we really are," Lev joked.

"Seriously, we're trying to solve the little puzzle of the bunker," Jim said. "So far, we've got a good suspicion, but not much else. We were hoping to reinterview some of the women, but now that this fiasco broke out, we don't know if we will be able to do so."

"I know some of them live here in Baghdad . . . if I remember correctly," the major volunteered.

"From what I can see in this investigation report, I think they all do," Jim answered.

"I don't know how well you know this town, but it can be pretty bad out there," the major cautioned. "You have to watch where you're going and what you say. If you do or say the wrong thing in the wrong area, you'll end up in an alley somewhere. They don't fool around. They're very serious people. I suggest you ask for an interpreter to go with you so you don't get lost and end up in the wrong place."

"We both speak Farsi," Jim informed.

"The interpreter will be there to show you around and make sure you don't stray into the wrong areas."

"Good idea. Where do we go to ask for one?" Jim inquired.

"I would start with the ambassador's secretary," the major said. "You might as well start at the top."

Jim chuckled. "You're right. We'll get upstairs and see what happens."

They said good-bye to the major and took the stairs to the ambassador's office.

When they entered the ambassador's outer office, they could see the secretary was on the telephone, so they stood back at a discreet distance. When she finished, they walked closer to her desk and informed her of what they wanted. She had a puzzled look on her face.

"Are you the only ones that don't know what is going on here?" she asked sarcastically. "We are extremely busy, and I can't help you now. Try the office downstairs. Maybe the legate can help."

They said "thank you" and headed for the stairs again.

When they entered the legate's office, there was a flurry of activity going on. People were on the phone; some going from desk to desk and shuffling papers. Most of them look worried and they did not notice when Jim and Lev entered.

"Excuse me," Jim said, trying to catch the attention of the man at the closest desk.

The man looked at Jim and then Lev and said, "Can I help you?"

"Yes," Jim said. "We are here on a special assignment and are in need of an interpreter who can help us."

The man smiled and said, "We're all here on a special assignment. What's so special about yours?"

Jim was annoyed. "Who can help us? Who do we have to see?"

"My boss has the authority to assign an interpreter. I'll buzz him."

The man talked on the intercom and then stood and said, "This way, gentlemen."

He led them through the office and knocked on a door at the end of the room and waited for a response. They entered the small room, which contained a desk, three small chairs, and a small conference table. The walls were adorned with pictures of presidents with the person sitting behind the desk.

"My name is Bob. What can I do for you, gentlemen?"

"Hi, my name is Jim, and this is Lev," Jim said, noting that last names were not being used. "We need an interpreter or a guide. We have to interview some people here in Baghdad, and, unfortunately, we don't know our way around."

"I'm afraid I'm going to have to know more than that before I can help you. Whom do you work for, and what is the nature of your business here?"

"I'll give you a number to call in Washington. They will give us clearance," Jim said as he wrote down a telephone number on a pad that was on the desk.

"Very well. If you, gentlemen, don't mind, please wait outside and help yourselves to coffee or drinks. I hope this will only take a few minutes."

Jim, Lev, and their escort went back into the main office, where they refused a drink.

Jim looked at his watch. It was 3:00 p.m. That meant it would be around three in the morning in Washington. He figured he would have to wait another day before the call went through to satisfy the legate. He was surprised when they were called back into the office in less than twenty minutes.

They reentered the office, and Bob had a smile on his face. "You men have been cleared, and I will give you whatever you need."

"How did that happen?" Jim inquired. "It's in the middle of the night in Washington."

"We never sleep at the CIA," Bob responded. "However, they do sleep in Baghdad, so I won't be able to get your interpreter until the morning."

"That will be fine. Can you send him around to our hotel?"

"Yes, but let me warn you, he is more than an interpreter. He is very knowledgeable about what goes on in Baghdad and knows who the good guys are and who the bad guys are. I strongly advise that you pay close attention to what he tells you."

"Thanks. We will," Lev said, and they left the room.

They returned to the hotel, and Jim called Doris. He was lonely and missed her terribly. They talked about what they would do when Jim returned and made plans for the future as if nothing was going happen.

Chapter 19

The next day at 7:00 a.m., there was a knock on the hotel room door. Lev answered, and a slight man with a very dark tan entered the room.

"My name is Abdul Kabir," he said with a grin on his face. "You can call me K—everyone else does."

"OK, K." Jim had a rough time trying not to laugh.

"I understand you would like me to interpret for you."

"Not exactly," Lev said. "We both speak Farsi. However, we do not know our way around Baghdad and we'll need help finding some people."

"Ah,"—K smiled—"that is my specialty."

"Great, then let's get started, shall we?" Lev said.

They sat at a small table in the room, and Jim spread out the papers he had obtained from the FBI. "We want to locate and speak to these women."

"That may be a little more difficult," K said. "These addresses are in a Shiite area run by an Imam who imposes a strong code of conduct. You will not be able to speak with them without their husband being present, and you should pay your respects to the Imam before you even try."

"But they worked for the government by themselves without their husbands being present," Jim offered.

"They must have obtained special permission from the Imam. Perhaps an exchange of some sort was accomplished. Perhaps a quid pro quo," K responded.

"Maybe so, but that doesn't help us. We have nothing to offer."

"We may not need anything, I have a good relationship with him, so we can give it a try," K offered.

"Great. Let's get going," Jim said.

They stopped for breakfast, after which they hailed a taxi and headed for the location of the Imam.

On the way, K schooled them on how to act. "Do not say anything until you are introduced and the Imam starts the conversation," he told them. "If he does not like what he sees, he may just leave the room without speaking, which means we are dismissed."

"Then what?" Jim asked.

"Then we leave, and you don't get to interview anyone," K told them.

"That's garbage," Lev offered.

"That is how powerful the Imam is," K responded.

They arrived at a mosque, where they exited the taxi. K motioned them to follow him. He entered the mosque, where he took off his shoes and motioned Jim and Lev to do the same. K had words with an attendant, and they were ushered into a side room, where they were searched. Jim and Lev handed the attendant their guns and then they were told to wait. A few minutes later, they were ushered into another room. This room was painted with religious sayings on the walls. K motioned them to kneel on the floor on a mat that was there for that purpose. In front of the room was a large chair. The rest of the room did not contain any furniture.

Jim had a sense that they were being observed but did not want to look around for fear of annoying someone.

A side door opened, and a man entered followed by the Imam. He was a tall gaunt-looking older man with a long gray beard and dark piercing eyes.

He said something in Farsi to his attendant that Jim and Lev could not hear. The attendant motioned toward Jim and Lev, and the Imam looked at the two of them.

"What brings you here?" the attendant said to K.

K responded by complimenting the Imam and saying how wonderful he was to allow them in his presence. The Imam dismissed what K said with a wave of his hand.

"We come to ask permission to interview six women who live here," K answered.

"Why?" the Imam spoke directly to K.

"We have reason to believe that they killed two people and stole a very important disc from our facility."

"Why should I allow this?" the Imam asked.

"What they stole was very important to the government."

"Which one do you suspect?" the Imam asked.

"We would like to talk to all of them with the Imam's permission," K responded.

"I will grant you to speak with one. I do not want you upsetting my people," the Imam said empathically. "You must have suspicion of one over the others."

K looked at Jim and Lev. Jim took out a paper and pointed to Naaz's name.

"With your permission, we would like to speak with Naaz," K responded.

"Come back tomorrow morning, and she will be here along with her husband." With that, the Imam rose and left the room.

They left the mosque, and Jim was shaking his head.

"It was like we weren't even there," he said to no one in particular.

"He knew you were there, and by tomorrow morning, he'll have complete dossiers on both of you," K said in response.

"Well, I'm impressed," Lev offered.

The next morning, they hurried to the mosque. They were greeted by the same person as they were the day before. As before, they were relieved of their weapons and waited in an outer room. This time, the Imam's attendant escorted them into the next room, where the Imam, Naaz, and a male, presumably Naaz's husband, were present.

The Imam looked at his attendant and nodded. The attendant then addressed Jim, Lev, and K.

"You may speak now," he said without any emotion. "Naaz has been told that she must tell the truth in the presence of the Imam."

It had been decided beforehand that Jim would do the questioning. Jim nodded to the Imam and decided that "good mornings" did not seem appropriate at this time.

"Naaz," Jim started, "you did work at the building with the Marine major, didn't you?"

"Yes," she answered in a very low voice.

"Do you remember when the two men in the building were killed?"

"Yes," she said in a barely audible tone.

"Did you have anything to do with the murders?" Jim pressed on.

"Yes," she repeated.

Jim was surprised at the admission.

"What, if anything, did you do?"

"I shot them," she admitted, causing Jim to pause at her naked honesty.

"Why?" he pressed on.

"Because I needed the disc."

"Why did you need the disc?"

"I promised Abdul I would get it for him."

"Who is Abdul, and why does he need the disc?"

"He is my cousin and he made me do it so he can give the disc to the Imam in Iran to whom he owes his life."

"Where is the disc now?"

"I gave it to Abdul yesterday," she offered.

Damn, Jim thought. *We were so close.*

"Enough!" the Imam shouted. "I have heard enough."

Jim, Lev, and K were shocked by the Imam's outburst.

"You have killed two infidels for which there is no penalty," the Imam said, pointing at Naaz. "You have stolen a disc, which was not yours." He then looked at Naaz's husband and said, "Take her out and cut off both her hands as a penalty for stealing the disc."

"Please," the husband talked for the first time, "she is useless to us without hands."

"Very well," the Imam said. "Stone her until the life has left her, and let that serve as a lesson to anyone who steals."

The husband thanked the Imam and was satisfied with the sentence, to the surprise of Jim and the others.

The husband took Naaz by the arm and took her away. Jim and Lev were dumbfounded. They stood there not knowing what to do. K took it matter-of-factly and just shrugged his shoulders and motioned to the others to leave.

When they were outside, they discussed what had just taken place. Lev asked Jim if they should try to save Naaz, but K told them that they could not.

"What's the difference?" he said. "If you had her in court, she would be put to death for murder anyway."

"Yes, but at least she would have had a trial, and, besides, her husband seemed almost happy that she should be stoned to death, and it was for stealing, not murder," Jim said.

"Think about it. What good would she be without hands? She would just be a burden on the rest of the family. You Westerners have a weird sense of what is right, wrong, and what is practical," K offered. "Besides, there are politics involved here. The Imam in Iran is not at all friendly with this Imam, so he is also sending a message to him."

Lev looked at Jim and shrugged his shoulders as if to say, "There is nothing we can do about it, so let's drop it."

Jim just shook his head as he walked away in disbelief.

Chapter 20

They returned to their hotel with the intention of formulating plans for recovering the stolen disc.

Jim first called Doris, and they spoke of mundane things because both knew Jim could not reveal what he was up to. He wanted to tell her about the Imam and what had happened in the temple, but he could not because he feared that the phones in the hotel were tapped. He told her he loved her as he hung up the phone and turned red when he realized the other two present were listening to his call.

K had an idea. If the Imam was "unfriendly" with his counterpart in Iran, perhaps he would help them. The others said it was worth a try, since they obviously couldn't get any more information from Naaz.

Jim asked K if he thought questioning Naaz's husband was possible and if it would be fruitful. K thought it would be a bad idea to attempt to talk with Naaz's husband but said he would attempt to speak with the Imam and that Jim and Lev should not be there, in that the Imam may be more forthcoming without them being present.

They decided to let K try, while they tried to get some intelligence on Naaz's cousin Abdul.

Jim and Lev decided to head to the embassy, while K would go to the mosque, and they would meet back at the hotel that evening.

At the embassy, they were treated better by the clerk they originally met. He tried to be very helpful. They explained to him that they needed to find an Abdul, and the only information they had on him was that he was a cousin of Naaz. He brought them to a computer, and the clerk punched in a password. He then entered into an intelligence program and got up and left so Jim could sit and try to ascertain Abdul's identity.

First, Jim typed in the name Abdul and received over a thousand hits just for the city of Baghdad. Next thing he did was put in Naaz's name and address. He received a hit. *At least she's in there,* he thought to himself. He tried relatives of Naaz but got nowhere. He got an idea. He got out of the intelligence software and on to a browser. He then typed in family tree and put Naaz's information in. He smiled when the asked for a credit card number and was only too glad to put in his government credit card information. The next thing he knew, he had her family tree and was able to identify Abdul. He got Abdul's last name and typed it into the intelligence software and he was given his address and other information. It seemed that from time to time, Abdul provided information to the embassy. *He was probably working both sides of the aisle,* Jim thought. He retrieved a piece of paper and a pencil from the desk drawer and wrote down the information he needed regarding Abdul. He handed the paper to Lev and smiled broadly. Neither one realized at that time that K had already had the information.

"Some of the old detective juices are still flowing," he said.

Lev smiled and read the information on the paper. "I guess we better take K with us because I have no idea where this house is," Lev informed.

They thanked the clerk and left. They decided to check back at the hotel in case K was waiting for them. When they returned, K wasn't there, but he had left a note saying he was following up on some information he received at the mosque and would meet them at around five at the hotel. Since it already was three thirty, Jim and Lev decided to wait.

They didn't have to wait long, as K arrived at around four thirty.

"What is going on?" Jim asked.

"I got Abdul's address and decided to go to his residence. I spoke with his mother, who told me that he wasn't home and that he would be gone for three days. When I pushed her as to where he was, she told me that he was going to Iran to meet friends and to pray. She gave me the name of the town in Iran, but I don't think we can go there."

"Why?" Lev asked.

"It is in very hostile area, and if we were caught, they would probably summarily execute us," K said. "One good thing I found out was that he was meeting some friends halfway there, so that would give us a little time to catch up."

"OK, then let's go," Jim said emphatically.

"I guess we better get to the embassy and get a car," Lev offered.

"No time for that. I'll take care of the transportation," Jim offered.

"How?" K asked.

"Never mind," Jim shot back. "Meet me in front of the hotel in five minutes."

K looked at Jim and shrugged his shoulders as if to say, "If you say so."

Jim left the room and went to the underground garage. He spotted a Mercedes, which looked like it would do fine. He noted the parking spot number and returned to the lobby. Just outside the hotel was an area that the valet parking attendants used containing a small cabinet in which they hung the car keys. Jim waited for someone to use their service, and when the attendant left to retrieve a car for a guest, he looked in the cabinet and took the keys that were on a hook with the number of the parking place for the Mercedes. He reentered the lobby and went to the underground garage and entered the Mercedes, utilizing the keys he had just taken. He drove out of the garage and to the front of the hotel, where Lev and K were waiting for him.

"Nice wheels," Lev said. "Any problem getting it?"

"No. The owner was only too happy to lend it to us," Jim kidded.

They drove away from the hotel, and Jim followed the directions K provided.

They drove for about an hour and a half until they came to a small town that seemed to appear out of nowhere.

"This is it," K informed.

"OK. Where to from here?" Jim asked.

K pulled out a piece of paper and studied it for a minute.

"Pull over when you can. I'm going to have to ask for directions."

Jim spotted a middle-aged man walking down the street and pulled over next to him.

"Excuse me, sir," K asked. "Can you tell me where this address is?"

K handed him the paper. The man perused it for a minute, and then his eyes lit up in recognition. The man gave K directions, and they were off again.

K explained that it was the address of one of Abdul's friends that he was able to get from his mother.

They pulled up in front of a nondescript house that appeared to be very small. K got out of the car and knocked on the door. An elderly man answered and eyed K with a wary look on his face. He then looked over his shoulder at the Mercedes and became more apprehensive.

"Excuse me, sir," K said. "I'm looking for Abdul. We are friends of his, and he forgot something at his mother's house, and since we were coming this way, we thought we could deliver it to him." K lied.

"He is not here," the man replied.

"Do you know where I can find him? His mother will be very disappointed if we don't give it to him. It is a gift for him to give to the Imam."

The old man warmed up at the mention of the Imam, as only a friend would know where he was going.

"You just missed them," the man replied. "They left about an hour ago."

"Thank you," K replied. "Whose car were they driving?" K asked.

"They are in my son's car."

"What color is it so that I might see him and catch up to him?" K said.

"It is a white Opel," the old man responded.

"Thank you," K responded and turned and got back into the car.

After explaining his conversation with the elderly man to Jim and Lev, they decided to try to catch the Opel. They drove as fast as the streets would allow,

193

dodging push carts and people strolling through a market they happened upon. Finally, they were on the open road again, and Jim floored the Mercedes.

After about a half hour, Lev received a call. He told Jim he had to get back to Baghdad as soon as he could. Jim realized that it must be someone in Israel giving Lev orders, as Lev seemed very concerned.

K offered, "I think there is a town about another fifteen or so kilometers ahead. Perhaps we can find our way back to Baghdad from there."

"What do you mean *we*?" Jim asked.

"I told you I am not going into Iran, and at the rate we're traveling, we will be there soon. I will return to Baghdad with Lev, and if you're smart, you will also come."

"I can't. I have to get that disc," Jim replied. "I'll drop you off at the next town, and then you guys can take the Mercedes, and I will borrow another car."

When they entered the town, they looked around to see where they could get another car for Jim. They found an old wreck of a car, and Jim thought it would fit the bill. The last thing he wanted to do was to drive into Iran in a Mercedes. He paid the man who sold it and kidded Lev and K about having the only legitimate car between them. He then admonished them to dump the Mercedes as soon as they could because it was hot, and by the time they got back, the police would be looking for it.

Seeing Jim's determination to continue on to Iran, K explained to Jim the best way to enter the country without being noticed and avoiding checkpoints. He told him he had to continue down the road they came in on until he saw a checkpoint, at which time he would make a U-turn and proceed back on the road until he saw a dirt road on his right. The road was not marked, and that was why he had to go until he spotted the checkpoint. At the dirt road, he was to travel about twelve miles and then take a right turn and enter Iran. He could then continue for a few miles and he would come to a rundown shack where he was to make a right, again on a dirt road, and that road would eventually lead him onto the paved road he had left but beyond the checkpoint. The town the Imam was in whom Abdul wanted to see was about another two hundred kilometers up the road.

Jim checked the fuel gauge on his newly purchased vehicle and was satisfied that he had enough for his journey. He said good-bye to his friends and watched as they drove away in the stolen Mercedes. He turned his car around and headed for Iran, following the instructions that K had given him.

He drove for about an hour until he could see the Iranian checkpoint K told him about. He immediately made a U-turn and headed back in the direction he had come from. About a mile down the road, he made out the dirt road and made a right onto it. He drove on the dusty road for about twelve miles where the road made a sharp right. He followed the road for about ten miles and came to the shack, where he made a right. *That shack would be a perfect observation post,* he thought to himself. He was certain that the Iranians must know about the road. It was just too easy to enter the country that way. Maybe they just don't care.

After another twenty minutes, he came to the paved road and made a left, heading deeper into Iran. Jim could feel the sweat on his back wetting the back of his shirt. He wasn't certain whether it was the heat or nervousness on his part.

As he drove, he was deep in thought as to what he would do if he was caught by the Iranians. He formulated different scenarios in his mind as to what he would say and do.

Then he saw it! It was a white Opel on the side of the road with its hood up. Two men were standing in front of it, staring into the engine compartment. Jim immediately pulled his car off the road about one hundred feet in front of the Opel. He exited his car and walked toward the two men, who turned and looked at him and smiled, expecting assistance with their broken car.

As Jim approached, he called out, "Abdul."

One of the men said, "Yes. How do you know me?"

Jim pulled out his gun and pointed it at him. Fear spread across Abdul and his companion's face as they tried to comprehend what was happening.

"Let's get to the point," Jim said. "You have a disc that I want. Hand it over now before I am forced to hurt you."

Abdul's companion put his hands up and stepped back away from Abdul.

"I have no disc and I don't know what you're talking about," Abdul said, his voice trembling.

Jim fired a shot into Abdul's leg, causing him to buckle and fall down on his knees. He let out a scream as the pain surged through his body.

"The next one goes into your head," Jim said as he put the gun to Abdul's forehead.

"I can get it off your dead body if you like," Jim said.

"No, no," Abdul said as he reached into his shirt pocket and handed a disc to Jim.

Jim took a few steps backward and examined the disc. On it were imprinted the words "Property of the U.S. Government." Satisfied, he began to walk back to his car after taking the men's cell phones and admonishing them to stay put until he was out of there.

Jim entered his car, started the engine, and made a U-turn, heading back toward the dirt road that had brought him there. He felt the adrenaline ease in his body as he put distance between him and the two men with the Opel.

His relaxed state did not last long. A military jeep passed him going in the opposite direction and made a U-turn upon seeing him. Jim opened the window on the passenger's side of his car and threw out the two cell phones he had taken from Abdul and his friend.

The jeep, which was still a distance away, illuminated a blue flashing light and was speeding up. Jim realized they were coming after him and waited for a curve in the road where he could have a few minutes out of the sight of the jeep. The road curved to the right, and there where houses that would give him some cover. He broke the disc into four pieces and threw them one at a time out the window. Then he threw out his gun, followed by his government identification.

A few minutes later, the jeep caught up to his car. Jim pulled over to the side of the road, took a deep breath, and waited as two men dressed in military uniforms approached.

Before Jim could say anything, they pulled him out of his car, and one of them punched him hard in the stomach. Jim felt the air go out of him and, for a minute, thought he was going to vomit. He was spun around and pushed roughly onto the truck of the car, and his face was pushed onto its hot metal surface. His hands were cuffed behind him as he lay there defenseless. They stood him up, and he tried to speak, but that only got him a slap in the face. His ears started to ring.

"Try to outrun us," one of them said as he sneered at Jim.

"No, no," Jim responded. "I didn't know you wanted me to stop."

That got him another slap in the face. They searched Jim and took everything he had including his wallet, wristwatch, and even the few coins he had in his pocket. They left him his belt, which Jim was grateful for. They half walked him and half dragged him to their jeep, where they threw him onto the backseat. Then they did a systematic, careful search of the car Jim had driven. Finding nothing, they returned to the jeep. Jim was relieved that they didn't find anything in the car and hoped that they would release him. It didn't happen. They started the jeep, made a U-turn, and headed back in the direction Jim had come from, away from the border.

As they drove, Jim saw Abdul and his companion on the side of the road. He ducked down in the seat in hope that they would not see him. They were waving at the jeep. Jim was relieved when the two soldiers ignored them and continued on their way.

They drove for about an hour and entered a small town, which appeared to be on the outskirts of a much larger city, which was on a hill above them.

The jeep came to a halt, and one of the soldiers got out and entered a building, which appeared to be a police station. When the soldier returned, he said something to his partner that Jim couldn't make out, and then they told Jim to get out of the vehicle. The soldiers grabbed Jim, one on each arm, and brought him into the building.

They entered what appeared to be a small office-type room with only one desk and one chair. The room was dark and painted a dark gray, which gave Jim a feeling of foreboding. There was one person behind the desk who got up when they entered and removed a set of keys from the desk drawer. In front of the desk was a prison cell with other cells further down the hallway to the right. The guard opened the first cell, which faced the desk, and the two soldiers literally threw Jim into it. They forced him facedown onto the floor, one of them placing his knee into Jim's back, and removed the handcuffs. Jim was relieved, as the cuffs had been cutting into his wrists and hindering the blood from going into his hands, which felt cold and numb. One of the soldiers then kicked Jim in the side as they exited the cell. The guard, looking bored then, locked the cell and went back to his desk, where he sat down and removed a newspaper from a drawer and began reading.

Jim slowly tried to move. His body ached from the blows he suffered. He moved his head to one side and saw nothing but a dark-gray cement wall with a bucket in the corner. He slowly brought his arms under him and lifted his chest from the floor. His side was very painful from the kick he had received from the soldier. He hoped he didn't have any broken ribs. He slowly got to his knees and then tried to stand on unsteady feet. He decided to crawl to the wall and use it to steady himself as he got to his feet. Finally, he was able to stand, leaning with his back against the wall. He could taste blood in his mouth, and his jaw ached.

He looked around the jail cell. Nothing there but three dark-gray cement walls with no windows and the front of the cell having steel bars that made up his cage. The only other thing in the room was the bucket, which was probably his bathroom. No cot or blankets, not even a chair. On the concrete ceiling was a bare light bulb that dangled precariously from a wire. The bulb was lit and it was about five feet above him, just high enough so that he could not reach it. *Welcome home,* he thought to himself. *I hope I can get out of here soon.*

The guard was engrossed reading his newspaper and did not even look at Jim. Jim tried to engage him in conversation, asking where he was and why he was there, but the guard totally ignored him and did not even look up from his paper. It was clear to Jim that this was a casual experience for the guard, who probably has had many prisoners here before.

Jim let himself slide down the wall and onto the floor where he sat. The cement was cold, but since it was very hot outside, it was tolerable. *Think,* he told himself, *Why am I here? Why did they just arrest me and didn't even ask who I was or what I was doing? It obviously wasn't the shooting with Abdul because they didn't even slow down when he tried to hail them to stop.* Jim had to chuckle to himself when he thought about all the scenarios he worked on for just this type of occasion and not one of them fit what was happening.

He sat in the corner of his cell for hours. Then a new guard came in. He looked more Oriental than Iranian. He was short and thin and was clean shaven as opposed to most Iranian men, who sported long beards. He tried to engage him in conversation.

"Hello. Can you tell me why I'm here, and when I will be let go?" Jim said.

The guard looked at him and said, "I don't know and I cannot speak with you."

Well, Jim thought, *at least he speaks.* "Why can't you speak with me?" Jim inquired.

"Rules say no speak with prisoners," the guard responded. "You be quiet." The guard looked serious, so Jim thought he would be quiet for a while. He thought that perhaps he could work up a rapport with this guard, as he at least talked to him.

Hours went by when finally two military officers entered the small office. They asked the guard for his keys and then motioned for him to leave the room. The guard immediately left. The soldiers opened the cell and stepped inside.

"Why have you violated the borders of our country?" one of them, who appeared to be an officer, asked Jim.

Before Jim could say anything, the officer slapped him in the face. Jim rolled his head with the blow, easing its effect.

"I didn't know where I was. I was lost, and the next thing I knew you pulled me over." Jim lied.

"You are a smuggler and you brought in narcotics with you," the officer said, his face getting red with anger.

"No, I never smuggled anything," Jim said. "I just got lost. If I were a smuggler, I would have narcotics or money with me. I just got lost," Jim repeated.

"Do you know what we do to smugglers?" the officer snarled as he removed his pistol from its holster. He placed the revolver on Jim's forehead. Jim could see that there were no bullets in the revolver's chamber but decided the best course of action for him was to go along with the charade.

The officer pulled the trigger, and the gun clicked on the empty chamber. Jim fell to his knees and forced a shudder in his upper body. This seemed to satisfy the officer, who smiled broadly and holstered his weapon.

"The next time you may not be so lucky," he said. He left the cell, locking the door behind him.

The guard returned to the office and looked in at Jim. He shook his head as if to say he was sorry. This gave Jim some hope.

A little while later, another guard entered the small office carrying a metal plate that contained food. Jim was ordered to the rear of his cell, and the other guard opened the cell door, placed the plate on the floor, and retreated back out the cell.

Jim looked at the plate and saw it was a small pile of what looked like mush with no discernible meat or vegetable. He decided that he had better eat it, as he had not eaten in some time. It tasted awful. He had nothing to wash it down with and almost gagged halfway through the meal. He noted that the guard was watching him closely as he ate.

"Can I have something to drink?" Jim asked.

The guard got up from his desk, went outside, and brought him back a metal cup that contained water. He once again motioned Jim to the rear of his cell and unlocked the door and put the cup on the floor. He relocked the door as he left.

The water tasted cold and was an aid in getting the food to settle in his stomach.

That night, Jim tried to sleep. He curled up on the floor but had no blanket to cover him and shivered through most of the night, as the cement floor was cold. The light was always on, but Jim faced the wall and was able to black out most of its effect by placing his arm over his face. He wasn't sure whether he slept.

The next morning, the guard, whom he decided to call Chan, left and was replaced with the mean-looking original guard. He decided to call him Fang, as he had a tooth protruding from his upper lip. A few hours later, two more guards entered, and Jim was ordered to take his plate, spoon, cup, and bucket and was led outside where there was a spigot and he was ordered to wash them. Jim looked around to try to find out where he was but saw nothing but a vehicle that the two guards probably came in, what looked like a shack, and then open country. *There's nowhere to go,* he thought to himself as he washed the utensils. After he finished, he rinsed his mouth out with the water, which did soothe his jaw a bit. He was then taken back to his cell, carrying his utensils and a cup of water he had taken from the spigot.

As he sat in the back corner of his cell, he took note as to his situation and planned an escape. He could take the guard if he could get his hands on him, but that would require the guard making a mistake and either entering the cell alone or letting him out when the guard was by himself. He felt the odds of that were not good. He would have to bide his time and hope the guard would make a mistake.

His stomach started to hurt, as he nothing to eat since the gruel he had been given the night before. He asked the guard for food, but, as before, the guard totally ignored him. He wondered what time it was and how he could make the day pass faster. *Certainly,* he thought, *they can't keep me here very long. What's the sense? I don't think they have any idea who I am and must be mixing me up with a drug smuggler, and, besides, why am I the only one here? This must be some kind of temporary jail they use. There at least a half-dozen cells here, yet I think I'm the only one occupying a cell.*

He decided that he would break the day into segments to try to make the time pass and to forget about his hunger. He would use few hours to consider his plight and try to make sense of things, an hour or two to exercise, the best he could under the circumstances, and a few hours to plan his escape. At night, he would concentrate on Doris, imagining what she was doing, smelling her perfume, and recounting the good times they had together. Then he will plan their future and try to think of what they will do minute by minute.

Finally, the guards changed. Fang left, and Chan took over. He thought at least he could talk to Chan, even if only a few words. It would help him keep his sanity. An hour or so later, the food was delivered. It was the same gruel, only this time Jim thought he could make out that some of it was rice. He ate it, trying to eat slowly but failing due to his hunger. He sipped the water he had left. He only allowed himself a few small sips at a time so that it would last. He looked up and noticed that Chan was watching him closely. Then Chan got up from his desk and removed a paper bag from one of the drawers. He took out an apple, walked to the cell, and handed it to Jim. Jim couldn't believe it. It was the first time he was shown any kindness since he arrived in Iran. He thanked Chan profusely and sat on the floor and savored each bit of the red delicacy. He ate the entire apple, including the stem and the pits. It was a feast.

He tried to make conversation with Chan but he could not find anything they had in common. Finally, Jim figured he would make up a story about his life and feed it to Chan, who seemed to enjoy it, especially when he told of the United States and the tall buildings and the beautiful cars. Chan found it difficult to believe that there could be such decadence, and it was available to all and that the average person could afford a car.

Their relationship developed, and Jim found himself growing fond of Chan. He especially was grateful for the few morsels that Chan gave him every evening. Sometimes it would be a tasteless cookie, a piece of fruit, and, once, a sandwich, which consisted of cooked vegetables.

The time went slowly, and Jim was getting depressed. He was losing weight rapidly and could not exercise very much. He came down with dysentery and grew weaker by the day. Chan gave him some bitter herbs, which did help him get better.

Then one day, while Fang was guarding him, there was a knock on the door. Fang hesitated but then finally decided to open it. A tall thin man asked Fang for directions to the city. As Fang was explaining, the man looked into the room and saw Jim in the cell. The man then thanked Fang and left.

A few days later, Chan did not show up for work, but another guard took his place. When Jim asked him what happened to Chan, the guard told him that he had been transferred. Jim became concerned, as he knew that he could not exist on the small bowl of gruel he was given nightly. He became further depressed and just sat in the corner of his cell day after long day. He became so weak that he could no longer wash his dish and cup. No one cared, and they just dumped the gruel into the dirty dish, causing Jim to get dysentery and grow weaker by the day. The stench in his cell became unbearable.

Chapter 21

About a week after, Chan left Jim heard a loud noise outside the building. It sounded like a helicopter. There was a knock on the door, and when Fang opened it, he was thrown to the floor by a man armed with a submachine gun. Behind the man was another male who also entered the prison. To Jim's surprise and glee, it was Lev. Lev grabbed the guard, pulled him to his feet, and told him to get the key to the cell. Fang meekly obeyed and retrieved the key from the desk drawer and handed it to Lev. Lev unlocked the cell door and lifted Jim to his feet. He half walked and half carried Jim out to the waiting helicopter. They entered it, and when the man with the submachine gun got in, they immediately took off. They flew low to avoid being detected by radar and, within a matter of minutes, were out of Iran and in Iraq, heading for Baghdad. Jim was not sure whether all this was really happening or if he was a figment of his delirium.

They arrived in Baghdad, and Jim was carried from the helicopter and placed on a stretcher. An IV was inserted into his arm. He was quickly evaluated by a medical team who went with him as he was carried into a large four-engine aircraft. Within minutes of their arrival, they were airborne again.

Jim still wasn't sure all this was really happening. He tried to clear the cobwebs in his head but could not. Then sleep came.

He tried to open his eyes, but his eyelids felt very heavy. Finally, he was able to open them. At first, the glare from the bright lights caused him to close his eyes again, but as he slowly got used to them, he was able to see. He looked around and realized he was in a hospital, a nurse standing nearby.

"Where am I?" Jim asked with a raspy voice.

"Well, hello," the nurse answered, a smile on her face. "It's good to have you with us. You are in a military hospital in Germany. How are you feeling?"

"I feel like I've been run over by a Mack truck," Jim answered. "How long have I been here?"

"Only a day. You were brought in yesterday."

"How did I get here?" Jim asked.

"I don't know. You were brought in on a medevac flight from Baghdad, I understand."

"How am I?" Jim asked.

"You are extremely dehydrated, and we're running tests on you to see if you have anything else wrong with you."

Jim wanted to make some telephone calls but felt extremely weak and fell asleep before he could reach the telephone, which was on the table next to the bed.

He woke up hearing conversations taking place around him.

"Good evening," a man's voice said. "How are you feeling?"

"OK, I guess," Jim replied.

"I'm Dr. Frederick. I'll be taking care of you while you're here visiting with us," the doctor said with a smile in his voice. "Do you have any questions for me?"

"Yes. When can I get out of here?" Jim inquired.

The doctor chuckled. "You just got here and you want to leave us already? We'll have to wait on the results of the tests we took, and if everything looks all right, we'll have you out of here in no time. In the meantime, you have to rest so that you can get stronger and let your body help you. I'm prescribing a strong sedative to help you sleep."

"Doctor, may I notify anyone that I'm here?"

"Of course you can. I understand that a man named Corcoran made arrangements for you to be brought here, and also your significant other, a Doris Macon, was notified. Is there anyone else you want notified?" the doctor inquired.

"No, that's it. Thanks, doc. I think I'll get some sleep now." Jim's eyes were getting heavy as the sedative started taking affect.

The doctor smiled and left the room.

Jim felt warm and comfortable for the first time in a long, long time as he relaxed and let the medicine do its work.

He woke in a haze and felt something on his hand. Was it one of the many bugs that roamed freely in his cell? No, it was warm and soothing. He forced his eyes to open slightly and could make out the figure of a woman. Doris . . . was it Doris, or am I still in my cell dreaming? Then he smelled her perfume. *If I am dreaming, I do not want to wake,* he thought to himself. Then darkness came again as he once more drifted off to sleep.

He woke up again. This time, he could open his eyes. It was her in all her magnificent beauty. "Doris, my love," he said, gazing at her.

"Yes, sweetheart, I'm here with you."

"Oh, thank you, thank you, thank you," he repeated. "You don't know how I dreamed of this and how much I missed you."

"I missed you too, sweetheart. Promise me you'll never leave me again."

"The thoughts of you were the only thing that kept me alive. Through all the days of loneliness and starvation, you would come to me in my dreams and kept me going. The thought that I might see you again was my only way to survive. I couldn't give up. Now I know I love you so very much."

She bent over and kissed his forehead and wiped away a tear that formed in the corner of his eye. Her heart was full of love for this person along with the worry about his health. She silently swore she would care for him all the days of his life.

"Please don't leave me," he said.

She smiled at him and said, "Where could I go without you? I will be here until we walk out together, arm in arm." *He looks so weak and vulnerable,* she thought.

He drifted off to sleep again; this time he was calm and serene, and his heart was filled with love and peace.

Doris settled into one of those convertible chairs that could also serve as a bed that hospitals are famous for. She covered herself with a blanket that a nurse had given her. She too was filled with love and felt a closeness to Jim that she had never experienced in her life. *God, do I love this man,* she thought. For the first time in her life, she prayed for someone.

Chapter 22

The next day, Jim woke up and felt a little stronger. He didn't move too much because of the tubes protruding from his arms. He looked over and saw Doris asleep in the chair next to his bed. He figured she didn't get much sleep due to the nurses constantly checking on him and taking his blood pressure, temperature, among other things, throughout the night. He was so happy she was there.

She heard him stirring and woke up.

"Are you OK, darling? Can I get you anything?" she said.

"I'm fine. I feel much better today. Maybe we can get out of here today," he said without much confidence in his voice.

"The doctor should be in today to give us the results of the tests they took. So who knows—maybe we can escape."

"Maybe I can promise him that I'll stay in bed. I intend to do that as long as you're in there with me."

It made her feel good that he was already joking.

Breakfast came, but it wasn't for Jim. The nurse told him that they had been feeding him through the tubes, and perhaps today, if the doctor OK's it, he could start on whole food. Doris asked the nurse if she could give him some orange juice, and she said she thought it would be OK as long as he could tolerate it. Doris opened the wrapper on a straw, placed it in the container of juice, and held it to Jim's mouth. He dragged on it, and it felt cool and moist in his mouth. One sip was all he wanted, and it seemed to satisfy him.

After Doris finished her breakfast, she read a newspaper to him. It was a paper that was a few days old that she had brought with her from New York. It made no difference to Jim, as he had been out of circulation for months. It was just so very nice to hear her voice.

After a while, the doctor entered the room.

"Well, Jim, I've got good news and bad news," he said. "Which do you want first?"

"I don't really care," Jim responded. He looked over at Doris, and she looked worried.

"The bad news is you have a bug in your gut. The good news is it's very curable with a regimen of pills."

"Great, doctor. When can I leave?" Jim asked.

"Not so fast. We'll start you on the medication for the bug and try to put a few pounds on you and then we'll make sure you have plenty of fluids in you. In the meantime, as soon as you feel strong enough, I want to see you walking the halls. The sooner you get out of bed, the sooner you'll leave us."

Doris and Jim were relieved at the prognosis. They smiled at each other, and Doris assured the doctor that she would take care of Jim and make sure he takes his medicine and walks the halls.

As soon as the doctor left the room, Doris picked up a glass of ice water and put the straw to Jim's lips. He took a little sip and pushed it away.

"You have to drink more than that," she scolded him.

"I will, but right now, I want to rest some more." He closed his eyes and promptly fell asleep. Doris went downstairs to the restaurant and ate breakfast. It was not the usual fare she was used to, but it wasn't bad for hospital food.

When she returned to the room, she was surprised to see Jim sitting up in bed.

"The nurse helped me sit up and put these pillows behind me," he said. "Can walking be far off?"

She smiled at him and was happy that he was making progress.

"I want to know how I got here," Jim blurted out. It was obviously on his mind.

"Don't you remember anything about it?" she inquired.

"Everything seemed to be happening in a fog. I think I remember Lev being there and then a lot of scurrying and a long airplane ride. That's about all I can remember. Do you know anything about it?"

"No, darling," she responded, "but if you like, maybe we can call Tony and see what he knows."

"OK, let's do it."

She reached into her pocketbook and took out a cell phone. She found Tony's home number, but before she called, she looked at her watch.

"I think it's six in the morning there," she said.

"Tony won't mind unless he has company," Jim answered. "Go ahead and dial."

Doris pushed the button and waited for a ring. She handed the cell phone to Jim.

"Hello," a groggy-sounding voice on the other end answered.

"Tony, it's Jim."

"Where are you?" Tony asked.

"I'm in a hospital in Germany."

"I heard about it. Are you OK?"

"Yes. I'll be out of here very soon. Tell me, who got me out of that hellhole?" Jim asked.

"Lev, of course," Tony answered matter-of-factly.

"I thought so. Can you get him to call me? I want to thank him and find out what took him so long," Jim kidded.

"You have to give me a little time—who knows where in the world he is."

"OK. Thanks, Tony."

"Take care of yourself, boss," Tony said as he hung up.

He still calls me boss after all these years, Jim thought to himself.

He handed the cell phone back to Doris, who placed it back in her pocketbook. The following day, Jim received the call he was waiting for.

"Hello, Jim?" Lev asked.

"You son of a gun," Jim said into the telephone. "You'll do anything to get even."

"Don't blame me," Lev answered. "I'm not the one that can't stay out of jail. You went and got locked up and were having such a good time in there that I thought I'd get in on the fun too. Seriously, Jim, how are you doing?"

"I'm fine, just a bug in my gut, which I probably caught from you. Nothing the doctors can't fix. I should be out of here in a few days."

"Glad to hear it, Jim," Lev answered. "Be well, buddy. I might need you again."

"By the way," Jim asked, "where did you get that helicopter, or was I dreaming?"

"The Iraqi government was only too happy to let me borrow it," Lev answered with a smile in his voice.

"I thought I was bad grabbing that Mercedes. You just had to show me up, didn't you?"

"And what about the flight to Germany?" Jim asked.

"Your friend in Washington, Corcoran, made the arrangements," Lev answered.

"OK, we're even at two rescues apiece. Let's hope we don't need to do that again."

"Take care of yourself, friend," Lev said as he hung up the telephone.

After lunch was delivered and consumed, Jim wanted to try to walk. Doris was against it. He assured her that he was all right and he could do it. She made him promise to get back in bed if he felt tired or dizzy.

Jim put his feet over the side of the bed and sat for a few minutes. Doris held on to his arm as he slowly slid off the bed and stood on his feet. He looked at Doris and almost laughed at the concerned look she had on her face. He slowly moved one foot and felt shaky. He stood there for a while and then moved the other foot. He was grateful that Doris was giving him support. He took a few more steps and slowly turned and headed back to the bed, where he once again sat with his feet dangling over the side of the bed for a few minutes and then got back into bed. He lay down, and Doris put the covers on him.

"Thanks, darling," he said. "I think we made a little progress. Tomorrow I'll race you around the hall," he joked and promptly fell asleep.

As he slept, Doris left the room and made some business calls. She informed her partners that she would probably be out of the office for two more weeks, if not three. She then asked one of the partners if the beachfront apartment in Boca Raton, Florida, was available. When she was told that it was, she told them that she will be using it to help Jim recover and that if there was any urgent business, she could be contacted there.

Jim was right. The next day, he felt much stronger, and the color was returning to his face. After breakfast, he insisted on getting out of bed. He did take one lap around the hall, which was about one hundred feet. Doris was holding on to his arm, while he glided the stand, which was on wheels and contained the fluids that were connected to his arm. When he returned to his room, he sat in a chair rather than getting back into his bed. Although exhausted, he felt great that he was able to walk and was happy with the improvement he was making.

The next couple of days, Jim was feeling stronger and stronger until he was able to walk freely around the halls.

Six days after his admittance into the hospital, he was finally released. Doris had made arrangements for them to fly from Germany to Florida. She had to go and buy Jim a new wardrobe, as the only clothes he had were the ones he was wearing when he entered the hospital. Those were the same clothes that he wore throughout his period of incarceration in Iran.

They arrived in Boca Raton, Florida, on a nice, sunny, warm day. Jim was feeling very well and couldn't wait to get to the beach and feel the sand between his toes. The apartment was beautiful. It had new modern furniture, and the bar was filled with top-shelf liquor. Jim immediately wanted to sample all the bottles that were on the bar, but Doris stopped him, telling him that he was still weak and needed more time to recuperate.

They walked hand in hand along the beautiful beach, and Jim was feeling very well. After a couple of days, Jim went out and bought himself a bathing suit and decided to go for a swim. Doris was very nervous, fearing that he was still in a weakened condition.

They went down to the beach, Jim walking to the edge of the water while Doris had wrapped herself in the towel. When she took the towel off, Jim saw that she was wearing a scanty bikini. He joked with Doris, saying that he had to get into the water because just looking at her made him perspire. She laughed, and they frolicked in the water for the next hour.

LOUIS DE MARTINIS

The week went by quickly, and Doris had to get back to New York and her business.

They said a tearful good-bye at the airport, and each went their separate ways. Doris knew that Jim was back to his old self but still was afraid that he was pushing it too soon to be fully recovered. As for Jim's part, he felt stronger than ever and wanted to get back to Virginia to his house where he could start living a normal life again. They made arrangements that they would see each other every weekend possible, and Doris vowed to take any extra time she could when not working an important case to get to Virginia to see Jim.

Jim arrived at Dulles Airport and took a cab to his house. He was happy to be home and had to rely on the key that he had hidden in the shed to get into the house, because he was stripped of all his property when he was taken prisoner in Iran.

After relaxing in his home for a day, Jim decided to call Corcoran to bring him up to date on what occurred in Iran and Iraq.

"Hi, Jim," Corcoran said. "How are you? I've been keeping track of you and I am so happy that you have made such great progress."

"I'm doing pretty well now. Thanks," Jim responded. "It was pretty hairy and touch and go for a while, but I made it."

"I heard about it. How did you get into such a mess?"

"It's a long story. How about I come down and see you one of these days?" Jim said.

"Just let me know when you feel up to it, and we can meet in my office, or I can meet you somewhere that's convenient to both of us," Corcoran said.

"How about I come down to your office tomorrow?"

"That would be fine. How about 2:00 p.m.? Will that be OK with you?"

"I'll see you then," Jim said as he hung up the telephone.

The next day, Jim went into the city to the Department of Justice, where he saw Corcoran. He told Corcoran what had happened while he was in Iraq and Iran. Corcoran inquired about the disc, and Jim told him that he had to destroy it. Corcoran was happy to hear that it could not fall into enemy hands. They decided that Jim would take a couple of months off until he was he felt he was in good enough condition to come back to work at which time he would call Corcoran.

Chapter 23

Jim took the next couple of months to join a gym and work out regularly. On the weekends, he would either travel to New York to see Doris, or if she could, she would come down to Virginia to visit with Jim. During the two months, their relationship got stronger; however, it was very frustrating for them to have to part on Sunday evenings.

Jim felt that he was in tip-top shape, so he called Corcoran and met him in his office.

"I have another assignment for you, Jim, if you feel up to it," Corcoran said.

"I am in the best shape I have been in the past four years," Jim said.

"Very well. Take a look at this folder," Corcoran said as he handed Jim a folder marked "Top Secret."

Jim took a folder and opened it to reveal a picture of a young woman.

"This woman—her name is Susan Wilson but she goes by Arda in Iraq—works for the government and she was undercover in Iraq. She was feeding back information regarding ISIS. The location she was at was overrun by ISIS, and we have to extricate her," Corcoran said. "Your job will be to get in there, locate her, and bring her back."

"Why not use the Navy SEALs? They are experts at this sort of thing," Jim said.

"As you may or may not know, the president has a 'no boots on the ground' policy. If we send the SEALs in and one of them is wounded or captured, the media would have a field day, and it would embarrass the administration."

"What about me? What if I get wounded or captured? I guess you're saying I don't count in the grand scheme of things."

"I have full confidence in you, Jim. I know you can handle this and bring her back. Read over what's in the folder and let me know when you'll leave. I have a contact over there that will assist you. His name is Mosaud, and you can meet him in Mardin, Kurdistan. He is a sergeant in the Kurdish army, and it has been cleared to the highest levels that he will help you while you are there. I understand he is a tough old-timer."

"How do I get in country with ISIS running all over the place?" Jim asked.

"You will have to land in Ankara, Turkey, and make your way into Kurdistan. I don't have to tell you, time is of the essence. We have information that she was hiding with the Christians, but they are being slaughtered. I hope she is heading to the mountains with the others," Corcoran said, a worried look on his face.

"Today is Friday. I'll see if I can catch a hop to Ankara tonight. Doris isn't going to like this."

"Sorry, Jim, but it has got to be done," Corcoran said. "I'll arrange for our guys from the Turkish embassy to meet you and take you to the Kurdish border. Remember, the Kurds and the Turks do not get along. I'll also try to get Mosaud to meet you at the border, if I can reach him. If not, you'll be on your own. I'll have my secretary get you a flight to Ankara."

There was a flight at eleven that night, so Jim barely had time to go home, get his passport, some money, and clothes, and head for the airport. On the way, he called Doris. He could not contact her, as she was on her way to Virginia to meet with him.

As he entered the ramp that led to the airplane, he tried once again to call Doris. This time, he was successful.

"Hi, sweetheart," Jim said into the telephone.

"Hi. Where are you? Doris asked.

"I'm sorry, dear, but I got a last-minute job and had to leave right away."

"Oh, no," she said. "I'm in your house."

"I'm so sorry, dear. I was looking forward to being with you this weekend, but Corcoran gave me a job that I couldn't refuse and is very time sensitive."

"Not again. You're just getting over your last assignment. Can't you pass it up?" she asked, sobbing. "I'll be worried sick until you get back."

"I'm sorry, dear," Jim repeated, "but I'm boarding the plane now."

"Promise me you'll be very careful, Jim," Doris pleaded.

"I promise, dear. I'll be home before you know it."

"Where are you going?" she asked.

"You know I can't tell you," Jim responded.

"Oh, please, please hurry home to me. I love you," she said, and then the phone went dead.

"Hello, hello," Jim tried to reconnect to the call but without success. He dialed the number again but could not get a connection. He felt terrible that he didn't get a chance to tell her how much he loved her. *Maybe I can get a connection when I get to Turkey,* he hoped.

Doris sat on the couch where she loved to cuddle with Jim. She sobbed and brushed away her tears with a hanky. *Stop it,* she told herself. *I'm a big girl and I knew what I was getting into when I decided to get involved with him, but I never thought I could love a man so much. My heart is breaking.*

She decided to head back to New York and bury herself in work until Jim returns.

She tried to get a flight out of Virginia, but it was too late. She would have to leave in the morning. The worse part, she thought, was sleeping in his bed alone. When she went to bed, she cuddled his pillow and languished in his aroma. She did not get much sleep that night.

He arrived in Turkey early the next afternoon after a restless night on the plane. He couldn't get Doris out of his mind and the way they had parted without him being able to tell her he loved her.

After leaving the plane and heading down the exit ramp, he was ushered with all the other passengers to customs. As he approached the customs desk, two men approached him.

"What is your name?" one of them asked.

"Who wants to know?" Jim asked.

"We're from the American consulate," one of them responded.

"Jim Vara," he answered.

"Good afternoon, Mr. Vara. We are from the American embassy and we are here to see that you get to your destination as quickly as possible. Would you please come with us?"

They walked down a long hallway and passed the customs desk without stopping and into the main part of the airport. Jim was impressed as to how huge and modern it was.

"Can we stop and get something to eat?" he asked his escorts. "The food on the plane was inedible, and I haven't had anything to eat for the past twenty-four hours."

"Certainly. We can eat here in the airport. There are several fairly good restaurants in here," the taller of the two remarked.

They entered a hamburger restaurant and sat at a small table.

After ordering and feasting on hamburgers and french fries, Jim was filled and ready to go. He was surprised at how good the food was.

The two men from the embassy tried to ask questions of Jim, but he evaded answering most of them. They explained to Jim that it was eight hundred miles to the Kurdish border, and it would take more than a day to get there by car, as a mountain chain had to be crossed. They told Jim they hired a plane and a pilot to get him to Mardin in Kurdistan and that he could leave whenever he was ready, as the pilot was on standby. Jim was surprised and happy, as he did not look forward to a long car ride in a desolate country, and he would be taken to his final destination without having to bluff his way in when he crossed the border into Kurdistan.

The plane was a small single-engine two-seater. The pilot was a gruff-looking man whose breath smelled of alcohol. As soon as Jim buckled up, the pilot offered

LOUIS DE MARTINIS

Jim a drink of vodka from a bottle that was more than half empty. Jim declined the offer and hoped that the pilot had not drunk the amount missing from the bottle.

As the engine revved up and they started to taxi, Jim looked out his window at the two agents from the consulate. They gave him the thumbs-up sign and turned and started to walk away. Jim wondered if they knew the condition of the pilot.

The plane taxied down the runway, and after receiving clearance from the control tower, the pilot pushed the throttle to full speed. The engine strained as it pushed the aircraft forward. It took a screaming engine and a lot of the runway to finally lift off and get airborne. *Too much runway,* Jim thought.

At the beginning of the flight, all seemed to go well as the plane lumbered its way up to cruising altitude. The pilot throttled the engine back, and the deafening noise subsided. The pilot then retrieved his vodka bottle and motioned to Jim if he wanted to drink. Once again, Jim declined, and the pilot put the bottle to his mouth and took a large swig of the contents. Jim was not happy.

As they lumbered along, Jim could see the mountains ahead of them. The pilot noticed Jim looking at them and said, "Thirteen thousand feet. We will have to dance in between them because I don't have any oxygen. Don't worry, I do this many times and I have a special route."

Jim was not reassured.

The closer they got to the mountains, the more the aircraft started to bounce. Jim held on, and the pilot smiled, noticing his discomfort. They headed straight for the first peak, and for a while, it looked like they were going to crash into it. At the last second, the pilot veered to the left, just missing the mountain by what seemed to be a few feet. *Too close,* Jim thought. *I wonder if he's putting on a show for me or if he is drunk.*

This went on peak after peak, zigzagging between the mountains for the next half hour. Jim noticed that he was drenched with sweat. Finally, the mountains became smaller, and the plane settled down. *Now to survive the landing,* Jim thought.

The pilot brought the plane down to a much lower altitude and was barely a few hundred feet above the ground. Jim could see what looked to be an airport ahead.

"We not go there," the pilot blurted out. "Too much security and paperwork. I have my own airport," the pilot said, a big grin on his face.

Jim just sat back and decided that whatever was going to happen, he had no control over, and he resigned himself to the fact that his life was in the hands of a drunken pilot.

They flew a little further when the pilot motioned to Jim that they were over "his" airport. Jim looked out and saw nothing but a small piece of level earth.

The pilot circled it one time and throttled back, and the plane started to lose altitude.

Jim braced himself as he saw the ground getting closer and closer. To his amazement, the landing was relatively smooth except for a few minor bumps caused by the ruts in the ground.

The pilot turned the aircraft around and came to a stop. Once again, he reached for the bottle of vodka and held it toward Jim, offering him a drink. This time, Jim took the bottle and took a swig of the raw-tasting liquor. The pilot smiled his approval and motioned to Jim to look to his right. To Jim's surprise, he saw an old World War II jeep heading for the plane. The jeep had a lone driver and came to a dusty screeching halt next to the aircraft.

"Your next ride," the pilot said. "Good-bye, Mr. American." He laughed as Jim unbuckled and opened the airplane's door.

"Thanks for the ride," Jim said tongue in cheek.

"You Mr. Vara?" the driver of the jeep said.

"Yes, and you are?" Jim inquired.

"My name is Mosaud. I am a sergeant in the Kurdish army. I'm here to take you to where my outfit is, in the hills outside of Mosel."

"Yes, Mosaud, I've been told about you."

"All good, I hope, Mr. Vara," was Mosaud's answer.

"All good, and please call me Jim."

"OK, Jim. We have about a five-hour drive, so hang on and make yourself comfortable."

"How can one get comfortable in this jeep?" Jim responded.

Mosaud laughed, put the jeep in gear, and sped away from the airplane.

The ride was bumpy and loud. Mosaud had to yell at the top of his voice to speak with Jim. He explained that his platoon was holding a mountaintop outside of Mosel and were trying to protect the Christians who were feeling the town. The problem was that the ISIS troops were in the valley below and taking potshots at the Christians as they tried to flee up the mountain. They were using the Christians for target practice, and no matter how hard his platoon tried to stop them by firing at them if they exposed themselves, they were usually successful in shooting a woman or child. It was getting to be a killing ground.

Jim shook his head in disgust.

"How can they kill defenseless people?" Jim asked, already knowing the answer.

"They are animals," Mosaud answered.

They arrived at the mountaintop after leaving the jeep further down the hill. What Jim saw amazed him—people lying on the ground trying to sleep, men and women crying obviously for lost ones who were killed on their trek up the mountain. Some of the people were trying to continue down the mountain where Jim and Mosaud had just come. *It's controlled chaos,* Jim thought.

Mosaud motioned to Jim to follow him. With Jim in tow, Mosaud found his commander, a captain, who was introduced to Jim. They shook hands, and with Mosaud acting as interpreter, the captain tried to give a synopsis of what had been taking place on the mountain. The ISIS troops were encamped at the bottom of the hill and had tried several times to attack his fortifications but were repelled each time with heavy losses. The captain explained he had forty men with him, but many of them were caring for the Christians who were fortunate enough to make it to the top of the hill. They were, however, available should the ISIS troops try to storm the hill again. Jim requested permission from the captain to speak to the Christians in an effort to obtain information on the whereabouts of Arda. The captain was all too willing to assist Jim and told Mosaud to stay with him and act as interpreter and bodyguard, to which Jim requested a weapon, as he was unarmed. The captain ordered Mosaud to get Jim a weapon and took his leave.

Mosaud led Jim to the edge of the mountain, where he took a rifle that was on the ground and handed it to Jim along with a bandolier of ammunition. The rifle was an M1, which was as old as Jim. He had used one while in the Marines, so he was familiar with its operation. He put the bandolier over one shoulder and slung the rifle over his other shoulder. Mosaud watched him closely and was satisfied that Jim knew his way around the weapon.

"When can I get some target practice?" Jim asked.

"Don't worry, you'll have plenty opportunity here," Mosaud said, motioning toward the valley where the ISIS troops were.

Jim walked over to a young man who was sitting on the ground.

"Do you know Arda?" he asked through Mosaud.

The young man nodded yes.

"Do you know where she is?" Jim asked.

The young man shrugged his shoulders as if to say that he had no idea.

Jim went from one person to the next, but with the same results. They all seemed to know Arda but had no idea where she was.

All of a sudden, Jim felt exhausted. He realized he hadn't slept for two days and was feeling very tired. He explained to Mosaud that he needed to rest, and Mosaud took him to a tent that had two cots in it. Jim flopped down on one of the cots and immediately fell asleep.

He was awoken by the thump, thump, thump of helicopter blades. He slowly got up and tried to shake the cobwebs from his brain. He opened the tent flap and looked out and saw a helicopter landing about 150 yards from where he was. The helicopter kicked up a great deal of dust as it softly came to rest on the ground. The engines were slowed to an idle, and a soldier inside the cabin began to throw boxes out the side door. People started to scramble toward the helicopter as the soldier, who was then accompanied by the copilot, quickly finished throwing out the boxes, which were carried away by the Kurdish soldiers and the civilians who were in the area.

Then the rush started. People were pushing and shoving each other to enter the helicopter. The soldiers in the helicopter helped some women and children climb into the ship, and when it was full, two Kurdish soldiers held the remainder of the crowd back as the helicopter revved its engines and took off. The whole operation was done in a matter of a few minutes. Jim marveled at the efficiency of the helicopter personnel.

He wondered how long he had slept. He felt a little refreshed and realized he was hungry. He wandered over to where the boxes from the helicopter were stacked. Soldiers were emptying them and giving MPGs, packaged meals, to persons around them. Jim reached out and was handed one by a Kurdish soldier, who seemed surprised that he wanted one. Jim sat on a rock and began to eat when Mosaud came over to him.

"How did you sleep, Jim?" he asked.

"Not bad," Jim answered. "There wouldn't be any coffee around, would there?"

"When you finish eating, we can go see if the captain has any."

"Thanks. How often do the helicopters come?" Jim asked.

"Hard to tell. There is no pattern. Some days they come four or five times, and other days they don't come at all. I guess they take care of different areas and not just us."

"I would like to give them a message next time they come. I'll write it down and maybe you can see that it is delivered to them."

"Sure, no problem," Mosaud responded.

Jim finished his meal, and he and Mosaud walked over to where the captain was.

"Do you have any coffee for our American friend?" he inquired.

"Yes. Go over by my tent." The captain motioned toward his rear. "There is usually a pot on the burner. When you're finished, I have some news for you."

Jim walked to the captain's tent and observed a Bunsen burner with a coffeepot on it. Next to the burner were some tin cups. Jim took one and poured some liquid from the pot into it. He looked around but found no cream or sugar, not that he expected any in these environments. He took a sip of the hot liquid and almost spat it out. It tasted like lye. *Oh, well,* he thought to himself, *it's better than nothing, but not by much.*

As he sipped at the coffee, he glanced over at the captain and Mosaud and saw that they appeared to be in a heated discussion. He threw the rest of the liquid onto the ground, returned the cup, and headed to where the two were standing.

"The women you are looking for, Arda," the captain said through Mosaud, "I think we have located her. She was seen in the basement of a schoolhouse down there." The captain motioned toward the bottom of the hill where the city of Mosul stood. "Unfortunately, the area is controlled by ISIS. There is no way we can get her out. I don't have enough men, and a platoon of ISIS stands between us and the village. The village is heavily patrolled by them, and I doubt she can make it out without being observed. As you know, if they capture her, they'll kill her. I'm sorry, but there is nothing I can do."

Jim stood for a minute, contemplating what the captain said. "One man can make it. It would be better if I tried to sneak in rather than confront them with a force." Jim was trying to convince himself as well as the captain.

"I understand what you're saying, and Mosaud was telling me the same thing. I can't, in good conscience, let you go. Besides, you don't even speak the language."

"I speak Farsi," Jim informed him.

"Yes, but this is a different dialect. They may not understand you."

"I think I'll take my chances," Jim responded. "With all due respect, Captain, I do not fall under your command, therefore I will take full responsibility for my own actions."

"That's why we love you Americans—you can never take no for an answer." The captain smiled. "Very well. I will send Mosaud with you, and God help you if you're ever caught."

"Thank you, Captain. We will leave as soon as it gets dark. Do you have any night vision equipment I could borrow?" Jim asked.

"Yes. Mosaud can get it for you. Good luck."

Just then, gunfire broke out about a hundred feet from where they were standing, and the captain hurried to the location.

Jim and Mosaud headed back to the tent that Jim had slept in.

Jim took out a pencil and paper and wrote out a note to Corcoran, explaining the situation and asking him to call Doris. He wrote that his cell phone was dead and he would be in contact as soon as he returns from Mosul with Arda.

Chapter 24

Darkness came quickly. Mosaud had gotten night vision lenses for both of them. He also fitted Jim with fatigues, a pistol with holster, and belt, which contained extra ammo. Included on the belt was a full canteen of water. He gave Jim a floppy hat and a backpack containing food and other essentials. Jim was happy to change his clothes, since he had been wearing them for four days. There was no facility to bathe on the mountain, so he felt pretty grubby.

Mosaud discussed with Jim the path they would take to try to bypass the ISIS contingent on the mountain and the road that would take to Mosul. Mosaud had interrogated some of the Christians who knew where the schoolhouse was and the best way to get there without being observed. The problem was that they were about eighty miles from the schoolhouse, and the trek would be on foot unless they got lucky and could commandeer a vehicle. The area was unknown to Mosaud, and he thought about taking one of the rescued Christians as a guide but then thought better of it. He figured it wouldn't be fair to ask them to return to the area that they had just escaped from.

Jim, Mosaud, and the Kurdish troops were located on top of a hill with about a twenty-foot sheer drop that was straight down. That was how the Kurds could keep the ISIS troops from charging their position. The ISIS troops would make it to the wall and then have to fall back as the Kurds would fire down on them. The Kurds knew that it was only a short amount of time before ISIS gets enough equipment to scale the walls. In the meantime, the Kurds held out and served as a sanctuary to the Christians who could make it up the wall.

The Kurds used a rope ladder, which they threw over the side to aid the Christians in climbing the wall. A couple of large Kurdish soldiers would climb down the ladder and help the women with children negotiate the rope. If an ISIS soldier tried to fire at those climbing the rope ladder, he would be met with machine gun fire from a bunker that was placed nearby the makeshift ladder.

Of recent worries to the Kurdish soldiers was the introduction of mortars that could lob shells on their mountaintop position. They had taken fire for a few days, and then inexplicitly the shelling stopped. The captain thought that perhaps they ran out of shells and were waiting a resupply.

Finally, it was time to leave. The captain came to say good-bye and to caution the men not to take any unnecessary chances and to stay in touch via walkie-talkie. He wished them good luck and escorted them to the rope ladder.

Jim clamored down the rope, almost losing his balance. *This would be some mission if I fell and broke a leg before I even get started,* he thought to himself. Mosaud had led the way and was waiting for Jim at the bottom of the ladder. They adjusted their equipment and put on the night vision lenses and looked around. It was eerily quiet.

No movement of any kind. They figured there had to be some form of coverage for the rope ladder, as the enemy soldiers knew it was there. But nothing was stirring. Mosaud slowly moved away as the ladder was pulled up. Jim followed closely behind, looking from right to left and listening for any movement. He heard nothing.

They cautiously moved forward and had covered about one hundred yards when they finally saw some movement off to their left. They slowly inched forward and saw a small campfire with three men sitting around it. Jim had to remove his night vision lenses, as the campfire created a glare, temporarily blinding him. Mosaud looked back at Jim and placed a finger over his lips, indicating "quiet." They slowly moved away, putting distance between themselves and those around the campfire.

What they saw next sickened Jim. It was a group of bodies rotting on the ground where they were obviously executed. There were men, women, and children lying in grotesque positions in a macabre death dance. The stench almost made Jim sick.

When they had moved far enough, they stopped and rested. They had not gone far, but with the adrenaline pumping through their bodies, they quickly tired and decided to take a ten-minute breather.

It was very slow going, as the terrain was very rough and unforgiving. Jagged rocks along the path caused them to stumble a few times, and they decided not to rush it, as the last thing they needed was a twisted or, worse, a broken ankle.

It took most of the night, but, finally, the terrain started to level off, indicating that they were out of the mountains. Only small hills were ahead of them and then level farmlands.

As dawn approached, they decided to find a place where they could hide and maybe get some sleep. They were exhausted from the forced trek. They looked around but did not see any structures of any kind, so they settled for a small clearing under a few trees. The area was fairly hidden from view and would have to serve as a hiding place until nighttime. They took turns, one acting as a lookout while the other tried to sleep. It was a long day with neither of them getting much sleep.

Finally, the sun set, and darkness began creeping over the land. They started out, leaving their hiding place behind. It was pitch black with very little moonlight, and had it not been for the night vision glasses, they would have been completely disoriented. Mosaud had a difficult time trying to figure out where they were. The Christian had told him that after he exited the mountains, he would find a small dirt road that he should follow south for about fifteen miles. They hadn't come across any road, and Mosaud was concerned that they had made a mistake. He checked his compass for the fifth time that night and convinced himself that he had taken the right path.

They walked for another two hours when they discovered a small dirt road that did not look as if it had been used much. *This has to be it,* Mosaud thought. They did not speak much, only when necessary and then in a whisper for fear that they could be overheard, so Mosaud motioned to Jim, pointing to the dirt road. Jim nodded that he understood and gave Mosaud a thumbs-up signal. They started walking down the road, feeling a little better.

After about eight hours of slow walking, they looked for somewhere to spend the day.

Finding nothing that was of interest, they decided to walk into a cornfield and use the cover of the stalks to hide them. They walked in about fifty yards and trampled down some of the stalks and made a suitable area in which to spend the day. A problem arose when the sun was high in the sky and began searing them with its burning heat. They decided that they had to move and find better shelter. They did not like the idea of exposing themselves during the day but felt they had no choice.

They returned to the road and continued their trek. After a half hour, they came upon a farmhouse that had a barn about forty yards behind the small house. They decided to try to use the barn for shelter for the day. They cautiously entered the barn, and Mosaud motioned to Jim to climb the ladder to the second level, where hay was stored. As Jim started to climb, he heard a noise. It was a baby's muffled cry. He took out his pistol and scanned the haystacks. He saw movement and would have fired except that he was certain that it was a baby's cry he heard.

"Put your hands up and come out from behind there," he commanded.

"Please don't shoot," a woman's voice responded.

Just then, about ten people stood up with their hands in the air. Men, women, and three children, including the baby, all stood there seemingly paralyzed.

"Don't shoot, please don't shoot," one of them repeated.

Jim quickly realized that they were probably Christians fleeing from ISIS. Mosaud, who was still on the ground below the ladder, asked Jim what was going on. When Jim explained, Mosaud quickly climbed the ladder, and they all introduced themselves. They asked if Mosaud and Jim had any food, as they hadn't eaten in two days. Jim and Mosaud shared what they had left in their backpacks with the Christians, leaving virtually nothing for themselves.

After they ate, they asked the Christians about Arda and were told that she had been wounded and was in the basement of an old schoolhouse the last time they saw her. The schoolhouse was just on the outskirts of Mosul with ISIS patrolling the area. They explained how to get there using the best possible route through the ISIS patrols, but they were still five days away by foot. Mosaud then told the Christians the best route to get to the mountain where the Kurdish forces were encamped. After the exchange, they all tried to get some sleep, but the temperature in the barn was extremely hot and almost unbearable, and the baby kept crying. They were grateful that the farmer did not come to the barn that day.

When night finally came, they were set to depart, the Christian group going north and Mosaud and Jim heading south. As they parted, Mosaud stopped them and gave them his night vision glasses, telling them to tell the captain they got them from Mosaud and that all was fine with them. At that point, Jim realized that for all his toughness, Mosaud had a heart of gold.

Jim and Mosaud started on their trek again, taking the dirt road. Jim had thought about stealing a vehicle from the farmer but then thought better of it, as it would probably bring ISIS there and spoil it for future escapees. He decided to put distance between them and the farm before he attempted to find transportation.

As usual, the walk at night was slow going, with Mosaud staying close to Jim, who had the only pair of night vision glasses. They walked until dawn and found an orchard, which would serve as a resting place for the day. They sat under the trees, which gave them shade. It was quiet, and one could almost forget what was ahead waiting for them.

Chapter 25

Corcoran received the message from Kurdistan. He was elated to hear that Jim had made it that far into the mission. He had expected it to take much longer due to the terrain and the logistics of getting to the front lines. Jim never ceased to amaze him. He did not, however, cherish the idea of calling Doris, since he knew that there would be a lot of questions he could not answer. She has to understand; after all, she did work in the Group for over five years and knew the type of work they did. She was the one who recruited Jim, and no one could fathom her falling in love with him. She was a tough broad and knew how to handle people and problems and had no compunction sending them on super dangerous missions. *Still, she is a woman in love, and I guess that changed everything.*

After checking to see that he had her number, he picked up the phone and dialed.

The secretary on the other end of the line sounded very professional and asked what the call was about. He told her just to say Mr. Corcoran is on the line. Doris picked up immediately.

"Hello, Doris. How are you?" Corcoran started, knowing full well she wasn't interested in small talk.

"I'm fine. How is Jim?" she said, getting straight to the point.

"He's fine and doing well," Corcoran embellished.

"Where is he? When is he coming home? Why hasn't he called?"

Corcoran could feel the tenseness and concern in her voice.

"You know he's on an assignment and his cell phone is dead, and that's why he asked me to call you."

"If he can call you, then he could have called me," she opined out loud. "He's not hurt again, is he?" Her heart was in her throat.

"No, no," Corcoran responded. "He's in an area where he could not charge his phone and got a message through to me via the military." Corcoran decided that that was all he would say.

"When is he coming home, and when can he call?" she asked.

"I don't know, Doris. I suspect he'll be out of touch for a while, but as soon as I know something, I'll call you. I've got to go now there are people waiting for me." He lied.

"Please let me know as soon as you hear something." Doris heard herself pleading, which was something she swore she would never do.

"I promise," Corcoran said as he hung up the phone.

She stared at the phone she just hung up. *I can't do this,* she thought to herself. She realized she was shaking. Tears welled up in her eyes. *Love is not supposed to hurt so much. Oh, God, please keep him safe and send him home to me,* she pleaded again. Then it came, uncontrolled sobs and a gusher of tears as she cried and cried. She wanted to take the rest of the day off but knew in her heart that it would only be worse sitting at home alone and worrying.

Chapter 26

They took turns again, one keeping watch while the other tried to sleep. Jim was getting hungry and he reached up to pick an apple even though it was green and not ripe. Then he heard voices. It was a few men walking through the orchard and talking about the bugs that were plaguing the crops. Jim crawled to where Mosaud was sleeping and placed a hand over his mouth to wake him up and keep him quiet. Mosaud knew immediately what was happening and picked up his rifle, which lay next to him, and quietly took the safety off. He lay down in a prone position, pointing the weapon at where the voices were coming from. Jim did likewise.

The men were about two rows away from where Jim and Mosaud were and continued walking and talking until the voices faded away. Jim relaxed and thought to himself that those men will never know how close they came to dying that day.

Jim and Mosaud discussed their situation as they sat under the apple trees. They decided that it would take forever to continue to walk at night. They had to chance a daytime walk and to try to get some form of transportation to speed up their journey to Mosul. After all, if Arda was wounded, then they had to get to her as quickly as possible to give her aid and get her out of Mosul. They decided to head out immediately, as they were wide awake after the adrenaline rush caused by the farmers walking nearby.

They began walking near the road but staying as close to the side as possible in case they would have to take cover. They hadn't walked more than a half mile when they came upon a farmhouse. Some distance away from the house was a barn, and parked nearby was a tractor. Jim and Mosaud looked at each other and nodded. They decided that riding a tractor was better than walking. They slowly approached the barn, keeping low to avoid detection. When they were at the tractor, Mosaud climbed up into the driver's seat. The key was in the ignition, where most farmers kept it. He glanced over at Jim, who climbed onto the fender, then, with a prayer, turned the key. The engine started immediately, and Mosaud put it in gear, and away they went toward the dirt road. They tried to drive on the shoulder of the road or in the field itself, feeling that it was the safest way to go. Jim had to hang on to the driver's seat in order not to be bumped off the vehicle. The tractor could only do about ten miles an hour, but it still beat walking.

They weren't gone more than forty minutes from the barn when a car came down the road toward them. The car pulled in front of them and stopped, causing the tractor to stop. Jim opened the flap to his pistol and put his hand on its grip. Out of the car came an irate farmer raising his hands and yelling at them. It was as though he didn't care that Jim and Mosaud were armed; all he wanted was his tractor back. *He must think we're ISIS,* Jim thought, *but he has a lot of guts confronting us like this.* Jim and Mosaud got off the tractor, and the farmer got on it and made a U-turn and drove away.

Jim and Mosaud couldn't believe their luck. In the farmer's haste to retrieve his tractor, he left his car, thinking that as long as he had the key and the car was locked, it would be safe until he could return. It was old and beat with a fender being held on with wire, but it was better than a tractor.

As soon as the farmer was well out of sight, Jim went to work. First, he forced the door, which came open with a hard pull. Then he got to work on the ignition. Within minutes, he had the ignition wires shorted and the car running. Mosaud got behind the wheel, and they again started down the dirt road, this time feeling much better.

They drove for a while, feeling certain that they were on the right road heading south and, best of all, were doing at least thirty miles an hour. They came to an intersection that had a paved road that was perpendicular to the road they were on. Mosaud remembered the directions given him by the Christians and made a right turn onto the paved road. As he turned, a truck carrying ISIS soldiers almost hit him. Mosaud swerved to his right and thanked God when the truck kept going.

They drove for about fifty miles when they observed another turnoff to their right. It had a sign indicating a school.

"This is it," Mosaud said to Jim.

"Take it easy and let's see if we can find the rear entrance," Jim responded.

Mosaud made a couple of turns to the rear of the building where there were a couple of old school buses that were parked. They looked like they had been wrecked. One had a front that was smashed in; the other had charred marks on the back that were probably the result of a fire. To their surprise, there was an abandoned American tank parked near the buses. Looking at the tank, Jim said out loud, "I wonder if that thing can run."

"Forget it, Jim. We can't make it up the mountain in that thing." Mosaud laughed.

They saw a back door to the school, and Mosaud parked the car far enough away so as not to arouse the suspicion of any soldiers that may be passing. Jim examined the door and saw that it was locked. He took out the lock picks that he always carried with him and began manipulating the barrel of the lock. It was an old lock and took an inordinate amount of finagling to get it to open. They entered the dark rooms of the abandoned school. Jim donned his night vision glasses and walked to the nearest door with Mosaud in tow.

"We're supposed to find stairs to a basement and then a sub cellar," Mosaud whispered to Jim.

"I don't see any signs of a stairwell. Let's walk down the hall. Maybe it's in the other end of the school," Jim answered.

They walked about one hundred feet when Jim spotted a sign indicating a stairway. He motioned to Mosaud and opened the door that led them to a set of stairs that went both up and down. Jim moved to the right and took hold of the handrail. Mosaud followed close behind.

The stairs were littered with debris. It was slow going with no lights. Finally, they were at the door to the basement. Jim opened it and slowly peered in. He couldn't see anything but garbage strewn about. Mosaud tugged on Jim's sleeve and whispered, "There is supposed to be in a subbasement somewhere."

"I know, but I thought we'd better check out this level, just in case. It looks abandoned enough, so let's continue down the stairs," Jim said.

They continued their slow-moving decent one step at a time in the total darkness. After descending two more flights of stairs, they came to another door. Jim looked around, utilizing his night vision glasses, and saw that there were no more steps going down.

"This must be it," he said to Mosaud, who was still clinging to Jim's shirtsleeve, being completely disoriented by the darkness and the strange area.

Jim opened the door and looked in. He saw nothing but walls and more debris scattered about.

"There's nothing here," he whispered to Mosaud. "We'd better go in and take a closer look."

They entered the subbasement, which was large and had many rooms partitioned off. As they slowly moved forward, Jim looked into each room. Still he saw nothing.

They came to an intersection of hallways. One went to Jim's left and the other to his right, while the hall they were in continued straight ahead. He decided to take the hall to his right first. They continued down the hall, checking out some rooms, but still no signs of life. They turned around and went straight past the original hallway. They again checked rooms as they slowly moved forward. Then Jim heard it—muffled sounds of children's voices. Jim moved as swiftly as he could while not getting away from Mosaud. They opened a door, which was at the end of the hallway, and stepped into a room lit with candles. Jim immediately took off his glasses and couldn't believe what he saw. The room was inhabited by about twenty-five people—women, children, and a few young men.

When Jim entered the room, there was a collective gasp. Women grabbed their children and tried to protect them from the strangers who entered their sanctuary.

"We are friends," Jim said out loud. "We are not here to hurt you but to help you. We are looking for Arda. Is she here?"

Immediately, most of the room's inhabitants looked to the rear of the room. Against a back wall was a homemade stretcher on which a person was lying.

"That must be her," Jim said to Mosaud as they walked into the crowded room and headed toward the back wall and the stretcher.

The people in the room moved away and left a path for them.

Jim knelt down next to the stretcher and looked closely at Arda. She appeared to be awake and looked at Jim intently.

"My name is Jim Vara, and I came here to take you home," Jim said with a smile.

Arda looked at him in disbelief. "How did you find me?" she asked.

"It's a long story, and someday I'll tell you, but right now, I need to know what your condition is. Can you walk? Are you hurting?"

"I don't think I can walk. Two weeks ago, I was hit with some shrapnel from an explosive that struck my home. I am feeling a great deal of pain in my right hip area. These good people who were my students and my neighbors have been caring for me ever since. If it weren't for them, I don't think I'd be alive."

"What are you all doing in this room?" Jim asked.

"This is sort of a halfway house. They come here on their way to Kurdistan. Some wait for other friends or relatives, while others make their way north at night. I haven't been able to go north with them. My condition is too bad, and I would just hold them up and probably get them killed, so here I wait."

"I'd like to take a look at your wound if I can," Jim said, taking a light sheet off her.

She nodded yes, so Jim lifted her blood-dried skirt, while Mosaud held a candle close by. He undid the waistband on the skirt and lifted her blouse. She had some sort of slip on, and Jim knew he would have to cut it to get at the wound.

"Does anyone have scissors?" Jim asked, looking around.

A woman held up a tiny pair of scissors, and Mosaud took them from her and gave them to Jim. They were small but would have to do. He felt that if he cut the slip with a knife, he would probably hurt her and cause her pain.

He cut away at the slip and slowly removed it. The wound looked terrible. It had dried blood crusted on it, and Jim could not really see much.

"We need clean water and a cloth to clean it and then something to dress it with," Jim said to Mosaud.

"I have some water left in my canteen, but I have no idea where we'll get a clean cloth or bandages," Mosaud answered.

Jim looked at the sheet that had been covering Arda and decided to cut a small piece of it to use as a swab to clean the wound. It was not clean but would have to do for now. He wet the piece of cloth and slowly rubbed the wound. The crusted blood was difficult to remove and took many passes at it before it was removed and he saw fresh blood. There were no bones protruding from her hip, so he took that as a good sign. He rinsed the cloth again and placed it over the wound.

"Arda, I want to put my hand under your hip and lift a little so that I can see the extent of your wound."

She looked at Jim and nodded yes.

She's a brave one, Jim thought to himself.

He bent over her and slowly slid his hand between the stretcher and the back of her hip. He felt around, barely moving his fingers, but felt no broken bones. He lifted her hip slightly feeling the soft flesh of her backside, and she let out a moan. He pulled his hand out, satisfied that he could not feel anything broken as far as he could tell. *Perhaps it is a dislocated hip or just a serious flesh wound,* he thought.

Jim motioned Mosaud to come away from Arda. When he thought they were out of hearing, he discussed the situation with him.

"She is in obvious pain, and I can't tell the extent of her wounds," Jim said.

"We have to move her. She can't stay here," Mosaud responded.

"I know . . . I have an idea. You find out what you can from these people,"—Jim waved his arm around the room—"and I'm going outside to see what I can come up with."

"OK, but be careful—who knows what's lurking out there," Mosaud cautioned.

Jim donned his night vision lenses and started up the debris-clad stairs. When he got to the outer door, he took off his glasses and exited. He looked around and observed the two buses, the abandoned American tank, and the car they came in. He went to the closest bus, entered, and looked around. The entire back of the bus had been on fire, and there was nothing of any value there. He then went to the driver's seat and reached underneath, hoping to find tools or something he could use, but there was nothing.

He exited the bus and went to the next one that was parked next to it. The bus appeared to be in good condition except for dirt and dust that covered it. He looked around but found nothing. He wondered if it would run. Once again, he put his NYPD experience to work and shorted out the ignition. The engine turned over once and then died. The battery was obviously discharged to the point of being useless. *Still,* he thought, *if I can get a charge, it might run.*

He exited the second bus and turned his attention to the tank. He climbed atop it and opened the hatch. He climbed down into it and looked around. It looked as though everything of any use was already taken from it. Instruments were

227

damaged and various parts broken as if to dismantle it and make it useless. A lot of the damage appeared to be just plain vandalism. His search was rewarded when he spotted a small metal compartment attached to the ceiling that must have been overlooked by those that were there before him. He opened the compartment and smiled as he pulled out a small box with a red cross on it. He opened the first aid kit and found its contents in order. He fumbled through the contents until he saw a few small vials. Jim knew instantly that it was the morphine he was looking for. He replaced the contents back into the box and climbed out of the tank and returned to the school basement.

He was greeted by Mosaud, who noticed Jim was carrying something under his arm.

"Find something good, I hope?" Mosaud said, pointing to the box Jim was carrying.

"Yes, it's a first aid kit and it has clean bandages and other equipment we may be able to use."

"What's the story with all these people?" Jim asked.

"They want to go north but are waiting for someone to guide them. A dozen or so leave every week, and more pile in. It's a miracle that ISIS doesn't know about this place yet. It was a girls' school, and that's why it's abandoned. It's bound to be discovered sooner or later," Mosaud mused.

"Any ideas on what we can do?" Jim asked.

"We're going to have to leave, but I don't know how we can take Arda in her condition and I don't know what to do with the rest of them. How about you? Did you find anything besides a first aid kit while you were out there?"

"Well, as you know, there are two school buses in the back, and I may be able to get one to run. It has a dead battery, but I was thinking maybe we could get a jump from the car we brought with us. I'm not sure it will run or if it has gas, but it's worth a try. I don't know what else we can do unless we take Arda in the car and head back ourselves," Jim responded.

"We can't do that and leave all these people. If necessary, we'll have to walk out with all of them," Mosaud offered.

Jim marveled at Mosaud's caring. For all his toughness, he was a softy at heart.

Jim questioned one of the young girls who had been a student in the school. She didn't have much to offer, but Jim kept asking about where she thought the maintenance office was in hopes of possibly finding some tools. He could only establish that she thought it was on the first basement level.

While Jim questioned the girl, Mosaud was lining up the strongest of the young men in case they needed muscle to carry Arda. He was impressed at how eager they were to help. They all seemed to know Arda and respected her very much.

AN AMERICAN ASSASSIN

Jim donned his night vision glasses once again and headed out the door to try and find the maintenance office. He made his way up the stairs to the first basement level, where he entered through the gray metal door. He perused the hallway and spotted a sign protruding from over one of the doors that read "Maintenance." He smiled to himself that he had found the location without any problems. He pushed away some debris and entered the office. It smelled of oil and was in pretty bad condition. It looked as though people had been through it and took anything of any value and destroyed whatever was left. He foraged around the floor and cabinets, hoping to find something he could use. The only thing he found that he could possibly use was an old pair of pliers, which had been buried under some papers on the floor. He had hoped he could find some wires that he could use as jumper cables but was out of luck. Disappointed, he headed back downstairs.

After Jim arrived downstairs, they ate whatever was around that was provided by the Christians, checked on Arda, and then tried to sleep. The room was hot and stuffy with practically no air circulation, making it difficult to sleep.

The next morning, two more Christians arrived, swelling the already crowded room. Jim and Mosaud knew they had to make their move soon. Jim explained to Mosaud that the pliers was all he could come up with from the maintenance room and that he did not find anything he could use as jumper cable. Mosaud came up with the idea that they could cut some electrical wires that would normally be running the different electrical systems in the building and use them. Jim thought it was a great idea and starting looking around to see what was feasible.

The wires leading to what should have been the lights in the room were covered by a metal shield that looked like it could be breached. Because they had no ladder, they opted to try the line that went from the switch to the ceiling light fixture, as they were reachable. Jim, using the pliers, started twisting the shield that was covering the wires back and forth until it came loose, exposing three wires. He pulled away the shield and was going to cut one of the wires when Mosaud cautioned him.

"You don't think there's juice in the wires, do you?"

"I doubt it. The lights would come on if there were," Jim said, flicking the switch back and forth to make his point.

He then placed the pliers on the first wire, smiled, held his breath, and snipped. The wire broke without incident, and all were relieved. He then snapped another wire. Now the problem was to get enough length; they would have to climb the wall about eight feet to make the cut. One of the boys, realizing the problem Jim was having, volunteered to climb on Jim's shoulders and cut the wire from above. The plan worked, and before they knew it, they had two perfectly good pieces of wire that could be used as jumper cables.

Jim and Mosaud then huddled together to plan their next moves. They realized that if there plan worked and the bus started and it had enough gas, they would have to move all those who wanted to head to Kurdistan rapidly out of the school and into the bus. They formulated plans using some of the young men who could act as lookouts, while Jim worked and others who would escort the Christians out of the school and into the bus. They counted eighteen boys, women, and children who wanted to leave with them. They also assigned two of the strongest-looking boys to carry Arda on her stretcher. It had to be done quickly lest they are spotted by some curious passerby or, worse yet, an ISIS soldier. Fortunately for them, the work would take place in the rear of the school, mostly hidden from public view.

Satisfied with their plan, they told everyone present what they intended to do and admonished all to get some sleep, because if their plan worked and they were lucky enough to get going, it may be a while before they sleep again.

Chapter 27

The next morning, they got up quickly, and all were excited at the prospect of leaving the school and escaping ISIS. Jim immediately went up to the bus, taking a young man with him as a helper. In the meantime, Mosaud made a dry run with those who would try to escape with them, hopefully on the bus. The stairs were still cluttered with debris, and it was slow going, as they had only candles to light the way. Mosaud had them hold on to the person in front of them so as they would not get lost or misstep.

When he finished the exercise, he went upstairs to join Jim. He found him feverishly working on the bus.

"How's it going?" he asked.

Jim looked up from the bus's engine compartment and gave Mosaud a shrug of the shoulder.

"I don't know yet. We'll find out in a minute," Jim responded. "I've attached the cables, but I'm not sure the car has enough output to charge the bus's battery. I don't think the bus's battery is that dead, but we shall see. Do you have everyone inside ready to go?"

"Yes," Mosaud responded. "Do you think I should bring them upstairs?"

"I hate to have them go through that especially if we can't get the bus started and with Arda still on a stretcher. On second thought, maybe we should. If I'm lucky enough to get it going, we won't have any time to spare, especially us not knowing how much gas is in the bus. I was thinking of trying to siphon some gas from the car, but if the bus doesn't run, we'll need it in the car."

"OK. I'll start them up the stairs, and hopefully by the time we all get up here, the bus will be percolating," Mosaud said as he headed for the school door.

Jim started the car and drove it as close to the bus as he could. He opened the hood to the car and prepared to hook up the cables. He showed the young man with him how to rev the car's engine, as he had to stay with the makeshift cables to make sure they didn't come unhooked.

Then the moment of truth! He hooked the last cable to the car's battery and signaled the boy to rev up the engine of the car. When he was satisfied that the cables would not come loose, he entered the bus and tried to start it. The engine turned slowly but did not start. He waited another few minutes and tried again. This time, it turned over and let out a burst of dark smoke, and the engine, clanging and sputtering, started. Jim immediately checked the gas gauge and was elated to see that it was half full. He motioned to the boy to come into the bus and told him to tell Mosaud that the bus was running and to get everyone up as soon as possible.

The boy ran down the stairs, tripping and falling a couple of times. At the end of the first set of stairs, he came upon some of the people heading up. "Hurry!" he shouted as loud as he could. "The bus is running. We're going to Kurdistan."

Mosaud, hearing the boy's shouts, went back down the stairs to make sure that the boys carrying the stretcher containing Arda knew what was happening. He had earlier given Arda an injection of morphine, which was taken from the tank's first aid kit. He was wearing Jim's night vision glasses, so he took the front of the stretcher in an attempt to move faster.

The first of the Christians reached the door and propped it open to allow light to flow into the stairwell. When Jim saw them, he waved his arms in a motion indicating he wanted them to hurry. As they entered the bus, he told them that only the boys can have window seats because if they were observed by ISIS, they would be suspicious if they saw females, as girls were not allowed to go to school. He further admonished that if ISIS were observed, the women were to duck down so as not to be seen.

As soon as all the Christians were on the bus, they brought in the stretcher with Arda. They had a hard time getting it through the door without jostling Arda too much. They decided that the safest place for the stretcher was on the floor in the rear of the bus.

Jim took his seat behind the wheel and put the bus in gear, causing a loud clunk. The bus slowly rolled forward, and Jim made a U-turn and headed for the road that would take them north.

Mosaud counted eighteen people on board, nineteen counting Arda, and then took his seat behind Jim. Jim had laid his rifle next to him on the floor, while Mosaud held his between his legs just in case it would be needed in a hurry.

The bus moved very slowly, and if Jim tried to give it more gas, it would just bog down. They were doing only about twenty miles an hour so any other vehicles on the road would either pass them or go as slow as they did. Neither Jim nor Mosaud liked the idea of going so slowly, but at this point, there was nothing they could do about it.

About five minutes into the drive, Jim observed, through the rearview mirror, a pickup truck with a gun mounted on the back. The truck was catching up to them. He yelled for all the women to duck down. The truck gained on the bus and eventually started to pass them. In the bed of the pickup were three soldiers sitting down. They looked at Jim and Mosaud as they passed. Both Jim and Mosaud then gave them a V for victory sign with their fingers. The soldiers smiled, and the truck passed them and continued on. There was a collective sigh of relief when Jim told them that all was clear.

It took them quite a while to finally get to where the dirt road they had to take intersected with the road they were on. Jim made the left turn onto the road and relaxed a bit. He knew that there would be very little traffic, if any, on the rural road.

They drove for another hour without incident. Then it happened! A pickup truck with a mounted gun on the bed was closing in on them from the rear. Once again, Jim yelled for all the women to duck down. As the truck passed, Jim and Mosaud gave the V sign in hopes that it would satisfy the inhabitants as it did before. Jim noticed that it was the same truck with the three ISIS sitting in the bed. This time, the truck pulled in front of them, cutting them off. The truck came to a halt, causing the bus to stop, and the three men jumped out of the back and came toward the bus. Jim took out his pistol and held it low so that it could not be seen until the bus door was opened. Mosaud also took his weapon out and braced himself for the battle that was about to take place.

As one of the men approached the door, Jim opened it and fired two shots into the man's chest. Mosaud then jumped through the door, knocking the man Jim had just shot to the ground. Mosaud then pointed his pistol at the man who was about six feet away and apparently had frozen. He fired three shots into the man, who fell backward onto the ground. The third man from the truck, seeing what was happening, jumped back into the bed of the truck and was attempting to swing the large gun around when the bullets from Mosaud's weapon struck him, killing him instantly. In the meantime, Jim grabbed his rifle and jumped out of the bus. The driver of the truck, seeing what was happening, for some unknown reason, made a quick U-turn and sped down the dirt road followed by a hail of bullets fired by Jim and Mosaud. The truck veered to the left and then to the right and drove off the road into a ticket and came to a halt.

Jim told Mosaud to take a couple of the young men and see if they could hide the truck. In the meantime, Jim dragged the two soldiers, who were lying in the road into the orchard that was on the right. He threw some brush on them in an effort to hide them.

Mosaud and two young men cautiously approached the truck. Mosaud looked into the bed and was sure the soldier lying there was dead. He then slowly went to the cab of the vehicle, and, pointing his pistol inside, he slowly opened the door. The occupant lay across the seat with his head half blown off. The truck was still running, so Mosaud shoved the driver over and got behind the wheel and accelerated, moving the truck deeper into the brush. Satisfied that the truck was well hidden, he shut off the engine and returned to the road. Just in case someone could catch a glance of the truck, he had the boys throw some more brush on it as he headed to the bus to help Jim.

Jim was already in the bus, trying to calm down its occupants. Many of them were upset over what had just transpired. Seeing that Jim had already taken care of the two bodies, Mosaud waved at the boys to come to the bus. When they arrived, Jim put the bus in gear, and they started out again. Jim and Mosaud looked at each other and smiled as if to say, "Well done, and I'm glad that's over with."

They drove for a few more hours, and it started to get dark.

"What shall we do?" Mosaud asked. "Do we try to make it tonight or hide out tonight and start late afternoon tomorrow?"

"I'd love to go tonight, but I'm afraid these people are tired from all the excitement and I'm a little worried about Arda," Jim answered. "It's going to be tough on her and on us carrying her."

"OK. Shall we try for the barn we stayed in on the way down?" Mosaud asked.

"Yes. I think it's about another hour or so away. We'll be traveling in the dark by then, and I can't use the headlights. We will also have to ditch the bus somewhere as far away as possible."

"OK," Mosaud agreed. "Park away from the barn, and we'll walk in so that no one hears the motor."

"Fine. I'll drop you off and then turn around and ditch the bus, probably in the orchard. I can walk back by the light of the moon, so you keep the night vision glasses."

"Sounds like a plan." Mosaud smiled. "But, wait, how will you know when we're near the barn?"

"I do remember a pole next to the road. If we spot it, fine. If not, I'll have to pass the barn and come back. I don't like driving on a road I'm not familiar with without headlights, but I don't think we have a choice."

They drove for another hour. Jim drove slowly, and they had all those sitting on the right side of the bus looking for the pole. No one saw the pole, and Jim spotted the barn as they drove past. He continued up the road until he found a place where he could turn around. He made a U-turn and drove just past the barn, where he let everyone out. Mosaud took the lead, and everyone followed closely behind him. Two of the young men carried the stretcher with Arda. When they reached the barn, most of the people climbed the ladder, while some, including those with Arda, stayed on the ground level.

Jim drove the bus about another mile down the road until he came to the orchard. He drove the bus off the road and in between the rows of trees until he was satisfied that the bus could not be seen from the road. He shut the bus off and climbed out and started to walk back to the road. As he walked, he noticed that the bus had left tire tracks where it knocked over small scrubs. As he neared the

AN AMERICAN ASSASSIN

road, he attempted to cover the tracks as best he could in the darkness. He made a mental note to return tomorrow to finish the job.

As he walked down the road, he spotted headlights coming in his direction from the north. He dashed into the orchard, keeping his eye on the headlights and hoping the vehicle did not stop at the barn. He was elated to see that the vehicle just kept going south down the road. As the vehicle passed him, Jim could see that it was a huge military truck probably carrying ISIS soldiers.

When he arrived at the barn, most of the people were settling down for the night. Jim felt pretty confident that there would be no problems for the rest of the night, but he worried about the daylight the next day. The children in the group behaved remarkably well and were very obedient. He hoped that they would remain that way when they got close to the ISIS lines.

The next morning, all arose to a very rainy day. Jim was happy with the rain, as he figured the farmers would probably not be working the fields and orchards, so the likelihood that they would be discovered decreased. Jim and Mosaud decided that the rainy day would be a perfect time to prepare the group for the trip ahead. They slowly drew a picture of what they faced ahead. They explained the flat terrain ahead, which would be followed by hills that would get steeper and steeper as they neared the Kurdistan fortifications. They then explained the rope ladder at the end of their journey. Most of all, they cautioned them regarding the ISIS soldiers that were dug in near the end of the trip and taught them different hand signals they would use to communicate in lieu of oral communication, although most of the trip would take place in the dark, so hand signals would be useless.

Finally, evening came. The rain had let up, and Jim and Mosaud decided that it was time to leave. It was decided that Mosaud would lead the group because he had the night vision glasses, and Jim would bring up the rear behind the stretcher that was being carried by two young men, who would be relieved by another two young men at intervals of about an hour, depending on the terrain.

They swiftly crossed the road and were covered by some foliage that would protect them from being seen. The first hour, things seemed to be going well, and the stretcher carriers changed hands. The people started to relax, but Mosaud warned them that the worse was ahead of them and to stay vigilant as they neared ISIS territory.

The path they were on started to become rocky, and the caravan slowed down to avoid falls and possible sprained or broken ankles. They stopped and took a rest as night began to close in on them. Jim gave Arda another injection of morphine to help ease the pain of the arduous journey. He had only two left but estimated that it would be enough to get them to their destination, as the injections lasted for about three or so hours.

They resumed their trek, entering into the steeper part of their journey. The rocky territory had turned into small mountains with many boulders to climb over. It was especially difficult to maneuver the stretcher over the rugged path. Jim helped the young men with the stretcher as much as he could but felt that he would better serve the group by protecting the rear and keeping a lookout lest they be surprised from the back.

All of a sudden, the group stopped. Mosaud heard voices and decided to call a halt to the trek until he was satisfied that the voices were not those of ISIS soldiers. The voices were difficult to make out, so Mosaud decided to go alone toward the voices to identify them. After moving about one hundred feet toward where the voices were coming from, he could make out what they were saying. It turned out that they were farmers who were searching for a lost sheep. Relieved, he returned to the group and started them off again toward the Kurdistan outpost.

The darkness of night enveloped the travelers, making the dangerous and difficult march even more arduous. Mosaud was in the lead, going very slowly with those that followed holding on to each other. The stretcher carriers found it almost impossible to keep up. Jim decided to assist the carriers, as he felt that no one would be overtaking them from the rear in the dead of the night. The worst part was that Mosaud knew they were closing in on the ISIS position, and traveling at such a slow pace was going to give the ISIS soldiers all the more time to discover them, and that would mean certain death in the most gruesome fashion for those he were leading. His only hope was that the ISIS soldiers were sleeping or occupied and not paying attention or being too alert.

The trek slowly moved forward with an occasional cry from someone who tripped on a rock, causing everyone to stop and listen to hear if they were found out. Each step was getting painful especially for those who had only sandals on their feet. Jim and the two young men were doing the best they could moving the stretcher forward over the unyielding terrain. At times, they had to lift the stretcher over their heads to try to keep it level. It was extremely difficult, and Jim was sweating profusely. He decided to give Arda another shot of morphine lest she cry out in pain and alert the ISIS troops. This left him with only one vial left of the pain-relieving medicine.

The sun started to rise in the east, and Mosaud could see the rock formation that he recognized, indicating that they were arriving at the steep hill that served as a fortress for the Kurdish forces. *Only a few hundred yards left to go,* he thought to himself. He marveled at their luck in getting through the ISIS forces without being seen. But now, the hard part of getting up the rope ladder without being shot, and how were they going to get Arda up the rope ladder? He said a silent prayer.

They arrived at the base of the cliff where the Kurdish forces were entrenched. At the base was a large boulder capable of hiding many people while they waited to transit up the steep cliff. Mosaud waited until the entire group including Jim and the stretcher arrived. Jim put down the stretcher and took his M1 rifle off his shoulder and, using a rock for cover, aimed at where he thought the ISIS soldiers may fire from.

Mosaud clicked his radio three times, which was the signal to the men above to lower the rope ladder. Staring up at the top of the cliff, Mosaud saw one of his men looking down on them. The man waved at Mosaud and flung the rope ladder over the edge of the cliff.

As if on cue, when the ladder was dropped, an ISIS soldier stepped out from behind a small hill, weapon at the ready, and looked at the rope ladder, waiting for someone to climb it. Jim took aim at the soldier and fired a shot, killing him instantly. He regretted having to fire, as he knew it would alert other soldiers, who will probably come to where they were in response to the gunshot.

A large Kurdish soldier came scrambling down the ladder, and he and Mosaud exchanged greetings. The soldier then unceremoniously grabbed a child and, placing her under his arm, swiftly climbed the ladder. Another big Kurdish soldier came down the ladder, and gunfire erupted from both the hill where the ISIS fighters were and the top of the cliff as the Kurdish machine gun responded. Jim, spotting some exposed soldiers, also opened fire. The Kurdish soldier, ignoring the gunfire, grabbed another child and started up the ladder when he was hit by a bullet. He hesitated for a moment and then continued his climb until he was at the top.

Now it was time for the women to make the dangerous climb. The first women to try tied her baby to her chest using a scarf. She made slow progress on the swinging ladder. When she was near the top, a shot rang out, and she and her baby, obviously hit, let go of the ladder and fell to the ground with a thud. Mosaud, seeing what happened, ignored the danger and ran to her and dragged her behind the rock. He examined her and saw that she was dead, but the baby was still alive, as the woman, whether on purpose, fell on her back. Mosaud cursed the ISIS under his breath and vowed to himself that he would make them pay.

Jim had seen what happened and felt responsible, as he had missed the soldier that had shot the women. His blood boiled. *How could they shoot a woman who was carrying a child?* He had heard of their savagery, but this was the first time he actually witnessed it.

As the next woman approached the ladder, Jim stood up and charged the hill hiding the ISIS soldiers, firing his rifle as he ran. The weapon emptied, and he reloaded as he continued his charge. There were about seven ISIS soldiers behind the hill, and Jim fired at them, striking four, while the other three ran for cover. He kept up the firing until he was satisfied that there would be no more firing at the ladder from that position.

In the meantime, the rest of the women and young men climbed to safety. Now there was only the baby and Arda left. Jim retreated back behind the rock shielding them as one of the Kurdish soldiers descended the ladder to where they were.

Jim took out the last shot of morphine and injected Arda. The Kurdish soldier, seeing their dilemma and without hesitating, picked up Arda off her stretcher and started up the rope ladder, carrying her on his shoulder. Mosaud and Jim just looked at each other as the soldier ascending the ladder made it to the top without a problem.

Now it was their turn. Mosaud motioned Jim to go ahead, but Jim motioned Mosaud to go first. They looked at each other and smiled. Jim pulled a coin out of his pocket and said, "Heads you go first, tails I go first." They agreed, and Jim flipped the coin.

It landed heads, and Jim took his rifle and pointed it at the hill where he shot the ISIS soldiers and was prepared in case they had returned. Mosaud slung his rifle over his shoulder and, with a quick glance back at Jim, grabbed the baby and started to climb. He made it up without incident. Now Jim slung his rifle over his shoulder and grabbed the end of the ladder. He started to climb up when rifle fire caused pockmarks around him. He climbed as fast as he could and could hear the machine gun above, giving him cover fire. He realized he was sweating as his hand slipped on the rope. He recovered quickly and continued to the top, while the rattle of the machine gun continued. After he got over the edge, a Kurdish fighter helped him up over the edge of the cliff and then pulled on the rope ladder until it was completely on the top of the cliff.

Jim lay on the ground for a moment to catch his breath. He wiped the sweat from his face and looked around for Arda. Mosaud, who was standing over Jim, grabbed his hand and helped him up.

"They took her to the medical tent," Mosaud said.

Jim wiped his hands on his pants leg and followed Mosaud to the medical tent.

He tried to enter but was unceremoniously barred by a female nurse, who told him to wait outside until the doctor was ready to let them see Arda.

Jim peeked in and saw that they had Arda undressed and were examining her wound.

About a half hour later, the doctor exited the tent, and Jim approached him and asked how Arda was doing. He told Jim that her wound was serious and there was not much he could do and that she needed to be in a hospital. He told Jim that he would see that she gets on the next helicopter for evacuation.

Jim entered the tent and knelt next to the cot where Arda lay. He held her hand as she awoke. She attempted to smile at Jim but was obviously in too much pain. He told her that she would be evacuated and be in a hospital before long. She lipped a "thank you," as she could not speak, and then fell asleep. Jim figured the doctor must have given her more drugs.

After leaving the medical tent, Jim and Mosaud went to the mess tent to get some food. They were starving, as they had not eaten in quite a while. When they entered, they saw most of the people they helped escape from ISIS eating. Some of the women got up and came to Mosaud and Jim and tried to kiss their hands as they thanked them. Embarrassed, Jim and Mosaud pulled their hands away and smiled and hugged the thankful women. They felt it was all worthwhile as they looked around the room at the grateful people who started to applaud. Jim's thoughts went back to the only woman who didn't make it and inquired about the baby. He was told that one of the other mothers had her and would take care of her. Jim went over to the woman and saw the beautiful child in the woman's arms and felt a sensation of love sweep over him. He asked if he could hold the baby, and when the woman handed her to him, he cradled her in his arms. "I'm sorry," he whispered to the child. "I'm so sorry." Jim handed the baby back to the women and fought off the urge to cry. He told the woman his name and said if there were anything she needed for the child to not hesitate to contact him. He then got her name and said he would try to keep in touch with her.

Chapter 28

The helicopter kicked up a cloud of dust as it landed on the makeshift dirt pad. Jim and Mosaud held each end of the stretcher as they headed for the helicopter. A Kurdish soldier pushed back the horde of people hoping to get onto the flight and made a path for the stretcher bearers. They gently lifted the stretcher into the helicopter, and Jim got in and sat next to it. He looked back at Mosaud and said, "Good-bye, my friend, and I can never thank you enough for all you did for us."

Mosaud smiled and said, "It was my pleasure, and I hope we meet again someday."

The soldier in the helicopter then let the women and children in until the helicopter was full. There were still many people left out who were disappointed in not being able to get on the flight and out of harm's way. Jim looked out the door and saw the woman with the baby he had held just a short time ago.

The helicopter started to rev its engine when Jim yelled, "Stop!"

The soldier looked at him as if to say, "What's the matter with you?"

Jim opened the door and shouted to the soldier, "Her name is Susan Wilson." He quickly wrote Corcoran's phone number on a piece of paper and handed it to the soldier and then jumped out of the helicopter. He then helped the woman with the baby climb aboard and take his place.

"God bless you," she said as the helicopter roared and lifted off.

"God bless both of you," Jim said silently to himself.

As the dust cleared, Jim saw Mosaud standing there, his hands on his hips, and shaking his head. "I didn't think we would meet again so soon." He laughed.

"Well, I missed you so much, I decided to stay awhile." Jim laughed and put his arm around Mosaud, and they walked away from the helicopter landing pad.

Mosaud and Jim decided to report to the captain what had transpired over the last several days. They entered the captain's tent and were offered a seat and some refreshments. The captain was intrigued by their exploits and commended them for a job well done. As they spoke, an explosion close by caused them to hit the deck. When they got up, the captain cursed and told them that the ISIS soldiers must have gotten another mortar or additional ammunition for the one they had.

He opined that the helicopter would not return if the mortar fire continued. When Mosaud asked why the helicopter could not take the mortar out, he was informed that the Americans had strict orders not to fight or get involved in any of the warfare. Jim shook his head in disbelief. The captain explained that they can go on humanitarian missions such as rescuing people from the mountain, but they cannot get involved in any skirmishes while doing so, and if they were fired upon, they will retreat.

"Here's one American that is not restrained by those orders," Jim said. "I think I would like to take a shot at getting those mortars out of service so the helicopters can return and get some of those poor people out of here."

"With your permission, Captain, I would like to go with Jim," Mosaud offered.

Before the captain could say anything, another mortar round landed nearby with a deafening roar.

"We won't be able to stay here and defend this mountain with that incoming fire raining down on us," the captain answered.

"Then what will happen to the Christians that are trying to come here?" Jim asked.

The captain shrugged his shoulders and said, "I honestly don't know. They will probably be slaughtered by those savages down there," he said, motioning toward the bottom of the hill. "You have my permission to do whatever you can to stop those mortars. Take as many men as you think you'll need," the captain continued.

"Thank you, sir, but I think, on a mission like this, we are better off just going ourselves," Mosaud answered and smiled at Jim and said, "Here we go again."

"Yes," Jim answered. "But this time we're on the attack and we don't have civilians to worry about."

Another mortar round hit nearby, causing all three men to flinch.

Mosaud and Jim decided to go to the edge of the cliff to see if they could spot where the mortar fire was coming from. They had field glasses they had borrowed and scoured the area below. They didn't see what they were looking for until another mortar round was fired. Mosaud spotted the puff of smoke coming from the discharge of the mortar.

"Over there," he said to Jim, pointing in a direction a little to his right.

"Where? I don't see anything." Jim had missed the puff of smoke.

"You see that large flat rock near the path that we had come up here on?" Mosaud said, still pointing.

"Yes," Jim responded.

"It's behind that large flat rock. They are using the rock for cover, and that's why we can't knock it out from up here."

"I think I see where you're talking about. We can take the path back where we came from the other night, and when we hit that area with the small shrubs on the right, we can hang left and we should be pretty close to the mortar position," Jim said, pointing down the hill.

"I agree," Mosaud answered as they backed away from the edge of the cliff.

"We'll leave as soon as it gets dark. In the meantime, let's get some chow," Jim responded.

"OK. Then we can get whatever equipment we'll need and rest up until nightfall."

After eating, they went to the supply tent, where Jim took another bandolier of ammunition and three hand grenades along with another pair of night vision glasses.

He noted that the tent contained very little supplies, and if it will not be replenished soon, the Kurdish soldiers would be out of weaponry very soon.

Later, Jim asked the captain about the scarcity of weapons and ammunitions and was told that they only get supplies when the American helicopter smuggles them in against their orders. With the mortar raining fire down on them, he opined that they may run out of ammunition before long. He further stated that he had to hold back enough ammunition to fight their way off the mountain and back toward Kurdistan. The situation was rapidly becoming a crisis.

Chapter 29

Darkness came, and Mosaud and Jim were ready. They donned their night vision glasses and climbed down the rope ladder without being harassed by the ISIS forces.

When they got to the bottom, they went behind the large rock that had hidden them the last time they came with the Christians. They adjusted their weapons, and Jim was unhappy with the old M1 rifle he had because it could not fire automatically and only had an eight-bullet clip, which meant he had to reload after firing eight rounds, but he knew he had to make the best of it. After all, the Kurdish soldiers had no better, and partly thanks to the terrain, they managed to hold off the invaders, who outnumbered them.

They slowly moved forward toward where they thought the mortar was secreted, following the trail as they went. The weather was warm with a cool breeze blowing every so often, which made it manageable. When they got to the area where they thought the mortar was, they heard voices and froze. It sounded like there were many men talking, so Mosaud motioned Jim to fall back away from the position.

When they were far enough away, Mosaud said to Jim, "It sounds like there are a lot of them near the mortar."

"Yes," Jim agreed. "I think we should wait awhile to see if some of them go to sleep so we can crawl closer and get some damage done to the mortar before they realize what happened."

"Sounds like a good plan to me," Mosaud quipped.

They settled down and made themselves as comfortable as possible considering the situation.

"Why don't you get some shuteye?" Jim offered. "I'll keep watch."

"I don't think I can sleep so close to our friends," Mosaud said, motioning toward the ISIS camp.

They stayed where they were for three hours, taking turns crawling toward the enemy and reporting back their disposition.

Finally, Jim returned from one of his trips to the enemy camp and told Mosaud that all was quiet.

They decided to wait another hour to make sure that the soldiers were asleep before attempting their raid.

After spending a wrestles hour, they slowly crept toward the enemy encampment. As they approached, one of the ISIS soldiers who could not sleep heard them approaching. He was not certain whether it was some of his comrades or the enemy approaching. He called out to them, waking some of the soldiers that were sleeping nearby. Mosaud tried to answer, but his accent gave him away. The soldier lowered his weapon, but Jim shot him where he stood. This woke the entire camp, and shots were being fired wildly, sometimes hitting their own men. Jim and Mosaud hurled grenades in the direction of the small arms fire and started to retreat back to where they came from under the cover of darkness.

One of the grenades must have hit a cache of ammunition and set off a secondary blast, which caught Mosaud and Jim by surprise. They were literally swept off their feet and thrown into the air. Jim was slammed to the ground, and his head was pounding, and he realized he could not hear. He started to run again but could not hear his feet as they crunched the ground beneath them. It was surreal.

* * *

Doris was working late with one of her associates, Bob. Bob always liked Doris and thought she would make the perfect date for him. He hadn't tried to make any advances toward her because he knew she was an item with a guy named Jim, who was some sort of civil servant. *Probably works for IRS and is a pencil pusher,* he thought. He studied Doris as she talked and was intrigued by her. *I could show her a great time in Manhattan. I know all the "in" spots, and we could have a blast.*

Just then, Doris stood up, and her face contorted, and she grew pale and swayed and had to lean against the desk to keep her balance.

"What's the matter?" Bob said as he rushed to her side.

"I don't know. My head is aching, and I can barely hear you."

"Come on, I'm taking you to the emergency room."

Bob held on to Doris to support her, and they slowly walked out of the office and headed for the medical center.

* * *

After running as best they could for about a half mile, they slowed down to catch their breath. Their hearing started to return.

"We'll never be able to destroy that mortar now," Mosaud said between breaths.

"Not tonight, that's for sure," Jim answered.

They had to look at each other and read lips as they spoke, knowing that neither one of them could hear properly.

"I don't see how we can attack it during the day. We probably won't be able to get within a mile of the place. They'll be on high alert," Mosaud mused.

"I doubt we get near it tomorrow night either. They may even move the mortar if they figure out that is what we we're after," Jim offered.

"Damn," Mosaud said. "What shall we do now?"

"I guess we had better head back to camp while it's still dark."

"I guess so. I hate to disappoint the captain."

"I'm sure he heard the grenades and will realize we gave it a good try. Besides, they may have more than the one mortar. We can't really stop them. They're getting stronger, while we're getting weaker. Let's head back," Jim said almost to himself.

"That's what I mean. If the helicopter can't come in to resupply us, we're finished. What about the Christians? I hate to think what will happen to them if they come to our camp and the ISIS is waiting for them. They'll all be slaughtered," Mosaud said.

Chapter 30

After a careful examination, the doctor could not find anything wrong with Doris. He advised her that she should go for a brain scan in case she had a mini stroke. Her hearing had returned, and her headache was almost completely gone.

Bob insisted on taking her home, and she agreed, fearing the symptoms might return.

When they entered her apartment, she thanked him and was about to close the door when Bob made his move. He grabbed her and attempted to kiss her. She shoved him away only to have him push her against the wall and hold her even more tightly.

"What are you doing? Are you crazy? Leave me alone," Doris spat the words out.

"Come on, Doris, you know you want it. Your boyfriend has been away a long time, so I thought I could fill in for him," Bob responded. "He doesn't have to know. It'll be our little secret."

She tried to get away, but he was too strong for her. He wrestled her to the bedroom and threw her on the bed and tore at her blouse. She fought as hard as she could but was completely overpowered. She finally kicked him as hard as she could in his crotch, and he let go of her, rolling over in pain. She rolled off the bed and retrieved her automatic from the nightstand drawer and pointed it at him.

"Get out!" she screamed. "Get out before I shoot you."

Bob made a hand gesture as if to plead with her. He was in a great deal of pain.

"I don't ever want to see you again. Don't even come into the office. I'll send someone to your house with your belongings," she threatened while pointing the gun at him and trying to catch her breath.

"Get out now!" she screamed and waved the gun toward the door.

Bob slowly got off the bed and limped toward the door.

"I'm sorry," he said. "I thought you were interested in me."

"Get out!" she screamed again as he left and she locked the door behind him.

She leaned against the closed door and began to shake uncontrollably and then she cried, sobbing hard between deep breaths as she slid to the floor.

*   *   *

The next morning, Jim and Mosaud told the captain what had transpired the night before. The captain had heard the explosions and had worried that the two men may have been hurt. He opined that they would wait and see if the mortar fire started again, hoping that the explosions might have damaged them.

They didn't have to wait long. As if to answer their question, mortar fire began raining down on them. It was obvious to them that the incoming fire came from more than one position, indicating that they had more than one mortar. The captain ordered that all should prepare to abandon the hilltop and retreat to the next chain of mountains to the north. He explained that the trip would be extremely hazardous, as they would have to descend the mountain to the rear of their position and march on a narrow path through a valley that was probably occupied by ISIS troops.

The captain, Jim, and Mosaud spent the morning formulating plans for the march. It was decided that the captain would lead the way with thirty men, some going ahead with ten on each side of the trail followed by the Christian civilians, who will be led by Jim and Mosaud, bringing up the rear with the remaining ten men after the path was cleared and he ensured that they were not being followed by the ISIS troops below. To do this, he would fire bursts of machine gun fire from time to time until he got the signal from the captain that it was safe to leave the position and follow.

The next day, all rose early in preparation for the trip that lay ahead. Jim checked his weapons and went to the mess tent, ate, and loaded a backpack with as much food as he could carry. He made sure that the Christians took all the food that was available and gathered them in a group away from where the mortars would soon begin their hellish fire. He told them that he expected them to stay together and keep an eye on him for signals telling them to either run, hide, or stop.

At 9:00 a.m., the captain led his men down the mountain and onto the path below. His men spread out, fanning both sides of the path.

Jim followed about fifteen minutes later with the Christians close behind watching his every move . . . He could hear sporadic gunfire that probably was Mosaud and his men pinning down the ISIS troops below them.

A quiet half hour passed when, all of a sudden, gunfire erupted from in front of Jim. He signaled the Christians to take cover, but it wasn't necessary, since they had already left the path and were in hiding at the sound of the shooting. Jim slowly crept forward, carefully looking around, but saw nothing. He radioed the captain, who told him that it appeared a lone ISIS soldier had wandered into their path and was taken out. He warned Jim that the sound of the gunfire could attract other ISIS troops. He told Jim to start forward again but remain very vigilant.

LOUIS DE MARTINIS

In the meantime, Mosaud and his men caught up with Jim and now positioned themselves directly behind the Christians, following them closely.

They no sooner started forward than gunfire broke again. This time, it was automatic weapons along with rifle fire. Mosaud radioed the captain, who told him that they were under heavy fire and to fan his men to the left to try to flank the insurgents. Mosaud and his men quickly obeyed the order, leaving Jim and his band of Christians to fend for themselves.

The fighting appeared to be coming from Jim's left, so he was surprised to see three ISIS soldiers appear from his right and crossing the path and were headed toward the rear of Mosaud and his men. Jim, who was kneeling down behind some bushes, quickly fired his rifle at the soldiers. He saw the last one crossing the path fall to the ground. The other two jumped into the brush and immediately opened fire toward Jim's position. The bullets buzzed all around him as he quickly lay flat on the ground. He slowly crawled to a tree and used the trunk as cover. He fired several more shots toward where he thought the soldiers might be. They were hidden, and Jim did not know if any shots found their target. Then it became quite, and he feared they may be circling around to better find him and he feared, in doing so, they may come upon the Christians, who were not armed and could not defend themselves. He crawled to his rear toward the Christians when more gunfire broke out. He had a sickening feeling that the ISIS soldiers had discovered the Christians and were shooting them.

"Jim, Jim, it's Mosaud. Don't shoot."

Mosaud had heard the shots and realized what had happened and headed back to Jim's position when he came upon the soldiers and shot them.

"Thank God you showed up. I was afraid they were going to shoot the Christians." As they spoke, more gunfire erupted ahead of them.

"There are quite a few of them. We are barely holding them off," Mosaud said. "I circled around them to try to outflank them, but they had enough men to engage both us and the captain. We're afraid they may be getting reinforcements, so we don't know how long we can hold them off. The captain wants you to take the Christians and make a run for it behind our men, who will try to give you cover. After you pass, keep going until you get to our lines, which are about ten miles up the path. Once we know your clear, we'll follow."

"Is there anything I can do to help?" Jim asked.

"Yes, just get the Christians out of here as I said. Then we'll take up a rear position and keep them back as we head for our lines. Now get going."

"Good luck," Jim said.

"And to you," Mosaud answered as he headed back toward his men and the fight.

Jim gathered the Christians around him and explained the situation. He told them to follow him, and then when they were behind the captain's men, they were to run up the path as fast as they could until they were clear of the fighting.

They made their way up the path until they saw the captain and his men. There was a lull in the fighting, so it was eerily quiet. Just as the Christians made their way up the path and passed the captain and his men, the fighting broke out again. Bullets were whizzing by them. Jim egged them on to keep running as fast as they could, but the women carrying children slowed them down. Finally, they were out of range and slowed a bit. Jim then took the lead in case there were ISIS soldiers further up the path.

The remainder of the journey was quiet for them, even though shots could be heard from the fighting that continued behind them. Before long, they arrived safely in the Kurdish city. At last, they all relaxed and waited for the captain, Mosaud, and their men to arrive.

After waiting for an hour, the captain's men started to arrive. They looked torn and tattered and exhausted from their fighting and trek back to the Kurdish city. Finally, the captain arrived near the end of the group. Jim immediately went over to him and asked about Mosaud and his men. The captain shook his head from side to side, indicating they did not make it. Jim stared at him in disbelief.

"It must be a mistake," Jim said, hoping for a positive answer.

"No, Jim. I lost some of my best men, including Mosaud. They were ambushed on their way here. They put up a hard fight but were outnumbered and completely overrun. By the time we got back to them, the fight was over. My only hope is that none of them were taken alive, as that would be worse than death."

The captain slowly walked away from Jim, his head bowed.

Jim felt as if his heart was torn out of him. He knew Mosaud for only a short time but liked him very much, and a bond had formed between them, the kind only known by those who fought side by side and relied on each other for survival. Jim said a silent prayer for his friend.

Chapter 31

The next day, Jim awoke still feeling depressed thinking about the loss of his friend. He knew he had to put it behind him, but he was felt devastated even though he knew that this was to be expected in war; when it actually happens to someone close to you, it takes its toll. He had to get out.

He approached the captain, who made arrangements for him to get transportation to Turkey and the nearest airport where he could arrange for a flight out of Asia. In the meantime, he thought of Doris but could not get a telephone call out of the small town they were in. Unfortunately, he had lost his cell phone during one of his forays into the ISIS camp.

He said his good-byes to the captain and the Christians he had led out of ISIS territory, and with a sad feeling in his heart thinking about Mosaud, he climbed into the jeep and started the long drive to the Turkish border.

The drive was very difficult. Many times they had to traverse narrow mountain roads and sometimes they had no road at all to drive on. A few times when the road was washed out, the jeep seemed as if it was going off the edge of the mountain and would be hurtling down several thousand feet. Jim marveled at the driver's ability to keep his cool and control of the vehicle.

Finally, after ten hours of the harrowing drive, they exited the mountains and onto a more level plain. Jim relaxed a bit. His hands hurt from holding tightly on the roll bar of the jeep. He began to feel excitement at the thought of going home and seeing Doris, whom he missed dearly. He hoped she understood that he had to take the mission and, having worked for the "Group" herself, knew he had very little notice to say a proper good-bye.

They arrived at the Turkish border where the Kurdish driver left him, not being allowed to enter that country. Jim got out of the jeep, shook hands with the driver, and walked to the nearest guard. He took out his American passport and showed it to the guard. The guard looked at the passport and then Jim and motioned for him to wait. He then entered a small guard shack and picked up the phone to make a call. Jim could not hear what was being said, but the guard seemed calm and glanced over at Jim through a small window. When the guard exited the shack, he walked back to Jim, handed him his passport, and motioned him to cross the border.

Jim walked through the gateway and onto Turkish soil. He tried to ask the guard about transportation to the nearest city, but the guard could not understand what he was saying. Frustrated, he decided to wait to see if he could hitch a ride or if a bus would show up. He waited for over an hour, but there was no traffic at all. Finally, a small car came to the border station, and as would luck have it, it was a British national behind the wheel. Jim waved the car over, and the driver opened the window.

"Can you give me a ride? I'm sort of marooned out here," Jim asked.

"Which way are you going?" the driver asked with a thick English accent.

"I'm trying to get to a city with an airport," Jim responded.

"Jolly well, hop in," the driver offered.

The driver introduced himself as Quinlan Foxel and said that he was returning to England after a skiing vacation in the mountains of Kurdistan. Jim smiled to himself, thinking it wasn't a very likely story as to who vacations in Kurdistan during a war? Jim told Quinlan that he was a salesman and just returned from Kurdistan, where he purchased rugs for his company.

They drove for about an hour, exchanging small talk. Jim liked Quinlan, who asked to be called Quin, even though he knew he was lying, but after all, he was also lying.

"I wonder where those guards at the border stay?" Jim queried. "They seem to be in the middle of nowhere."

"I don't know for sure, but I understand there's a barracks of some sort a few miles up the road to the north," Quin said.

"Seems like awful duty," Jim responded, still making small talk.

"Yes, it does." Quin's response was interrupted by the sound of a helicopter overhead. They both looked up and saw a helicopter closing in on them, appearing to get a closer look at them.

Quin stomped on the accelerator, and the car leaped forward, causing Jim to brace himself. He looked over at Quin, who appeared to be studying the helicopter and speeding as fast as he could.

Within minutes, the helicopter caught up to the speeding car and, without warning, spewed machine gun fire at them. The bullets kicked up bits of tar on the road in front of them and were making pockmarks as they came rapidly in their direction. Quin spun the wheel of the car hard to avoid the bullets and certain death.

Jim held on to the door handle as the car careened off the road and into a ditch. The car then rolled over a couple of times, throwing its occupants out as it rolled.

Jim was about six feet from the car and was lying flat on his back in the dirt.

He heard Quin let out a yell as the car came to a halt.

Jim felt a sharp pain in his back and, for a second, thought he was going to black out.

Meanwhile, the helicopter was circling above them. It started spitting out bullets again. Jim rolled to his side to avoid being hit and realized he was physically OK.

Quin was trapped with his leg caught under the car, which was lying on its side. He couldn't move.

He called out to Jim, "The boot, man, get the lift from the boot."

Jim groggily got to his feet and limped around the car until he was able to reach in the open window and retrieve the ignition key. As he leaned on the car, Quin let out another moan. In the meantime, the helicopter circled around again, taking in the scene and preparing to fire another deadly blast.

Jim hurriedly went to the trunk of the car and opened it. He assumed Quin wanted him to get out the jack and try to lift the car so he could extract his leg. He was surprised to see an AK-47 inside with several clips of ammunition. It appeared to have been secreted in the trunk, and the rolling of the car had obviously uncovered it from its hiding place. Jim slammed a clip of ammunition into the weapon just as the helicopter was coming in low to finish them off. As the helicopter started firing, Jim wildly and, without aiming, fired the AK-47 in its direction. As luck would have it, he must have hit something, as the helicopter started spewing smoke from its engine and was bucking wildly, causing the bullets it was firing to completely miss its intended target. The pilot was struggling with the craft and finally got it under control and flew away.

Jim replaced the AK-47 in the trunk and reached for the jack. When he went to the side of the car where Quin was trapped and in pain, he tried to find a place to put the jack to lift the car. It was impossible to place the jack, as the car was on its side with no understructure strong enough to support it. He abandoned the jack and tried to lift the car by hand to give Quin enough room to free his trapped leg, but to no avail.

"I'm going up to the road and see if I can flag down someone who can help," Jim said to Quin.

"Hurry," Quin said. "I'm in terrible pain."

Jim ran up the small embankment and stood in the center of the road and looked both ways. There weren't any vehicles coming in either direction. He waited for about ten minutes when, at last, a small bus came from the direction of the border. Jim stood his ground directly in the bus's path and waved frantically at it. The bus slowed down and finally stopped. The front door opened, and a short thin man got off and walked toward Jim. He was dressed in dirty clothes and was obviously a laborer or someone who worked in the fields.

Jim tried to talk to him but without success. They could not understand each other's language. He finally motioned for him to come with him and took him to the car where Quin lay trapped. The man took one look and ran back to the bus. Jim's heart dropped, fearing that he was going to take off. To his surprise, several men exited the bus and ran down the embankment to the car. They each took a grip and lifted the car until it was on all fours. Then they scooped Quin up and gently carried him to the bus. Jim followed and was motioned to enter.

They rode on the bus for about forty minutes. Then they arrived at a very small village, which was miles from the main road. The bus stopped in front of a small stone home. They carried Quin into the home, followed by Jim and a few of the riders from the bus that were obviously curious.

A woman came out from the back of the house and spoke with the men. She retrieved a pair of scissors and started cutting away at Quin's pant leg. She gently removed Quin's shoe and sock, causing him much pain. The leg had a lump in it where the bone was broken. She spoke to the men from the bus, and they held down Quin as she went about resetting his leg. Quin's face was soaked with sweat as he moaned and strained against the men holding him. After the leg was set, he relaxed a little, and the men loosened their grip. The women spoke to the driver, and he went to the rear of the house from where the woman had originally come. He returned carrying a folded cot, which he opened and placed on the floor near Quin. The men then helped Quin up and eased him onto the cot. Jim could tell he was still in a lot of pain.

"It looks like she got it back in place," Jim offered.

Quin didn't answer but tried to smile through the pain.

The driver motioned to Jim to come with him.

"I guess I'm going with him, but I'll be back and I'll give you a heads up on where we are," Jim said to Quin, who just nodded in return.

Jim followed the driver out of the house and back onto the dirt road in front. He looked around for the first time and saw several small houses along the road and what looked like an intersection ahead. The driver and the workers got back into the van and slowly headed up the road. The driver stopped at the intersection, and three men got out and started to walk up the unpaved road. A few more stops were made, and the rest of the men were dropped off either at their houses or near enough to walk home. After all the men had left, the driver pulled the van in front of a small house and stopped and shut the vehicle off. He motioned to Jim to follow him. They entered the small house, which looked like it was made up of brown stones. It reminded Jim of the adobe houses he once saw in New Mexico.

The house was small and had a dirt floor. There were a few old-looking, rickety wooden chairs and a table in the middle of the room that appeared to be the only room in the house. Along one wall of the room was an old potbelly stove that served as a cooking stove and a heater. Against the same wall was a tub that had a spigot, which seemed to be the only source of water. Obviously, there was no hot water or other amenities Westerners are used to.

LOUIS DE MARTINIS

The driver went to the sink and, with a rag that was hanging over the side, began to wash himself. After he finished, he motioned to Jim to use the sink. Jim took a brown soap from a tray on the sink and washed his hands. The soap left an odor, so Jim decided to just splash water on his face.

After he was finished, he sat at the table and watched the driver stoke the coals in the stove. It was hot, and Jim couldn't figure out why he was doing that when the answer came in the form of one of the men who was in the bus with them earlier entered and put a pot on the stove. He was followed by another man who brought in a cot and placed it on the floor in the room, which was rapidly becoming crowded.

After the men left, the driver stirred the contents of the pot and looked over to Jim and made a motion as if he were rubbing his stomach, indicating that the food was going to be good to eat. Jim smiled at the gesture and wondered about what he was about to eat. He realized that even if he didn't like the food, he would still have to eat so as not to insult his host.

The driver spooned out the contents of the pot into two dishes and handed one to Jim. He retrieved a loaf of bread from a cabinet and cut huge chunks, placing them on the table, and sat down opposite Jim.

The food in the plate looked like a stew with small chunks of meat and some vegetables. Jim took a spoonful of the stew and was surprised at how good it tasted. He finished his meal and, with a slice of the bread, cleaned his plate. The driver looked at Jim and smiled, realizing that Jim enjoyed the meal.

After the meal, the driver went to the sink and started to clean the plates. Jim motioned to him that he was going to see Quin and hoped that he understood.

Jim left the house and started for the place where he had left Quin. When he entered the house, he observed Quin sitting up on his cot. Quin greeted Jim warmly and was happy to see him again.

"How are you feeling?" Jim asked.

"I'm sore, but I'm not aching too badly," Quin responded.

"It's good to talk. All I've been doing is using hand signals and grunting," Jim mused, smiling.

"I know what you mean. I've been doing the same," Quin answered.

"How are we going to get out of here?" Jim asked, getting down to business. "We seem to be in the middle of nowhere. And, by the way, who were your friends that were shooting at us?"

"I don't know." Quin lied. "I thought they were shooting at you."

"OK, let's cut the bull. What are you—007?" Jim asked sarcastically.

"And what are you?" Quin answered. "I saw how you handled that gun."

"Army training." Jim lied.

"OK," Quin responded, "let's cut the bull and figure out where we are and how to get out of here. There is a telephone in my car, and it should be in the glove compartment if no one has stolen it."

"The car is on a pretty remote area and it is off the road," Jim offered. "Do you think your friends in that helicopter will come back?"

"I don't know. If they do and this area is as remote as you say, it won't take them long to find us. You have to try to get to the car and either get it running or get the telephone. I am assuming that there is no other way out of here except that van that brought us in, and I'm not about to take the only means of transport these people have."

"Spoken like a true hero and a decent human being," Jim joked.

"I'll see what I can do to get to the car as soon as they leave for work in the van. Get some sleep, and I'll see you tomorrow—that is, if your friends don't show up tonight."

With that, Jim left and headed back to the driver's house.

When he arrived at the house, he saw that the driver had taken one of the rickety chairs outside and was sitting on it, leaning back against the building. Jim figured he was trying to get away from the heat that the stove emitted.

"I would like to go to the car," Jim said.

It was obvious to Jim that the driver had no idea what he was saying. He decided to try sign language again and made motions as if using a steering wheel and then with his hands indicated the car that had rolled over.

The driver looked puzzled for a while and then smiled and nodded his head as if he understood and shook his head, motioning yes.

Jim had a restless night. The cot was not comfortable, and it was very hot in the house with no air circulating. At one point, he got up in the middle of the night and was tempted to bring the cot outside but thought better of it, as he had no idea of what creatures may be lurking out there.

Finally, morning came. He marveled at how the driver seemed to know what time it was but didn't even have a clock. The driver placed a small coffeepot on the stove and stoked the embers and threw in another piece of wood. That was enough for Jim, who was sweating already. He grabbed one of the chairs and went outside to sit and try to breathe some cool air.

About ten minutes later, the driver emerged carrying a small cup, which he handed to Jim. It was coffee but looked and tasted like tar. Jim gulped down the concoction with one swallow and tried to smile at the driver, who retrieved the now empty cup and reentered the house.

About twenty minutes later, the driver came out again and headed for the van. Jim called to him and again made the steering motions. The driver smiled and nodded yes to Jim and motioned for him to wait. Jim, thinking he would be right back, sat back in the chair and waited. About ten minutes later, he observed the van loaded with the workers drive down the road and out of the village. He was going to chase after them but knew he didn't stand a chance to catch it. Perplexed, he headed for the house where Quin was.

Quin was asleep but woke when Jim entered.

"Good morning, at least I think it's morning," Quin greeted Jim.

"It's seven thirty," Jim responded.

"I thought you were going to get to my car this morning."

"I was, but they left without me."

"You don't think they're working for, er . . . er." Quin caught himself in midsentence.

"For who?" Jim smiled.

"Never mind."

Just then, the inner door opened, and a woman entered the room carrying two cups and some cookies on a small tray. She placed the tray on a small table next to Quin's bed. She smiled and quickly left the room.

The cups contained the coffee Jim had a problem swallowing at the driver's house that morning.

"Have you tried this stuff yet?" Jim asked.

"Yes," Quin responded. "I had some last night. Not good but not bad."

"Good, then you can have mine," Jim answered, picking up one of the cookies.

After Quin finished the two coffees and a cookie, he got down to business.

"We have to find a way of getting out of here or at least find a place to hide in case they bring some bad guys back with them," he said, deep in thought.

"Can you walk?" Jim asked.

"Get me that crutch," Quin answered, pointing to a stick in the corner.

When Jim brought it to Quin, he took it and tried to stand. With a lot of help from Jim, he was able to stand, putting most of his weight on his good foot. He grimaced in pain and tried to take a step, but it was much too painful, and he fell back onto his bed.

"Look," he said after he caught his breath, "you get out of here. No sense the two of us getting caught."

"Getting caught for what?" Jim asked, annoyance creeping into his voice. "I think it's about time you leveled with me."

"OK, OK. I guess I have no choice but to trust you. I am with MI6 and was on an assignment here in Turkey when everything went haywire. Somehow, the people I was looking at caught on to me. Before I could make a clean break, they tried to kill me. I managed to get away and I guess they sent the helicopter."

"What were you looking for?" Jim asked.

"First, tell me whom you work for, and I don't want to hear you're a rug salesman."

"I work for the government, much like you but not as formal."

"Are you CIA?" Quin asked.

"No, but a similar agency."

"Right," Quin continued. "It was a drug cartel, and they run this part of the country. They have corrupted many government officials and can pretty well do as they please. My job was to ascertain whether they had infiltrated the British embassy. There were many rumors that they had, and I was to prove or disprove them using some confidential informants we had placed inside the cartel."

"What did you find out?" Jim inquired.

"Nothing. When I called the first informant, they had him killed before I could meet with him, and then came after me. It was a stroke of luck that I managed to get away."

"You sound like you really have a leak, and probably in the embassy. Who else knew you were coming?"

"Never mind, I've told you too much already."

"Of all the people I could have gotten a ride from, I had to get you," Jim mused.

"You were a gift, old man. When I saw you waiting for a ride, I thought that my adversaries may pass me by because they were looking for a person all alone. Obviously, it didn't work."

"Obviously," Jim said. "What do we do now?"

"As I said, old boy, you get out of here in case they come back for me. I'm not going anywhere. If you can somehow get to the car, but as I recall, it was pretty far."

"OK., I'll see what I can do. In the meantime, don't go anywhere," Jim said with a smile.

"Yes, I think I'll stay here for a while." Quin returned the smile.

With that, Jim left.

He walked back to the driver's house, mulling over in his mind what had happened. *Surely,* he thought, *if the driver was a bad guy, they could have gotten rid of us right away. But then why did he leave this morning when he knew I wanted to go to the car? Maybe he didn't understand me?*

Jim decided to find a place where he could hide and still observe the building that Quin was in. He looked around but didn't see any natural foliage he could hide behind. He opted for a gully that passed along the road but was not too far from Quin's house. He surmised that he could lie in the gully, which appeared to be dry and not be seen by anyone passing by. He looked at his watch and realized that he had at least eight hours before the workers would return and decided to try to take a nap in the driver's house.

The day went by slowly, and Jim was bored. Finally, the time came for the workers to come home, so he walked to the gully and sat at its edge, waiting to hear the van.

It was another half hour before he heard the van lumbering down the road, trailing a cloud of dust. Jim jumped into the gully and lay on his stomach as he peered over its side at the oncoming vehicle. The van slowly made its way into the compound, and Jim almost burst out laughing when he saw that it was towing the car. *The driver must have misunderstood my hand signals,* he thought to himself. With a sigh of relief, he got out of the gully and followed the vehicles into the compound. The van pulled off what was used as a road and stopped the vehicles. The driver jumped out of the van and went to the back of it and began to untie the heavy rope he had used to tow the car. The rest of the men exited the van, and some headed up the road, while others watched the driver working to untie the rope.

Jim approached the driver and smiled at him. The driver returned the smile and pointed to the car and made motions as if to say he was proud of his ability to retrieve the car. Jim patted him on the back to acknowledge his accomplishment.

After the driver freed the car, he motioned Jim into the van, but Jim pointed to the house where Quin was and tried to let the driver know he would be along in a few minutes, but, first, he wanted to see Quin. The driver nodded and got into the van and headed home. The rest of the men who had been watching walked off, obviously going home. Jim looked over the car and was convinced that it could not be driven due to it being smashed on one side and the wheel was bent in. He marveled how the driver made it back towing the damaged car.

Jim entered the house where Quin was to explain what had happened. Quin was surprised to see Jim, as he thought Jim had left. He told Quin the whole story of the towing and that the car was right outside. He explained the damage to Quin and told him he thought the car was useless. Quin muttered that he wished he could walk to see it for himself. He then told Jim to search the car, as he had a cell phone with him before the accident and, with a little luck, it was in the car.

Jim left Quin and crossed the dirt path that was used for a road. He entered the car and searched it. He looked in the glove compartment and the pockets on the doors, to no avail. Finally, he bent down and tried to look under the seats. He saw something but wasn't sure what it was. He reached in and pulled out some papers, candy wrappers, and the cell phone. Elated, he ran back to Quin to give him the good news.

Jim handed the phone to Quin, who had a big smile on his face.

"This could be our ticket out of here, old chum," he said to Jim while gazing at the phone. "Pray that the battery has enough charge to make the call."

Quin turned the phone on and was elated when it showed life. He smiled at Jim and dialed a number.

"Hello, hello," he said into the phone. "Yes, it is Marcy Man. I am injured and need a ride out of here. Can you follow the beam to me? Good, good. I have another passenger who also needs a ride. No, he is not a bad guy." Quin smiled at Jim again.

"He is from the other side of the pool. Bring some money if you can for the local villagers who saved me. Cheerio, yes, I'll leave it on." Quin then laid the phone on the bed and looked at Jim.

"Well, old chum, it looks like you may be going home."

Jim smiled at the thought, and visions of Doris immediately flooded his mind.

"I can't wait. How long before they get here?" Jim inquired.

"I would imagine it will take at least three or four hours. We're in a foreign country, don't forget."

"Yes, I know. It's just the thought of home is making me anxious. I'll go explain to the driver. How do you think they'll get here—helicopter, car?" Jim inquired.

"I haven't the foggiest, old chum. I don't really care if they come by Pony Express, as you Westerners say, as long as they take us home."

"Roger that," Jim said as he left the house.

Jim returned to the driver's house and tried to explain to him in sign language that someone was coming to get them. He became frustrated not being able to communicate how they were to be removed when he was not certain himself. He did manage to inform the driver to remove the car as quickly as possible, fearing that the drug cartel may see the car and take Quin's escape out on the townspeople.

An hour had not passed when Jim heard the unmistakable sound of helicopter blades in the distance. Not knowing whether it was their rescuing party or the drug cartel, he decided to stay hidden until the copter came into view.

The helicopter circled the village twice, obviously looking for a safe place to land. The sign on the helicopter brought relief and a smile to Jim's face; it read "Extraction Ltd." It was made to look like a business vehicle and not what it really was used for.

Jim hurried to the aircraft and was greeted by a rough-looking man who had jumped out of the still-running aircraft.

"Where is he?" the man growled at Jim.

"Follow me," Jim responded, heading for the house that Quin was in. Jim looked over his shoulder and noticed another man exit the helicopter carrying a machine gun.

When they entered the house, the rough-looking man went directly to Quin and whispered something to him. Quin responded in kind, and they both turned and looked at Jim, who was standing by the door. Jim had an uneasy feeling and thought for a minute that he would either be left or killed. At that moment, the women who had been caring for Quin entered the room. Quin waved at her as the rough-looking man physically picked him up and headed for the door. Quin was obviously in a lot of pain at the sudden movement but tried to not let on.

They exited the building with Jim following. The man who was carrying Quin eased him onto a seat in the helicopter and motioned for Jim to get in. Jim

259

was relieved and gladly entered the helicopter and sat next to Quin, who was being strapped in. The man who had carried Quin moved to the seat next to the pilot and buckled his seat belt. The man with the machine gun straddled the door and placed a belt around himself as he sat in the open doorway with his feet dangling out of the copter door and resting on the skid that was used for landing the aircraft.

The engine on the helicopter revved up in preparation for liftoff. The rough-looking man who was sitting next to the pilot bent down and picked up a briefcase and flung it out the door onto the ground. "Money," Quin said, trying to smile through his pain.

As the helicopter rose, Jim could see the people of the village enter the streets to see what was happening. He saw the driver and waved at him but wasn't sure the driver saw him, as he did not respond.

They flew for two hours, and Jim was elated to find out that they were taking Quin to a hospital in Ankara. This meant that Quin would get immediate care and that he wouldn't be too far from the airport.

When they landed on the helipad at the hospital, medical personnel were waiting with a gurney. They gently removed Quin from his seat and gently laid him on the gurney and began wheeling him away. Quin looked back at Jim and, through his pain, said, "Keep in touch, old boy."

Jim smiled and said, "Will do," as Quin disappeared behind the swinging door that led into the hospital.

The rough-looking man who was sitting in the copilot's seat told Jim to get out of the helicopter. Jim unbuckled his harness and got out. Then to Jim's surprise, the helicopter revved up its engine and took off, leaving him alone on the helipad.

Jim looked around and decided to enter the hospital and try to find out where he was and how he could get to the airport or the American embassy. He tried to talk to several people, but they did not understand him. Finally, he came upon an elderly gentleman near the front desk who spoke English. The man directed Jim to the U.S. embassy, which, fortunately for Jim, was only seven blocks away. Jim thanked the man and hurried out the hospital and headed for the embassy at a very fast pace.

When he arrived at the embassy, he had a bit of a problem with the Marine guard not letting him enter until the guard got the word from inside the embassy to let him in.

Just inside the door, Jim was greeted by a man wearing a three-piece suit that looked to be two sizes too big for him. The man either borrowed the suit or was on a diet that was obviously working.

The man ushered Jim to the second floor, where they entered an office that was empty and contained only a desk and three chairs. The man nodded for Jim to sit down and promptly left him alone in the deserted room. Jim looked around the office, which was bare; the only decoration was a picture of the president hanging on the wall. Thankfully, it was only a few minutes when the inner door opened, and a man entered and looked Jim over from head to toe. He sat behind the desk, looking over his eyeglasses, and inquired, "What can we do for you, Mr. Vara?"

"Who are you?" Jim asked.

"I'm the deputy legate," he responded, taking out identification and showing it to Jim.

Satisfied, Jim said, "I need to make a phone call and transportation back to Washington."

"That can be arranged, but do you realize that it's three o'clock in the morning in DC?"

"I'll leave a message," Jim responded.

"Do you need a safe phone?"

"Yes, that would be best."

The legate smiled at Jim and motioned for him to follow as he got up and entered the inner door of the office and into a much larger room where several people sat at desks doing various jobs. They continued through the office and into a smaller office, where they were greeted by a woman who nodded at the legate and eyed Jim.

"We want to use the telephone," the legate said to the woman, who smiled as if to say, "I understand," and left the room.

Jim called Corcoran's office and left a message. He could have been forwarded to a situation room that was used for emergencies but thought that it would be best to use Corcoran's answering machine. He left the message that he was all right and would be back in Washington as soon as he could get a flight out of Ankara. He also asked Corcoran to contact Doris and tell her he was all right and would see her soon. He hadn't realized that it had been months since he was in touch with them. He wondered how Doris was taking his absence and if she gave up on him. His heart jumped thinking about seeing her again. Suddenly, a rush of emotions flooded his brain, thinking of how she felt to his touch and her softness and her smell. He again was reminded of how much he loved her and wanted and needed her.

When he finished his call, he opened the door and was greeted by the woman.

"My name is Margaret," she said as she held out her hand.

"I'm Jim. I hope I didn't disrupt you too much by having to use your telephone."

"Not at all, I'm used to it, although I don't know why this phone is in my office."

"I can see that it would be a problem," Jim responded. "By the way, how can I get a flight out of here to DC?"

"I'll call the legate. I'm sure he can help," she said as she picked up a phone other than the one Jim had used to make his call.

LOUIS DE MARTINIS

Within minutes, the legate entered the room, and Jim explained to him what he needed. The legate told Jim to follow him, and Jim nodded good-bye to Margaret as he exited the room. The legate made arrangements for Jim to sleep in one of the embassy's rooms and wait for the next day for his flight out of Ankara.

Chapter 32

He landed at Dulles Airport after a daylong flight. As soon as he could, Jim headed for the nearest telephone. He dialed Doris's number and felt an excitement as he waited to hear her voice. He was very disappointed when her secretary informed him that she was in court and not available. He left the message that he was home and to call him as soon as possible.

He took one of the taxis that waited on the arrival ramp for passengers to his office.

He had to leave the cab a few blocks from the office to keep its location secret. When he finally arrived, he was met by Tony to whom he gave a briefing as to what had happened to him in the past few months. Tony was happy to see Jim and was always delighted to hear Jim's past adventures. After completing his story, Jim asked Tony to get him a new cell phone, as he had lost his in Iraq. Tony went to a nearby drawer and gave Jim a phone, telling him that it was capable of sending scrambled messages. He showed Jim which buttons to push in case he wanted to use the secure system. Jim thought he would give it a try and dialed Corcoran's number.

He spoke to Corcoran and told him he would be in the next day to brief him regarding his recent exploits. When he hung up, he called Doris's office again and left his new cell phone number for her to call. After that, there was nothing more to do but go home, take a shower, and get some rest while he waited to hear from Doris.

He didn't have to wait long. Doris had checked with her secretary for messages, and when she found out Jim had called, she called him immediately. She missed him so much and couldn't wait to hear his voice and be with him again. She admonished herself knowing that this affair was killing her slowly. She was perplexed. She loved Jim and wanted to be with him forever but knew in her heart of hearts that it could not be. The months of not knowing where he was and if he was alive or dead or, God forbid, lying injured somewhere was taking a heavy toll on her. It wasn't fair. Why did she have to suffer for love? *Other people are so lucky; they marry and have children and carry on daily seeing each other and loving each other. It's not fair!*

Jim sounded groggy when he answered the phone.

"Darling, it's me," she said, anticipating his response.

"Hi, sweetheart. I've missed you so much and I can't wait to see you," Jim responded.

"I've missed you to. How are you? Are you OK?"

"Yes, I'm fine, except for a little jet lag. When can I see you?"

"I have this darn trial, but I'll get out of it somehow and fly down this weekend."

"Today is only Wednesday. How can I survive to the weekend knowing you're so close?"

"I know, I know," Doris answered, "but this is our life and how we have to be as long as you're in that job."

"I can't quit, you know that better than anyone. You know it's impossible to walk away. They'll never let me do it."

"Maybe someday if a new administration . . ." Doris's voice trailed off.

"We can only hope," Jim answered.

"Maybe I can fly up and see you tonight."

"No, no, don't do that. I'm in the middle of this trial and won't be able to get away. I'll be working through the night, especially if I want to get out of it."

"Damn," Jim answered.

"I know, darling, but just keep busy until the weekend."

"Can I at least call you?"

"Let me call you when I can, again because of this trial and the meetings and brainstorming sessions and research it requires. I have to go now, they're calling me. Love you," she said and hung up.

Jim was fuming as he placed the phone back on the console. *I've been away all this time, and I can't even get to see her,* he thought. *She sounded a little uptight. I guess it's that damn trial she is working on. I hope she isn't getting tired of our situation and me being away for long periods of time. She did say she loved me, so I guess I'm worrying about nothing. If I lose her, I don't know what I'll do.*

His thoughts were interrupted by the telephone ringing.

"Hello," Jim answered.

"Can you come in today and brief me?" It was Corcoran.

"I might as well. I've got nothing else to do," Jim responded.

"You sound a little miffed. Anything I can do?" Corcoran inquired.

"No, it's just that Doris has a trial, and I can't see her until this weekend."

"That's the pits. I just got a call from MI6, and when you come in, we'll talk about it."

Now Jim was very interested, and for a minute, he forgot his situation with Doris.

"OK. I'm on my way."

"See you when you get here," Corcoran said as he hung up.

Chapter 33

Corcoran was waiting for Jim. He motioned Jim to a seat and spoke into his intercom, telling his secretary to call MI6.

Within a few moments, the secretary informed Corcoran that MI6 was on the line.

After a few niceties, Corcoran asked the person on the other end if they were on a secure phone. When he was reassured, they began their conversation in earnest.

"I hear you have a message for one of my people?" Corcoran asked.

"Yes, I was told to forward a message to a Jim Vara."

"He's right here, and if you don't mind, I'll put you on the speaker phone."

"Not at all" was the response.

Corcoran pressed a button and said, "Can you hear me?"

"Yes, I can. Are you there, Mr. Vara?"

"Yes, I'm here," Jim responded. "How is Quin? Is he in England?"

"Yes. We flew him in, and he is in a very good hospital here in London. In fact, the message is from him."

"Go ahead, I'm listening."

"He wanted you to know that the village you were both in was destroyed. It seems that you no sooner left than Aslan, better known as the Lion, attacked the village and all were killed."

Jim was in shock. He couldn't believe what he was hearing.

"You mean they destroyed the whole village?"

"Yes, sir, I'm afraid so. From what we learned, there were no survivors. It must have been a slaughter."

"Who is this Lion?"

"He is the head of the narcotics cartel in that part of the world. Quin said he told you about him."

"He mentioned him, but I didn't think he was that ruthless or dangerous."

"Quin asked that you remember his name and, if you ever get a chance, to take care of him."

"Believe me, I will," Jim responded, looking at Corcoran, who shrugged his shoulders.

"That's all from this end. We would appreciate it if you have any contact with Aslan that you let us know."

"We will," Corcoran answered as he ended the call.

Jim sat there trying to process what he just heard. His thoughts went to the driver and the women who nursed Quin and the other men that helped them.

"I want to go back and get the son of a bitch," Jim said, looking at Corcoran.

"I understand," Corcoran responded, "but I need to be briefed on what happened, and you can include what transpired in the village."

Jim briefed Corcoran, going back to saving the "teacher" and the battles he fought with Mosaud at his side and his escape, thanks to the Kurds. He told him of Quin picking him up and the helicopter that nearly killed them. He tried to paint a picture of the village and the warmhearted people who cared for them and shared their food and homes with them. As he finished, he looked into Corcoran's eyes and said, "I've got to go back and see this for myself."

"What you really mean is that you want to go back and kill this Aslan. I can understand how you feel, but I think you should get some rest and maybe you'll see this in a different light—after all, you've been out of the country for a long time. You need some time to reenergize."

"No, I'm ready to go right now," Jim responded.

"I can't justify a trip to Turkey. We can't just take off and do what we want. Don't forget, we have a chain of command. If anything comes up in that area, I promise you'll be the first to know," Corcoran said in a conciliatory tone.

Jim slammed his hand hard against the chair arm as he rose to leave.

"Try to relax and keep in touch," Corcoran said without much conviction in his voice.

"Right," Jim said with a bitter taste in his mouth. He nodded at Corcoran as if to say, "I know it's not your fault, but I need to get out of here."

Chapter 34

Sunday finally came. Doris could not come on Saturday because of the trial. She arrived on the first flight out of New York. Jim anxiously awaited her arrival at Reagan Airport. When she got off the plane, she looked around, and, spotting Jim, she ran into his arms. They embraced for several minutes, dispersed with deep longing kisses. Finally, they separated slightly, and Doris took in Jim's looks from an arm's distance.

"Darling, you look so tired, and you lost weight."

"Yes," Jim responded. "I was in an area where we didn't get much to eat—speaking of which, let's go get some breakfast."

"That sounds wonderful."

"I know a place not too far from here that's famous for its brunches."

"Sounds great." Doris smiled. "I think I can eat a cow."

"Save some for me," Jim kidded as he escorted her to the parking area where he left his car.

They both ate a hearty breakfast.

Jim sensed that there was something uneasy in Doris's conversation. It seemed forced and not easygoing as usual. Perhaps he thought that it was because he didn't take her home and to bed first as he usually did after being away for a long time. He actually was afraid that because of all that happened and his losing weight, he may not be able to satisfy her. He couldn't shake thoughts of Mosaud and the driver, and he knew that if he couldn't, it would affect his lovemaking.

After breakfast, Jim told Doris that the cherry blossoms were in full bloom this time of year and suggested that they take a walk and enjoy the day. Doris was all for it, and they left for the Tidal Basin.

It was absolutely beautiful. Jim was not much for romantics, but the weather was perfect, and strolling with his loved one, hand in hand, made for a great afternoon. He couldn't remember the last time he was so relaxed and happy. The white petals from the trees blew in the wind and covered their hair. They smiled at each other and took turns brushing the petals from their head and shoulders.

"Jim, we have to talk," Doris said, her voice almost a whisper.

"Must we?" Jim asked, fearful of what was coming. "This is so beautiful. I want it to last forever."

"I'm sorry, darling, but I have to get it off my chest."

"It's my job, isn't it?"

"Yes, I can't take it anymore. You leave for months, and I have no idea where you are or what you're doing. For all I know, you could be wounded, lying in a ditch somewhere. It just hurts so much being in love with you."

"I know, sweetheart, but what choice do we have?"

"It is even affecting my work. How can I continue when I constantly have you on my mind?"

"I know, I know, but what can we do?" Jim asked.

"I have to get away from you. I do not want to leave you, but you and your job leave me no choice. We need to separate for a while."

Jim was shocked even though he expected something was up. This was the worst-possible scenario for him.

"Doris, I love you and want to be with you always. Let's get married and run away somewhere . . . where they can't find us."

"You know neither one of us can do that. We would live with regrets the rest of our lives, and it would affect our relationship."

"I'll do anything to be with you," Jim said emphatically.

"I feel the same way, but it just will not work. Every time your phone rings, I'll think it's Corcoran, and off you'll go, leaving me behind and alone."

They walked silently for a while, pondering what to say next.

"I guess what I'm saying is that the next time Corcoran calls, I'm leaving," Doris said sadly.

Jim didn't answer but motioned toward a bench, where they sat down and watched a young couple stroll pass with their arms around each other.

"I wonder if they know how lucky they are," Jim said.

"I hope so," Doris answered. "I am envious."

Just then, Jim's phone buzzed. It was a one-word text from Corcoran. All it said was "Turkcy."

Edwards Brothers Malloy
Thorofare, NJ USA
October 12, 2016